Mary McGreevy

Mary McGreevy

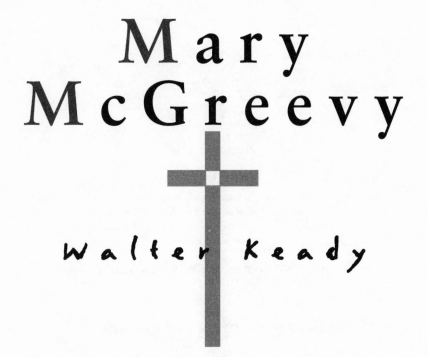

Walter Keady

MacMurray & Beck
Denver

Copyright © 1998 by Walter Keady
Published by:
MacMurray & Beck
1649 Downing St.
Denver, CO 80218

Printed and bound in the United States of America

2   3   4   5   6   7   8   9   10

Library of Congress Cataloging-in-Publication Data
Keady, Walter, 1934–
Mary McGreevy : a novel / by Walter Keady.
        p.   cm.
    ISBN 1-878448-83-8 (hardcover)
            I. Title.
    PS3561.E16M37   1998
813´.54—dc21   98-17137
                                        CIP

MacMurray & Beck Fiction: General Editor, Greg Michalson
Mary McGreevy cover design by Laurie Dolphin,
interior design by Stacia Schaefer.
The text was set in Granjon by Chris Davis, Mulberry Tree Enterprises.

To
My wife, Patricia
My siblings, Mary, Jim, and Bridie.

ACKNOWLEDGMENTS

My very special thanks go to Hilma Wolitzer, whose wise direction at a critical point put me on the right track.

I am particularly thankful to my brother, Jim, whose reminiscences of our childhood provided invaluable background material for this book.

I am most grateful to the Southern Dutchess Writers' Group for their constructive criticism throughout.

Many thanks to Frederick Ramey and the staff at MacMurray & Beck for their enthusiasm, kindness, and continued faith in me.

May 15, 1950
Mater Dolorosa Convent
Dargle Road
Drumcondra, Dublin

V. Rev. John Mulroe, P.P.
Parish House
Kildawree, Claremorris
Co. Mayo

Very Reverend Father,

It has come to my notice that Sister Mary Thomas of this Order of Mater Dolorosa is currently residing in your parish. She is doing so in direct defiance of her vow of Holy Obedience.

I would be most grateful, Father, if you would counsel Sister and admonish her severely to return immediately to her convent and her sacred commitments.

Yours in Jesus and Mary,
Matilda, Mother Superior

PART ONE

1

The parish of Kildawree rests in the low, ridged hills of south Mayo. On all but rainy days—of which there are far too many—you can see the Partry mountain range to the west, with the cone top of Croagh Patrick peering up from behind. Sometimes, when the air lightens after a cleansing shower, you can even see the pilgrims' path that winds to the top of Ireland's holy Reek.

To Father John Patrick Mulroe, newly appointed parish priest of Kildawree, those mountains were too far away. He had been born and raised in their midst and, apart from his seven years in Maynooth seminary, had spent his entire life surrounded by them. There was great comfort in the protective presence of their towering bulk. They made a person feel strong and safe and that God was looking solicitously down. In the couple of months since he had come to his new parish, Father Mulroe had been suffering from a feeling of vulnerability to the elements in the midst of these flat fields and puny hills and unending gray stone walls.

His new parishioners, however, went out of their way to make him feel at home. Good practicing Catholics, the most of them, as far as he could tell, which was a great consolation to a new P.P. Not a ripple of scandal or hint of trouble had disturbed the parish since his arrival. Not, that is, till the letter arrived from the mother superior. He would ever after recall exactly where he was and what he was doing on that momentous occasion: sitting in his dining room in his shirt sleeves, finishing his dinner of mutton, potatoes, and carrots at twenty past one on a Wednesday afternoon in May. He remembered even that it was the day before Ascension Thursday. There was a knock at the front door that brought his housekeeper padding down the hall. Then the voice of the postman: he had gotten to know the lilting tone of Paddy Joe Keohane, who had moved up from Kerry, it was said, to avoid being shot by the natives after the Treaty was signed in 1921. And then Bridie May floated in and left the letter by his plate and departed without a word. A silent woman, the same Bridie May, but a great housekeeper. He opened the envelope immediately, he remembered.

Since he was still getting to know his parishioners, Father Mulroe might have been expected to have not the foggiest idea who on God's earth the Reverend Mother was talking about. However, just the week before he had been called out to the townland of Kilduff to administer the last rites to an old man by the name of Michael McGreevy. There at the deathbed was a nun who introduced herself as the moribund's daughter, Sister Mary Thomas. "I came home to see him off," she explained. "We don't normally leave the convent," she added, as if a parish priest couldn't be expected to know about such an arcane practice.

"Very good," said Father Mulroe at the time. "Very good indeed." How was he to know she had no permission to be there?

"We're a very strict order," she continued. "We observe the monastic silence. Except of course when we're in school teaching the children. Or outside the convent like this."

"Yes, of course." Father Mulroe himself, because he was always fond of a good chat, had never entertained the slightest inclination to join a monastic order. It was sort of unnatural, he felt, to cut yourself off for life from the benefit and pleasure of your God-given gift of speech.

He had met her again three days later at the graveside. "I suppose I'll miss him," she said. "Though I hadn't seen him for sixteen years. And he never wrote to me until after Mammy died. He was the kind of man," she added, "whom you thought of as living forever, if you know what I mean."

"I do," Father Mulroe said. His own father had died two years ago. He shared his big black umbrella with her as they walked back from the graveyard in the rain.

"I didn't get home at all when Mammy died," she told him as they were passing Queally's public house. And then she cried a little, softly, her hand to that part of her face that wasn't covered by her veil. On Sunday morning she was at mass and communion, and then he didn't see or hear of her again until the letter arrived. As soon as he finished his jelly and custard and his cup of tea and biscuits he got up from the table and put on his soutane and biretta.

"I'm going back to Kilduff to see the nun," he told Bridie May. "So you know where I am in case the archbishop should be looking for me." He winked at the housekeeper: it had been a standing joke between them ever since His Grace had decreed that all priests of the archdiocese must leave word of their whereabouts whenever they left their residences. Outside the front door he got into the black Ford motorcar that his parishioners in Doogort had run a raffle to buy him on the occasion of his elevation to parish priest. It was his first car, and he was still a bit shy about driving it. In Doogort he had gotten around on a bicycle except when, which was fairly often, his parishioners would come to fetch him in a horse and trap or sidecar, or even on occasion an ass and cart.

He drove up the village now, very slowly and carefully. Past the post office on the left, then on the right Garvey's two-story residence, the bottom level of which housed the grocery shop. Followed by Queally's public house on the left again, painted a jarring bright yellow as if the color alone would attract every drinking man for miles around. Beyond Queally's he turned right onto the sandstone road that led to the parish of Castletown. The potholes and protruding boulders exercised the springs of the Baby Ford as he rolled by grim-looking Kildawree National School, with its gray limestone walls and long sloping slate roof, flanked on either side by concrete outhouses.

A mile and a half later he turned into the boreen for the townland of Kilduff. The grass grew down the middle of the narrow, winding track and the stone walls loomed close on either side, with hardly enough room for a hen to pass between them and the car. He counted five thatched houses and one rather new-looking bungalow, all of them close together, before he came to the one-story slate-roofed house that belonged to the deceased Michael McGreevy and where now, according to Mother Matilda, resided the nun Sister Mary Thomas. He drove through the gateway leading to the yard, to the great consternation of the hens that were nibbling there.

"Good afternoon," he said to the woman who came to the front door. "I'm Father Mulroe, the new parish priest."

"Of course you are, Father!" She smiled at him. "It's nice to see you again."

"Ah, yes," he said agreeably. She would have seen him at the altar these past few Sundays. A fine-looking woman indeed. Even if her red hair was cut terribly short and she was wearing a very plain gray dress. Although always very correct in his dealings with the opposite sex, Father Mulroe admitted—to himself only, of course—to an appreciation for God-given feminine pulchritude. "I was looking for Sister Thomas. They tell me she's still here." And the smile left his face, for beneath his calm and pleasant manner there lurked all the firmness of a parish priest fully bent on giving a delinquent nun a piece of his mind. If you belonged to a convent, you should be in your convent. If you took vows, then you kept your vows.

"Ah," said the pretty woman, "you don't know me, Father, without the habit."

"Good God!" was all the parish priest could manage at that instant.

"I think you'd better come inside, Father." Sister Mary Thomas led the way into the kitchen, where a fire burned brightly in the open hearth and a big black pot hung over the flames. Father Mulroe said nothing: his mind was grappling with the notion of a nun walking around without her habit. It seemed unnatural on the face of it. "We'll sit back in the room now, Father." She ushered him into the tiny parlor just off the front end of the kitchen. "Would you like a cup of tea?"

"No, thank you. No tea now." The room was dim and musty. Sister pulled back the heavy curtains on the window and let in some light. Two olive-green armchairs stood one on either side of the fireplace, and a small sofa was set back against one wall, a piano against the other. "We have things to talk about." He settled himself comfortably into one of the chairs.

"Well, I'm glad you came now, Father." She remained standing. "I had intended going back to see you all week, but there has been so much to do. My poor father, the Lord have mercy on him, wasn't able to take care of things these last few years. The house is a bit of a mess, as you can see, and the——"

"Sit down now," the parish priest interrupted, and Sister Mary Thomas sat obediently on the edge of the other chair. Her dress, he noticed, didn't fit her too well, as if it had been stitched together in a hurry. "I had a letter from your mother superior." He paused then, the way he liked to do in his sermons when he wanted to give the congregation time to absorb a particularly important point.

"Mother Matilda!" Sister Mary Thomas's face took on a look of great animation, which made her terribly good-looking. "How is she at all, the creature? She wasn't well when——"

"She tells me in the letter that you are here in disobedience to your vows." Father Mulroe gazed sternly at this nun without habit. It was a look he had had to practice a lot in his younger days. When he was a curate straight out of Maynooth his parish priest, a dour old dodderer, had admonished him for smiling too much. "You'll never be a good shepherd of your flock if you grin at people like that," the old P.P. had said, so Father Mulroe had begun to cultivate a stern visage in his morning mirror.

"I suppose I am, Father." Sister averted her eyes humbly to the shiny linoleum floor and said no more.

"Well, then," said Father Mulroe, searching for words to fill the sudden silence. "Isn't it time you were getting back to your convent? Obedience is the lifeblood of the religious life, you know." A great phrase that! He wondered as it came out of his mouth where it was he had read it or if he had just made it up on the spot himself.

"I don't know, Father," Sister Mary Thomas murmured, still staring pleadingly at the floor, as if guidance from the Holy Ghost Himself were to be found there.

"What don't you know?" The parish priest looked sharply at the top of the nun's head. Though short, the hair was a lovely tint of red.

"I don't know if I want to go back, Father." The head remained in its position of humility, but there was just the slightest hint of rebellion in the voice.

"Ah!" said Father Mulroe. And a satisfied *Ah!* it was. Here was the cue for one of his favorite homilies. Coming over in the car he had thought of it as appropriate for the occasion and had run over its main points in his head. It was a sermon he had given many times over the years when asked to conduct one-day retreats for nuns. He titled it "Fidelity to Commitments" in his notebook of sermons, and it was unfailingly a great success with the Sisters. "A commitment to Almighty God," he began now, "is the most solemn undertaking a human being can ever engage in." That was the opening line, and every time he used it he could feel the atmosphere charge with electricity. The nuns would sit a little straighter on their hard wooden benches and the already perfect silence would deepen, and Father Mulroe would know that he held his audience in the palm of his hand. It was a great feeling and one that filled him with a profound humility at the power for good that Almighty God had placed in his hands.

Sister Mary Thomas looked up suddenly from the floor. "No sermons, Father, please." And she said it rather sharply. "In sixteen years I've heard them all, and most of them are not worth the paper they're written on."

Now, Father Mulroe was as kindly a parish priest as you'd find in the archdiocese. Too soft for his own good was what people had often said of him behind his back in Doogort—especially when he went around in an old suit or soutane because some of the rich people in the parish would give only five shillings for their Christmas and Easter dues. Be that as it may, if there was one thing that he had developed in his twenty-one priestly years, it was a strong intolerance for lay recalcitrance in matters of faith or morals. The priest stood *in loco Dei* for his parishioners and any other members of the laity who came within his purview. And nuns, especially those who resided in *his* parish in defiance of their vows, most certainly belonged to this class of persons. They owed him the same obedience they owed to Almighty God Himself. He bristled, searching his brain for a quick mot juste that would recall this disobedient nun to her duty. As a preamble, he looked her sternly in the eye, the same practiced stare he had bestowed on her a little earlier. But this time Sister Mary Thomas did not glance humbly at the floor. She gazed back at him with eyes that were moist with pain. And that were full, too, of another quality that stopped John Patrick Mulroe the man from uttering the sharp retort that the parish priest was on the point of delivering. "Would you mind telling me why you don't want to go back?" he asked, in the mildest of tones, as he desperately tried to recover his priestly composure.

"I'm sick of it all!" Sister Mary Thomas spoke in a forthright tone, still looking straight at him with those luminous eyes. "I don't believe for one instant that this is the way Almighty God wants us to live our lives. In the convent we are children and we are treated like children and we act like children. And in the name of holy vows we no longer act as Christians or even as human beings." She got up from her chair and stood over the priest. "When my mother was dying and asked to see me, do you know what Mother Matilda said to me? She said it was more important for me to deny myself in the name of holy obedience than to honor my dying mother's last wish. That's what she said, and that's what I did, and the memory of it gives me a pain in the stomach every time I think of it. So when the word came a fortnight ago that my father was dying I just got up and walked out without telling anyone and came home to spend his last few days with him. And I'm glad that I did, and I don't believe that God will hold it against me." And she sat down abruptly and covered her face and cried.

The remainder of Father Mulroe's homily on fidelity went out the parlor's tiny window. He was familiar with the phenomenon of the crying woman, having come across it many times in his priestly ministry. But familiarity did not bring with it facility in coping. Being a man himself and as such never having engaged in the practice he couldn't decide whether he should console the weeper so as to hasten the process or leave her in peace to let nature take its course, as it were. Previous attempts to console having resulted in embarrassment to himself and fresh paroxysms to the criers, he decided this time to sit it out. So he sat back in his chair and folded his arms and lowered his head and gritted his teeth and tried to relax his shoulder muscles. He glanced briefly again at Sister

Mary Thomas's undulating red head before turning away and staring un-seeing out the window.

"Sorry, Father." He was surprised at how quickly it was over. The eyes were still damp, but she was trying to smile through them, and the effect sent quivers through the parish priest's entire nervous system. He straightened in his chair and shook himself like a dog coming out of water. He had been tempted a few times in his day by women's eyes, but he had always been firm in his reaction. He was a priest, a man of God, with the strength of his calling to shield him from such temptations. And he was not about to succumb to the charm of a nun with badly cut hair and a frumpy frock.

"So what are you planning to do?" was what he heard himself say to the disobedient sister. And in the gentlest of tones. The old dodderer had been right, of course: Father Mulroe needed to be more stern. "You must return to your convent immediately," he added sternly.

"I'm not going back, Father, and that's that now," the nun retorted with equal severity. She settled back into the armchair and crossed her legs defiantly.

"I see," said Father Mulroe. But of course he didn't see at all. It was just something to fill the silence at a time when there was nothing intel-ligent he could say. He was in fact nonplussed. He had come across the occasional parishioner who was bold or reluctant or evasive or even ar-gumentative, but never could he remember anyone who had defied him face to face.

"You don't know," said the nun, "what it's like to spend sixteen years locked up behind those walls. It was only when I came home and saw this place again and talked to the neighbors that it dawned on me what I had done with my life." She leaned forward confidentially. "Do you know, Father, what it was that really opened my eyes? The clouds. Would you believe that? In sixteen years I had never once seen them. Always going around with my head down in the bent of humility till I forgot they were up there. As a child I loved looking at them. I used to lie down in the fields for hours at a time and watch them rolling across the sky. And some days when there was rain on the wind they'd race across so fast and so dark that they'd frighten the wits out of me and I'd be afraid to look anymore. And on stormy nights they'd whip over the face of the moon and I'd think it was the moon itself that was chasing across the sky. But I forgot all this in the convent. And I forgot what it was like to have the freedom to stop on the road and talk to a neighbor. It was always silent in there. Except when we were teaching, of course. And the pressure of holiness weighing you down. To be more perfect. To avoid distractions. To live only for Jesus and Mary. To be always aware of my faults. To deny myself everything in the world that I liked. That's no way to live, Father. Do you really think that God put us on this earth and surrounded us with the beauty of nature and gave us our individual gifts for seeing and hearing and doing and enjoying only to have us reject them all for a life of sterility and abnegation? Well, I don't anymore. And from now on, with the help of God, I'm going to live like a real human being and I'm going to enjoy the good things that God has given us."

"I see," Father Mulroe said again. But he wasn't a bit nearer to knowing what he ought to say to this rebellious nun. Worse still, he was inclined to agree with her. Not the part about renouncing her vows, of course, but her view that it was unnatural to lock yourself up behind convent walls for your entire life. Being an honest man, he could not encourage anyone else to do what he wouldn't do himself. On the other hand, he had to recognize that Sister Mary Thomas had freely taken vows. And vows to Almighty God must be kept at all cost. He himself had taken on the obligation of celibacy, and, despite all temptations to the contrary—and they had been many over the years—he had managed to keep it and would keep it for the rest of his mortal life. So he said, "What about your vows, Sister? You have taken perpetual vows, I imagine?"

"Yes, yes, of course." She glanced briefly at him and then stared back down at the floor. "But you can get a dispensation from them. From the pope himself. We had a sister three years ago who had a nervous breakdown, and she got a dispensation."

Father Mulroe well knew that it was the duty of a parish priest to defend the teaching of the church at all times. Every last doctrine and practice, from the divinity of Christ down to the nightly recitation of the family rosary. And including fidelity to religious vows. Now, dispensations for nuns might be possible in extreme cases—though they never were for priests—but there was always fault in the petitioner when that occurred, and confessors like himself must dissuade their penitents from seeking such relief. And while it was true that Father Mulroe was not, by the letter of the law, Sister Mary Thomas's confessor, since she had never gone to confession to him, nevertheless it could clearly be held that at this moment in her spiritual life he stood *in loco confessoris*. And therefore it was his duty to direct her against the course of action she was proposing. In light of this, then, the response of the parish priest of Kildawree was inexplicable, and maybe even culpable. "You could do that, I suppose," Father Mulroe said mildly. And then he compounded the felony, as it were, by adding, "I'll have that cup of tea now if you don't mind."

It was only much later, after the unfortunate events that were yet in the future, that he asked himself why he had not been more firm and forthright. And even then, with the gift of hindsight, he couldn't give himself a satisfactory answer. Maybe, he considered, it was compassion for the pain in the sister's eyes. And maybe, he reflected in a moment of self-accusation, he selfishly wanted her to stay in his parish. Or worse, he goaded himself in pitiless denunciation, he was bewitched by short red hair and a pretty face. Anyway, whatever the reason, he did not properly use his pastoral powers that afternoon to persuade the reneging nun to go back to her convent. Instead, over a cup of tea and some freshly baked currant cake, he discussed his new parish with her.

"Ah, sure, it's a great place to live in, Father. I appreciate it more and more every day since I came home. It's the land, you see. The smell of mother earth. And the people are grand. This is where we belong, Father—not cooped up in convents."

"So you intend to stay here, then?"

"Where else would I go?"

"And what will you do? I mean, how will you keep body and soul together?"

"I have a farm to take care of." There was a puzzled look on her face. "Daddy left me the place in his will, you know."

"Well, is that a fact, now?" He gave the idea a moment's thought. "You'll have to get married, then, I suppose." A woman couldn't manage a farm by herself, now could she?

"Don't be too sure of that, Father." The nun arched an eyebrow at him and sipped her tea. "I've been thinking that it might be foolish for me to exchange the tyranny of one mother superior for another."

Father Mulroe blinked. "I don't quite understand that," he said a bit obtusely. He had been noticing her hands, with their long white, slender fingers, and wondering what a few years as a farmer's wife would do to them.

"Do you think for one minute that I'd let a man in here so he could tell me what I could do and what I could not do? I might as well go back to the convent." She extended the plate to him. "Have some more currant cake, Father."

"Well, now, maybe you *should* go back to your convent." Father Mulroe made one last belated stand for God and church and perpetual vows as he took a piece of cake. It was a long time since he had met anyone who so challenged the norms of civilization. Not, in fact, since Frank Cunnane. Frank was a stubborn confrere of his in Maynooth who challenged every doctrine taught by every professor until they sent him away in the middle of his second year of divinity. The last Father Mulroe had heard of him, he was preaching atheism on a soapbox in Hyde Park in London. This woman, he was beginning to think now, who wouldn't stay in her convent and wouldn't think of getting married, might be as big a thorn in his side in Kildawree as Frank Cunnane had been to the professors in Maynooth.

"I thought we had settled that, Father." The set of her mouth and chin said, don't argue with me any further. "I may as well tell you that I wrote a letter to Mother Matilda yesterday and cycled back to the post office with it this morning." Then she hit him with a sudden smile that had the parish priest clutching his empty cup more tightly. "So I'm here to stay, for better or worse. Anyway, Father, I'm sure that you and I will be good friends."

This was a fear that had already briefly entered Father Mulroe's mind. And it troubled him quite a bit on the drive back to the parish house. He went straightaway to his study and composed a letter to Mother Matilda.

Reverend Mother,

On receipt of your letter I visited Sister Mary Thomas at her home in Kilduff. Sister advised me that she does not intend to go back to the convent and that she has written you to this effect.

It is my considered opinion, based on a long conversation with Sister in which I advanced the most cogent arguments as to why she should return to the practice of her vows, that any further attempts to change her mind on this subject will be fruitless. I therefore suggest that the process of seeking a dispensation for Sister Mary Thomas be begun immediately.

As her parish priest I will, of course, provide Sister with all the spiritual direction she needs in this time of special trial to her soul.

> *Sincerely in Christ,*
> *John Patrick Mulroe, P.P.*

2

Tom Tarragh was having a heated discussion in his upstairs flat in Drumcondra on a wet, blustery Saturday afternoon in March 1940 when the letter came through the front-door mail slot. He had been appointed! It was a momentous occasion for him, one he had dreamed of ever since the day, when he was only fourteen years of age, that he had decided to become a national teacher. He was going to have his very own school and teacher's residence, and the respect of an entire parish. No small achievement for a ladeen who went barefoot to school on the westernmost tip of Achill Island. Mr. Thomas Aquinas Tarragh, principal of the National School in Kildawree.

In truth, however, it must be admitted that when his landlady brought the letter, the rap of her knuckles on his door brought panic rather than jubilation to the then thirty-five-year-old bachelor teacher. At that very instant he was in the midst of serious negotiations regarding the removal of a young lady's knickers. 'Twas a battle won and a battle lost. It required only the briefest of moments to get his shirt back on, open the door a smidge, receive the letter, exchange a little banter with the landlady, close the door, and return to the fray. Alas, during that moment not only had the knickers returned to their proper place but the frock that had been recently thrown on his bed was now restored to its owner's body. Thereafter the lady's bargaining position hardened. Without prior wedding bells, she averred, there would be no divestment. The result was that he and Maggie were married in July. They moved west to Kildawree as soon as they got back from a week-long honeymoon in Killarney, so that Tom could be ready to take up his new post on the first of September.

He was delighted to get out of Dublin. A country man—a *culchie*, as Dubliners called the men from Mayo—he had a fierce hatred for the city he was forced to live in—with the exception of its bookshops. And its theaters, which he loved to attend and in which he had a strong desire to participate himself someday. His other abiding passion was Irish history. It was his ambition to write a compelling account of Ireland's greatest heroes, both mythological and real. Though he didn't think much of a distinction needed to be made between those two categories.

It was not surprising then that the minute he got settled into the teacher's residence in Kildawree he decided to start a dramatic society and to write a history of the parish. The history he completed in three years, and it was greeted with much delight by the local population and no small praise by the history critic of the *Western People,* who proclaimed it a treasure of its kind. His attempt, however, to start a dramatic society was less successful. Father Moran, the parish priest at the time, was dubious about such innovation. The theater was a tool of the devil, he had learned in his seminary days back in the '80s, and even though it had now become an accepted facet of life in many parts of the country, he was extremely concerned about its effect on the spiritual health of his flock. "We'll have no plays here," he pronounced. And that was that until, nearly ten years later, he completed his dotage and died peacefully in his bed on a Sunday morning.

It would be unkind to say that Tom Tarragh cheered the old man's passing. But it would not be untrue to assert that he looked forward to the arrival of Father Moran's successor. Tom's hopes were heightened the minute he set eyes on Father Mulroe's puckish grin, and they were fulfilled a few months later when the new man not only approved of his putting on a play but even volunteered to announce the auditions from the pulpit. Father Mulroe prided himself on being a forward-looking man, but even *his* limitations were displayed when after last mass Tom let him know the name of the play he was putting on at Christmas.

"*The Playboy of the Western World,* is it! You can't be serious, Thomas?" The two of them were standing in the vestibule of the sacristy, looking out at the rain.

"It's a very fine play, Father," Tom said stoutly. "A very fine play indeed. You might even say a great work of literature." He had been afraid of just such a clerical reaction and was prepared to defend his choice.

"They tell me it's a bit dirty," said Father Mulroe, looking out somberly at the downpour.

"Ah, not at all," said the schoolmaster. "Not at all. Not in the least." He spoke nonchalantly, as if such an accusation were not to be taken seriously. "I've read it five times myself already, and there's not a dirty word in it."

"But didn't they have riots up in Dublin when it was put on at the Abbey Theatre?" The priest was a bit distracted, his mind mostly on how to reach his house through this lashing rain without being soaked. He hated getting wet. "I seem to remember reading about that somewhere."

"There was a bit of a row all right," said Tom, "but not because it was dirty."

"I think it's lightening up a bit," Father Mulroe said. Then he added the crucial words, "Well, if you think it's all right, go ahead so," before exploding into a sprint down the path to his house, one hand holding his soutane high above the knees and the other tightly gripping his biretta.

Tom Tarragh lost no time at all. On Friday night he was over in the school at seven o'clock waiting to see who would turn up for the auditions. He didn't have long to wait. Scarcely had he lit a fire in his classroom and finished moving the front desks over against the wall when he heard the crunch of bicycle tires on gravel. Jack Banaghan it was. A great footballer, Jack, and an intelligent fellow: a clerk with the Bank of Ireland in Ballinamore. He'd make a good Christy Mahon, was Tom's first thought. "How are you, Jack?" he said. "Will we beat Claremorris?" Kildawree was playing its old nemesis in the first round of the south Mayo football championship on Sunday.

"We could." Jack put on a sly grin as he pulled off his bicycle clips and shook out his trouser cuffs. It was said that half the girls in the parish were mad about him. And why wouldn't they? Tall, with a great physique and jet-black hair and big brown eyes, and he thirty years of age and a bachelor with plenty of money.

"I don't suppose you've done any acting before?" The schoolmaster was resigned to dealing with raw talent.

"I did a little bit when I was stationed in Tulach." Jack tried to sit in one of the desks. "Cripes, but they're small," he said in amazement and sat on the top instead. "They had a fairly good dramatic society over there."

"Watch out for the inkwell," Tom Tarragh warned, and Jack Banaghan jumped to his feet just as Kitty Malone walked in the door.

"No need to stand, now," said Kitty. "We'll keep it informal." She winked at Tom, and the principal of Kildawree National School felt the warm blood of embarrassment in his cheeks. A single woman of striking appearance and indeterminate age whose father had the biggest farm in Kildawree parish, Kitty Malone had been looking at him now in that certain way of hers for the past six months or more. And the more she looked, the more nervous he became. Not that he was terribly averse to her attention; on the contrary, he was flattered that such a fine-looking and cultured woman would single him out. And he had indeed been on the lookout for a wife ever since Maggie, the Lord have mercy on her, had died. What disturbed him about Kitty was the feeling that she, not he, was the hunter. He was a man who liked to be in charge of his own destiny.

"What play are we doing?" She faced him directly now, her back turned conspicuously to Jack Banaghan.

"*The Playboy of the Western World*." He only very briefly met her eye. "By J. M. Synge. It's about—"

"Oh, I'm familiar with it." She gave him the raised eyebrow. "I saw it in the Abbey Theatre in Dublin last year when Daddy and I were up for the Horse Show." Her voice had a brittle quality that suggested it might break at the very next syllable, though it rarely did. "It's a wonderful play indeed. Marvelous language." She smiled at him, and her blue eyes were soft, and Tom Tarragh felt the butterflies all the way to the pit of his stomach. "Pure poetry. I want the part of the girl, of course." She put her hand on his shoulder to emphasize her point. "What's her name at all?"

"Pegeen Mike." He said it without thinking. "Ah, no, probably you're thinking of the Widow Quin." She was a bit old to be sweet, innocent Pegeen, despite the long blond hair and trim, almost boyish figure. But she'd make a fine sharp-tongued widow all right, with her straight, thin nose and determined mouth.

"I mean the young one that the fellow falls in love with." She batted playful eyelids at him. "I'm not going to be any old widow, Tom. Can you imagine me!" And Kitty Malone laughed in a forthright sort of way that made Tom Tarragh feel his widower status was slipping out from under him. "I suppose," she added, "you'll be playing the leading man yourself?"

"Ah, no, no," he said quickly, his defenses rising to the occasion. "I won't be acting in the play at all. I'll just be doing the directing."

"Really? Well, that's a pity." She looked around to Jack Banaghan, who had his back turned to them examining a map on the wall.

"Who else is coming?" Jack called out.

"A lot more, I hope," the schoolmaster said fervently, and at that very second, as if in answer to his prayer, in walked Paddy Carney and Mick Burke.

"How are ye?" said Paddy, a rather stolid middle-aged farmer who had a wife and six children. The last man on earth Tom Tarragh would expect to audition for a play. He was dressed in his Sunday-mass suit.

"Ah, the thespians of Kildawree," Mick Burke declaimed with a flourish of his arm. Mick was the type Tom was looking for: curate and jack-of-all-trades at Queally's and a great talker and well-known wit. "And how is your ladyship this evening?" Mick, his quiff gleaming with brilliantine, bowed grandiosely to Kitty Malone.

"Very fine, your lordship." Kitty gave him half a smile and half a bow. "And how is Queally's this fine autumn evening? Has it been destroyed by fire and brimstone yet?"

" 'Tis just waiting for your presence, ma'am, waiting for your presence."

"It'll be a cold day in hell when Kitty Malone puts a foot inside Queally's, I can tell you that. Imagine! Making your living getting poor *amadhans* drunk."

"Arrah, what harm is there in the odd pint?" Paddy Carney put in sourly, looking down at his boots. He might do nicely for the part of Old Mahon, with his paunch and his jowls.

"It's not the odd pint," Kitty retorted, and there was a combative edge to her voice. "It's the too many odd pints the eejits have that cause the problem."

"Pegeen Mike is a barmaid, you know," Tom Tarragh pointed out.

"Yes, but she's a lot more than a barmaid, I'd say." Kitty walked away from them and looked out the darkened window at the back of the room.

"I've never been in a play myself," said Mick, hands deep in his pockets, looking admiringly after Kitty. "But I always wanted to. When I was a nipper I saw the Conway brothers do *The Plough and the Stars* back in Glenmore."

"I remember them lads well," Paddy Carney put in. He had his back to them, looking at a picture of a duck on the wall near the fireplace. "They used to come here too. With their big tent and an engine that gave them their own electric light."

" 'There's nothing derogatory wrong with me,' the fellow said," said Mick. "I always remember that line. He was fierce funny, the same lad."

" 'Twasn't long they were here, faith," Paddy said. "The second night Father Moran came up with a stick and told them to get out. Blasphemy and sacrilege he said they were committing just a few yards from the church itself."

"Someone's coming," Kitty called from the window. "I see a flash-lamp." Then she shouted, excitement in her voice, "It's the nun! Can you believe it?"

There was complete silence in Tom Tarragh's classroom then until Mary McGreevy walked in. The former Sister Mary Thomas had already been much talked about in the parish; great speculation as to whether she was fish or fowl, as it were. She appeared at her father's funeral in her nun's habit, and she came to mass as a nun for two Sundays after that. But then she turned up the next week in a green frock and a red coat and high-heeled shoes and nylon stockings. And the week after that she was wearing powder and lipstick. So why wouldn't there be talk! Dan Queally, a man of great common sense, told his patrons that she came out of the convent because she was an only child and the father left her the farm. But that was too simple for those who liked their gossip. Some know-all claiming inside information said she had been defrocked, whatever that meant. Others said they knew for a fact that she had gone soft in the head. Mary herself of course said nothing about the one and showed no signs of the other, and no one had the cheek to ask her what a nun was doing out of her convent. Even Wattie Feerick's wife, Rita, her neighbor that she came to mass with, said she didn't know what was going on. But maybe she did and maybe she didn't—Rita Feerick never talked much anyway.

There was discussion, too, at the beginning about how to address her when you met her, but that question was soon resolved. Back in Garvey's grocery one evening shortly after she stopped wearing her habit she was overheard telling Mrs. Garvey that she was Mary McGreevy. "Michael McGreevy's daughter, don't you know, the Lord have mercy on him." As if Maureen Garvey didn't know very well who she was. And when Noreen Macken, the postmistress, called her Sister the first time she went in to buy stamps she was promptly told, "I'm not Sister anymore, if you don't mind. Just plain Mary McGreevy will do."

Then there were those who reported seeing her out in the fields, in Wellington boots and a man's shirt and trousers, herding the sheep and cattle the father had left her. And it was known that Wattie Feerick cut the hay for her and his three older boys helped her save it. She herself was seen on the tramp cocks with the lads forking the hay up to her. And everyone wondering was she going to get herself a husband one of these days instead of trying to do a man's work all by herself.

"How are you, Mary?" said Tom Tarragh when she walked in the door. The schoolmaster heard all the gossip, though he spread none himself. Mary McGreevy said she was well, thanks be to God, and took off her coat and scarf to display a tartan skirt and a white blouse. A fine cut of a woman. Trim figure, neat ankles, and the red hair growing nicely in.

Tom's appraisal did not go unnoticed by Kitty Malone. "I didn't know they let nuns act in plays," she said to no one in particular.

"Ah, sure now, maybe they'd be better at it than the teetotalers," said Mick Burke, and he grinning impudently at Kitty. "You'd need a little drop of the creature inside you, I'd say, to give of your best on the stage. They say—"

"We're talking about nuns, not drunks," Kitty said.

"And why are you talking about nuns?" Mary McGreevy asked. There was a coolness about the former Sister Mary Thomas that might have warned a lesser woman than Kitty Malone to mind what she was saying.

"I thought *you* were a nun," said Kitty, and she looking over at Tom Tarragh for support.

"Can't you leave it be, now, Kitty?" said Paddy Carney. You could taste the discomfort in the air.

"'Tis no one's business but her own, I'd say," said Mick Burke. And he jingled the pennies in his pockets to cover the silence.

"I *was* a nun," said Mary McGreevy, calm as Dan Queally drawing a pint. "But I'm not anymore. There were good reasons for my leaving, but I'd rather not go into them here. Suffice it to say that I am now a layperson like the rest of you. Does that clear the air a bit?"

"Arrah, why wouldn't it?" said Mick. "You wouldn't be the first nun to leap over the wall."

"We'll take a look at the play, then, if you're all ready." Tom Tarragh spoke loudly into the strained silence. "I have copies here," and he handed them out. "We'll try reading a bit of it."

"I'd like to do the part of what's-her-name," Kitty reminded him.

"Right so." Though he'd have preferred the nun for that part. The men said nothing. Jack Banaghan was alternating between looking at the text and watching Mary McGreevy. Paddy Carney was sniffing at his book as if it were some new kind of tobacco. And Mick Burke was staring mesmerized at the cover of his.

"I'd like to read Christy Mahon, if you don't mind," the former nun said. In a very soft voice. Almost apologetically.

"But . . . ," said the principal of Kildawree National School. His mouth opened and his lips moved several times, as if he were trying to formulate a sentence. Yet no words came out. "But," he tried again, and this time there was apology in both the voice and the face, for he was a kindly man, especially towards women the like of Mary McGreevy, "Christy Mahon is a man."

Kitty Malone looked tolerantly at the nun. "You should read the Widow Quin's part," she said.

"I'd *like* to read Christy Mahon," Mary said again, still very quietly, looking at Tom and ignoring Kitty entirely. "I know the character very well. I used to read the play to my Leaving Cert English class."

"But—" Tom Tarragh began again.

"I know he's a man." There was a testiness in Mary McGreevy's tone this time. "But there's no reason why a woman can't play the part?" She slouched suddenly, walked slowly, heavily, shoulders hunched, to the schoolroom door, turned and faced them, hands on hips, and took a deep breath. "'And I the son of a strong farmer, God rest his soul,'" she declaimed in a strong voice, "'could have bought up the whole of your old house a while since, from the butt of his tail pocket, and not have missed the weight of it gone.'" She straightened herself up. "Can any of you say it better?" They all just stood there looking at her as if she were an apparition, nobody saying a word. She looked at Tom. "I know a lot of the part by heart already."

"Well, now," said the schoolmaster after a silence you could cut with Christy Mahon's spade, "you did that very well indeed."

"And my voice is deep," said Mary McGreevy in a deep voice. "When I dress up as a man people will forget straightaway that I'm a woman."

"The same way, I suppose, that they forget she's a nun," said Kitty Malone to the window.

"Now, Kitty!" Mick Burke begged. "Will you hold your whist like a good girl."

"We used to do plays at school." Mary ignored the interruption. "And the girls always did the men's parts, and some of them were very convincing. Try me," she pleaded, and those green eyes that had so disturbed Father Mulroe several months back now held Tom Tarragh in thrall.

"I don't know," he said, afraid to look at her and afraid to look away. "It would be very strange, wouldn't it?" But you could see he was weakening all the same.

"Arrah, go ahead, Tom," said Jack Banaghan, standing quietly by the fire.

"Sure," said Mick Burke. "Why not?"

"Right, then," Tom agreed. He seemed relieved at getting support. "We can give it a try anyway, I suppose."

"You can't be serious?" Kitty Malone expostulated. "Isn't Christy Mahon supposed to be a big, rough farmer who kills his father with a blow of a spade? I remember well the fellow who played him in the Abbey. He was twice her size."

"Ah, yes," said Tom Tarragh, indecisive again.

"If you will take the trouble to read the directions for the part," Mary McGreevy said evenly, "you will find that Synge describes Christy Mahon as a slight young man."

"Will you try the part of Shawn Keogh, then?" the principal said to Jack Banaghan.

"Right," said Jack, his eyes still on Mary McGreevy. "Shawn Keogh it is."

"You're engaged to Pegeen Mike here." Tom nodded at Kitty.

"You should play Christy Mahon yourself," Kitty said plaintively.

"And you'd be just right, Mick, for the part of Michael James Flaherty," Tom said. "He's a publican, you see. You know a bit about that business, I'd say."

"Faith, I do," said Mick. "Will I be serving real porter on the stage?"

"You'll have us all drunk at the end of the night, by God." Paddy Carney grinned and gave Mick a dig in the ribs.

"Be patient for a bit," Tom Tarragh said quietly to Kitty. "We'll see how things work out. Paddy, we'll try you for the part of Old Mahon, Christy's father."

"Christ Almighty! Do you think I'll be able for it?" Paddy looked petrified all of a sudden.

"I kill you with a blow of my spade before the play begins," Mary McGreevy told him. With the first touch of a smile that any of them had seen on her face.

"You don't say!" said Paddy. "Well, is that a fact? I'm playing a dead man, then?"

"Bedad," said Mick, "I can see the headlines already in the *Western People*: 'Carney the Corpse, the Dramatic Hero of Kildawree.'"

"I don't know if I can hold my breath," Paddy said, a worried look on his face. "People might take fright if they saw the corpse breathing."

He looked quizzically at Tom Tarragh. "I won't have to say anything, then?" He seemed disappointed at this sudden realization.

"Oh, you'll have plenty to say," Tom said. "You come back to life in the middle of the play."

"'Carney the Corpse, Risen from the Dead,'" Mick declaimed.

"If *you* play Christy Mahon," Kitty Malone said to Tom Tarragh, "the nun could play the Widow Quin."

"I'll thank you not to call me the nun," Mary McGreevy said sharply.

"I was thinking of Noreen Macken for the part of the Widow," Tom said. "I'll ask her about it tomorrow."

"I still think—" Kitty began.

"We'll do a bit of reading, then," Tom continued. "I'll fill in for the parts we don't have. We'll start at page one. Shawn Keogh is a bit of a bosthoon," he explained to Jack Banaghan. "Not a bit like yourself, of course, so you'll have to imagine what it would be like to be a sniveling, craw-thumping sort of a lad."

"Frankie Dunne, begob!" Mick shouted. "The greatest craw-thumper of them all. You know Frankie, don't you, from over in Kilnamona? He has a hollow in his chest from—"

"Will you shut up, Mick, and let us get on with the play?" Kitty shouted, and this time her voice did crack.

"Calm now, Kitty." Mick waved his arms at her like a farmer herding sheep through a gap. "I was just explaining to Jack that if he pretends he's Frankie Dunne he'll do a great job entirely on the part."

"Begob, Frankie mightn't like that," Paddy Carney admonished. "Frankie is the boyo with the fierce temper when he gets waxed. 'Tisn't only his craw he can thump, I can tell you. I once saw him at the fair of Ballinamore and he laying into—"

"Will you all shut up!" Kitty screamed, and the piercing ring of her anguished tone brought sudden silence, like the aftermath of a thunderclap. "Thank you," she said quietly, and they all staring at her as if she had just gone mad. "Shall I start, Tom?" And without waiting she began to read. "'Six yards of stuff for to make a yellow gown. A pair of lace boots with lengthy heels on them and brassy eyes. A hat is suited for a wedding day. A fine-tooth comb. To be sent with three barrels of porter in Jimmy Farrell's creel cart on the evening of the coming Fair to Mister Michael James Flaherty. With the best compliments of this season. Margaret Flaherty.'" She read in the measured, cultured tones that had been knocked into her by the nuns of stylish Kylemore Abbey, where she had gone to secondary school a long time back.

"Faith, you're a powerful reader entirely, Kitty," Paddy Carney said admiringly. Kitty rewarded him with the faintest hint of a smile.

"Well, yes and no." Tom Tarragh reddened with the anticipation of what he had to say. "You read it very well indeed, but you were not quite Pegeen Mike, I'm afraid."

"Oh!" Kitty arched an eyebrow at him. "And what was wrong with the way I read it?"

"Well, Pegeen Mike is a very simple sort of country girl, you see, with a Mayo accent you could hang your hat on."

"Like one of them Gibbons girls, Kitty," Mick Burke offered. Kitty glared at him.

"She'll say 'shtuff' for 'stuff' and 'besht' for 'best.' That sort of thing," Tom suggested.

"I see," Kitty said. But you could see the temper rising in her face.

"In this opening scene," Tom spoke into his copy of the play, avoiding Kitty's eye, "Pegeen Mike is sitting at a table writing. So she'll be speaking very slowly, you see, getting the words out just as she is putting them down on the paper. And she's not a quick writer, of course: she's barely able to write at all, in fact. So if you could think of her that way, with her tongue sticking half out, maybe, and she making her letters. Would you try it again?" There was apology but also a dogged determination in the schoolmaster's tone. He was going to do this play right, by God, with or without Kitty Malone.

So Kitty read it again, more slowly this time, though still with her cultured accent and with a strained awkwardness that set Tom Tarragh's teeth on edge. But he let her go on for now and then let them all try their parts. He was surprised at how well they performed. Mick Burke was a natural actor, as might be expected, managing to be both himself and Michael James Flaherty rolled into one. And Jack Banaghan showed that he had indeed done some acting before with a convincing reading of the sniveling Shawn Keogh. But Paddy Carney was the surprise of the evening: the stodgy farmer from Balyglass turned Mahon into a real cranky old character that Tom Tarragh felt John Millington would be happy with. His biggest difficulty would be trying to change Kitty Malone into Synge's wild peasant Pegeen Mike. Though to give her her due, she knuckled down to it when she saw he wouldn't let her do it her way. She tried with fierce determination to match the rough cadences of Christy Mahon that seemed to explode so naturally from Mary McGreevy. But she was never at ease with Pegeen's kind of speech, and he had to be constantly reminding her of the character she was playing. To complicate matters, he himself was being distracted a bit watching her. Marriage was a state he would like to be in again, and the thought of it would enter his mind any time he came across a likely-looking girl. Kitty was a fine woman indeed, and he felt she would have him the minute he was ready to ask her. She was the kind of woman a man like himself ought to be proud of having for a wife. She wasn't just good-looking but intelligent as well, and a great talker—a wife he would never need to be ashamed of. In that respect she was totally unlike Maggie, the Lord have mercy on her, a beautiful girl if ever there was one, but a rough diamond who had been an embarrassment to him more than once with her uneducated talk and her heavy Kerry accent. On the other hand, he was a bit afraid of Kitty, and he might as well admit it. He was a fairly easygoing man in many ways, which was why Maggie had been able to talk him into marriage against his better judgment. And Kitty was a woman of even stronger opinions and beliefs, which she would most certainly want him to share. Like not eating meat, which she had a terrible set against, and he a man who liked his bacon and the occasional steak or mutton chop. And her positive hatred of drink. He'd never again be able to have a pint or a drop of whiskey. And that wouldn't do at all, would it, though it wasn't a lot of drinking he did anymore. But despite all these objections he was still tempted by some undefinable attraction in the woman. In his saner moments he would acknowledge that he must fortify himself against the day when she would corner him and force him to propose marriage to her. At this very minute he was half entertaining the hope that if he annoyed her enough rehearsing the play, maybe she'd never want to set eyes on him again. "Pegeen would say 'shneaky,' not 'sneaky,'" he interrupted her hopefully.

"'That was a *shneaky* kind of murder did win small glory with the boys itself,'" said Kitty, meekly for a change.

It was Mary McGreevy most likely that was making him so critical of Kitty tonight. He hadn't met her before, though he saw her in church every Sunday. An attractive girl, for sure. Intelligent too. And young enough to give him the children he wanted so much. Something he wasn't sure Kitty could still do. Listening to Mary read Christy Mahon, he let his imagination conjure up what it would be like to have her walking into church with him on a Sunday morning. Or sitting at his side by the fire on a winter evening. Or getting into bed with him on . . . No, he shouldn't be thinking of things like that right now. But a man couldn't help wondering what it would feel like all the same. She had lovely hands that turned the pages of Synge so gracefully. "Will I do, do you think?" she asked when he said that would be enough for tonight.

"How did *I* do?" Kitty put in without waiting for him to answer the nun.

"You were both great." What else could he say? "I'd like you all to start memorizing your lines," he said loudly to everyone.

Kitty put on her coat. "If you're going home now, Tom, I'll walk back with you."

The schoolmaster had been hoping to have a chat with Mary. "I have a few things to do here before I go."

"I'll wait for you," she said.

Mary McGreevy slipped away with the others. Tom shuffled papers and made notes for long enough to justify his lie, while Kitty waited patiently by the door. Finally he struggled into his raincoat, switched on his flashlamp, and turned out the electric light. "Mind the step down," he advised at the hall door. But too late—Kitty lurched suddenly, wordlessly, into the night. "Oh my God!" His flashlamp showed her crouched on all fours on the gravel. "Are you hurt? Are you all right?"

"Of course I'm not all right!" Her voice was tight with pain but under control. "I've torn my hands and knees to shreds on these bloody stones."

"Let me help you." He stepped in front of her and bent over.

"Will you get that bloody light out of my eyes, for God's sake!" He put the lamp in his coat pocket. In the sudden darkness he groped for her arms. "Mind your manners, Tom Tarragh," Kitty yelled.

"Sorry! Terribly sorry!" Small and soft they were. This time he found the arms and tried to lift her.

"Easy does it, now! I'll get up by myself." And she did.

Their hands touched briefly and he felt the sticky wet. "I think you're bleeding. Come back to the house and we'll take care of you." She didn't object and hardly said a word till they were inside the door and he turned on the electric light.

"Jesus!" she shrieked. "I'm a bleeding mess." And she laughed half hysterically.

"Bleeding is the word," he said. When she lifted her skirt her knees were a mess of crimson sand and tattered nylons. "If you'll come upstairs with me we'll get you cleaned up." He led the way to his pride and joy in the teacher's residence—just this past year he had had running water and a fully appointed bathroom installed. Despite all the gore she had just small cuts on three fingers of one hand and a gash on the palm of the other. "This'll sting." He swabbed iodine with a piece of cotton.

"Sting, my foot! Burn, scorch, crucify is more like it." But she didn't flinch.

"Now let's see the other."

"You just want an excuse to see my knees."

"I don't . . ." he began, flustered.

She raised her skirt and looked at the knees again. "The stockings will have to come off first. Your job, Tom. I can't do it with these poor fingers."

It was his turn to burn. His girl-chasing days had ended abruptly with marriage. Maggie, the Lord have mercy on her, had seen to that. And the respectability bestowed on and expected from a principal teacher had kept him from renewing such activities after she died. "I don't know," he mumbled.

"I'm sure you've often done it before." She hoisted the skirt till the tops of the nylons and the crotch of her white knickers showed. "Just unhook them from the garter belt and roll them down. And God help you if you tear my poor knees any worse."

He had forgotten the feel of a woman's inner thighs. Tactile memories of Maggie's soft flesh. He fumbled at releasing the stockings till she giggled. "What in God's name are you doing at all?" But she didn't move. He had to have hurt her in peeling the nylons off, but she said nothing. He cleaned and swabbed the wounds and bandaged both knees. "You'd make a fine doctor," she said when he finished. "Or even a good husband, maybe."

He was about to offer her brandy when he remembered her aversion to alcohol. "Would you like a cup of tea?"

"That would be grand." She stepped gingerly down the stairs ahead of him. "It must be awful for you having to cook and clean for yourself. You need a woman around the place." She sat primly at the kitchen table.

He stoked the range and added turf. "Sarah Brown comes in every day to take care of the house. Did you know that she's a great-grandniece of the late unlamented Lord Castletree?"

"I knew that. Daddy knows everything about everybody in the county. Sarah has to be a hundred by now. She was old when I was a child. It must be hard for her to get around, never mind do any work."

"She needs the money, God help her. Lord Castletree used to own the entire parish of Kildawree." He filled the kettle from the tap at the sink and put it on the range. "But Sarah doesn't have a penny to her name."

"Daddy said she was once engaged to an English lord, but he ran away with a London chorus girl instead. And she never got married afterwards. They tell me you were married yourself." She wasn't looking at him anymore.

"Ah, yes. Yes indeed. The wife died five years ago. In childbirth. The baby too. The Lord have mercy on them both."

"That's very sad. I'm so sorry."

That brought silence for a minute. Then Kitty said, "It must be terribly lonely for you without them. You know, I'm dreading the day when Mammy and Daddy will go. But I suppose you'll get married again?"

"I think the kettle is boiled." He jumped to his feet. "Do you like your tea strong?"

A strong pair of knuckles rapped the back door at the other end of the room. Father Mulroe. "I saw the light in your kitchen and I said to myself, the man is making tea. Was I right? Bridie May goes home after . . ." He was in the door before he noticed Kitty. "Oh, I'm awfully sorry. I didn't mean to . . ." He turned to head back out the door again.

"Not at all, Father. Not at all. Come right in. Kitty and I were just about to have some tea. We'll enjoy your company."

"We will indeed, Father." And Tom Tarragh had to admire Kitty Malone for that dissimulation.

3

Some said it was being the youngest of six boys with no girls in the family that made Jack Banaghan so shy with the women. And that might well have been the case. Especially since the mother died when he was only four, and he was reared without the benefit of a woman's touch. Others said he was just taking after the father in bashfulness before the opposite sex. And there could be some truth in that too. Michael Banaghan was forty years of age, with his own farm of land and well on the way to being eternally bachelor when Delia Farragher snared him before he knew what was happening.

At any rate, Jack's reticence with the girls was talked about—especially by the girls themselves. It was one of his most endearing traits, and certainly his most exasperating. It was not that he never met them, or talked to them. He had been going to the dances in Ballinamore with other lads of his age since he was eighteen. A great dancer too, and not in the least afraid to ask a girl out for a waltz or a foxtrot or a rumba. But that was it. He rarely asked to see one of them home. And only with two of these did he ever do a steady line. Several other young ladies did their level best to coax him out—short of outright asking, of course, which was not permitted by the social rules of the day—but without success. The two he did go out with were said to have been quite disappointed with the level of physical contact. Or rather, the lack of it. One of them,

Carmel Quinn, who had been daft about Jack for years, immediately afterwards started doing a line with his oldest brother, Packy, whom she
married within the year. There were those who said she did it just to live
in the same house with Jack. Which she did: the old man handed the
place over to Packy on his marriage and went to live with another of the
married sons in Ballinamore, and Jack stayed on to help Packy with the
farm in his spare time while he worked in the bank. That led to some talk
for a while about Carmel and Jack until Jack went to work at the Bank
of Ireland in Tulach and they didn't see him for a few years. When he
came back to the bank in Ballinamore and started to appear at Town Hall
dances again, those ladies that hadn't gone to England or Dublin or gotten themselves married in the meantime thought for sure he would be
different. But not a bit—he was just as skittish as before.

The nub of the matter was the squeezing and the kissing that were
the concomitants of seeing a girl home from a dance. It wasn't that Jack
was averse to these activities. On the contrary, the thought of engaging in
them tortured him day after day and night after night. But, unfortunately, there was sin. Mortal sin—always mortal, you see. Well had the
Christian Brothers done their duty of warning him about the dangers of
sex. There was no light matter when it came to sins of the flesh, Brother
Ciaran pontificated in catechism class. Dancing, he allowed in answer to
a question, was all right as long as it was done with a good intention—for
recreation and not for carnal titillation. The tango, he added explicitly,
was a dangerous dance and was to be avoided.

The conclusion for Jack was obvious: unless you were engaged to a
girl, or at least had the serious intention of getting engaged to her, you
had no right to be doing a line with her and risking occasions of serious
sin by so doing. So he danced chastely with the girls and kept his distance
from them and watched and waited for the right one to come along.

Until he renewed acquaintance with Mary McGreevy. He had
known her since he was a nipper. They were neighbors before she went
to the convent—she from the townland of Kilduff and he just a bit farther over the road towards Castletown in the townland of Gortmor. But
because she was four years older, he hardly ever talked to her in those
days. She would say hello to him and the lads as they walked back the

road to the National School and she passing on her bike to the convent school in Ballinamore. Then she became a nun herself and he forgot all about her. Since she had come home this year he saw her at first mass every Sunday. Once he even knelt beside her at the altar rail, and he said hello to her outside the church on a few occasions. But he didn't pay the slightest attention to her until the night of the play rehearsal.

The minute she walked in the schoolroom door that Friday evening the shivers rippled down his body. And he marveled as he tingled at how he could have failed to notice this gorgeous woman until now. He watched her discreetly all evening, making sure that she never caught him looking. And he daydreamed about her all week, to the point of several times forgetting his count of banknotes and having to start all over again. Occasionally, the imagination would go too far on him and he would feel the forbidden stirring in his body. Then he would have to utter silent ejaculations to the Blessed Mother to prevent the other kind from occurring. Saturday night he told Father Mulroe in confession about his bad thoughts and impure looks. At first mass on Sunday she was a few seats in front of him on the women's side, and he had trouble keeping his eyes to himself. At the end he waited till she got up to leave and then followed. It was his intention to cycle back the road with her. But Rita Feerick was waiting outside for her, so he joined the lads at the gate for a chat instead.

They were just finishing the dinner when Eamonn Reilly came by. Carmel gave the young man a cup of tea and he sat at the table talking with Packy, who was feeding his youngest lad with a spoon, while Carmel and Jack washed the dishes in their new scullery. It was at times like this that Jack wondered why he had let Carmel slip away instead of marrying her himself. He liked helping his sister-in-law with the housework, and he did it whenever he could. Packy would sometimes engage in good-natured jeering at him for doing what he called woman's work, although he himself was sometimes coerced by Carmel into helping out around the house.

When they were finished with the dishes, Jack got his togs and boots from the bedroom and tied them on the carrier. "There'll be great skelping today," Eamonn said happily as they got on their bikes. He was referring to the match against Claremorris. Kildawree was proud of its footballers. They were a small parish, backward maybe in many ways, but for several years now they had had one of the best teams in south Mayo. This year they were hoping to prove they were the best. Some of the young lads who managed to stay home rather than going off to England had turned into skilled and forceful players. Like Eamonn Reilly, their big, raw fullback, who was known as Iron Ned for the bone-crunching shoulders he inflicted on any unfortunate forward who got in his way. And among the older lads they had Jack Banaghan, who by common agreement was the best footballer Kildawree had ever produced. He had even played briefly for the county team a few years ago, and although he hadn't particularly shone in that capacity, the glory of his being chosen reflected well on the entire parish.

They were early for the three o'clock match. Only a few old codgers were standing by Queally's gate when they wheeled their bikes through and headed for the football field at the back. "Hit them hard, Ned," one man shouted at Eamonn. The Kildawree crowd liked a good robust game. Several of the lads were already togging out behind the wall at the back of the field. By the time Jack finished tying the laces tightly around his boots the Claremorris team had arrived. They picked a spot farther along the wall as their dressing room, and Jack as captain of Kildawree walked down to welcome them. Then he jumped the wall and got out on the field to join his own team for a bit of practice before the match.

The referee had just blown his whistle to line them up for the start when Jack spotted her. By this time there was a good crowd spread out along the sidelines—Kildawree turned out in force to cheer its own. What he saw first was the coat, the brilliant scarlet set against the green grass in the foreground and the gray stone wall behind. He knew it had to be her the second the red came into his peripheral vision. Who else could it be? Careful not to be seen looking in her direction, he waited till he was facing the Claremorris captain for the coin toss that decided who would play into the wind before glancing across. It was her all right. Standing near the middle with a man and a woman on either side. Wattie and Rita Feerick, neither of whom he had ever seen at a football match before.

He was conscious of her presence all through the match. You're too old to be showing off for a girl, he told himself as he leaped high for a ball. But he *was* showing off anyway, and well he knew it. And he didn't care. A wild sort of lightheartedness came over him at the thought that she was watching him do what he did best, and it made him play better than ever. Which surprised some of the old-timers on the sideline who had been saying for the past year that Jack Banaghan was slowing down. His performance seemed to inspire the younger lads, and when the referee blew the whistle for halftime they were leading Claremorris by a point.

He joined Eamonn Reilly as they walked off the field, making sure they were heading in the general direction of the red coat. He had his head down, talking nonsense to Iron Ned and wondering whether to say hello to her or just walk right by, when Wattie Feerick shouted, "Good on ye, lads!"

Eamonn stopped and waved. "How are we doing?" He and Wattie were neighbors.

"You keep it up now and you'll kick them lads all the way back to Claremorris," said Wattie, a slightly built man with carrot-red hair and a faceful of freckles. A talker to beat the band, this same Wattie, and equally well known for his nine children, his physical strength, and the amount of turf he could cut in a single day.

"You're great entirely," Rita added. She was a quiet woman, half a head taller than Wattie and about twice his weight. The fellows at Queally's said it was she that wore the pants in the Feerick house.

"Hello, Jack," Mary McGreevy said—casually, as if the match had not thrilled *her* in the least. But when he glanced at her he found a kind of excitement in her eyes that said otherwise. On Tuesday night she had ignored him, giving all her attention to Tom Tarragh. Now she was looking at him as if he were an old and valued friend. It was a good job he was already flushed in the face, for that look of hers would most certainly have made him blush. He had a propensity for turning red at the least provocation.

"How are you?" he managed to say, conscious of the sweat trickling down his face.

"I'm learning my lines." She waved her arms: "'I've seen none the like of you the eleven days I am walking the world, looking over a low ditch or a high ditch on my north or south, into stony scattered fields, or scribes of bog, where you'd see young, limber girls, and fine, prancing women making laughter with the men.'" And then she laughed herself, a deep and richly melodious sound that echoed and reechoed in the caverns of Jack's already excited sensibilities.

"That's great!" He wished Ned and the Feericks would go away and leave the two of them alone to talk.

"Is that the play ye're doing?" Wattie asked.

"It is," said Mary. "'You've a power of rings, God bless you, and would there be any offence if I was asking are you single now?'" She laughed again, and there was a teasing look in her eye that made Jack want to forget his religious scruples about flirting.

"'Tis a strange way to be talking," said Wattie. "Who do you think would say things the like of that?"

"It's a play about Mayo people," Mary said.

"Well, on my oath," Wattie declared, "I never heard anyone in Mayo talk like that. Making fun of us they are, I suppose. They do a lot of that up in Dublin, they tell me, make sport of the poor Mayo lads. *Culchies,* they call us."

"True for you, Wattie." Mary smiled at him. "Them Dublin jackeens are strange people. But this play is not making fun of us. It's a great poem about the people of Mayo, and someday we'll all be proud of it."

"Good on you, Jack!" Three young women passed by and waved at him. "We'll see you at the dance tonight." Jack was mortally embarrassed. He didn't want Mary McGreevy to know he might be going dancing with these young ladies. A sudden thought struck him to ask her if she'd like to go herself. But of course he couldn't here in front of everyone.

Father Mulroe and Tom Tarragh were talking to the lads behind the wall. They had both been footballers themselves in their days and were keen supporters of the Kildawree team. "Good man yourself," the parish priest greeted Jack. "You'll beat those lads if you keep it up."

"Well, it won't be for want of trying, Father," Jack said. "We could use your left foot out there today," he teased Tom Tarragh. Tom used to practice with them occasionally, though he claimed he didn't have the stamina anymore for a match.

The fellows at Queally's were saying all the next week that they never saw a man play as hard as Jack Banaghan did in the second half of the game on Sunday. But none of them knew the cause of Jack's inspiring performance. Mary McGreevy had wished him luck when he was going back on the field, and he vowed that come hell or high water he was going to win this match for her. And he did, almost singlehandedly. Claremorris was leading by two points with only minutes to go when Jack got the ball at center field, did a thirty-yard hand-to-toe run, and smashed the ball into the back of the net. The Kildawree crowd went wild, and his teammates carried him off on their shoulders at the end of the game.

It took him a long time to change out of his togs. The parish priest and the schoolmaster came back to congratulate them. Some of the younger lads who aspired to the team crowded around, wanting to relive the highlights of the game, especially that last goal of his. Then he had to go over to the Claremorris lads and say a few diplomatic words. By the time he finally escaped and went looking for her, Mary McGreevy was nowhere in sight. Eamonn Reilly wanted him to stop into Queally's for a pint with a few of the other lads, but Jack excused himself on the grounds of being tired and headed home instead. Normally his mind would be on the match just played, reenacting and savoring the high points. But not today. All the way back the road he was thinking how gorgeous Mary McGreevy looked in her red coat, and wondering why he hadn't ever paid attention to her before, and warning himself that he'd better do so immediately before she got interested in somebody else. Tom Tarragh, for instance, if indeed that hadn't already happened. Maybe she had left with the schoolmaster and was now being entertained to tea in his big teacher's house. On a sudden impulse as he was passing the Kilduff boreen he turned in, cycling slowly, wondering what he was going to say. If she was at home, of course.

She was. He was taken aback when she opened the door to him not more than two seconds after he knocked. "Well, isn't this a pleasant surprise!" And although her smile was wary, she said, "Come on in. I just put the kettle on to make some tea. I'm sure you'd love a cup after your hard match."

"I wouldn't mind." And he was suddenly overcome with a terrible shyness.

"Pull a chair over to the fire; it's getting cold out there." She poured water from the kettle into the teapot. "Did you win?" The tragic look on his face must have been comical, for she immediately added, "Don't mind me at all. Wattie and Rita had to go before the end to take care of a sick calf, so I had to leave with them because they gave me a ride in the trap."

"We won by a point," he managed to say. Though all he could think about at that minute was that his goal had been wasted.

"Isn't that great, now." She mustered enthusiasm. "You played awfully well yourself, I must say."

"Fair to middling." He wanted so badly to tell her about the goal, but of course he couldn't.

She smiled at him. "Oh, you're very modest, Jack."

It was her smile that gave him the courage. He'd better do it now while he still had the nerve. It was well he knew his own weakness: he'd talk around the subject all night and never make the actual overture. Sometimes, like now, he resented the fact that it was always the man who had to do the asking. "Will you come dancing with me tonight? Stephen Garvey is playing."

"Unfortunately, I don't dance at all." Her smile turned apologetic. "I never have, and I don't suppose now that I ever will."

"Ah, go on, give it a try." Forcing himself to be brazen.

"I'd love to oblige you, Jack, but I'm much too old now for that sort of thing. Do you know what I mean? I'd rather leave it to the young ones, if you don't mind." She brought two cups and saucers from the dresser and began pouring.

"Did you *never* go dancing?" He had to keep talking to hide his mortal embarrassment. "I mean before you went . . ."

"Before the convent? Just a couple of times when I sneaked out unbeknownst. Daddy, the Lord have mercy on him, would never let me go. He claimed that lads going to dances had only one thing on their minds. Dangerous places for a girl, he always said." She went back to the dresser and unwrapped a large piece of currant cake from a cloth. "Bring your chair over, now, and we'll have a nice cup of tea." She took a long carving knife from a drawer in the table and began to cut the cake. "I'll bet you have an appetite after that game."

"I do indeed," Jack said. "I—"

"Do *you* think dances are dangerous?"

"I—" Jack began.

"Help yourself to the cake."

"For me," Jack said, taking a piece, "dances are what you make of them. You can go to a dance and not get yourself into any kind of trouble, providing you go with the right intention."

"And what do you mean by a right intention?" She cut her piece of cake into dainty bite-sized squares and then put a tiny daub of butter on one square and placed it delicately in her mouth.

"The intention of avoiding sin." He could never say anything like this in front of the lads, or the girls for that matter, for fear they'd laugh at him. But he felt quite comfortable saying it to the ex-nun.

"I see." She buttered another square and placed it on her tongue. "But what kind of sins, if I may ask, are you likely to commit at a dance that you wouldn't be equally likely to commit anywhere else? Do you know what I mean?"

"Well!" He had a terrible fear he was going to blush. "You know the kind of thing that goes on at dances!" He waved his arms, almost hitting the jug of milk.

"It's so long since I've been." She was munching contentedly.

"There are those who dance very close, holding each other very tight. That's a definite occasion, I'd say."

"Uh-huh." Gazing at him with those gorgeous green eyes. "Is that it? They don't do anything else that you'd consider dangerous?"

He had a feeling that she was teasing him and enjoying his discomfort. "No, it's not!" The anger suddenly welling up inside him. "There's a lot of kissing and cuddling in the alley behind the hall. And a lot of things taking place on the way home, behind bushes and walls and inside hay sheds."

"And you think all that is bad?"

"It's mortal sin, isn't it?" He snapped the words at her.

"You think it's mortal sin?" There was a challenge in the deep voice that said he'd better be able to prove his assertion.

"Well, isn't it true that there is no light matter in those cases?" Feeling a bit exasperated at her questions. "At least, that's what I was taught. I wish it wasn't, God knows, but that's the way it is."

"And you don't think a bit of squeezing and kissing can be justified because people have a need for those things?"

"I do not!" he retorted fiercely. "Sins against the flesh are always mortal."

"Let me tell you a story." She finished chewing the last square of cake and took a sip of tea. "Once upon a time," she said, pushing back her chair from the table and crossing her legs and folding her arms, "an Irish monk by the name of Ganmny went to a far-off land to convert the heathens. He traveled the length and breadth of the country, preaching the gospel, fasting and praying for these poor pagans, and generally living a most exemplary life.

"But it was all in vain. Not a single soul did he convert. The people loved to listen to him, for he had a most mellifluous voice. They flocked in their thousands to hear him preach. But when he was finished they went back to worshiping their old gods and thought no more of Ganmny's exhortations. He asked one man why this was so. 'Because,' said the man, 'we follow only the religion of our queen. We worship only the gods she worships. Convert first our queen and then we will all become followers of your God.'

"So the monk went to the palace of the queen who ruled the land and begged to be allowed to preach the true faith to her and her court. The queen herself overheard his plea as she walked in her garden and, immediately bewitched by his golden voice, sent for him and had him preach to her. He gave her his finest sermon, and she listened enraptured. When he was finished she ordered a sumptuous feast prepared and invited him to her table. And after they had eaten and drunk, though Ganmny ate only a few vegetables and a little fruit and drank only water, the queen said in a loud voice before all her courtiers, 'I have fallen in love with this noble monk and swear before you all that I will grant him any favor he chooses to ask. I do, as is the custom in this kingdom, reserve the right to attach one condition to the granting of the favor.' Then she turned to Ganmny who sat by her side and said, 'Sir, what is the favor that you ask of me?'

"The monk was overjoyed. 'I beg only,' he said, 'the favor of your conversion to the one true faith.'

"'Granted,' said the queen immediately. 'And my condition is this— that you make love to me tonight. Then tomorrow I and all my subjects will convert to your one true faith.'

"'But,' expostulated the monk, 'I am a celibate priest. I have a vow of perpetual chastity. It would be a mortal sin for me to have carnal inter- course with you.'

"'Nevertheless,' said the queen, 'that is my condition. Think of what you have to gain. I and all my subjects and all our descendants forever- more will belong to your one true faith. Did you not say that that is the greatest gift of all, to belong to your only true religion? Would you deny millions of my people the right to eternal happiness simply because you will not make love to their queen?'"

Mary McGreevy stopped and sipped her tea. "There's no ending to this story," she said, "only a question to the listener—what would you do if you were the monk?"

Jack had been so mesmerized listening to her, so captivated by her voice, as the queen was with the monk, that he missed the conundrum. When she repeated the question he could only stutter while he tried to get his brain going. "I—well—" And he stopped to think some more. "What would *you* do?" he shot back at her in desperation.

"Never mind what I would do," she said. "You're the man who has been spouting dogma. So I'm asking you to apply your dogma and decide what is right and wrong in this particular case. If you were Ganmny, would you carry your rules to their logical conclusion by maintaining your chastity, and thereby condemn the souls of millions to the loss of Paradise? Or would you fornicate with the queen and become the Saint Patrick of that pagan land?"

"I'd do the right thing!" He suddenly felt decisive. It was the word *fornicate* that tipped the balance. "I'd trust to the providence of Almighty God to take care of the people." He looked at her challengingly.

"Right so," she said, not a bit put out. "But God helps those who help themselves. And it doesn't appear to me that divine providence necessarily cleans up after our blunders. Can I get you some more tea?" She went to the fireplace and brought back the pot. "So you would stick to your principles at any cost?" She filled his cup.

"You know, you're a very smart woman. We never had questions like that at school." He leaned back in his chair and stretched. "So what would *you* do if you were this monk, what's his name?"

"Ganmny. Well, I'm of the opinion that there are very few absolutes in life." She put her elbows on the table and looked him in the eye till he had to glance away. "I believe there are very few laws or rules that can't or shouldn't be broken if the particular circumstances demand it."

"Do you, now?" He was trying desperately to hang on to her train of thought.

"Let me ask you one question: In the matter of fornication or adultery, where is the evil? I mean, precisely what is it that is bad about them?"

Jack felt the warmth rising in his cheeks. In his entire life he had never deliberately thought about fornication or adultery, much less discussed them. So to be asked now to talk about them by this woman whose very nearness was creating within him the most exquisite sensations relating to those very sins was more than his nature could deal with. "The fact that they offend God, I suppose," was all he could manage.

"But why do they offend God?" That smile of hers was both delicious and malicious. "Take the act of sexual union. If the couple are married it is called the sacred consummation of holy matrimony. If they are not, it's the vile sinful carnal copulation of animals. Yet it is the same act. So what makes the one good and holy and the other evil and disgusting? Do you know what I mean?"

"You tell me." He had gone red as a beetroot at the awful words she was throwing around.

"Damned if I know!" Mary McGreevy laughed out loud. "Damned if I know!" And she banged the table with the side of her fist.

"But isn't it enough that God condemns it? Doesn't the gospel say it's sinful?"

"But why? I can understand the sin of adultery. The other spouses will be hurt by what the adulterers do—if they find out. But what's wrong with two single people making love if they don't do any harm to anyone else and face up to the consequences of their act? Tell me that, Jack Banaghan!" And she looked suddenly fierce, and Jack felt guilty because he had no answer to give her.

"You're a strange woman," he heard himself say.

"Amn't I, now?" And she chortled, a silvery tinkle that drove the embarrassing conversation from his head and sparked his imagination to float around the ballroom with her in his arms.

But she wouldn't go dancing with him, even though he asked her again. She made more tea and got out the frying pan and cooked him a decent supper. And he helped her milk the cows after that, and then they sat for hours by the fire talking. It was after twelve when he got up to leave, and she walked out to the road with him. It was just as he straightened up after putting on his bicycle clips that she kissed him, softly and firmly, full on the lips. She didn't say another word, and he pedaled home with a million devils of glee and fear and dread dancing inside his head.

4

It is incumbent on the parish priest, if he is to be a good shepherd
to his flock, to know all there is to be known about each of his sheep. And
it is an article of folk wisdom among the clergy that you cannot know
your parishioners unless you know their ancestry and their relations and
whom they're great with and whom they have fallen out with. It was this
onerous duty of knowing his sheep that Father Mulroe had in mind
when he asked Bridie May to determine discreetly who in the parish was
best equipped to supply, in strictest confidence of course, the requisite information. Bridie May listened in silence, nodded her head when he was
finished, and a week later told him as she was pouring his evening tea, "If
you want to know what makes this parish tick, you'll visit Henry
Malone." Then she left him to his toast and boiled egg without saying another word. Later on, when she was clearing the table, she added, "He
has a son, a priest, a missionary in South America."

Henry Malone was a rugged-looking, raw-boned, sprightly man,
close to eighty years of age as far as anyone could tell, with a big farm of
land and, everyone said, a lot of money in the bank. And he did indeed,
it was generally agreed, know more about the ins and outs of all the
human ties of blood and water and all the consanguinities and all the
affinities pertaining thereto, within and anywhere near the parish of
Kildawree, than any other living soul. Father Mulroe didn't ask him any

questions, of course. The information came by way of harmless conversation on the Sunday evening visits he paid to his parishioner's home in Curnacarton. He had only to mention someone's name in the most casual way for Henry to launch forth with a complete genealogical table of alliances, as well as past and present enmities and eventual prospects, and the effect of all this on current and future land ownership. He related all in the most objective manner, without the least hint of backbiting or rancor or of rejoicing in any way at a neighbor's misfortune.

And he was equally informative about his own family. The Malones came originally from County Carlow, he said, from whence they were driven west in the penal days, their lands confiscated because of their fidelity to the One True Church. But they prospered here anyway, thanks be to God, and today he himself owned a hundred acres of some of the best land in Kildawree, with three farm laborers to do the work for him and a maid to help the missus with the house. His only regret was that he had no son to carry on the family name. He *had* two sons once upon a time, but one was dead now, the Lord have mercy on him, and the other was a priest. He mentioned this in a tone of absolute resignation. Two daughters as well, but only one living, and she was getting on in years and showing no signs yet of settling down to rear a family.

Mrs. Malone would sit knitting by the parlor fire during these conversations, with hardly ever a word out of her. The maid would bring in the Jameson for the men as soon as the priest arrived and then later bring in the tea and cake on a silver tray. Kitty appeared only occasionally, but when she did she would immediately insert herself into whatever conversation was going on.

It was at the beginning of September, a couple of months after he started visiting the Malones, that Father Mulroe met the missionary son from Brazil. Father Stephen came home for six months every four or five years, the mother explained, adding with obvious pride, "He's a real saint, Father. Everybody in Kildawree will tell you that."

Father Stephen modestly pooh-poohed such pious exaggeration, as he called it, and said his homecoming was a time for renewing his spiritual energy as well as for raising funds for his desperately poor missions in northeastern Brazil. He then proceeded to regale them with tales of hunger and misery among the *caboclos* of Pernambuco that wrung great clucks of pity and sorrow from the mother and the parish priest while Henry sipped his Jameson in silence and looked into the fire. All the while Father Stephen was talking his sister, Kitty, kept looking at him with rapt attention.

"Isn't he a fine-looking man now, Father?" she demanded when her brother inadvertently paused for breath. The missionary instantly countered with a "Will you go on out of that, now, Kitty." But indeed he was a handsome man—big and broad-shouldered, with great white teeth and a deep tan from his years in the hot tropical sun.

It was that same Sunday evening, too, that Kitty happened to mention the play they were preparing for Christmas. More specifically, she brought up Mary McGreevy's role in it, for it was a subject that had been rankling all week since the rehearsal. "Imagine," she said, frowning and waving her arms, "she's playing the part of a man!"

"Glory be to God!" Mrs. Malone ejaculated. "Is that a sin, Father?" She directed this at the parish priest rather than her son. It was one of her very rare intrusions in the conversation.

"Ah, not at all, not at all, Mrs. Malone. Mary McGreevy is a very intelligent woman, you see. And a very exemplary Catholic too," Father Mulroe added, lest he be thought to prize intellect more than piety.

"She hasn't been to communion for a while," said Kitty, who hadn't been at the altar rails herself for many a year. "Did you notice that, Father?"

"We mustn't judge, now, Kitty," the priest said. "We mustn't judge." Though he *had* taken note himself of the former nun's recent backsliding.

"So you think it's all right for her to play the part of a man, then?" Kitty put down her cup and folded her arms and looked the parish priest straight in the eye.

"Ah, sure, what harm would there be in it?" Father Mulroe sipped his tea. "They say that the Blessed Virgin herself only escaped from Herod in the flight into Egypt by dressing up as a man."

"Is that a fact? Well, I never heard that," said Kitty. "I always thought it was a sin for a woman to dress up like a man. Father Stephen!" She turned to her brother. "What do you think?"

"In my parish, *a ghradh*," said the missionary, "neither the men nor the women wear much of anything most of the time. And some of them are very good Christians." Father Stephen showed his great white teeth in a delicious grin.

"I must say," said Kitty, "it's all very strange to me. But in that case I suppose I owe the nun an apology."

"Nun!" Father Stephen echoed immediately.

"The woman we've been talking about is an ex-nun. Mary McGreevy from Kilduff. Maybe," Kitty added slyly, "you'd like to meet her."

"I would indeed," said Father Stephen. "Didn't I go to school with her brother, Mikey McGreevy?"

"That would be her second cousin," Henry put in instantly. "From back in Puckaun. Michael McGreevy of Kilduff didn't have but the one child. Both he and the missus, the Lord have mercy on them, were a bit long in the tooth when they got married."

So that's how it came about that the following Saturday Kitty Malone and her brother cycled back the road in the early afternoon to visit Mary McGreevy. They didn't have to go all the way down the Kilduff boreen: just beyond the head of the road they saw her at the far end of a field flocking sheep into a corner with the help of a big dog and a small girl. So they leaned their bikes against the bank, scrambled over the wall, and walked across the field.

"God bless the work," Father Stephen shouted.

"You too." Mary McGreevy stopped chasing sheep and waited for them, leaning on her crook, wearing a man's overalls and Wellingtons and a battered caubeen. The little girl—she couldn't be more than six or seven—ran up and stood behind her. The dog barked at the newcomers a couple of times before coming to heel. "Well, if it isn't Kitty Malone herself," Mary noted when they came up close.

"This is my brother, Father Stephen," Kitty said very politely. "He's been dying to meet you."

"Kitty! Don't say things like that." A touch of annoyance in the priest's voice.

"Well, you were! He's a terrible ladies' man," Kitty added, hand to mouth as if imparting confidential information.

"Pleased to meet you, Father," Mary said quickly to cover his embarrassment. "I'd offer you my hand except it's not too clean after handling sheep all afternoon."

"What are you doing, anyway?" Kitty demanded.

"Delighted to meet you," Father Stephen said warmly.

"There's a sheep fair in Ballinamore on Friday, and I'm picking out the fattest of the wethers for selling."

"They all look in pretty good condition to me," the priest said.

"And this is my good friend Fidelma Feerick." Mary smiled down at the little girl shyly clutching her overalls.

"I'm sorry for being rude on Tuesday night." Kitty stood in front of Mary, hands on hips. "I consulted my theologian here, and he tells me it's all right for a woman to do the part of a man in a play. Isn't that right, Father Malone?"

"How do you tell the fattest?" the priest asked.

"Stephen!" Kitty yelled.

"Yes, indeed," he said patiently. "It's perfectly all right for a woman to take the part of a man in a play."

"Well, I'm glad to hear that," Mary said evenly.

"And I hope we'll get along well together and do a great play." The color was high in Kitty's cheeks.

"*You're* in the play?" Father Stephen yelled. "You!"

"Of course!" Kitty preened. "I'm the leading lady. *She's* the leading man." She smirked at Mary.

"Ye gods! I can't wait to see this performance."

"I told you he was a ladies' man," Kitty jeered.

"Stop it, Kitty!" Father Stephen glowered at her.

"Well, I have to get back to the post office before it closes," Kitty said. "So I'll leave you two to your theological discussions. Or whatever it is that priests and nuns talk about when they get together." She turned her back on them and set off with great dignity across the field.

"I have two more wethers to look at," Mary said. "And then we can talk. Sic 'em, boy." The dog raced around the edges of the flock, followed by Fidelma. He barked and nipped at hind legs and in a minute had the sheep herded tightly in the corner. Then he stood back, crouched, wary, tongue out, watching lest any try to break away. The little girl crouched beside him. Mary waded in among the sheep, looped the crook around a hind leg, and backed out, dragging one. With a flick of the crook and a pull on a front leg, she had the animal on the ground. Then she forced back the ovine lips and examined the teeth, stood the beast up while still holding on to it, spanned her fingers heavily over the arch of its back, marked its wool on the rump with bluestone, and let it go. "One more," she said, and repeated the process.

"You're a good farmer," Father Stephen said when she had finished.

"I suppose I am." She took the girl by the hand. "Though there's no shortage of people around here to say I should find myself a husband to do the farming for me."

"You'd make a good catch for a young farmer, I'd say all right. If my memory is correct, Michael McGreevy had a nice bit of land."

"You mean it's the land, not me, that would be the catch?" Mary McGreevy stared wickedly at the missionary.

"It's the way farmers tend to look at things, unfortunately," Father Stephen said smoothly. "It's not the view I would take myself, of course."

"Ah, but you're a celibate and you wouldn't be thinking about a woman anyway." She added quickly, "We'll walk back to the house, if you don't mind. I have pigs to feed."

"They tell me you were a nun." The dog trotted on ahead of them, followed by the girl.

"I was."

"So I suppose you *will* be looking to get married one of these days."

"Why so?" She stopped in the middle of the field and looked at him as if he were a stray sheep himself. "Do you think that the only reason a nun leaves the convent is to get married?"

"Well, if it's anything like the seminary, I would imagine it's the *primary* reason."

"Let me tell you, Father Malone, that was not *my* experience in the convent." She moved on and said nothing more for a bit. "Nuns used to leave for all kinds of reasons before they took perpetual vows. Some because of health. One, I remember, got out because she said she couldn't stand the hypocrisy of the vow of poverty. Others were asked to leave because they had difficulties with obedience. I knew of only one nun in my sixteen years there who left because she wanted to get married."

"And that nun wasn't you," said the missionary, with a touch of the sardonic.

"That nun wasn't me," she agreed. The girl and the dog had already climbed over the wall and were trotting back the boreen. Mary, brushing off Father Stephen's gallant offer of help, placed her right hand on the top and leaped lightly over without touching a stone.

"Pretty limber," the priest admired after he rather ungracefully scrambled over himself. "So that's how you leaped over the convent wall." He chuckled.

She smiled at him for the first time. "I taught physical education as well as English and French."

"So why *did* you leave the convent? Of course it's no business of mine, just curiosity." He recovered his bike and wheeled it alongside.

They walked for a bit in silence, till it seemed she had ignored his question. Then she said, "If you don't mind following me around while I'm doing some chores, maybe I can explain it to you."

"I don't mean to intrude in your private—" he began.

"You're not in the least. I don't mind discussing it. Though I'm liable to say things that will shock you."

"You can't—" he began.

"—shock a priest," she finished for him. That made them both laugh. "Well, there's always a first time. I don't bring the subject up with the neighbors. They might stone me if I told them the truth."

"Well, you have certainly piqued *my* curiosity." Father Stephen unbuttoned his jacket. "Have you discussed it with Father Mulroe?"

"I told him enough to satisfy his curiosity. But I think he'd be horrified if I told him everything. Of course he knows that I haven't been going to confession."

"Or communion either, I gather."

"Cripes! The gossip gets 'round, doesn't it?"

"So what's the big mystery anyway?" They turned in the front gate to the McGreevy house. The little girl and the dog were waiting by the door.

"You'd better go home now, Fidelma," Mary said, "so Mammy won't be cross with you for staying out too long."

The girl pouted. "I'd rather stay with you, Aunt Mary."

Mary smiled. "I'll be over tonight and then we'll play cards. Isn't she darling?" she noted when the little one had run off down the boreen with the dog trotting along beside her. "I'd love to have a girl of my own like her."

"I thought you didn't want to get married," the priest said dryly.

"There's more ways to kill a cat than to choke him with butter, my mother used to say. Let me see if the pigs' dinner is done first, and then we can talk." She headed around to the back door and into the kitchen. Father Stephen followed. A huge three-legged black pot hung from the crane over the open fire, with the brown bubbles sputtering up through the sacking that covered the potatoes. She pushed back the burlap with a long-handled fork and prodded the spuds. "They're done," she said, plucking an empty flour sack off a peg above the fireplace and wrapping it around the pot handle.

"Can I help you?" Father Stephen hovered near.

"Not at all!" She leaned forward and lifted the pot without so much as a grunt, carried it two-handed and spread-legged in front of her out the back door, and laid it down on the stone flags around by the gable. Then she turned it sideways and let the scalding liquid pour down the shallow trench that led into the bushes. The steam from the pot briefly enveloped her.

"You're a strong woman," the priest admired from the doorway.

"I'd rather be doing this than teaching school." She straightened. "We'll leave it there for a while to cool." She ran her fingers through the red hair hanging down on her forehead and pushed it back under the caubeen. "I hated teaching. I liked literature, but I hated to teach it."

"They say teaching is a vocation."

"Really!" She took an enamel basin that was hanging from a wooden peg on the outside wall and filled it with water from the rain barrel by the doorway. "What *is* a vocation anyway? I mean, how is it different from just wanting to do something?"

"A vocation is a calling from God," the priest began sermonically.

She brushed past him going into the kitchen. "And you think that God calls some people to teach English literature?" Putting the basin down on a small table just inside the door and taking a bar of soap from a dish on the table, she began to scrub her hands vigorously.

"I'm sure you could lead people to heaven through literature. Like Dante's *Divine Comedy,*" he ventured.

"Or Chaucer's bawdy tales!" She lifted her head to look around at him, without slowing down the scrubbing. "Or someday maybe even teaching James Joyce."

"Like any vocation," he argued, "it would depend on how you respond to it."

"But what *is* a vocation? Is it a permanent thing? Or does God call you at one stage and then maybe tell you later on to forget about it?"

"I suppose He could. Is that what you think happened to you?"

"I don't know what happened to me. What would *you* do if you suddenly lost your calling?"

"*Sacerdos in aeternum,*" he said sententiously.

"Well, there *have* been priests who left, you know. And of course some who were defrocked. Are they damned? Is God not allowed to tell priests to forget about it?" She reached for a towel hanging on the back of a nearby chair. "Or does God even care one way or the other?" She was looking out the door as she dried her hands.

"Do I detect a problem of belief?"

"Maybe. Or maybe for sure." She finished the drying and replaced the towel.

"And how long has this been going on?"

Mary McGreevy turned slowly to face the missionary from Brazil, and there was increasing menace in every degree of her turn. Her hands were on her hips, and her eyes were closed, and she took a deep breath. "Father Malone." She spoke very slowly, and there was the weariness of a lifetime in her voice. "I don't want to be examined, and I don't want to be analyzed, and I don't want to be preached at. Unless that's understood, this conversation is over here and now."

You could see the resistance arching the missionary's back. Then he relaxed and took a step backwards. "Of course. Of course. You know your theology, I'm sure. And there isn't anything I could tell you that you wouldn't know already."

"The truth of the matter is," she stared out the door again, "I don't think I believe in God anymore."

"Ah!" he murmured. "Loss of faith. I'd say that—"

"I'd prefer you didn't say anything at all for the moment. I'd like to let my thoughts just spill out. It'll be sort of like the confession of an atheist, if you know what I mean. Would you mind?"

"Not at all. Not at all." He had recovered his composure. "I won't say a word."

"You'll be like the goat that heard the sins of the Hebrews and then was driven out into the desert—you'll have to go right back to the jungle."

"Whatever you say will have the seal of confession around it."

"And I'm going to make some *caiscin* while I'm talking."

The priest made himself comfortable in a chair by the fire. Mary took a tin basin from the top of the dresser and scooped brown flour into it from a sack on the floor and white flour from another. The look on Father Stephen's face suggested a little more than purely priestly interest as he watched her cross the kitchen into the back room: his eyes ranged slowly all the way up her body from the Wellingtons to the caubeen. And they remained fixed on the door all the time she was in the other room. They did drop modestly when she reappeared with a jug of buttermilk and looked straight at him, but when she stood at the table with her back to him he turned in his chair to watch her again.

"I used to wonder," she said, "when priests would preach about having doubts of faith. I thought that the only people who could suffer such things were saints like John of the Cross or traitors like Judas Iscariot." She took a box of bread soda and a shaker of salt from a drawer in the table. "Faith, I think, is something that when you have you can't conceive of not having. Not even sin affects it." Taking a pinch of soda from the box, she crushed it between her palms before spreading it over the flour. Then, holding the salt shaker high over the basin, she shook it vigorously. "I was certainly not a sinless saint in the days of my unshakable belief. For one thing, I was vain because I was better-looking than most of the nuns."

After mixing the contents lightly, she dusted her hands over the basin. "Except for Sister Perpetua, who was an absolute smasher. And I was envious of her."

She made a deep well in the flour and poured buttermilk into it. "And I had the most wicked desires against chastity. I was so innocent then, it's hard to believe now." She pushed the mound of flour into the buttermilk-filled well and began to mix the soggy mess with her hands. "Thinking when I was going to the convent school and feeling my first licks of impurity that surely nuns couldn't possibly experience such things. I mean, physically couldn't. I thought they did something to them—I didn't know what, maybe a female version of castration, whatever that might be—when they entered so they were turned into pillars of purity for life. Of course, that wasn't why I entered, though it was an attraction. The real reason I became a nun was to keep a promise."

She looked around to see if she still had his attention. "About Kevin Kelly. I thought the sun, moon, and stars shone out of that boy's eyes from the first day I saw him in Ballinamore. Blue they were, and they went perfectly with his brown hair. And he had a spring to his walk like he was made of rubber. A townie, and I a country mug, and he said hello to me as I cycled past. Not in the snotty way townies did. With grace and charm. And poof! went poor Mary McGreevy's girlish heart. Am I boring you?"

"Not at all." He cleared his throat. "Not at all."

"I think the fire needs a little more turf. There's a few sods there on the hob. Throw them on, like a good man. I'll need them for the baking. Anyway, I had this terrible crush on Kevin Kelly. And he on me too." She kneaded the dough ever so gently. "He used to wait outside the convent gates—I don't know how he got there so fast because they got out of class at the Brothers the same time we did, and, as you know, the schools are at opposite ends of the town." She stopped kneading and stared out the window. "But anyway, he did. And he'd wheel my bike for me and we'd walk up through the town, ever so slowly. Sometimes he'd buy a bar of chocolate and we'd share. I used to dream about him in class and have bad thoughts about him at night. Then in the middle of my Leaving Cert year, Sister Mary Joseph asked me was I thinking of becoming a nun, and

I laughed in her face. I *had* thought about it before I met Kevin, but now of course it was out of the question. Afterwards, I used to think that God punished me for my irreverence to the sister. Because just a few days later Kevin got sick. Double pneumonia, the doctor said, and they rushed him to the county hospital in Castlebar in an ambulance. They said he'd probably die. I got on my knees and stayed on them all night, praying for his recovery. The next morning they said he was worse and it was only a matter of time. On the way home from school that afternoon I went into the church in Ballinamore and promised the Sacred Heart on my solemn oath that I'd become a nun if Kevin Kelly got well."

"The Brazilians," said the missionary, "are great for making promises like that. I remember—"

"Not now," she said. "Let me finish. Anyway, Kevin got better and I was left with my promise to keep. I got him back only to lose him. If only I wasn't so bloody logical. You know, they tell you, girls are not as logical as boys. Well, let me tell you I was more circumscribed by logic than any dozen boys. A promise is just a contract, right? And for good and valid reason, you can break a contract! Well, tell that to eighteen-year-old Mary McGreevy. My mother tried to talk sense into me. I was her only child, for Christ's sake, and going into the convent was the same as dying as far as she was concerned. My father was vexed at me too. He wanted me to get married and bring a son-in-law in to help him run the place. Kevin, needless to say, wasn't happy either. And I didn't really want to be a nun. So we all tried to talk me out of it." She lifted the mass of dough and shaped it into a loose ball. "But we couldn't. A promise is a promise is a promise, said the Sacred Heart every time I knelt down. So I said good-bye to them all, and in I went."

"Bravo," he said. "I suppose Kevin went on to become a priest." He was appalled then at the malevolence of her glare.

"I hoped he would, but he didn't, the rat. He married a girl in my class, and he's now a shopkeeper in Ballinamore. Maybe I'll visit him next Friday when I go in to the fair."

She went over to the fire, pulled out hot coals with the tongs, and placed them in a circle on the edge of the hearth. Then she took a three-legged baking pot from the floor by the dresser and put it on top of the

coals. She ran to the back room and returned with a lump of butter in a
wooden spoon. She tapped the butter into the oven.

"I'm not quite sure," she said, spreading it around the bottom and the
sides, "what exactly burst my bubble of faith. Was it something theological? Or did it have to do with morals? Or was it the liturgy? It's hard to
be sure." She took the dough from the basin, dropped it into the oven,
and pushed it down gently with her knuckles. "My first reaction when I
found it slipping was that I was losing my faith because I was a bad person. I hated my job, I was bored with mental prayer, and I was still full
of lustful thoughts at the ripe old age of thirty-three."

She cut a cross on the top of the dough with a knife from the table
drawer. "I discussed it with my confessor. 'Pride,' was what he said. 'It's
only your pride that's making you think you're having doubts of faith—
so you can be like the great saints, you see. So forget about it,' he said.
'Practice humility.' What an *amadhan!*" She put the lid on the oven and
covered it with more hot coals from the fire. "Anyway, in the end I decided the source was liturgical."

"Is that a fact? And what exactly does that mean?"

"We'll feed the pigs now." She headed for the back door. The priest
followed. "We used to get a French liturgical review in the convent. I
don't know where it came from, and nobody ever read it except me, so
nobody thought there was any harm in it." She grabbed two buckets from
beside the rain barrel and dropped them next to the pot of potatoes. "But
it was full of advanced ideas on liturgical reform, and about rows with
the Holy See and condemnations of innovations coming from Sacred
Congregations. Stay where you are! I'll be right back."

She walked quickly across the yard and disappeared into the nearest
shed, then returned carrying a sack of something and a hand shovel. "And
it dawned on me after a while that some of those people in Rome were
daft." She dug out spuds from the pot and dumped them into the buckets.
"They were condemning as heresy simple notions like performing the
liturgy in languages the people could understand." She scooped bran from
the sack and heaped it on top of the spuds. Then she looked up at the missionary. "And gradually it became clear to me that this wasn't just a few
unusually stupid Roman clerics: this was the church! Holy mother her-

self! The infallible one! Hold that thought now while I get the butter-milk." She swept by him into the house and was back in a few seconds carrying a white enamel pail. "And then the next thought came to me." She sloshed buttermilk into the buckets till they were full. "If she could be this stupid over things that were obvious even to someone like me, what of . . . ! Could you trust her in anything at all?" She moved the shovel up and down in the buckets until the buttermilk was mixed into the mash.

"I'd say," the priest said, "you're drawing conclusions that are un-warranted by the premises. I—"

Mary picked up the buckets. "The next thing I'm going to do is carry these tasty conclusions down to the *pigs'* premises."

"Let me help you," the chivalrous priest offered, though his act of leaning forward lacked any strong sense of resolution.

"No! No! Not at all. You'd only get your nice clerical trousers dirty. Anyway, I'm well used to it by now." She walked slowly down the yard, sagging a little beneath the weight of the heavy buckets. "Continue your argument, Father. I'm interested in hearing your rebuttal."

"We're dealing here," he said, picking his steps carefully through the muddy yard, "with forms of worship and matters of church discipline. Even if you disagree with the Latin liturgy, that doesn't warrant a con-clusion that the church is in error in a matter of faith or morals."

She stopped at the end of the hay barn and put the buckets down. "I always rest here so my arms won't fall off. But I maintain that a church that fails its members so badly in the matter of their essential suste-nance—and I'm sure you'll agree that the liturgy is their sustenance— can't be doing what's infallibly right." She picked up the buckets again and turned left around the side of the barn. "I mean, if I fed my pigs stones they'd die in no time. The church is feeding its people an indi-gestible mess of Latin gibberish and expects them to thrive on it. Do you know what I'm trying to say?" She put down the buckets in front of a stone shed that had a walled-in concrete area in front of it. "Don't come in here, now," she admonished, "or your clerical clothes will smell all the way back to Brazil." As she opened the gate and stepped inside carrying one bucket three pigs rushed out from inside the low shed. "Whoosh!" she shouted and kicked at the leader. "Back! Where's your table manners?" She dumped the bucket's contents quickly into a wooden trough. The pigs squealed and charged the trough. She stepped back and grabbed the other bucket and dumped it into a second trough. Two of the pigs immediately swung their attention to the newest feeding spot. Mary backed out and closed the gate.

"I know what you're trying to say," he said. "And I—"

"And I'm going to make you a cup of tea now," she interrupted. "You poor man, you must be famished." They headed back to the house. "I have an apple tart that I made this morning. Do you like apple tart?" And her smile wiped from Father Stephen's mind the entire theological argument he was just about to expound.

When he arrived home, late for supper, his sister gave him her best to-what-do-we-owe-this-tardiness look. "Did you have a good time? How was the theological discussion?"

"She's a good woman." He said it as casually as he could. "But she does need some spiritual guidance in her current state of transition. I intend to look in on her from time to time to see if I can help her along."

"Well, isn't that nice, now," said Kitty ironically.

5

Wattie Feerick was having a terrible dream about a herd of wild cattle chasing him through a long, narrow meadow. He was trying his damndest to scramble up a high wall of loose stones, but buckets of water tied to his shoulders kept him from climbing fast enough. The long, curved horns swung closer and closer, and he shook himself desperately to escape. It was then that he heard Luke's voice saying, "It's a quarter to three, Da!" And felt his son's hand on his shoulder. "We'll be late for the fair if you don't get up."

"Right so," he mumbled, relieved to be awake. He was always having bad dreams about those blasted cattle. "I'll be there in a minute." When he came down to the kitchen Luke had the pot of tea on the table and the *caiscin* cut and four boiled eggs sitting on a saucer. And the butter and the sugar and the milk out, and two places set. "Good man yourself," he said, still rubbing the sleep out of his eyes. You never had to worry about being on time as long as Luke was going with you. A fierce responsible lad, though he wouldn't be sixteen until December. The missus and himself used to wonder sometimes where they got him from. Rita said he was born a man rather than a child.

"We should be leaving at three," Luke said before his father had time to get the top off his second egg. "It'll take us over an hour to drive the sheep into Ballinamore."

"Don't forget we're bringing Mary McGreevy's with us too," Wattie reminded him. That was when Fidelma appeared in the kitchen, all dressed up, with her coat and shoes on. "And where are you going, miss?" Wattie looked at her quizzically. "It's a bit early for school, isn't it?"

"I'm going to the fair with Aunt Mary. She needs me to help her with the sheep." Spoken with the gravity of a bishop explaining the Lenten fast. "Marco is coming with us too."

"Well, I know the dog is going, but I'm afraid you can't come, *a ghradh*. You have to go to school."

Fidelma put on her best pout. "But Lukeen is going. Why doesn't he have to go to school?"

"Because," said Luke with great authority, "I'm over fourteen and I don't have to go to school anymore."

Fidelma thought about this for a while. "Well, some boys under fourteen stay home from school to go to the fair with their daddies." A touch of youthful belligerence in her voice.

"Ah!" said Wattie, sprinkling salt on his egg. "That's different. Boys can go to fairs, you see, but girls can't."

"Well, Aunt Mary is a girl, and she's going." Fidelma folded her arms in that determined way of hers. Her rebuttal caught Wattie with a spoonful of egg halfway to his gob, and between his puzzlement and his merriment as much of the yolk wound up on his face as in his mouth.

"Bedad, now," trying to clean his chin off with his fingers, "you're no joke at all when it comes to arguing." Truth to tell, he had been wondering for some time how he could tell Miss McGreevy discreetly that women didn't go to fairs. It just wasn't the thing for them to do. He had offered to sell her sheep for her, but she wouldn't hear of it, though she did consent to driving both flocks together into Ballinamore.

"Am I going, then?" Fidelma demanded.

"No," said Wattie. "I'm afraid not. You're too small, and anyway you have to go to school."

"Well, if you won't let me go to the fair I won't go to school either." And the seven-year-old sat down defiantly in the middle of the kitchen floor.

"Now, Fidelma, wouldn't that be a sin?" Wattie took a big gulp of tea. "And you just after making your first communion. You'd have to tell Father Mulroe in confession that you were a bold girl and wouldn't go to school."

"I'll tell Father Mulroe that you were bad and wouldn't let me help Aunt Mary bring her sheep to the fair," Fidelma shouted.

"Let's go, Da," said Luke. "We're late already."

"Bad cess to ye!" Fidelma yelled after them, and they going out the back door.

They herded their eleven sheep down the boreen. The animals were fairly docile at such an early hour: Marco scarcely had to growl. Mary McGreevy was waiting for them. "Open the gate," she shouted to Luke, and her sheep darted through and mingled with the Feerick flock. A last quarter moon gave plenty of light down the boreen.

"Six, is it?" Wattie asked, though well he knew how many she had.

"Yes. I marked their rumps with bluestone."

"Ours are marked on the top of the head," Luke said.

"You're a great girl to be out going to the fair at this time of morning," Wattie said. "I don't think I ever saw a woman at a fair before twelve o'clock. They come in on their bicycles or in the sidecar after the selling is done to get some money and do a bit of shopping."

"Well, I'm a farmer," Mary McGreevy said pointedly. "And farmers take their own animals to the fair."

"You're a farmer all right. And a good one too. I say that now because it's true, though not many men would be honest enough to admit it."

"You're a good man, Wattie."

"Your father, the Lord have mercy on him, was good to us when times were bad, so you can always count on me and the missus for help."

It was a long, slow drive: almost a half hour before they turned onto the town road at Kildawree and another forty-five minutes from there to Ballinamore. The sheep ambled and meandered from side to side of the road and would not be hurried. Ahead and behind them they could hear other sheep bleating and an occasional dog barking. It was nippy in the early morning: Wattie was glad he had put on his gabardine. Mary McGreevy had a raincoat on too, he noticed. And woollen stockings under her boots. And a dress that came most of the way to her ankles.

The darkness and the waning moon were still with them when they arrived at the high-walled boundaries of the old Burke estate that flanked the Kildawree road and Market Street. Along the wall from Market for more than a hundred yards sheep were huddled, some hemmed in by cart cribs, others just kept in place by farmers and their sons and dogs. Everything and everyone looked yellow in the dim light of the town's gas lamps. "We'll pen them here now," Wattie said. "Some people like to take them up the town, but it's more work, and the jobbers will come to look at them here anyway." They herded the sheep up against the wall next to a flock of about thirty that were jammed between several sets of cart cribs. The owner bade them good-morning and immediately turned his back on them. The two young lads with him nodded to Luke but then turned away as well and talked quietly to each other.

"I haven't been to a fair for sixteen years," Mary said to Wattie. "I used to always go with my father."

"See, Dad," Luke said. "Girls do go to fairs after all." He sniggered a bit, but Wattie said nothing.

"Why shouldn't girls go to fairs?" Mary challenged Luke.

"Fidelma wanted to come today, but Daddy told her only boys are allowed."

"Well, it's true for me," Wattie said. "Anyway, she'd get trampled on, the size of her."

"Ah, the creature!" Mary said. "She told me she was coming, but I didn't pay any heed to her. Sometime I'll take her with me."

A half-dozen sheep were herded in on the other side of them. "Cold morning," the owner said to Wattie. He was by himself, a heavyset man with a cap and oversized white woollen sweater. Not even a jacket.

"The winter will be here soon," Wattie said.

"Wasn't it smart of you to bring the missus along to help out." The man nodded briefly to Mary. "I wish I had thought of that myself."

"Ah!" said Wattie. "Yes. Well—"

"I'm not his missus," Mary interrupted. "Some of these sheep are mine. We just came to the fair together."

The man gaped at her like a fellow faced with a hard sum in arithmetic. He removed his cap and scratched his head. "I see," he said. "I see." He paused a bit. "I suppose himself is sick or something." He put the cap back on very carefully.

"No, that's not it either." Wattie had the impression she was enjoying the man's discomfort. "There isn't any himself, you see. *I'm* a farmer, and I have my own sheep, and I brought them to the fair, and I'm going to sell them."

"She's a farmer in her own right, you might say," Wattie shouted, as if by raising his voice he would better bring home the point.

"I see, begob. 'Tis a free country after all, I suppose. That's what we fought the Black and Tans for, wasn't it?" The man grinned briefly. But he didn't say any more, just stood there minding his sheep and whistling tunelessly.

They waited for more than an hour as flocks continued to line the demesne wall farther out and daylight appeared in the eastern sky and jobbers passed by with scarcely a glance before one came along who actually looked at their sheep. They were watching him from the time he turned in off Market, a tall, gangly fellow swaggering down the street surveying the animals from a distance, Wellingtons clopping, trench coat flung open, a wide-brimmed hat set way back on his head. Sometimes he'd move in and press a hand into a sheep's back, but he never paused and he made no offers. He stopped and looked hard at Wattie's and Mary's for a full minute. Then he moved in and felt the backs of a couple of them and examined the teeth of one wether.

"You won't get better this side of Athlone," Wattie said confidently. "Seven pounds fifteen a head for the lot."

"You're daft." The jobber moved away. But he stopped a little farther on and came back. "I wouldn't take them anyway," he said, "but if I *was* hard up enough I wouldn't give a penny more than five pound five." He swept away again.

"Seven ten," Wattie shouted after him. "Not a penny less."

The jobber stopped, turned, looked fiercely at Wattie, made as if to go on his way, then swung back. "You'll be driving them home again today and taking five pounds for them at the next fair. You wait and see.

Sorra jobber in Mayo would be daft enough to give you that kind of money." He walked off. From ten yards away he turned and yelled, "Five pound ten, take it or leave it." And he continued walking.

"Seven-five is me bottom dollar," Wattie shouted. The jobber waved disgust with both hands and kept on going.

"Don't you think we should have taken the five pound ten?" Luke asked. "Better than driving them home again."

"Ah, no, not at all. He's a cute lad," Wattie told him. "He'll be back."

"I remember," Mary said, "my father used to say that if you had the nerve to stick to it you could always get one-third more from the jobber than the first offer he made you."

"You might," said Wattie sagely, "and then again you mightn't." He removed his hat and ran his fingers through his unruly red hair. "You have to have the experience of dealing with them fellows or they'd build a nest in your ear. I'd say now we might get as much as six pound five from this lad."

"One-third more would be seven pound," Luke announced. He was a great lad for the sums.

"I think I'll take a walk up the town and see how prices are going," Wattie said. "That way we'll know better where we stand." He left Mary and Luke to mind the sheep, with instructions not to take any offers in his absence. Up on Main Street he met several farmers he knew; only a couple of them had sold animals yet, and the best anyone had gotten was six pound five for a couple of ewes. They all agreed it was a slow day and that prices wouldn't get much better. Maybe as much as six-ten for the fattest wethers. Too many sheep and not enough jobbers, they lamented. Coming 'round Market onto the Kildawree road on his way back, Wattie spotted the trench-coated jobber gesticulating in the distance. At Mary McGreevy, he discovered as he got closer. He broke into a run.

"Mind yourself, now, or he'll make a horse's collar out of you," the man beside them was saying.

"Is it this fine gentleman?" Mary asked. "Sure, I'd trust this man with my own money any day of the week."

"And it would be safe too, begob," the jobber said. "I never cheated a man out of a penny in my life!"

"Or a woman either, I'll bet," said Mary. "I'll let you have them for seven pound four."

"Ah, now, sure, that would be taking the bread out of my childer's mouths." The jobber grimaced like a man in serious pain. Then he leaned forward confidentially. "But seeing as you're a nice girl and all that, I'll make you an offer I won't make to anyone else. Six pound it is to you!" He raised his right hand and spat in it and held it out. "Put it there, *a ghradh*, and we have a deal."

"We'll have to—" Wattie began, but Mary raised her hand to stop him.

"I'll tell you what: I'll make it seven pound three." She ignored the jobber's outstretched hand.

The fellow hunched over as if in mortal agony. He turned away and faced the other side of the road. "This woman will be the death of me," he moaned. "I'm a decent, hard-working man trying to put bread on the table for seven childer and a sick missus. And she's trying to take the clothes off their backs. Six pound five, though I'll be in the poorhouse for it." His back remained turned to them.

"Look!" said Mary, and she raised her hand again to keep Wattie from interrupting. "Will you look at these sheep? You know and I know that these are the best wethers you'll come across at this or any other fair in Mayo this year. Raised on the best grass in the county and fed turnips and mangels all year 'round. They're fit for the butcher's knife this very minute. You won't need to waste two months in the midlands fattening them up like most of the sheep you'll see at this fair. So they're worth every penny of seven pound three to you. But anyway, since you're such a nice man I'll let you have them for seven-two." She spat in her right hand and held it out to him.

The jobber put on the surprised look of a man who has just been bowled over by a charging sheep. "You want to send me to the work-house, don't you? Well, I won't go. Do you hear me!" He pulled off his hat and threw it on the ground. "I'll find better wethers up the town for six pound a head." He picked up his hat. "Good day to ye." And he stalked off in the direction of Market.

"I think we lost him," Wattie said. "You should have taken the six-five."

"Maybe," said Mary. "And maybe he'll be back."

He was, almost immediately. There was an air of desperation about him, the look of a man who couldn't bear to be bested. "I'll tell you what," he said, "since you're a woman with a sick husband at home and I know what that does to a person, out of the goodness of my heart I'll give you six-ten."

"Take it," Lukeen whispered urgently.

"Seven-one," Mary offered.

"Oh, for God's sake, take six-fifteen and be done with it." The man was standing spread-legged in front of them, his hat off. Wattie nodded urgently at Mary. If she didn't take it now they were lost.

"Seven," she said, "and we have a deal." She spat in her hand again and held it out to the jobber.

He turned his back on her, put on his hat, made as if to go, then swung around and spat in *his* hand. "I'll split the difference, God damnit! Six-seventeen and six."

"Done," Mary said, then spat in her hand again and slapped the jobber's outstretched palm.

"Hurray," Lukeen shouted. Wattie said nothing.

"Well, you're the hard woman," the jobber said. There was sweat on his forehead below his hat. "I've never had to deal with a girl before, and with the help of God I'll never have to again. I hope himself will be happy with you when you get home."

"I'm sure he will," Mary murmured. Lukeen sniggered.

"Maybe ye'll help me drive them to the station and I'll pay ye down there," the jobber said. They did, and he did, and then the three of them made their way through the filthy sheep-filled streets up to Durkin's eating house on Main Street and ordered a big breakfast of fried eggs and mutton chops and fresh white bread and strong tea. The place was filled with hungry farmers and their sons and there was a lot of discreet gaping at Mary McGreevy, the only woman eating in the place.

"Well, you're a great woman entirely," Wattie said. "There won't be a better price at the fair today."

"I used to watch my father doing it," she said. "It all came back to me."

"If you don't mind," Wattie's head was bent over the plate as he cut his chop, "we won't say anything at home about who did the bargaining."

"Of course not," Mary said. "Why would we?"

"Well! You know how people have a habit of talking. If the fellows back at Queally's heard that Mary McGreevy did the bargaining for Wattie Feerick at the fair of Ballinamore, sure, I'd never hear the end of it. As I'm sure you'll understand."

"Absolutely," said Mary. "I'll never breathe a word about it."

"Me neither, Da," Lukeen said loyally.

"Well, that's that, then." Wattie slathered butter on a big piece of bread and stuffed it in his gob. "We can go home now with good money jingling in our pockets."

"I think I'll stay a while longer," Mary said.

"Why wouldn't you?" said Wattie. "You'll have some shopping to do, like all the women on a fair day."

6

It wasn't shopping Mary McGreevy had on her mind. No sooner had she shaken hands with Wattie and Luke than she headed up to Castle Street and stopped in front of Kelly's drapery shop. It was open already, though it wasn't much after nine. She stepped inside. The light was a bit dim, but she could make out a woman at the back folding a bolt of cloth.

"Good morning," the woman said, laying aside the bolt and moving up behind the long counter. "What can I do for you?" She was a bit on the plump side, with dark hair and lovely pale skin.

"Is it Brideen Costello?" Mary asked.

"Yes," said the woman. Not warmly. She came closer. "Do I know you?"

"Mary McGreevy."

"Mary McGreevy?" The woman's forehead knit in puzzlement. "Mary McGreevy? Now, where do I know that name from?"

"We were in school together, Brideen. Sister Perpetua's class. Don't you remember?"

"Mary—oh my God, but . . . !" The woman stopped, put her hands on her hips. "You can't be Mary McGreevy!"

"I am indeed."

"But aren't you a nun?" Brideen Costello looked thoroughly flustered. "The Mary McGreevy I knew joined the Mater Dolorosa sisters years ago and was never heard of again."

"I *was* a nun," said Mary, "but I'm not anymore."

"Well, glory be to God!" Brideen relaxed, smiled, and put out her hand. "Is it really yourself, Mary, that's in it? Sure, I wouldn't know you at all. You've changed a lot. But then, haven't we all." She laughed. "Well, anyway, it's grand to see you again. Come on in. Come on in the back and we'll have a cup of tea and a chat." She hurried to lift the flap of the counter to let Mary pass. "Eileen," she shouted, leading the way into a small parlor. "Sit down now and make yourself comfortable."

A girl of about ten or eleven appeared in the doorway almost immediately. "Yes, Mammy!" She looked at Brideen and then smiled shyly at Mary McGreevy.

"Would you be a good girl, now, and make a pot of tea for the two of us and maybe rustle up a bit of cake or some biscuits. This is Miss McGreevy, a woman I went to school with a long time ago. It's still Miss, is it?"

"Yes." Mary felt herself blushing as she sat.

"And this is my oldest daughter, Eileen. Run now, dear, and make the tea."

"How many children do you have?" Mary asked, more to make conversation than to find out how many babies Kevin Kelly had fathered.

"Six." Brideen settled herself comfortably in an armchair. "The oldest you saw. She's ten. The youngest is just a babby—three months old—you'll hear her squawking anytime now. And in between, four boys."

"Well, isn't that wonderful. And it's great to see you again, Brideen. How have you been keeping at all?"

"Musha, I can't complain too much. The children are all healthy and himself is behaving at the moment. What more could a woman want?"

"And how *is* Kevin?" The words almost lodged in her throat, but she managed to get them out.

"Well enough, thank God. He just went down to the railway station to pick up a few packages that were coming in. Faith, 'tis he'll be surprised to see you." She jumped up and went to the door. "John," she shouted and returned to her chair. In seconds a boy appeared. Mary felt her breath being suddenly whipped away: he was a younger edition of the Kevin Kelly she remembered. "John," said Brideen, "will you keep an eye on the shop for me like a good boy."

"But I was going down to help Mr. Tobin kill a sheep in a few minutes," the lad complained.

"You can do that later. For now you're needed here to mind the shop." He said no more, just closed the door quietly.

"He's the image of his father," Mary said.

"In more ways than one." There was a bite to Brideen's tone. "So tell me about yourself, Mary, and how you come to be here. If you don't mind talking about it, of course."

"Not at all." By now she had a well-honed tale to tell. About her change of vocation being in God's plan too. And there being other ways to toil in the vineyard of the Lord besides living in a cloister. Pabulum for the faithful—she felt strongly about not giving scandal. Of course, sometimes it was impossible to avoid. She mentioned nothing now of the hard doubts and liturgical disagreements she had expressed to Father Stephen. Brideen Kelly nodded and yesed and certainlyed and to-be-sured, and her eyes glazed a little at some of the more pious nonsense.

"Well, I'd say it has been a great experience for you, anyway," was her only comment when Mary ended her story. The door opened and a small boy came in carrying a low tea table, which he placed in the middle of the floor. "Good on you, Kevin," Brideen said, and the boy fled from the room. Eileen came in then with a large silver tray that she placed on the table. And right behind her came Kevin Kelly himself. "You'll never guess who's here," Brideen said. She didn't get up.

"Arrah, why wouldn't I! How are you at all, Mary? Sure, I'd know you anywhere?" He was bigger and heavier than she remembered him, and his face had changed quite a bit, but his grin was as beguiling as ever. She blushed again and stood and shook his hand.

"You'd know her after all these years?" Brideen demanded, almost belligerently.

"Why wouldn't I!" Kevin winked at Mary.

"I don't believe you," Brideen said. "I didn't know her from Adam when she walked in. Even after she told me who she was."

"Well, I suppose, tell the truth and shame the devil," Kevin confessed. "I met a fellow from Kildawree down at the railway station, and he told me you were in town. So when John told me we had a visitor I put two and two together. But I'd know you anyway, for God's sake."

"Let's have our tea now while it's hot," Brideen put in. "Do you want a cup?" she halfheartedly asked her husband.

"Sure!" He settled into the sofa.

"Is that everything, Mammy?" Eileen was still standing by the door.

"It is, thank you, Eileen. Maybe you would relieve John in the shop for a bit. He has to go help a man kill a sheep or something."

"Let John stay where he is, now," Kevin said sharply. "I don't like him hanging around Tobin's."

Brideen sucked in air as if she were about to expostulate. But she stopped herself and said, "That'll be all" to Eileen.

"Well, then! They tell me you're out of the convent for good." Kevin turned and leaned toward Mary while his wife poured the tea.

"For good or ill, I am."

"Are you sorry now you went in?" He was looking closely at her.

"Kevin!" Brideen stopped in the middle of pouring milk into a cup. "What kind of a question is that to ask?"

"Sorry!" He raised his hand. "Beg pardon! It's none of my business. Consider it not said."

"I'm not at all sorry I went in." Mary accepted a cup from Brideen. "And I'm not sorry I came out either," she added as she took a piece of cake. "It was a great experience. It made me the person I am today. And it has given me the strength to be the kind of person I want to be in the future. I wouldn't change a bit of it."

"Well, isn't that wonderful, now," said Brideen. She handed Kevin his tea, then bit into a piece of cake herself.

"And you're happy now, I suppose?" Kevin asked, still leaning towards her.

"I've got my own land and I enjoy farming. Why shouldn't I be happy?"

Kevin slapped his knee, almost spilling his tea. "That's what the fellow told me. 'She's a farmer in her own right,' he says." He sipped his tea and reached for a piece of cake. "But you'll be getting married one of these days, I suppose?"

"Kevin! You're a terrible man for asking people embarrassing questions. Don't pay any attention to him," Brideen said.

"Ah, sure, who's there left to marry now, given that Brideen got yourself?" Mary smiled and looked at Brideen to let her know she was only joking. Kevin grinned, but he reddened all the same.

"There are days, faith, when I'd let you have him." Brideen's tone was sour. Then immediately she said, "I'm sorry, Mary. We should keep our dirty linen to ourselves."

The door shot open and John rushed in. "Mammy, there's a man out here and he wants to buy the makings of two suits! On my oath, that's what he said." The boy's eyes were wide with excitement as the words tumbled out.

"John! You don't have to swear." Brideen spoke very calmly. "Tell him I'll be right there." John raced back out, leaving the door open behind him. Brideen rose reluctantly and put her cup down on the tray. "If you'll excuse me now, I have some business to attend to." She closed the door softly as she went.

There was silence for a bit. Until Mary said, "I think you got a bit heavier since I saw you last."

"It's been a long time," he said. And there was another silence till he added, "You know, I often wondered if I'd ever see you again."

"Did you really, now?" And she smiled at him.

"Did you ever wonder if . . ."

"If I'd ever see *you* again? Ah, sure, they train you well in the convent not to dwell on the past. Particularly on boys, of course."

"So you forgot all about me?" His tone held just a hint of plaintiveness.

"Well, I thought about coming to see you, didn't I? That's more than you did for me."

"On my solemn oath I didn't know until this morning that you were home."

"And you'd have come to see me if you'd known?"

"Why wouldn't I!"

"But you're a married man with six children! You can't be going around visiting spinsters on their farms." She said it without even a hint of a smile.

"I'd come to visit you any day, Mary. God forgive me, but that's the honest truth." There was a terrible sincerity in his face and a hint of moisture in his eyes.

"So how has life been treating you?" She said it in a hurry, anxious to change the subject.

"Fair to middling, I suppose." He looked towards the door and lowered his voice. "To tell you the truth, herself and myself don't get along terribly well. We're always bickering and having at each other like a pair of cats on a wall." He stopped and took a sip of tea and put his cup and saucer back on the tray. Then he looked down at the floor. "'Twas a sad day for me, Mary, I can tell you, when you went into the convent. And I only compounded the problem by getting married in a hurry so as to forget you. And that's what I did, married in haste to put you out of my mind. To be fair, now, she's a good woman, and I did come into a good business here, the draper's shop and all. We make a decent living and we're not poor. But money doesn't make you happy, you know." Then, looking at her with all the sincerity that self-pity could muster, he added, "I'd rather any day be married to you and be poor."

"And what makes you think I'd want your poverty?" She said it with an impish grin.

He smiled like the old Kevin she used to know. "Well, it's no use crying over spilt milk. The—"

The door shot open. John again. "Mammy said, where are the buttons you went down to the station for? She wants them in a hurry, right now." He stood there waiting, quivering with expectation.

Kevin looked at the boy and you could feel the animosity coming out of him. But he spoke quietly, almost too calmly. "Tell her I'll be right in with them. And close the door after you this time." John vanished, the door slamming in his wake. "They say," Kevin said, "that there's always one of your own children you don't like. Well, John is my cross." He stood abruptly. "If you'll excuse me for a minute now while I take care of the button crisis."

Mary got up too. "I'd better be going. I have some shopping to do, and it's a long walk back to Kilduff."

He looked horrified. "You're walking! Not even a bicycle? You were always a great woman for the bike."

"I had to drive some sheep in this morning. But—"

"I'll drive you out. I have a car now, you know."

She held up her hand. "No! No! Not at all. That would only cause trouble for you. Anyway, there'll be lots of carts and sidecars going out. I'll get a ride without any trouble. But thanks all the same."

He wavered for a bit, his mouth forming and rejecting words. "Well, I suppose it might be best," he admitted at last. "But I'll be out to see you one of these days, and then we can have a nice long chat."

"That would be grand." She repeated that phrase to herself several times on the way home.

7

Kitty Malone's announcement shouldn't have been a surprise to Mick Burke. But it was anyway. There are events a fellow sort of knows are inevitable, but as long as they don't actually happen he continues to believe against all the odds that they won't. Mick knew, or ought to have known, that he himself didn't have a prayer. For one thing Kitty was rich, and for another he was a public-house curate. Yet he was taken completely unawares by her announcement on Saturday night. They had just finished their final rehearsal of the play in the newly put-together stage in Garvey's wool loft. Kildawree not having a parish hall, this was the best they could do. Tom Tarragh had just said, "Ye'll need to be here at six o'clock tomorrow evening to get dressed and put the makeup on," when Kitty butted in. "May I have your attention, please!" In her best convent-bred voice. "I have a bit of good news to tell you all."

"Henry Malone is going to build us a parish hall," Mick hazarded wildly. Many was the time in the past few months he had proposed the idea to Kitty. Everyone knew Henry was rotten with money.

"Thomas has asked me to marry him." Kitty trod across new, creaking boards to take the arm of a very red-faced schoolmaster. "And I have accepted." Her smile would have lit up the stage without any help from Garvey's generator.

"Oooeee!" went Noreen Macken. "Isn't that grand!" A smile of forced cheer on her face that would have strangled a horse. It was a well-known secret that Noreen had pined after Tom for years.

"Bedad, that's great, now," Paddy Carney said.

"There's no wedding date set as yet," said Kitty. "But," and she smiled up at her new fiancé, "it will most likely be before Father Stephen goes back to Brazil."

Mick said nothing. There was nothing to say. When he recovered his equilibrium, he looked over at Mary McGreevy. There were stories down at Queally's that Tarragh was interested in the former nun. But if the woman was disappointed, she showed no sign of it. And that gave sudden new hope to Mick Burke, the eternal optimist.

He decided on the spur of the moment to walk her home, but by the time he got down the steps of the loft Jack Banaghan was already heading off with her. He retired morosely to his upstairs quarters at the back of Queally's. It was a tiny room, just enough space for the narrow bed and a wardrobe and dresser. Time he had a place of his own, was the thought running through his head a lot lately. There was something more insistent about it now.

He went to first mass in the morning, knelt in his usual place near the back, and spotted Mary McGreevy just across the way on the women's side. Sunday mass being the only time of the week that he gave exclusively to the Almighty, apart from the couple of minutes spent on his night prayers before going to bed, he always tried hard to think about what was going on at the altar. However, this morning he found himself continually distracted and his eyes all the time wandering across the aisle. He was only vaguely listening to Father Mulroe's sermon when he caught the phrase about John the Baptist: "The voice of one crying in the wilderness," the parish priest bellowed.

"Just like myself," thought Mick. Only crying for a wife he was. Forty-two years of age—forty-three next month, for cripe's sake—and not a woman in sight. Bad cess to him, anyway! When he was young he had the chances. But no, he wasn't interested then. Didn't want to be tied down. Forever wandering from job to job, all the way from Galway to

Ballina. He had more fun going to parties and dances and indulging in the kissing and squeezing that followed. Sometimes even a bit more when he found a girl who was willing. But the years went by all too quickly. And the girls went away to Dublin or England, or they got married. And before he knew it here he was, stuck in this backwater, an old bachelor that no young woman would be found dead walking out with. Which was why he had set his cap at Kitty Malone, who was no spring chicken herself. Mary McGreevy now might be his last hope. And a nice woman she was. She'd suit him very well indeed.

He followed her out of the church and watched discreetly as she got on her bicycle and pedaled up the village. Her friend Rita Feerick wasn't with her for once. They were saying in Queally's last night that Mrs. Feerick had just had another babby, her tenth, no less. A lot of crack about that by the patrons at Wattie's expense: every time that old ram hung his pants on the bed, one toper remarked with a grin, the missus found herself in the family way.

Mick gave Mary several minutes' start on him while he chatted with Paddy Carney at the gate. Then he said, "See you tonight," and took off slowly on his bike up the road towards Queally's. But instead of stopping at the pub, he continued on and swung over the Castletown road, arguing with himself as he went. Wasn't he mad out of his mind to be chasing Mary McGreevy back the road on a Sunday morning? What kind of an *amadhan* was he at all? Damnit, he hardly knew the woman, and she knew him even less. Well, now, that wasn't quite true anymore. They had spoken to each other quite a bit these past couple of months while they were rehearsing the play. But still! "Y'have no sense at all," the prudent side of him said.

"Maybe not," said the practical side, "but you lost Kitty Malone by not speaking out when you had the chance. If you don't do it now, next week might be too late. I've been watching that fellow Banaghan hanging around her for some time, and unless I'm gravely mistaken he has his hat cocked at her."

"But sure, you haven't a chance against a fellow like that," said Prudence. "A smart lad that did his Leaving Certificate, and you not getting past seventh class in the National School. And he a bank manager, to boot, wearing a swanky suit of clothes to work every day, when all you do is pull pints for farmers by night. He was a Mayo footballer in his prime, but you couldn't get on the worst team in the county when you worked in Ballyglass. They say, too, he has a power of money put away. And you—well, you do have a few pounds under the mattress, I suppose. But he's twelve years younger than you, and age counts a lot with the ladies. So will you go home now, like a good man, and have some sense!"

"Well, divil a one of me," said Practical. "Every dog has his day. And anyway, there are those that say no woman will ever marry Jack Banaghan. I've heard it said many's the time on the other side of Queally's counter. And them fellows that do be talking in their cups say many a wise thing that sober men wouldn't know anything about. I don't know why that's so, but I remember my father, the Lord have mercy on him, telling me. 'There's wisdom in the Guinness,' he used to say. 'It's in the porter.'

"So I hear a fellow say one night, and he drunk as a lord, 'Jack Banaghan may be a great kicker, but he'll never have a son to kick like him.' 'And why is that, Matty?' another fellow asks him. 'Because,' says the fellow, 'Jack would be mortally afraid to get into bed with a woman, that's why. And if he did get dragged in itself he wouldn't know what to do when he got there.' They all laughed at that, but mind you, not a man contradicted what was said. Which is most unusual in Queally's, I can tell you."

Mary McGreevy's gate was open and her bike propped against the front wall of the house. The front door was off the latch, so Mick knocked and called out, "God bless," before stepping into the kitchen. He immediately heard a frightened female scream and saw a brief flash of something white disappear into a back room.

"Who's there?" Mary McGreevy's startled voice yelled.

Good God Almighty! Mick turned around to run. He had made a right bollocks of it walking in like that, so he might as well give up right away. But then he turned back with the stoicism of a man who has nothing to lose. "It's only me," he called out as calmly as he could. "Mick Burke."

There was silence from the room for several seconds. Then, "Mick Burke!" echoed back at him. "What on God's earth are *you* doing here?" The startled tone replaced by a querulous one.

"Musha, I just came over for a chat," said Mick. It was the best he could think of at that moment. "I'm sorry if I frightened you. But I'll go away now and come back at a time that'll be more convenient for you."

"You'll do no such thing!" The response was immediate. "Sit down and make yourself at home, and I'll be right out."

And he was no length sitting over by the table when she appeared, wearing a gorgeous green frock and high-heeled shoes. She looked terribly fetching. "Good morrow to you," he said, jumping out of the chair. "I'm fierce sorry—"

"It's perfectly all right." And her smile almost knocked him back into the chair again. "I was just in from mass, you see, and changing my clothes in the kitchen, not expecting to have visitors at this time of day."

"I shouldn't—" Mick began.

"Not at all. Not at all. It's a perfectly good time to drop in. You'll have a cup of tea, now, won't you?"

"That would be grand," said Mick.

She picked up the kettle from the hob and carried it out the back door. He heard the water being poured and then she was back again, leaning over the fire. A wonderful shapely pair of hips and ankles, he couldn't help noticing. Then she swung around before he had time to look away. "And to what do we owe the pleasure of your visit?" Accompanied by the friendliest of smiles.

"Ah! Yes! Well!" Mick was now at a complete loss for words. The man who could out-talk the finest gossips, gasbags, or assorted spouters that ever lowered pints in Queally's public house was suddenly struck dumb. He swallowed, felt terrified, and swallowed again.

"I suppose you want a final run over some of the lines in the play?" she suggested.

"Well!" He was on the point of agreeing with her out of sheer cowardice when some small dose of courage dribbled out of him from God knows where. "Not exactly," he managed and then got stuck again.

"Let me get the cups down while you're finding the right words." She went over to the dresser.

"Were you surprised at Kitty Malone last night?" he asked desperately. There was a connection here to what he wanted to say if only he could make it.

"You mean about her engagement? Ah, not at all." She put two cups and saucers on the table. "I think everyone knew that was coming."

"I suppose." Then he added, a glimmer of light coming to him, "'Tis a while, mind you, since we had a wedding in the parish."

"Is that a fact?" She returned to the dresser and took down a blue-and-white delft teapot. "There haven't been any at all since I came home."

"They say," said Mick, seizing his opportunity, "that whenever there's one there will always be a second within the space of a month. Isn't that a strange thing, now?"

"It certainly is. Maybe you'll be getting married yourself one of these days." Mary took the teapot and a tin box over to the fireplace, turning her back on Mick in time to miss the look of consternation on his face.

"Well, now!" His voice was strangled with phlegm and confusion. "Maybe I would, bedad, if the right woman would agree."

"So there *is* a woman!" Her tone was casual as she bent over to stoke the fire with the tongs. "This turf is only half dry. And who is she, if I may ask?"

Beads of sweat were popping out on his ruddy forehead. "'Tis someone you know well," he rasped, his throat all tight with terror at the predicament he had gotten himself into.

"Honest to God!" She straightened and came back to the table. "Isn't that wonderful, now! Who could she be at all?" She pulled out a chair and sat across from him. "Not Noreen Macken, I suppose?" Her smile made Mick squirm even more. "I've seen her looking a lot at you during rehearsals. She's a nice girl indeed. I've often thought she'd make a good wife for—"

Mick couldn't stand it any longer. "'Tis yourself," he blurted. He ran the back of his hand across his forehead to get rid of the sweat.

It was Mary McGreevy's turn to look consternated. The hitherto calm face turned puzzled, shocked, aghast, and finally amused. "You have to be joking, Mick," she half whispered, half gasped.

"Faith, 'tis no joke at all, I can tell you." Mick splashed ahead, now that he had made the plunge. "It's dead serious I am. I've been thinking about it for a long time," he lied.

"But Mick, I hardly know you! And you hardly know me. Surely—"

"Faith, I know you well enough to know you'll make a great wife for a man. I'm getting on in years, as you might notice, and I understand what the important things are now." He had recovered his gift of the gab, and he pressed ahead. "I'm not looking for a *cailin aluinn*—not that you aren't one yourself, mind you," he recovered nicely—"but that's not what matters to me anymore. What counts for me now is a woman that has her head on straight, if you know what I mean. Not like those flighty young ones I used to meet in the old days at dances all over Mayo and Galway. And for sure, you're a woman yourself that has her head well set. I said the other day to—"

"Mick! Hold it for a minute, will you please? Give a woman time to breathe." But she smiled at him as she added, "And time to wet the tea." She went over to the fireplace, took the boiling kettle off the hook, and poured a little water into the teapot.

"Will you marry me?" Mick blurted from the table. She swirled the water around the pot and poured it gently into the ashes beneath the hob. Four pinches of tea from the tin box, and then she filled the pot with water and placed it on the hearth to draw. All the while Mick sat waiting in agony. She came back to the table in unsmiling silence. "Will you?" he repeated desperately.

Then his blood pressure rose with excitement, for the look on her face was the kindest he had ever seen on any woman in his entire life. "You're a grand man, Mick Burke," she said softly. "And if I was going to marry anyone at all, it might well be you. But I'm not going to marry anyone. At least, not in the foreseeable future." The tears that came into her eyes as she said this brought a lump to Mick's throat till he thought he was going to cry himself.

"That's too bad," was all he could manage. "That's too bad indeed."

"It's a great wonder you didn't get married years ago?" She got up again to fetch the teapot.

"'Tis many's the person has said that to me." He cleared his throat. "But I was waiting for yourself." He wasn't quite ready to let her go yet. "Will you think about it, maybe?"

She placed the teapot on the table and sat across from him. "I'll be honest with you, Mick. It would do no good at all holding you on a string. I've already thought about it a lot. I'm not getting married." She looked straight at him. "My mind is made up on that."

She poured a cup and passed it to him. And Mick, who always needed two spoons of sugar and a generous dollop of milk to sweeten his tea, drank the scalding liquid without additive. Later, as he cycled home against the wind, he decided that the bitter taste it left in his mouth was a perfect reflection of his miserable life.

PART TWO

8

Rita Feerick was upstairs resting in her bed, the baby sleeping next to her in the cradle, when she heard them coming in. It was after ten, very late indeed.

"Mammy!" Tess, the worrier. Whenever she left the house the first thing she had to do when she came home was make sure Mammy was still there.

"Tessie!" Deirdre shouted urgently from the kitchen. "Mammy's resting. Don't you dare go into her room."

"I'll be down in a minute," Rita called out. Deirdre, the oldest girl, had stayed home to take care of Bridie and Alphonsus while the others went to see what they called Aunt Mary's playboy. Wattie took the four middle ones in the trap—along with Mary McGreevy, of course—and Luke gave young Wat a lift on his bike.

"Aunt Mary came home with us," Fidelma shouted from right outside the door. "She was dressed just like a man."

"Come down, everyone, right now," Deirdre yelled, "or there'll be no supper tonight."

Rita was tired. A week after the birth and she hadn't gotten her strength back yet. She was getting too old to be having babbies. This was definitely the last, even if it meant Wattie Feerick had to sleep with the chickens from now on. She came slowly down the stairs, her body still hurting.

"Mammy! You should have seen Auntie Mary! She had a black mustache. She doesn't have it anymore. She took it off." Fidelma was dancing in the hall.

"Anybody who wants to eat tonight better sit at the table right now," Deirdre said. Everyone sat immediately. A great boss, this girl.

"How are you at all, Rita?" Mary McGreevy asked. She was sitting in the middle of the long bench on the wall side, wedged between Fidelma and Brian. Rita noticed that her eyes were bright with excitement, but she looked a bit tired.

"I'm well enough now, thank God. Is there a place for Mammy at the table?"

"Tessie!" Deirdre yelled. "You get out of Mammy's place right now and sit next to Fidelma."

"Aunt Mary is sitting in my place," Tess grumbled, but she moved anyway.

"I'm terribly sorry, Tessie." Mary made to get up.

"Don't mind her at all," Wattie said, sitting at the head of the table in an armchair. "We'll say grace now," he announced. And he did. They all answered, "Amen!" and blessed themselves.

"I'm afraid there's not much for supper," Deirdre, sitting next to her father, apologized to Mary. "Just bread and butter and jam and a bit of cold chicken."

"It's grand, now," the former nun said. "I love the *caiscin*."

"And how was the play?" Rita asked. She didn't feel like eating but forced herself to have a piece of bread anyway. She expected an instant chorus from the children, but no one said anything.

"It was good, mind you," Wattie said into the silence. But having said that, he said no more.

"I didn't understand a bit of it," Luke said, throwing a quick side glance at Mary McGreevy.

"They all talked in a funny sort of way," young Rita said, her head down. "I didn't know what any of them was saying. Except for Aunt Mary, of course." She looked up and across the table and smiled at their visitor. "I could understand you all right."

"I liked Aunt Mary's mustache." Fidelma giggled. "It moved up and down when she talked. And she wore trousers and a man's coat and—"

"Brian didn't know Aunt Mary when she came on the stage." Tess laughed. "He kept asking me where she was."

"I did so know her," Brian yelled. He stuck out his tongue at his sister behind Mary's back. "I liked when you chased the other lad out the door with a spade," he said to Mary. "That fellow was a real scaredy-cat. He looked like Mike Murroe."

"That was Jack Banaghan, you jackass," Luke said, offended. He waved a chicken leg at his brother. "You'll never be half the man he is. Jack is the best footballer in Kildawree."

"I liked the best when Paddy Carney stood there with his mouth open and he didn't know what to say." Young Wat did an imitation, displaying a mouth full of bread. "Somebody had to whisper to him from behind the curtain. He looked like he was going to lay an egg." Wat chortled loudly.

"Poor Paddy forgot his lines a couple of times," Mary explained, looking at Rita. "But I thought he did very well all the same."

"Give the man his due, now," Wattie said, slurping his tea. "I didn't think he had it in him."

"What did you think of the play yourself?" Rita directed the question at her husband. She was ashamed of the lot of them, all going off like that to see Mary McGreevy act in her play and then having nothing good whatever to say about it.

Wattie looked as if he'd been asked to swallow cod-liver oil. He cleared his throat a couple of times and looked hard at a piece of bread. "Well, I'll say this," he said finally. "Your woman here was a wonder entirely. That's a compliment to you, now, Mary." He waved his cup at her. "You were the cut of a man from the top of your head all the way down to the toes of your shoes. In word and in deed. I never saw anything the like of it in my entire life. I found myself forgetting you were a woman at all, and I watching you. Now, isn't that an outstanding thing?" He stuffed the bread in his mouth to stop himself from saying more.

"Well, thank you, Wattie. That's very kind of you." Mary blushed a little.

"But what did you think of the play itself?" Rita was annoyed at the way they were all avoiding an answer to her simple question.

"Ah, sure, I would say that for most of the people there it was a biteen hard to follow, you know," Wattie admitted. "No offense, Mary. I heard fellows saying during halftime that 'twasn't English ye were speaking at all but some foreign tongue that sounded a bit like it."

"And there's a bit of truth in that, now," Mary said. "The play takes place here in County Mayo, up in the mountains beyond Castlebar to be exact. But about fifty years ago, you see. It was at a time when the people were just learning English. They all spoke Irish before that, so what they were doing at this time was translating directly from Irish into English. And what came out was a mixture. Does that make sense?"

"Ah, yes, to be sure." Wattie waved his knife to indicate his ease of comprehension. "*I* understand it. Sure! But a lot of them *amadhans* that were standing in the back there tonight wouldn't know what in the name of God you were talking about."

"I must say they were all very quiet during the performance," Mary said. "Even in the parts that were supposed to be funny," she added with a smile.

"I didn't find any of it funny," Luke said. Rita could have strangled the lad for his adherence to honesty over politeness.

"Tell me, now," Wattie asked Mary, "why were Father Mulroe and Father Malone sitting at the side of the stage behind the curtain?"

"They were behind the curtain!" Rita echoed. "The two priests! Go on out of that!"

"Priests are not allowed to attend the theater," Mary McGreevy explained, a piece of *caiscin* in her raised hand. "The bishops have forbidden them to go in case their presence at a performance that had something bad in it might give scandal to their flock. So they go and they sit in the wings where they can't be seen by the faithful. And the bishops allow that." She spoke slowly and carefully, like Father Mulroe expounding a point of theology from the altar.

"*I* saw them behind the curtain," Tess called out.

"You're not part of the faithful," Luke jeered.

"Everybody saw them," Brian retorted.

"Well, now, doesn't that beat the band," said Rita.

"Priests, if you'll pardon me saying so"—Wattie was looking warily at Mary—"do some very queer things at times. I remember once—"

"Wattie! Not in front of the children, now, please," Rita admonished. He was always saying things against the priests and scandalizing the little ones.

"We'll say the rosary, then, if you're all finished," Wattie pronounced a few minutes later. The table was pushed out from the wall to let those on the inside kneel. There was a scramble to grab the rosary beads that hung on nails near the fireplace. Rita gave Fidelma a spare pair to give to Mary McGreevy. Wattie, kneeling low, his elbows resting on the seat of his chair and his backside to the fire, intoned the opening prayers and the first decade in a loud, monotonous voice. The responses from the children were singsong and serious until halfway through the decade, when a cricket chirped from somewhere in the hearth and several of the younger ones erupted in giggles. Wattie stopped in the middle of his Hail Mary. "There'll be sore backsides going to bed tonight if there's any more of that," he announced quietly but menacingly, without so much as looking around at the culprits. "Visitor or no visitor. Blessed art thou . . ." he continued in the same monotone.

There was no repetition of the giggles. Rita led the second decade, and then Wattie invited Mary McGreevy to give out the third. The fourth and fifth were said by Luke and Deirdre. After the Litany of the Blessed Virgin, there was the usual long list of prayers for various members of the living and the dead, including a special God-bless for their very good friend, Aunt Mary McGreevy, which the children pronounced louder than any other prayer of the evening. After the final sign of the cross they all stayed on their knees for a few minutes in silent devotion. When they were getting up, Rita noticed a suggestion of moisture in Mary's eyes.

"Everyone to bed, now," Wattie said, standing with his back to the fire. "Or you won't be able to get up for school tomorrow. The girls can do the dishes in the morning." There was an immediate bustle towards the stairs. "Would you like me to walk you back to the house?" Wattie asked Mary.

"No, thanks. That won't be necessary. There's a full moon, so the *pookas* won't bother me." She smiled at Wattie. He was always so kind to her. "I'd like to chat with yourself for a bit," she said to Rita. "If you're not too tired, of course."

"Arrah, why would I?" Rita *was* tired, but she would never miss a chance to talk with Mary. The return of the nun had given her a friend the like of whom she had never had before in her life. "We'll sit here by the fire and no one will bother us." But the children, clunking up the stairs, wakened the baby, who began to cry. "Would you bring her down to me, Deirdre, there's a good girl," Rita called up.

"I'm so glad," said Mary. "I did want to see her. I only saw her once, the day she was born."

"Would you like to hold her, Auntie Mary?" Deirdre asked when she brought the baby down.

"Oh! I'd love to." And Rita noticed the look of adoration on her friend's face as she held the squalling infant. But she rocked and cooed and made faces to no avail. The little one continued to bawl. Mary eventually looked helplessly at Rita.

"I'd better take her for a bit till she quietens down." But the infant cried even harder when her mother took her.

"I'll go to bed myself so," said Wattie, who had continued to linger silently by the fire. And off he went up the stairs.

"She wants to be fed," Rita said. "Would you ever mind if I do it here? It's warmer by the fire."

"Not at all." But it was clear that Mary didn't realize the manner of feeding until Rita undid her blouse. They both blushed a little then and smiled at each other.

"Not many women feed their babbies this way anymore." Rita arranged the infant comfortably. "But I have done it with them all." Suddenly the crying stopped and the kitchen was quiet except for the occasional sucking sound and the chirping of the cricket. "I believe it's the best nourishment for them."

"I suppose it is," Mary said. "Though I must say I never gave it much thought myself. It's not something we discussed a great deal in the convent." They both laughed at that.

"You're not sorry you left?" It was a question that Rita had wanted to ask her friend for months, but the opportunity just hadn't come up.

"On the contrary, every day I'm out I'm happier about it. To tell you the truth, I wonder why I didn't do it years ago. Especially," stretching her hand out to touch the baby's head ever so gently, "when I see herself."

"Well, maybe, now, with the help of God," Rita said devoutly, "you'll have one of your own someday."

"That is my intention." And the way Mary said it left a person in no doubt that she meant it.

"Isn't that wonderful!" Rita smiled at her. It would be great to see her settle down. "I suppose you have someone in mind?" She raised a waggish eyebrow.

"How do you mean?" Mary looked a bit puzzled.

"Well, 'tis something we can't do entirely on our own, you know. Not even an independent woman like yourself, as I'm sure you understand." For God's sake, surely they told nuns in the convent how babbies were made!

"Oh! You mean to be the father?" Mary blushed as she said the word. "Well, I will tell you that there are a number of candidates in the running, but I haven't decided who it will be yet."

" 'Tis great to have a choice anyhow, isn't it? There are plenty of bachelors around, to be sure, but not too many that would be suitably educated for a woman like yourself."

"You think the education would be important for the father?" Mary was stroking the infant's head with the tips of her fingers.

"Ah, sure, why wouldn't it? God help us, when you're sitting by the fire of a winter's evening and the children are gone to bed, 'tis nice to have a man that can talk a little bit of sense now and again. A lot of them around here can talk only farming. It's one of the great things about himself, mind you." She lowered her voice and pointed up the stairs. "The neighbors do laugh at him sometimes for using big words, but he's very smart and he can entertain you all night with his talk. He didn't have much schooling, mind you, but like myself he reads a lot and he's got plenty of the gray matter. Yourself now would need a very intelligent husband to keep up with you, I'd say."

Her friend was silent for a minute. However, it was clear she was trying to get something out, so Rita kept her mouth shut. In the end Mary said, "There are a couple of things I need to tell you, Rita. Which is the reason I kept you up so late. But I'd like to ask you first of all, if you don't mind, not to be mad at me when I tell you. And then I want you to promise not to tell a living soul a word that I say."

Rita felt the hair rise on her neck and the itch attack her toes. "Let me get herself on the other side," she said, "and then I'll be ready for you." The baby whimpered on being turned over but quickly accepted the new nipple.

"You promise?" Mary sounded terribly serious.

"Of course I promise. Why wouldn't I! Sure, I could never get mad at you, Mary. You're such a nice woman. And such a good friend to me too."

"And you'll never tell anybody?"

"On my word of honor! Nothing you say will ever pass my lips. That's the God's honest truth."

"I have decided not to get married." Mary looked up from the fire and straight at Rita. There was fierce determination in those eyes. They reminded Rita of the look on Deirdre's face the day she told her father she wanted to go to the convent school in Ballinamore. "That's the first thing I wanted to tell you. The other is that I do intend to have that baby."

It took a while to sink in. Yes, they had been talking about her having a baby. But then she said she wasn't going to get married. And now . . . "Jesus, Mary, and Joseph!" was all she could muster when the contradiction finally hit her.

"I've been doing a lot of thinking about it lately," Mary continued as calmly as if she were talking about the weather. "Especially when Fidelma comes to visit. And then it suddenly occurred to me after seeing herself here the day she was born that to have my own baby is what I want most in the entire world."

"But you said you weren't going to get married!"

"Yes." And that was all she said. They sat in silence. The cricket had quieted. Upstairs a bedspring creaked. The infant suckled contentedly. It was Rita's turn to look into the fire. She felt Mary's eyes on her still. "Are you shocked?" Mary asked after a minute.

"Are you saying?" Rita had to stop then to collect her thoughts. "Are you telling me that you intend to have a babby but that you don't intend to get married? Is that what you're saying?"

"Yes." In a terribly small voice from the former nun.

"But why?" Rita could feel her senses recovering, and it was her anger that was out in front of the pack. "I understood you when you said you'd like to have a babby. And then I had no problem when you said you were not going to get married." Her voice was rising. "But I don't know what on God's earth you mean when you say you want both at the same time!" Then she got hold of herself. "Pipe down, Rita Feerick; calm down, now; get a hold of yourself. Don't rush in to make judgments till you know all the facts, is what Father Mulroe is always saying to us."

"Now you understand why I asked you not to get mad at me," Mary said.

Rita looked at her. The woman's eyes were damp with pain. "I won't," she promised again. "No matter what happens. But can we talk a bit about it? I mean, it's—"

"Of course! I'd like to do that."

"Wouldn't it be a terrible sin?" This was what was foremost in Rita's mind.

"In the eyes of the church it certainly would, but in the eyes of God I'm not so sure."

Rita's head was spinning again. "But doesn't the church speak in the name of God? Doesn't Father Mulroe stand in the place of the Almighty for us?" But then, nuns knew almost as much as priests, they said. She felt her spiritual world tumbling around her.

"Well, I've something else to tell you that's even more difficult." Mary folded her arms and bent over till her elbows were resting on her knees. "I no longer believe in the church."

Rita felt numb. The situation was beyond her. "Are you an atheist, then? Or an apostate? Or what? Is there any cure for it? God help us all." She was just babbling to cover her confusion. "I had an uncle in

Bearnadearg who stopped going to mass because he said the priests were just skinning lies about heaven and hell. And he died that way too. And they refused to bury him in consecrated ground. But sure, what would we do without the faith? What would we teach the children? And what would happen to us when we died? I wish you hadn't told me this." She couldn't stop the tears then, and she cried softly while the infant sucked her breast.

"I'm awfully sorry," Mary whispered. She stretched out a hand to touch Rita's shoulder. "Maybe I shouldn't have put all this burden on you. But I had to tell someone. I wish I had your faith. It was a lot easier when I did. But you can't make yourself believe what you don't believe."

"But you go to mass!" Rita suddenly remembered with hope. "We cycle back together, the two of us, every Sunday."

"Ah, yes! I do like going to mass. Being with the people, taking part in the liturgy. But I don't believe in it the way I used to. Now it's just a social event for me."

"Is that why you haven't been going to communion?" She had been wondering about that for some time.

"Yes." Mary looked into the fire again. "And I'm going to have a baby without getting married. And people are going to look strangely at me. And say all kinds of things about me behind my back. And maybe to my face as well. And I'll need a friend or two to be on my side."

Another thought struck Rita. "Faith, you'll be lucky if Father Mulroe doesn't read you from the altar. The Lord save us! Father Moran read a girl from Kilmorrin that had an illegitimate babby, and she had to go to England in a hurry."

Mary straightened in her chair. "Father Mulroe won't say anything. I can promise you that. And Mary McGreevy is not going anywhere. She has a farm of land in Kilduff, and she's going to rear her child there until that child is old enough to run the farm for her."

"But why wouldn't you get married, Mary?" Rita pleaded. "It would be a lot easier for you. And there are some good lads around, too, that would be glad to have you."

"Who's the boss in this house?" Mary was on her feet, her back to the fireplace, hand on the mantelpiece in a good imitation of Wattie.

"Bedad, himself is, though I know there are some that think differently."

"Well, I'm the boss in my house, and that's the way it's going to stay. I don't intend to have to fight anyone for the title." She dropped to her knees suddenly in front of Rita. "Will you be my friend through it all?"

Rita detached the infant from her nipple. "She's asleep," she said and buttoned up her blouse. "I will be your friend, Mary, whatever happens." Then the mischievous thought crossed her mind, and she smiled. "Will you tell me who it is when you decide?"

Mary thought about that for a minute. "I won't," she said finally, still kneeling. Then she too smiled. "It might only get you into trouble."

9

Kitty, stepping into the car, felt nervous as a sheep going through a new gap. She was still terribly inept at coordinating clutch and accelerator. But she was going to do it anyway. She slammed the door and rolled down the window. "I'm going to Galway by myself today," she told Stephen, who was standing back a few feet and showing his big white teeth in a superior half grin. "And I don't want you hanging around the shops gawking at ladies' unmentionables while I'm buying my trousseau." It would be her very first time to drive Daddy's Vauxhall all by herself. Or any car, for that matter. She had driven to Ballinamore on two occasions and once to Castlebar, but always with her brother in the passenger seat, just in case.

"Well, good on you," he said. "Are you sure you'll be all right?" But she could feel the relief in his voice. The minute she was gone, back the road he'd be on the bicycle to visit Mary McGreevy. Which, for his own peculiar reasons, he didn't want her to know about.

Press the clutch, put the gear in neutral, open the choke, and turn the key. The engine crackled into life. So far, so good. Now to get it into first and moving. This was the part she had the most trouble with. And most embarrassment, though Stephen, to give him his due, had been very patient. Two feet down hard on clutch and brake and then shift into first gear. She waved at him and looked straight ahead towards the front gate away in the distance. Out with the clutch, nice and gentle, while the right foot slid off the brake and pressed the pedal. The car started to move forward, ever so slowly, but smoothly all the same. She had it now! No! Damnit to hell! She had let out the bloody clutch too soon. The car pitched and bucked like an unbroken stallion. The engine cut out.

"Take your time," he called. "You were in too much of a hurry." She glared at him through the open window but remained still, breathing deeply, for a full minute. He knew better than to say anything more. She tried again; it worked this time. She rolled away down the long curved, rutted path. In the rearview mirror she could see him heading back towards the house.

She should stop at the gate before getting onto the road. You never knew what might be coming—an asscart or a bicycle or even somebody walking. But if she stopped she might never get started again up that short, steep incline. Keep going, girl! Swing the wheel to the left and out with you without daring to look. Nothing in the way, thanks be to God. The next bad spot would be getting onto the tar road at Kildawree. Well, anyway, she could drive now, and she'd be good at it soon with a bit of practice. Ready for Tom's new Morris Minor after the wedding.

She really should have learned before now. Just after she came home two years ago, Daddy had wanted to teach her. But she wasn't interested. Too down in the mouth from what had happened to her life. And no one to talk to about it. Not even the priestly brother to whom she had always told everything that was going on in her life. Everything except those ten years that she hid from everyone. She did consider writing to him a couple of times but couldn't bring herself to do it. You never knew how he might react. And there was no one else. She could never tell Daddy anything. On the other hand, she had always been able to talk to Mammy about her problems. But not this. Definitely not this one. Imagine telling her! Mammy wouldn't know what she was talking about, never mind be of any help.

Better slow down. The potholes were getting worse every day on this blessed road. And Daddy would kill her if anything happened to his prize motorcar. Oh God! Nadinha! There was still a lot of pain at the thought of her. And why wouldn't there be! And fecking Alberto! God forgive her, she never used the word except in reference to that maggot Alberto Gomez. She had gone to London because she was tired of Dublin. Dear old dirty city where the girls were all so pretty and the pay was terrible and you couldn't sneeze without committing sin. Of course, Daddy would have sent her money if she had asked him. Which she wasn't about to. Not after what she had done to him. Declining to become Doctor Kitty Malone, M.D., daughter of Henry and Sara Malone of Kildawree. Headlines in the *Western People* it would have been. But she couldn't stand the sight of blood, or bear the thought of winding up as an old sawbones snob like Walsh in Ballinamore, the only doctor she knew at the time.

She had wanted to live and love and enjoy her life. Unfortunately, the nuns at Kylemore had taught her that such living was seriously sinful! And that was a problem for a while. Until she came to realize that their teaching denied her most of the worthwhile things in life. Stuffing yourself with the rich food she loved was gluttony. The exquisite sensation of losing your rag was the deadly sin of anger. The simple joy of thinking well of yourself was odious pride. And of course the pleasure of pleasures was declared totally off limits to the unmarried. Even drinking wine or sherry, for which she had developed a taste as soon as she left school, was wicked. Though she did learn from Nadinha that alcohol *was* bad.

Passing the boreen to Kilduff it struck her she'd like to visit Mary McGreevy. 'Twas early in the day yet. Plenty of time later to shop. Wouldn't Stephen be surprised when he arrived on his bike and found Daddy's car in front of the house! After a disastrous start she was beginning to get along well with the former nun. Since before Christmas she had been paying her occasional visits. And inviting her back to the Malones' for tea and long chats. But there would be no more of the latter until Stephen went back to Brazil. The man was always there when Miss McGreevy was in the house, hovering around her like a bee after honey and constantly intruding on their private conversations.

When she put her foot on the brake the engine stalled because she forgot to shift gears. With trial and error she managed to back the car up and head down the boreen. Tom Tarragh's Morris Minor was sitting in

Mary McGreevy's front yard. It had to be his. There were only a handful of cars in the entire parish, and no one else that she knew of had a Morris Minor. Nobody in the kitchen when she knocked on the door. Very suspicious! What were they up to at all? A few shouted hellos got no answer. Down the yard at a gallop, ignoring the effect of mud and muck on good shoes. She found them in the stable behind the hay shed, Tom standing in the doorway looking in, Mary inside with a pitchfork in her hand.

"Hello." Trying to keep the suspicion out of her voice.

Tom was so busy talking he didn't notice her coming. He turned like a startled sheep. "Hello! Hello yourself! What brings you here?" Babbling and turning red in the face.

"I might ask you the same thing!" Trying not to be too snotty.

"How are you, Kitty?" Mary never paused in her smooth motion of flinging the straw-laced dung into a wheelbarrow.

"I was on my way to Galway and thought I'd stop in for a chat."

"Well, isn't that a coincidence, now," Tom said. "I was doing just the same thing myself."

She was about to remark that he had picked a rather roundabout way of getting from Kildawree to Galway. Instead she said, "I'm glad you did, now. I get to see my two favorite people all at the one time." It was all she could do not to scream at him, What was he doing visiting Mary McGreevy on a Saturday morning, and he an engaged man?

"I'll be finished here in a minute and then we'll have a cup of tea." Mary dropped the pitchfork and wheeled the loaded barrow a bit unsteadily out the door. "I'll be right back," she shouted, heading down the yard.

"I'd best be going," Tom said.

"You may kiss me before you leave." She liked the way he kissed— gentleness liberally dosed with passion. She liked passionate people.

"So long!" He waved at Mary as she came back up with the empty barrow.

"Did she chase you away? Well, you're a terrible woman, Kitty Malone."

"No! No! Not at all!" Tom disclaimed. "I have a lot of things to do in Galway. I'll be seeing you all." And off up the yard he raced as if a swarm of bees were after him.

"Come and have a look at my stall-feds," Mary said. "I've got six black pollies in here. They'll be nice and fat for the April fair. That's the time you'll get a good price for them."

Kitty looked in politely at the cattle. "Fine-looking beasts." How awful for the poor creatures! One of these days she'd have to talk to her friend about the immorality of slaughtering animals for food.

They walked in silence up the yard to the kitchen. Mary put the kettle on the fire. "If you're thinking what I think you're thinking," she said with her back turned, "you don't need to worry."

"Oh, I'm not in the least bit worried." Kitty pulled a chair out and sat at the table. "I'd split his head open in a minute if he stepped out of line, and it's well he knows it." When Mary came over and sat next to her she added, "In a backwater like Kildawree, if you want to be respected you must have not only a husband but a well-behaved husband."

Mary folded her arms. "And where does that leave the likes of me, may I ask?"

How to answer that without giving offense? She traced invisible letters on the table with her right index finger. "You're cut from a different bolt of cloth, Mary McGreevy. I'd say you'd create your own respectability no matter what you chose to do."

"We'll soon see about that." Mary got up and stoked the fire.

"Do you remember the first time we met back at the school?"

"Will I ever forget it? I thought you were going to physically assault me." Mary put down the tongs, sniffed her hands, and made a face.

"It was because you were a nun. I hated all nuns ever since I was in Kylemore. But do you know, before the night was out I was beginning to like you. And I hated you all the more for that. I didn't sleep a wink thinking about you and trying to understand how I could like you and hate you at the same time."

"I'd better wash my hands before I touch anything." Mary went to a table by the back door on which there was a basin of water. "And do you like me now?" Soaping her hands, bent over, backside facing Kitty.

"You'll do, I suppose."

Mary dried her hands, sniffed her armpits. "I'd better take a bath before I go into town. I smell like a stall-fed." She went to the dresser and took down cups and saucers and put them on the table.

"Why don't you come to Galway instead? I can give you a lift."

"Ah, not at all. It'll be a while before I'm ready to go. But thanks all the same." She went over and stirred the fire again with the tongs.

"I'm not in any hurry." Folding her arms and leaning back in the chair, trying to be casual. "That way we'll have plenty of time for talking. And we can have dinner at the Great Southern."

"Easy now, *a stor*." Mary took half an apple tart from the cupboard. "Some of us have to mind our pennies. The Great Southern is only for those with money."

"It'll be my treat. Henry Malone can well afford it."

So they had tea and apple tart and a lot of talk while the pot of bath water heated up. When it was boiling Mary carried in a big galvanized tub from the back room, put it on the floor by the fireplace, and emptied the steaming water into it. Then she went outside and came back with a bucket of cold water that she poured in as well. She stuck her hand in. "Just about right, I'd say. You can sit in the parlor now if you like while I'm getting myself cleaned up." She had her back turned as she began to take off her shoes.

"Would you mind if I keep you company?" Kitty had been planning on this from the minute she heard mention of a bath. Though now she was feeling nervous of the former nun's reaction. "That way I can scrub your back for you."

Mary looked at her with a sort of dark puzzlement. "I'm not used to having my back scrubbed." She removed her left boot and struggled with the thick woollen stocking. "In the convent we were allowed a bath twice a week, but it was in and out as fast as you please. In case the sight of your own body would give you temptations against purity, you see. And God forbid you should see someone else naked." She removed the other shoe. "So I don't know if I'm ready . . ."

Nothing for it but to get up and say, of course I understand, really, and I'll go and sit in the parlor. But then Mary went on, talking to herself: "Arrah, what are you worried about? She's not going to bite you." And she hoisted her dress up over her head.

She had a fine, shapely, smooth-skinned body. Breasts smaller and haunches slimmer than Nadinha, who often remarked that she was well designed for begetting and feeding babies. "Not that you'll ever catch me doing it," she would add fiercely. Running a soapy sponge on Mary

McGreevy's back and shoulders revived memories whose sweetness matched their pain. Out of habit and without thought she suddenly bent and kissed her friend where shoulder melded into neck.

"What are you doing, Kitty Malone?" But Mary was busy scrubbing her toes with a nailbrush, and the question was only a quiet murmur.

"Can I tell you a secret?"

"I love secrets." Mary lifted her left leg out of the water and began washing it with a cloth. "If I was a man I'd have been a priest and spent all my time in the confession box."

"You don't shave your legs!" Nadinha would occasionally let hers go for a couple of weeks, and that would be a bone of contention between them. But Mary McGreevy's left leg looked as if it had never been shaved. "Is it the convent? Aren't nuns allowed?"

"I'll remind you again, Kitty Malone, that I'm no longer a nun. I can shave my legs if I want to." The smile appeared just long enough to take the sting out of the words. "You shave yours, I suppose?"

"Of course!" She squeezed the sponge and watched the soapsuds trickle down the former nun's breast. "Everybody does these days. I mean all women do." She smiled bleakly. "At least nearly all."

"How far up?"

"As far as is needed, of course." She probably wasn't allowed to do it in the convent and never learned since she came out.

"Do you shave *all* your body hair?" Mary's question came so fast it took her by surprise.

"No! Of course not."

"Just your legs?"

"And armpits."

"But not between your legs?"

"Aren't you the innocent one? I'll have to take you in hand one of these days and teach you a few things."

"You'll have even more to teach me after you get married."

Not much that she didn't know after Nadinha. Not to mention fecking Alberto. "Which brings me back," she said, "to my secret."

"Ah, your secret, yes, tell me about it." Mary's right leg came up out of the water. Lovely toes. She'd like to suck them.

"I suppose you might have wondered why I never got married before this." Up off her knees, drying her hands on Mary's towel, smoothing down her frock, escaping to the front window to look out at the neat flower garden. "Not that I'm terribly old or anything, but . . ."

"Arrah, there are lots of women your age and mine in Kildawree who aren't married."

"Anyway, there *was* a particular reason. You know I lived in London during the war?"

"His reverence, your brother, told me that."

"Speak of the devil! Stephen is coming down the boreen on his bike."

"Cripes!" Mary wailed. "The whole Malone clan wants to watch me taking a bath."

"I'll stop him." Kitty rushed to the door. But by the time she opened it he was turning around in a great hurry at the gate and heading off back up the boreen again. "He saw the car. He doesn't want me to know he comes to see you. Not that it's any of my business, of course."

"Sorra bit of harm is in it, Kitty. Priests are only human too. They like a bit of female companionship from time to time like any other man."

Kitty watched him disappear around a bend in the road, then closed the door and came back and stood by the tub. "One of my secrets is that I lived with a woman for five years."

"And I lived with fifty-three of them for sixteen years." Mary stood, the soapy water dripping from her.

"We had a sexual relationship," Kitty said, as bleakly as she could say it.

Mary dried herself with great vigor and in total silence. She hung the towel on the back of a chair and stood naked by the fire, facing it, rubbing her hands together. Then she said, "Excuse me now while I put some clothes on," and headed back to her bedroom. From inside she shouted, "Tell me about it."

Moment of purest bliss! Kitty had never told anyone in all of Ireland about her relationship with Nadinha. She was over by the bedroom door in the swish of a cow's tail. "You're not shocked?" The door was open, but she refrained from looking in.

"Of course I'm shocked." But Mary's tone was casual. "It's something I've only read about in theology books, and what a heinous sin it is and all that. You could knock me down with a feather this minute to think that someone I know had done such a thing."

"Didn't you ever have a particular *gradh* for any of the nuns yourself?"

"Come on in and help me with this thing. It's a terror to get on." Mary was struggling into a green frock. "Would you button it up for me like a good girl? Now, what was that you were saying?"

"I was wondering," Kitty picked her words carefully as she fastened the buttons, "whether you ever felt attracted in that sort of way toward any of the other nuns. Not that you would have *done* anything, of course. I'm just talking about feelings. I mean, nuns are human beings too, I suppose."

"Well, thank you for granting us that. And as a matter of fact, I did have a special liking for one particular nun. But that was as far as it went, I can tell you."

"You never indulged in a little bit of surreptitious touching? You know, like this?" Reaching around and running the palm of her hand ever so lightly over the bust of the green frock. Oh! The delicious shock of that touch!

"Good God Almighty! 'Tis the Malones are free with their hands on a person's body!" Mary grabbed a pair of nylons from the top of a small chest. "Just forget that I said that, please." She sat on the bed and started to pull on a stocking.

"Sorry! Terribly sorry. I didn't mean—"

"It's all right, *a stor*. No harm done. As a matter of fact, you have nice hands. I liked the feel of them when you washed my back."

"So Stephen has been misbehaving, has he? I had a feeling he was up to no good."

"Arrah, 'twas nothing. Just a momentary loss of control. It could happen to anyone. And for God's sake, don't ever let on I told you." Then, standing and bending and pulling the stocking up over her knee, she asked, "Why are you getting married, so? I somehow thought that condition was not reversible."

"I was in love with a man before I met Nadinha."

"Were you now? Nadinha was your . . . ?"

"My woman lover. Yes. I met her after I went to Brazil."

Mary McGreevy's nose wrinkled. "I'm confused now. I thought you lived in London." She ran a garter up her leg.

"I went to Brazil from London with fecking Alberto—Oh, God! I'm sorry. I—"

"It's all right. I've heard the word before. But who is effing Alberto?"

Kitty slumped onto the bed. "The man I was in love with. I met him just after I went to London. God! He was gorgeous."

Mary ran her hands up her leg to straighten the stocking. "So what happened?"

"We lived together. It was the thing to do in London at the time. For a while it was great—the sex and the booze and the high living. Alberto had pots of money. Then the war broke out and the bombings and the shelters and the sirens and the rationing. It was totally miserable. So as soon as Alberto could get a passage to Brazil, he was off. And silly, inno-cent Kitty went with him, thinking this was the grand adventure of my life. I never told the family. Not even Stephen, although he was stationed at the other end of Brazil. I used to send my letters to a friend in London to mail them home for me."

"Tell me," Mary picked up the other stocking from the chest and ex-amined it carefully, "did the sin part ever worry you?"

"It bothered me in the beginning. I went to confession after the first time I slept with fe—excuse me—Alberto. When I said I had committed fornication the priest nearly had a conniption. He gave me three rosaries and made me promise never to go near that occasion of sin again. I wish to God I had taken his advice. But then I'd never have met Nadinha."

"And to think I was praying for you every day!" Mary pulled on the second stocking. "We said special prayers every night for the poor bombed people of London."

"Fat lot of good it did me. When we got to Rio his family would have nothing to do with me. They called me a whore and told Alberto he'd better find a virgin to marry or he'd lose his inheritance. He used that as an excuse to get rid of me."

"You poor thing. What did you do?"

"Got a job as an English tutor in São Paulo. That's where I met Nadinha." The tears were coming on.

"If it's too personal, now, tell me to mind my own business. But how do two women, you know, discover that they're—how do I say this?" Mary ran the second garter up her leg.

"In love? No different than with a man and a woman. Nadinha was my student. I fell in love with the way she said 'Keetchy.' She needed a place to live and I took her in, and she never left until she died." This time she couldn't stop the tears from filling her eyes.

"So sad." Mary's arm came ever so briefly around her shoulder. "And now you love Tom Tarragh."

"I do. Honest to God, I do." She desperately wanted this to be true. But she was going to marry him no matter what: Tom Tarragh's good name and her father's land and money were vital to her future well-being. She'd have leisure to deal with her feelings later.

They had great wick in Galway all afternoon, she trying on brassieres and knickers and corsets and petticoats and camisoles and nightgowns and garter belts, while Mary—under mild protest, and "only in deference to your insistence," she said—looked on, embarrassment in her face at times and hilarity at others, and she passing withering judgments on the necessity or suitability or desirability for free, civilized women to wear such ridiculous harness. "Thanks be to God," she said, "we didn't have to endure such things in the convent. They're worse than hair shirts."

"Did you wear a hair shirt?" Kitty was trying to fasten a too-tight corset.

"Some of the nuns did. Yours truly has never believed in inflicting corporal punishment on herself. Life does enough of that for you."

Kitty bought gobs of the things anyway, the need to please Tom Tarragh overriding, for the moment at least, a newly burgeoning suspicion that maybe indeed there was something to what her friend was saying. Afterwards they went to Ford's, where Miss McGreevy bought her groceries. And then they adjourned to the Great Southern Hotel, where Mary had roast beef that she said was delicious and Kitty insisted on being served a meal containing no meat.

That night, drifting off to sleep, Kitty's last waking thoughts were of Mary McGreevy.

10

The evening before Kitty Malone was due to marry Tom Tarragh, she rode her bike back to Kildawree to go to confession, a duty she undertook only because Father Mulroe said it had to be done if she wanted to get married. It would be her first time at the sacred tribunal in about twelve years. As she approached Kilduff, preparing in her mind a plausible rendition of the state of her soul, a motorcar—a Morris Minor—came out of the boreen and headed back towards the village.

The colossal gall of that man! She stood on the pedals, in hot pursuit, her mind no longer sifting through the mentionable sins of her life. Tom Tarragh was a dead man if ever there was one. After all she had told him. After all the warnings and threats. She would flay him alive. She would pull out his fingernails one by one. Tar and feather the blackguard. Stretch him on the rack. Every torture that English soldiery ever thought up for Irish rebels she would inflict on this lecherous, treacherous schoolmaster. When she was finished with him he'd know the price of infidelity.

The Morris was outside his house when she steamed up the driveway. She hammered the door knocker the way Mick Graney hammered horseshoes on his anvil. The door opened and there he was. But the grin came off his gob when he spotted the thunder on her face. "What's the matter, Kitty, *a ghradh?*" All solicitous, *mar dheadh*.

"Very well you know what the matter is." She wasn't going to beat about the bush. And her voice was high and cracking and loud enough to be heard all the way up to Queally's.

"Well, come in anyway and let's talk about it. Whatever it is," he added as he managed to get her inside and shut the door.

"What were you doing back visiting Mary McGreevy this evening?" The words almost choked her, so inadequate were they to express her anger.

He held open the door to his sitting room. "Musha, is that all that's bothering you? Sit down and I'll tell you all about it." As innocent as a newborn lamb, the rotten schemer.

"I'm not sitting down." But she stepped into his parlor anyway. "I want an answer to my question, and it better be a good one." If there wasn't fire coming out of her nostrils, there ought to have been.

"Take it easy now." He closed the door, calm as a cow chewing the cud. "Mary asked me to get her a couple of books from the county library in Castlebar. I was down there yesterday, as you well know, and I got them. So I drove back this evening and gave them to her." He sat in an easy chair. "Not much to get excited about there, I'd say."

She might have calmed down if it weren't for that last sentence. "Not much to get excited about," she screamed. "You're supposed to be getting married to me tomorrow and what are you up to this evening? Off visiting a good-looking spinster that you've paid more attention to for the past three months than you have to me! And I'm supposed to think it's nothing to get excited about. Well, I'll tell you this, Thomas Aquinas Tarragh! I *am* excited about it. Though *excited* is not the word I'd use. I'm furious, do you hear me? Furious!"

It was clearly the occasion for the soft word and the mollifying speech, and Tom Tarragh was noted for his ability to quell conflicts with his *plamas*. Unfortunately, the physician often can't heal himself, nor does the priest always attain the sanctity he preaches. And neither could Tom Tarragh in this instance bring the calm to his fiancée that he so often brought to others. "You're always getting fired up over something," he said now, with a touch of badly misplaced asperity. To make matters worse, he stopped right there, his very silence an incitement to the woman to increase the tempo.

"I don't believe it's all that innocent," she yelled.

"If you don't," he retorted, "then we might as well call the whole thing off."

"Hah!" All the anguish of a martyr on the wheel in that cry. "So that's what you're up to! That's what you wanted all along, wasn't it? That's what these visits to Miss McGreevy were all about!" The worms that had been torturing her intestines ever since she saw the Morris come out of Kilduff increased their activity. But she was a proud woman. Her life was about to be destroyed. So be it. She would not beg. She turned her back on him and opened the parlor door. "We'll go over to Father Mulroe so and tell him it's off."

The parish priest's broad welcoming grin vanished quickly beneath their fearful gloom. "You can't be serious, now," was his startled comment when Kitty, bent on getting first licks, told him the wedding would not take place tomorrow as planned.

"Nor ever," she added ferociously, glaring at her erstwhile fiancé. And into the priest's parlor she dragged her feet, like Wellingtons through muck. Oh, God! What had happened all of a sudden to her plans for a happy life? But she would not crawl. Her only futile consolation now was that she wouldn't have to face confession.

"Will someone tell me very calmly what happened?" Father Mulroe eased himself into the far side of the sofa, Kitty being at the other end and the schoolmaster taking the easy chair. But neither did. Only the ticking of the mantel clock relieved the deadly silence. "There must be a reason," the priest persisted.

"I'll tell you the reason," Kitty exploded. "He's seeing another woman, that's why. Before he even married me, for God's sake!" Then she burst out crying.

"I am no such thing!" Tom Tarragh shouted at the priest so he could be heard above his fiancée's *caoineadh*.

"You are so!" She managed to stifle her blubbering just long enough to issue the retort.

"Father!" There was the patience of Job himself in the wretched man's sighing of that word. "Mary McGreevy asked me to get her some books from the county library. And I did. And I brought them back to her this evening. And that's what the woman is mad at me over."

"You're always going back to see her." Kitty shut off the sobbing for good this time. "I've begged and I've pleaded with you, and—"

"Tell me, are you both determined this marriage will not take place?" Father Mulroe was staring into the grate, where a warm turf fire was burning. But again only the clock's tick-tock gave him answer. He stood then. "Thomas, could you and I talk privately?" And seeing the glare in Kitty's eyes, he added quickly, "Then you and I, Kitty, will talk privately as well."

She stared vacantly into the fire and felt the tears begin to flow every time she thought of her vanished bliss. Maybe she shouldn't have followed him back the road. Anyway, too late to undo that now. After the wedding she could have kept him out of harm's way. Overimpetuous as usual, her besetting sin. And one she *could* have confessed to Father Mulroe. She never could have told him about Nadinha, of course. Arrah, why not? It was all over and likely never to be repeated. Especially now that Tom had set his cap at Miss McGreevy. She might even feel better if she confessed all. Religion, they said, was the cure for an unhappy life. And hers was destined for misery, that was for sure.

They were gone a long time before the door opened again. Tom, head bowed and shoulders hunched, walked in slowly and sat in his chair, never once looking at her. "We'll talk now, Kitty," the priest said. He closed the parlor door behind her. "In the kitchen, if you don't mind. Bridie May is out." They went silently down the hall. He closed the kitchen door as well. "Tell me." He sat on the well-scrubbed deal table, his right foot touching the floor. "You don't really want to cancel this wedding, do you?"

"It was his idea." She plopped like a wet dishrag into Bridie May's armchair and stared at the fire.

"I've talked with Thomas." Father's left leg swung back and forth like a pendulum. "He sincerely regrets what he said to you about ending it all. He doesn't know what got into him to say such a thing. And he most certainly never meant it." The priest got off the table and stood looking into the fire as well. "Now, in the light of that, and if Thomas would apologize to you for what he said—which he expressed a most sincere intention of doing—would you be willing to reconsider?"

It was the damndest thing, and she could recall the sensation years later. All she had to say was yes, and her future happiness would be restored. And yet at that minute the urge welled up in her to say no. It was the thought of herself and Mary McGreevy that did it. Tom had set his cap at her, had he? Well, not if *she* got there first! Maybe she could share the house with her, like Nadinha did with herself. Especially since she'd never get married now, and in that case Daddy would likely give the place over to one of the nephews. But oh, God! Daddy! She could never face Daddy and tell him the wedding was off. Enough that she had reneged on being the doctor in the family and that she would never give him a grandchild, which he didn't know about yet, of course. Was she now about to deny him even the son-in-law he had grown to like and respect—a fact he had let her know many a time in the past few months?

"Yes," she answered. Regret and resignation and sadness, even a dollop of despair, in the saying of it. But she couldn't let Daddy down again. She was still his little girl, no matter what she had done in the past. This time she would sink her own feelings to please him.

And Mary McGreevy would still be around, was a thought not too far from the surface of her confused and bedraggled consciousness as she cycled home in the dark after making her confession.

Hard work and a good head had made Henry Malone the richest farmer in Kildawree, but he remained a simple man at heart. And a friendly one, a man who liked to visit with the neighbors and have them visit him, a man who knew nearly every other farmer in the parish and hardly ever passed up an opportunity to chat with them, and a man who still enjoyed the occasional pint or half one with the lads up at Queally's. Never mind his daughter's abhorrence of drink or her standoffishness from Queally's patrons. Henry, despite his wealth and prestige in the parish, had never, as Wattie Feerick once remarked, gotten too big for his britches. And he never would either. So it was a good job he didn't find out that his daughter's wedding was almost canceled.

He had been looking forward to the event the way a schoolboy looks forward to holidays ever since Kitty had made the announcement. And he had invited nearly half the parish to help him celebrate. Much to Kitty's chagrin, it should be noted, since she had wanted just a small and very select list of guests. The only concession he made to her was to allow the reception to be held at Moran's Hotel in Ballinamore. His own original plan, which he unveiled at dinner one night just after Christmas, was to empty out the biggest barn, whitewash it, and . . . Well, that was as far as he got before Kitty stood up and put her foot down and said if that was what he was going to do, she was going to elope and he would have to celebrate without her. Then, having wrestled Moran's out of him, she demanded that he rent himself a morning suit in Galway for the occasion. Henry put *his* foot down on that. So on the morning of the last Saturday in April, in the year of our Lord 1951, he wore a navy-blue suit and a bright red tie as he walked his daughter up the aisle of the parish church to be united in holy matrimony to Thomas Aquinas Tarragh, N.T., Kildawree, the Reverend Stephen Malone, M.H.S., Henry's own son and brother of the bride, officiating, assisted by the Very Reverend Father John Patrick Mulroe, P.P., Kildawree.

"Begob, she's a credit to you," Mick Burke told Henry after the mass and ceremony. They were standing outside the church waiting for the happy couple to come out of the sacristy, where they had gone to sign the register.

"She took long enough, anyway," Henry said. "But 'tis done now." He had the mien of a satisfied man.

"She's a fine-looking woman," Mick added. "Mr. Tarragh is a lucky man." To give Mick his due, there was no more than the barest trace of envy in his tone. "I had an eye on her myself, you know," he threw in on impulse.

Henry, thumbs hooked into his vest, looked sideways at the man. "You're better off without her. She wouldn't suit you at all." He lowered his voice. "That woman would drive any ordinary man cracked. My advice to you, Mick, is to find yourself a nice, easygoing girl who doesn't have big ideas." And he nodded his head and winked confidentially at Queally's curate.

"I was thinking of having a go at your woman," Mick half whispered, pointing a thumb at Mary McGreevy, who was standing on the steps a few yards away talking to Henry's missus. "Maybe since you're great with her you'd put in a word for me."

Henry looked straight ahead toward the distant Partry mountains. "Musha, sorra word, Mick; sorra word." He hawked and then looked at the missus, who was talking to the ex-nun but watching himself. He refrained from spitting. "Matchmaking is the devil's own work, believe you me. By the time you're done, the two parties are snapping like dogs at your heels. I know because I brought people together a couple of times myself. Never again, I can tell you that. Every man should do his own courting. That's my belief." Then Henry stepped briskly forward to meet Father Mulroe, who had just come through the outside door of the sacristy.

"Well, Father John Patrick, you tied the knot good and tight, I hope."

"I did indeed, Henry. Tight enough to hold them, anyway." The parish priest shook Henry's big, knobbly-knuckled hand. "He won't get away from her now, I can guarantee you that."

Henry was watching the happy couple appear out the back door of the church. "It isn't him I'd be worried about, but herself. She's always been a bit wild, Father. Ever since she was a nipper."

"She'll settle down now," the priest said comfortably. "They always do. Even the wildest of them. A couple of babbies and she'll be right as rain."

"He's a good lad himself, mind you."

"Ah, there isn't a finer man in the parish than Tom Tarragh. Present company excepted, of course." Father Mulroe smiled genially.

Henry leaned toward the priest and spoke just above a whisper. "It's the babbies I'm worried about. I need the grandchildren to carry on the line and take care of the farm. And the girl is not getting any younger; that's the problem."

"She's young enough to have a few, anyway, I'd say," Father Mulroe said confidently.

"Parents of the bride to the right of the bride," the photographer called out. Kitty had insisted on getting the fellow down from Galway so she'd have, as she said, some decent photographs of the occasion.

"Stephen, you stand next to Mammy," the bride shouted. Stephen kept an eye on Mary McGreevy during the interminable arranging of poses. It was occasions like this that made celibate life most difficult. Especially with a woman like herself standing there looking absolutely ravishing in her red coat. God forgive him, he shouldn't let the thought so much as enter his head, but on a day like today he wanted to shed his clerical garb and walk her home and close the door behind them.

"Father Stephen, will you come over here and stand between Tom and me for a picture?" *There's a place reserved in hell for priests who play fast and loose with their vows. Even after . . . No more now!* He leaned into Kitty's shoulder but refused to smile on cue.

"Stay right there for a shot of just you and Tom." At least Tarragh would no longer be competition for Mary. He positively scowled at the camera.

Jack Banaghan was something else again. Over there this very minute talking to her; the old man had gone overboard inviting everyone in the county. He couldn't have her himself, of course, that was a fact: next week he was off back to Pernambuco. But he had grown terribly fond of her, and he didn't want anyone else to have her in his absence. "How are you, Jack?"

"Fine, thanks, Father." He couldn't quite make the lad out—was he as innocent as he looked and talked? Although there *was* a kind of defiant edge behind the soft-spoken respect.

"I suppose you're all packed for the journey," Mary said.

"Not much to pack. I travel light." He wished Banaghan would take off so he could talk to her.

They were discussing banking, Mary said. "Jack says he can help me get a loan. I'd like to improve the land a bit and buy some more stock."

"You'll soon be as good a farmer as Henry Malone," Stephen teased.

"Better!" Not a trace of a smile. "Your father is a bit old-fashioned in his ways. Don't tell him I said that, of course."

"I was thinking of taking up farming myself," Jack said. Awkwardly. The lad was terribly shy.

"Good on you, Jack. And here's a nice lady farmer that could do with a husband. There's your chance!"

Jack blushed. He didn't know where to focus his eyes. "If you'll excuse me now," he managed, "I need to talk to a fellow." And he walked away in a great hurry.

"You're a terrible man, Father Malone," Mary McGreevy said. "The creature! You embarrassed the life out of him."

"He'd make a good husband for you, all the same."

"Ah, sure, the poor lad is too shy to make a move. Not like some other people I know." It was Father Stephen's turn to feel the blood in his cheeks.

Jack Banaghan was more than embarrassed; he was furious with the missionary. Spoiling everything just when he was making a bit of headway with Mary. That loan would be the way to her heart, if he could get it. God damn him to hell, anyway; priests shouldn't be snooping and sniffing around women. "Hello there!" He recognized the fellow standing by the church gate; he saw him now and again in Ballinamore, though he had never spoken to him.

"You're the footballer, aren't you?" Kevin Kelly responded. They watched the bride and groom get into the Morris Minor and talked a bit about Ballinamore and how the town wasn't prospering because too many people were leaving the countryside and going to Dublin and England. It was all the government's fault, Kelly said vehemently. Mr. Malone was a good customer of his, he noted as Henry got into the Vauxhall. And Mary McGreevy was a great woman altogether, he added as the former nun and Father Stephen eased into the back seat.

"I don't know her all that well myself," Jack said cutely. There was a fervor about the way Kelly mentioned her name that disturbed him. "Is she a friend of yours?"

"Arrah, why wouldn't she? Between you and me," he said out of the corner of his mouth, "I damn near married the girl."

"Go on!"

"Divil a lie."

"And why didn't you?"

"She went into the convent on me. I wish to God I'd married her before she went in. I'd be a happy man today."

"You could marry her now." Casually, though the words nearly choked Jack.

"I'd be a bigamist if I did." Kelly looked around like a spy in the pictures. "For God's sake, don't ever tell my missus I said that. She'd be here herself today, only she had to mind the shop." He started to move away. "Can I give you a lift in to Moran's?"

"And do you think she'd have you if you weren't married?" Jack got into the passenger seat.

"I'd say she would, now. You can tell when a girl is stuck on you. And that girl is stuck on me. Didn't she . . ." but he stopped suddenly in mid-sentence. "God blast it to hell," he exploded suddenly, and roared through Kildawree at a speed that was unsafe for man or beast. And most unfortunate for Sarah Brown's favorite hen, which chose that precise moment to cross the road. Jack, looking back, saw a cloud of drifting feathers.

They drove the four miles to Ballinamore almost in silence while Jack meditated on Mary McGreevy's awful powers of attracting men. And he himself couldn't even get her to go dancing with him. Well, he'd dance with her today, that was for sure. And all that talk of hers about not wanting to get married. Maybe she'd change her mind when he got her in his arms on the dance floor. And got her the loan for her stock. He'd take up farming if she'd have him. Of course, he knew a lot about it already.

The ballroom at Moran's was decorated with streamers and bunting that hung from ceiling and walls and windows and practically hid the small stage where the band members were already tuning their instruments. The tables were laid out along the walls, lovely to look at with their spotless white linens and fine blue-patterned china and gleaming silverware and crystal vases of flowers. The center of the floor was shining parquet, all ready for the dancing feet. "Well, isn't it grand," Rita Feerick whispered to her husband.

"Why wouldn't it?" Wattie was feeling ever so grand in a place like this. "Sure, Henry Malone would only have the best."

Mrs. Feerick was still looking around in wonder after Wattie wandered off into the crowd when she heard, "Hello, Rita" from behind. Kitty, looking absolutely gorgeous in her white wedding dress. With enough lace in it to cover all the windows in the Feerick house.

"Musha, isn't it yourself that's the beautiful bride. And you look so young." She did, too.

"Thank you, Rita. You're looking young yourself."

"I look my age now." She had noticed that in the looking glass this very morning. "Who'd ever believe that you and I were in the same class in—"

"Ssshh, Rita! We women have our secrets that we wouldn't want this crowd to know about."

"Well, you were wise to wait, anyway. You won't have as many children to worry about as some of us."

"With the help of God I won't have any to worry about. I'll see you later, Rita," and Kitty swept regally away across the dance floor in the direction of her new husband, leaving Rita Feerick to ponder the absurdity of a Mary McGreevy wanting a child but no husband and a Kitty Malone wanting a husband but no child. What was the world coming to at all?

Which was the very question Tom Tarragh was asking himself, though for a different reason. "I think they're all waiting for us to sit down first," Kitty said when she arrived at the table.

"I was waiting for you." He knew as the words came out that he had said the wrong thing. Kitty smiled at him with her lips, but her eyes were slits of annoyance. The marriage was getting off on the wrong foot, that was for sure. Which was only to be expected, he supposed, given the nature of the two of them. They all stood while Father Mulroe said the grace and then sat with a great waving of hands blessing themselves. Even before the explosion last night, the relationship had been a bit shaky. What was the world coming to anyway when a man was practically forced to marry a woman he hardly liked? Ah, now, he wasn't forced. And he did like a lot of things about her. The soup was in front of him before he had time to put his napkin on his lap. But he was pres-

sured all the same. "Fine, Mick, and yourself?" Now, who but Henry
Malone would invite the blacksmith to a wedding? Not that he himself
was a snob or anything, but at the same time . . . "Oh, I'm fine, thanks,
dear. It is indeed. Most delightful. Well, I didn't taste it yet." All very sub-
tle, you see. The invitations back to the house. The elegant teas with the
family. Being treated as important and yet as a friend. That was a big part
of it. A schoolmaster got a lot of respect from the parish but not much in
the line of friendship. A bit like the parish priest in that way. All of which
made you a bit lonely. Especially when you didn't have a wife. "Great
soup indeed, Mrs. Malone. Mother! Of course. From now on, certainly."
But there was the price to go with the privilege. From being treated as
family you were expected to *become* family. And you gradually began to
accept that fact. Till it seemed the most natural thing in the world one
cold Sunday night, after a delicious supper and a couple of glasses of
Henry's best Irish and being left alone with Kitty before a roaring fire
after everyone had gone to bed, that you should ask her to be your wife.
And here you were today, tied for life to a woman you had sworn you
would never marry. "Dance, dear! Well, now, I'm not much of a dancer,
I have to admit, but I suppose we are expected to make a spectacle of ourselves on occasions like this." Light as a feather in his arms. Not a pick of
fat on her, your hand on her back could tell that. But a body to stir a man's
blood all the same. Mind you, if that part worked out well, they might get
along yet. That and a few children. He'd settle for a couple, given her age.
Though he still didn't know exactly how old she was. Why women
wanted to keep those things secret, anyway . . . "I'm sorry too, dear. We
won't ever mention the whole wretched episode again. Exactly. A fresh
start. Absolutely, beginning right now." And he would make a fresh start.
Solemn oath. "Do you think it would be proper? Here on the dance
floor? But England is a different place, you know. Well, if that's what you
want, dear . . . I suppose they must have liked it if they're clapping." He
could hardly wait for this whole miserable thing to be over so they could
get away on the honeymoon. Never been to London! He was looking forward to it. The British Museum especially. George Bernard Shaw, they
said, educated himself just from reading there. Great plays. Too bad the
old rascal had died last year. Might have gotten to see him . . .

Wattie Feerick was trying to recall the last occasion he got drunk. But he had too much in him now to remember. It was a long time, for sure. So he was entitled to get a little bit jarred today. Mind you, the way herself was looking at him you wouldn't think so, but a man needed it now and again. That was what weddings were for, anyway. It wasn't as if he were obstreperous or anything like that. Just feeling happy. And talking a lot. That was what he liked about it. You could chat with anyone after a few whiskeys and a couple of Guinnesses and say exactly what you liked, to them or about them. Great wick altogether. Just like he was having now gabbing with Father Mulroe. A grand man, the parish priest. You could say anything to him and he wouldn't mind.

"My father, God rest him, Father, had a match made for him with my mother."

"Well, is that a fact, now, Wattie? Isn't that—"

"In those days, Father, it was the blood that counted, you see. None of this fancy romance that young people are talking about nowadays. Blood! That's what mattered. You married good blood and you produced good children."

"There's something to be said for that, all right. Was there a match made between you and the missus?"

"Well, yes and no. Herself took a shine to me first. I was kicking football for Castletown against Kildawree when she spotted me on the field. I was a good kicker when I was young. Anyway, we did a line for a bit. But her old fellow, I can tell you, when it started to get serious, was over asking questions about my family. TB, of course. And some other things as well that I'm sure you're well aware of, Father. Anyway, my breeding passed muster with him."

"And you have fine, healthy children, thank God."

"Thank God. Thank God for that. And with the help of God we're not finished yet."

"She's a fine woman, herself."

"And there's another fine girl for you, Father." Mary McGreevy floated by, dancing with young Jack Banaghan.

"She is indeed, Wattie. A fine girl. I expect she'll be getting married herself one of these days."

"Faith, I suppose she will, Father. And 'tis her will have the fine children too, with the help of God." He belched loudly a couple of times. "With the help of God indeed."

The next thing Rita was at his side, pinching his arm. "We'd better go home now, Wattie," she whispered fiercely into his ear, "before you disgrace us entirely." He protested loudly, but Rita could be very firm when she had to. The trap was heading out the Kildawree road before he knew what had happened to him.

11

Kitty couldn't decide whether the honeymoon had been a modest success or a miserable failure. She leaned on the rail of the mail boat watching Dun Laoghaire harbor getting slowly nearer. Tom was down below looking green and feeling wretched from the moderately choppy sea. He had been eager to see what he called the greatest city in the world, even in its still devastated condition six years after the war's end. And she had been worried that memories of past experiences might affect her relationship there with her new husband. Both expectations had been fulfilled as she showed him around London by day and he made love to her by night. The sightseeing gave him such obvious pleasure that after two weeks she had practically forgotten the sounds of the air-raid sirens. As for their carnal coupling, they just about survived it. Recollections of Alberto's fierce and tender passion provoked comparisons she knew to be unfair. And when fidelity banished that faithless fraud from her mind, she was invaded by thoughts of Nadinha's *volupté*. Indeed, on more than one occasion after he dropped off, well comforted and knowing nothing of her frustration, she gave herself up to thoughts of her Brazilian woman lover and cried herself to sleep. She would try to educate him by degrees. And if she didn't succeed—even if she did, maybe—there was always her friend Mary McGreevy living alone just over the road. It would be quite appropriate for the wife of the principal teacher of Kildawree to visit the lady farmer of Kilduff.

It was, then, a terrible shock to her, on the day after they arrived home, to hear in Garvey's grocery shop the whispered tattle that Miss McGreevy, the ex-nun if you don't mind, was said to be in the family way. What was gone wrong with the world at all? the pious gossiper asked Mrs. Garvey. To which the grocer responded, nodding knowingly as she wrapped string around a parcel, that she wasn't in the least bit surprised. That very same person, by all the accounts that she, Maureen Garvey, was privy to, had been encouraging every eligible man in the parish to court her. There were stories that she wasn't averse even to the attentions of married men, God help us. And got that attention too, if even half of what one heard was true. Well, thanks be to the good God, her Mr. Garvey would never be party to such goings-on. Furthermore . . .

Kitty was so shaken that she left the women to their talk and went home without her groceries. Denial came first. It couldn't be! She sat at the table in her new kitchen. Hadn't she seen Mary and talked to her the day of the wedding? And wasn't she dancing around the floor as frisky as a month-old lamb? A woman in the family way couldn't be doing that, could she? She banged the table half triumphantly with the side of her fist. At least, she didn't think so. But then, what did she know? She had never spent time around expecting mothers. On the other hand, there was no smoke without fire. Old biddies gossiping maybe, but even *they* picked up their information from somewhere. And who would ever invent something like that?

It was then that the thought struck her. Oh, dear God! She'd kill him! Bludgeon him! But hold it, now! The matter was too serious for that. And he couldn't have, anyway. Regardless of whatever else he might be, Tom was an honorable man, a decent man, a good man. Hadn't she said this to herself a dozen times in the past two weeks to compensate for his shortcomings in the marital bed? It wasn't possible. No, definitely not. Anyway, he had implicitly denied it himself. Remember? This was the very first time, he had said on their first night together—and she had thrilled to the words—that he was making love to a woman since his wife, the Lord have mercy on her, had died. That was good enough for her. Maybe Mary McGreevy *was* with child, or maybe she wasn't. But Tom Tarragh was not implicated. And when her husband came from school she kissed him fiercely and then had him drive her into Ballinamore to get the groceries. She couldn't face Maureen Garvey again today. But neither could she tell Tom the reason, so she invented an excuse for going to town.

Later that very same day Rita Feerick heard the gossip from Noreen Macken. She was appalled, not at the news itself but at its being common knowledge. "And where did you hear this from, Noreen?" she asked casually as she licked a stamp for a letter to her sister in England.

"'Twas Maureen Garvey told me. She got it from one of her boys, who heard it at school if you don't mind."

"Well, is that a fact? That would be the boy in seventh class, I suppose." Rita was pasting the stamp ever so carefully in the top righthand corner of the envelope.

"Seamus. She said it was Seamus. I was wondering myself who he got it from, but I didn't think to ask her."

"Musha, you never know where gossip starts. And the most of it isn't true anyhow." But as Rita Feerick pedaled home at a fierce pace there was murder on her mind. The boys were kicking football in the meadow next the house. "Wat!" she shouted before she even got off the bicycle. "I want to talk to you inside this minute."

"We're in the middle of a match, Mammy," he shouted back.

"You'll be in the middle of a funeral if you don't come in right away." And she stormed through the back door. He came panting in behind her. Deirdre and Fidelma were in the kitchen. "Upstairs to your room," she shouted at him. "You and I have something to talk about. Deirdre, will you make sure herself doesn't follow us up."

"What did he do?" Deirdre shouted as Rita slammed the door leading into the hallway.

"What did I do?" Wat wailed as she closed his room door behind them.

"You know very well what you did. And you'll pay for it, my lad."

"But I didn't do anything, Mammy. Honest to God!"

"The night before last when you were supposed to be asleep you came down to the kitchen."

"I was thirsty! I had to get a cup of water."

"And how long were you standing outside the kitchen door before I opened it and found you there?"

"No time at all. I only just came down. Honest!"

"Do you know what happens to liars? We're talking about a big lie, now. Not a venial sin, let me tell you. A red-hot mortal sin. Now tell me this: What happens to boys who die in their sleep with mortal sin on their souls?"

Wat, head down, said nothing.

"Tell me!"

"They go to hell." A crackled mutter. The lad's voice was beginning to break.

"For how long?"

The head sank lower, as if too heavy for his thin shoulders. "For all eternity."

"And is that where you want to go?"

His "No" was positively sepulchral.

"Then tell the truth now and shame the devil. What did you hear me telling your father when you were standing outside the kitchen door the night before last?"

A great, gaping silence broken by a shuddering sob from the lad. "I didn't—"

"Stop!" A scream of anguish. "Are you going to stand there and crucify Jesus to the cross again with your lie? Remember that's what you do when you commit a mortal sin. Come on, now, tell the truth. What did you hear?"

Another long pause. "I—" said Wat and stopped.

"Go on, say it."

"I heard you saying . . . Do I have to say it?" The most miserable tear-stained face you ever saw looked up at her.

"You had no trouble telling it to Seamus Garvey at school, did you?" And Rita slapped him hard across the side of the head. "You'll stay here now till your father comes in, and then you'll get the strap." She slammed his door and went to her room and cried.

Later she walked back to Mary McGreevy's. "I'm awfully sorry. I don't know what else to say," she sobbed after making her confession.

Mary didn't seem in the least put out. "Don't worry a bit about it. They'd have to find out sooner or later anyway. So it might as well be now as then." Small consolation to Rita for a terrible breach of confidence. But she didn't protest when, after she told Wattie about it, he decided not to use his belt on their son. That night she offered up her rosary for the salvation of Mary McGreevy and her unborn child.

Kitty rode up on her bike just as Mary was carrying in an armload of turf from the stack.

"Is it true?" Not even a hello or how-are-you as she walked in the kitchen door.

"It is." Mary looked straight at her, and she dusting bits of turf mold from her sleeves.

"I don't believe it!"

"Don't so." Mary turned her back and put a few sods on the fire.

"But!" Kitty strode right up to the fireplace. "How could it happen?"

Mary stood there watching the turf begin to smoke. "You know about the birds and the bees, don't you?"

"God blast it to hell, Mary! We're friends, aren't we? Tell me about it."

"There's not much to tell." Mary poked the fire with the tongs, then put the implement down and faced her. "I am, as the gospel says quaintly about my namesake, with child. I'm going to have a babby. It's a common occurrence with women. Has been since the beginning of time. You might have one yourself one of these days."

"If I were to have one—which I won't, I can tell you right now—people would rightly say that my husband was the baby's father. Who are they going to say is the father of yours?"

The woman had the gall to actually smile at her, as if the whole thing were a laughing matter. "That would be telling, now, wouldn't it?"

"Well, I hope," Kitty began, and then had to stop and take a couple of deep breaths to control herself. "I hope that whoever he is, he will be man enough to own up to it."

"You'll have a cup of tea." Mary grabbed the kettle from the hob and went out the back door to fill it. "I'm glad you dropped in," she said on her return. "I want to hear all about the honeymoon."

What could Kitty do except sit down and wait for the tea? "Who is it, anyway?" Confidentially, when both their cups were filled.

Mary added milk and sugar and stirred. "I wish I could tell you. Honest to God, I do."

"Do you mean to tell me you don't know? Sweet Jesus! What have you been up to at all?"

Mary slowly spooned tea from the cup and sipped. "Oh, I know all right. I just can't tell you."

"Go on! You can tell me. I'm not about to say a word to anyone if you don't want me to."

"I told one person that I was pregnant. Just one. A person I absolutely trusted. And in two days the entire parish knew."

"That was terrible altogether. Just awful. I agree with you on that. But Kitty Malone—Kitty Tarragh now—won't tell a living soul. You have my word of honor on that."

"If I could tell anyone it would be you, Kitty, *a stor*. But I can't take a chance. Other people's lives would be affected, you see. At the very least, a good and honest and decent man would be branded a blackguard. It wouldn't be fair to risk that, now would it?"

Kitty sipped her tea in silence. All she really wanted to know was that it wasn't her Tom. Her Tom! That sounded almost funny. As in tomcat. Well, tomcat her Tom wasn't. But she still needed assurance that he wasn't the father of Mary McGreevy's baby. "All right, then," she said. "I understand. Now, I know it wasn't, but just tell me anyway to keep me happy. Tell me it wasn't Tom Tarragh and I'll be satisfied."

"This parish," Mary said bleakly, placing her spoon on the saucer, "will very likely accuse half a dozen lads, married and unmarried. With some reasonable basis for suspicion, that is. They may even throw in another half dozen *without* reason. And do you know something? That's the way I want it to be." She sipped her tea, staring steadily at Kitty all the while.

Kitty felt the skin tightening on her skull and her intestines twisting into a painful knot. "Oh my God! I'll kill the two of you!" She shot to her feet, spilling her tea across the table, some of it onto her own dress.

Mary didn't move, not even when the tea dripped down on her lap. "Calm down, *a stor*. I didn't say that Tom *was* the father. Let me get you something to wipe your dress." She got up slowly, went over to the cupboard, and came back with a dish towel. "Dry it with that."

Kitty ignored the cloth. She stood there transfixed like the statue of the Blessed Virgin in the parish church. "You said it *wasn't* Tom, didn't you?" In a high-pitched monotone, as if she were in a trance. "You said it wasn't him."

"I said I didn't say that Tom *was* the father."

"Well, there, that means he isn't, doesn't it? That's all I wanted to know." She smiled with relief and sat down again.

"I didn't say that either, Kitty." There was a sharp edge on Mary's voice. "I neither affirmed nor denied that Tom is the father. And that goes for anyone else you might ask me about as well."

"What are you trying to do to me at all?" She heard herself screaming again. "He either is or he isn't. Now which is it, for Christ's sake?"

"First of all, there's Jack Banaghan." Mary tapped her thumb on the table. "Probably the prime candidate. The romantic old biddies will be putting their money on him. Handsome young bachelor with an eye on a farm. But then there's Kevin Kelly." She slapped her index finger against the wood. "Married with six children but known to have a roving eye. A long shot all the same because most of them don't know him. Next we come to Thomas Aquinas Tarragh, N.T., newly wed." Her middle finger touched the table. "Those who like serious titillation will take the long odds on—"

"You're a very rotten mean person, Mary McGreevy," Kitty shouted. "I don't know why—"

"The fellows up at Queally's will be torn between Mick Burke, who let it be known he had set his cap at me, and Wattie Feerick, who has been around here a lot helping out with the work." Ring and little fingers together thumped the table. "And to cap it all there are the holy priests themselves. Father John Patrick has put himself in the running by coming to see me more often than a parish priest is wont to visit spinster parishioners. Father Stephen's fondness for the ladies is generally known, and his interest in yours truly has been particularly noted." Thumb and index of her right hand rapped the edge. She looked at her fingers and counted. "That makes seven, if I'm not mistaken." Her smile was enigmatic, almost cruel, it seemed to Kitty.

"Well, you can't be serious about Father Stephen anyway, whatever about the rest. Oh, my God, don't . . . ! No! Nobody could possibly . . . ! Jesus Christ, they would, too! Wouldn't they ever? Oh, shite!" She slumped in her chair and covered her face with her hands. She felt totally numb; the brain shut down entirely. There were no thoughts. Only silence. For the longest time. Then slowly, imperceptibly, something began to move within. Life pulsed again, a quiet, rhythmic interior motion. Balmy and soothing, it seemed. But how could that be? Her whole life was in turmoil. She ought to be screaming in despair. Yet she felt only peace. Then she wanted to laugh. Life was so ridiculous. The laughter erupted suddenly from that hidden volcano deep inside where it always lay smoldering, waiting for a weakness in her ever so serious crust. Starting with a wispy giggle, advancing to a staccato chortle, exploding into uncontainable paroxysms. One following another till her sides ached, her stomach hurt, the salt from her tears burned her eyes. And still she couldn't stop. Several times she looked at Mary for help, but the woman's wide-eyed stare of incomprehension only set her off into worse explosions of hilarity.

Then it changed, as quickly and unpredictably as summer weather. One instant she was choking with merriment like she was enjoying all the circus clowns of the world; the next she was crying her heart out as if she had lost everyone who was ever dear to her. A gentle hand was rubbing her back, stroking her neck, fingering her hair. And a soothing voice said, things will be all right, *a stor*. But she couldn't contain this second eruption any more than she could the first, till it ran out of steam itself. She remained still then, forehead on the table, hands like blinkers blocking out the light. Dimly she heard Mary's voice: "Are you all right? Maybe another cup of tea?"

"That would be grand." Parched from it all. She raised her head. The table had been wiped and a fresh cup of tea put in front of her.

"Thanks awfully," she said. "Then I must be going."

"You'll tell me about the honeymoon another day," Mary said when she was leaving.

On the way home, breathing hard as she cycled into the wind, she vowed she would prove that Tom Tarragh was not the father! With or without the help of Mary McGreevy.

12

"I'll miss you," Father Stephen said. And his sincere, sad gaze said he meant it. They met in town on Saturday evening. Mary McGreevy was in doing her weekly shopping when she ran into himself and Kitty on Market Street.

"We're finally getting rid of him on Wednesday," Kitty explained.

"I'll drop in to say good-bye before I leave," he said. And he did, on Sunday evening. His stay was brief, but he held her hand for a long time after she extended it to him. Then, going out the door, he turned and said, "They're giving me a sort of formal send-off on Wednesday morning. Mass and speeches and the like. And Father Mulroe is putting on a breakfast. Maybe you'd like to come?"

"I won't," she said firmly. She didn't go many places these days because of the knowing looks and the surreptitious whispers. She mightn't even go to mass anymore, though she had gone every Sunday since she left the convent. This very morning the gaze of the parish had weighed her down with a gravity she hadn't felt before. It wasn't just her imagination, either. Coming out of the church with Rita Feerick—God bless Rita anyway for staying with her—she had bumped into Noreen Macken at the door as both were reaching for the holy-water font. Normally that would be an occasion for a polite good morning, Noreen, good morning, Mary, how are you at all. Not this time. Noreen had pulled her hand away as though Mary had just settled the plague on the font with her touch, and off with her without a word. Going down the steps outside she was talking with Maureen Garvey a mile a minute, and it was an easy guess from the backward nodding of her head who was the subject of their conversation. She was the object of avoidance by almost everyone else as well. Over the past year a lot of people had thawed out and become friendly, but that was all gone again. Even though it was the month of May she now felt the chill of a January morning in the air whenever she passed a neighbor on the road.

Father Stephen dropped in to say good-bye again on Tuesday evening. This time Kitty was there before him. Mere coincidence, she claimed, though Mary didn't believe her. But anyway there she was, sitting in the kitchen drinking tea, when her brother rolled up in Henry's Vauxhall. She already had several suspects, she told Mary. And it was apparent soon after her brother's arrival that he was one of them.

"Three sugars," Mary murmured as she poured the missionary's tea.

"She knows all my bad habits," he told his sister out of the corner of his mouth.

"And a tiny dollop of milk," the ex-nun added.

"Thank you, *a ghradh*," he said.

"And your two slices of currant cake, of course."

"You two are beginning to sound like an old married couple." Not a trace of humor in the sister's voice.

"Musha, a woman could do worse," Mary said with more than a touch of malice.

"I know who you *should* be marrying," Kitty shot back.

"Who?" Mary handed a plate with cake on it to the priest.

"Stephen, tell her."

"Oh, I'd marry her in a minute if she'd have me." Head down, cutting his currant cake into small squares.

"Stephen! Don't you think she should marry the father?"

"I think that's for her to decide." He put a square into his mouth and chewed and looked out the window.

"But it's your duty to tell her what's the right thing to do."

He turned and stared sardonically at his sister. "Do you think your woman here would do anything anyone told her?"

"Thank you, Father," Mary said. "At least someone understands me."

Saturday afternoon Father Mulroe came back to see her. She was up in the field her father used to call the long garden, getting the potatoes sown with the help of an army of Feericks. Wattie and Luke had opened the drills in the morning and now they were scattering cartloads of manure on them from the dunghill behind the sheds. Mary was sitting on a sack at the headland cutting slits while four of the junior Feericks—Brian, Tess, young Rita, and Wat—were spreading them a foot apart in the dung-filled drills.

"God bless the work," said his reverence from behind.

"You too," she said, startled, getting up in a hurry. "Though you look like a man of leisure." He was leaning over the wall sporting that half-impish grin of his.

"Faith, 'tis many a field of spuds I planted when I was a young lad." He examined his hands: very white, long, slender fingers, clean nails. "I had great calluses in those days."

The children came running up. "We need more slits," Tess said, out of breath. It was obvious they came to be seen and noted by Father Mulroe.

"You've got plenty of help, anyway," the priest said.

"The best in the world, Father." The children giggled. "There's plenty of slits in that sack, but maybe you're too tired to do any more."

"Oh, no, Aunt Mary!" Like a well-trained chorus. And they filled their buckets and off with them again.

"They're great," she said. "I don't know what I'd do without them."

The priest climbed carefully over the wall. "They're the Feerick children, aren't they?" Dusting off his hands and slapping at his trouser cuffs. He looked so neat in his black suit and roman collar.

"Wattie and Rita's. The best neighbors anyone could have." She resumed cutting. "We're trying to get all the planting done today while the children are off from school."

"Good people, I believe." The priest sat on a large flat stone that had fallen off the wall and wrapped his arms around his knees. "Though I haven't seen too much of himself."

"Well, he's at mass every Sunday, if that's what you mean."

"He is, I'm sure. But not much at the altar rails. That's where you get to know them. Herself, I must say, is quite regular in that respect."

"He does his duty."

"He does, I suppose. Though I don't remember seeing him there Easter Sunday."

"Don't you, now?" Her tone was almost belligerent.

He plucked a thrawneen and started chewing on it. "Almost everyone goes for Easter. Though, mind you, not all. Not all. Which is unfortunate."

She said nothing to that. Tess came running back for more spuds. "I'm faster than anyone else," she said breathlessly, looking out of the corner of her eye at the parish priest.

"You're marvelous," Mary said, and the girl dashed off again with her bucket full.

"I'd say we're going to have a shower." Father Mulroe was staring back toward the Partry mountains and the big black clouds that were looming over them. "But in the end, you know, it's the sacraments that count."

The small, sharp knife she was cutting the slits with slipped. "Damn," she shouted. "Excuse the language, Father."

"You're bleeding!" He was on his feet, pointing at her thumb, a mess of dirt and blood. "You'll need to wash that straightaway. Clay is dangerous in a cut, they say." He pulled a clean handkerchief from his trouser pocket. "We'll wipe it with this for the time being." And before she could say a word he was cleaning off her thumb and wrapping the white linen around it.

"Your hankie is destroyed," she protested.

"It's not important. You have iodine at the house, I suppose?"

"I do, but sure, it can wait. I—"

"No waiting. I'm told you can get tetanus from clay in a cut. And tetanus is fatal. We wouldn't want you dying on us, now, would we?" So after she shouted to the children that she'd be back in a few minutes, they headed for the house. At the end of the next field they met Wattie and Luke on their way out with a load of manure. "God bless the work," the priest said again.

"You too," Wattie replied. The look on his face asked, What was going on at all?

"A good man," Mary said after they passed. "He'd give you the crust out of his mouth if you needed it."

"The mark of a true Christian," Father Mulroe said a bit unctuously. "I must go back and visit him one of these days. Sometimes it only takes a word to get people back on the tracks."

"And what makes you think Wattie is off the tracks?" Brazenly, as if spoiling for a fight.

"Well, now—and I say this in confidence to yourself since you understand these things—confession and communion once a year is hardly enough to earn a medal."

"It's better than no confession or communion at all," she said sharply. "Which is what some of us are guilty of." If she didn't pull it out in the open he'd talk around the subject till the cows came home. She had gotten to know John Patrick quite well this past year.

"True for you," he said. "True for you indeed. But let us take care of your wound first and then we can talk." They were a hundred yards from the house when the rain came down. Father dried himself by the kitchen fire while she got iodine and bandages from her bedroom and scrubbed her hands. "Let me do it, now," he said. His fingers were cool and gentle, and the pleasure of his touch almost made up for the sting of the iodine. He wrapped the thumb in a neat bandage and held it in place with a strip of plaster.

"You'd make a great doctor," she said, taking the dirty handkerchief and soaking it in the basin of water. "I'll wash this for you later on."

"Did you know that priests are not allowed to practice medicine?" The grin was back on his face; he seemed pleased as Punch with his handiwork.

"Is that a fact? Healers of the soul but not of the body! Will you be excommunicated for this?" She held up her bandaged thumb.

"I don't believe something as minor as that would qualify." He seemed to take the question seriously.

"Anyway, you were really trying to heal my soul, weren't you, Father? After all, it was your sermon on the sacraments that made me cut myself."

"How are you doing, anyway?" He straightened his back and dug his hands into his trouser pockets, a sure signal he was about to get down to serious business.

"Musha, fair to middling, Father. Can we talk while we walk back to the field? I think the shower is over." It was easier to deal with this sort of thing if you were on your feet and moving.

"I don't listen to gossip, as you might expect." They crossed the yard, he in his shiny black shoes avoiding the puddles, she splashing into them with her muddy Wellingtons. "But there are some things one can't help hearing. And there's some serious talk going on about Mary McGreevy being . . ." He scratched his nose urgently and lengthened his stride.

"Yes?"

"With child," he managed. They walked out into the field in silence. "Is it true, I wonder?" he asked as she was closing the yard gate behind them.

"It is."

They traversed most of the field without another word being exchanged. "Well, I would never have thought it of you, Mary," he said as they approached the stile. His voice deepened with a kind of melancholy reproach.

"Thought what?"

He stopped dead. She stopped with him. "Now, Mary, we won't beat about the bush any further. You know, and I know, and the Man Above knows too, what kind of behavior gets you into this condition. There's sin involved. We know that. Grave sin. Unless of course . . . Good God! Did anyone force you? That was it, wasn't it? The blackguard! He'll go to jail for it. I'll see—"

"There was no blackguard, Father. Nobody forced me. I did it of my own free will. As a matter of fact, it was I who planned it in the first place."

She felt sorry for him as soon as she said it. He didn't know where to turn or what to say. Almost comical he looked, trying to show moral horror and indignation, his not being the kind of face that was designed for tragic expression. "Well, you're a great woman entirely for the joke," he tried feebly. "But I don't think that—"

"I'm not joking."

He walked away abruptly and perched on the top step of the stile. There he sat, head between his hands and not a word out of him. She inspected the bandage on her thumb. No sign of blood seeping through. It was stinging a bit still from the iodine. After a while she began to get annoyed at him, sitting there like Rodin's Thinker, ignoring her completely. But just as she thought of climbing the wall and heading back to the potato field without him, he shouted down at her, "What got into you at all?"

"It's a long story."

He was off the stile in a flash. "Tell me about it."

"I need to see how they're getting on with the spuds first. I'm already late with the planting. Wattie has had his in for the past couple of weeks."

"I'll walk with you," the priest said, as if afraid she might disappear and never come back.

Wattie and Luke were at the far end of the field spreading dung. Tess was sitting on Mary's sack with the knife in her hand trying to slit a potato, the other children standing around her watching. "I know how to do it, Aunt Mary," Tess said.

"There's half a sack of slits still there. Maybe you should plant them first."

"That's what I told her," Brian said. "But she wouldn't listen. She never listens to anyone."

"Did you cut yourself, Aunt Mary?" Tess asked.

"I did, so be very careful with that knife. And remember, there's tea and currant cake when we're all done." They grabbed their buckets and raced back to work.

"Now tell me everything," Father Mulroe said after they climbed back over the wall.

"Everything, Father?"

He blushed. "Just what's fit to be told, of course. I don't need the salacious details."

They wandered slowly across the field in the direction of the herd of black pollies grazing at the far end. "So what *do* you want to know?" she asked him.

"I suppose, for a start, why did you do it?"

"Because I want a child of my own, that's why. I don't want to be just Aunt Mary for the rest of my life."

He stepped carefully around some cow dung. "That's all very well. Indeed a legitimate and even a holy aspiration. But why in God's name couldn't you wait till you got married? Like your friend Kitty. I suppose she'll be telling us good news one of these days."

"Faith, you'll be waiting a long time to hear anything like that from Kitty." The words were out of her mouth before she could stop them.

"Mother of God!" The man appeared to be in anguish. "I don't want to hear about it."

"Well, don't tell her you heard it from Mary McGreevy." One of the cattle spotted them and started to move slowly in their direction. Two others followed. They ambled right up to Father Mulroe. He shied away. "Arrah, they won't bother you, Father," she said. "They're just curious. It isn't often a man of the cloth pays them a visit."

"You're a gas woman." He put her between him and the cattle. "Now, tell me why you didn't want to get married first."

"I think we have talked about that before. I have no intention of getting married." The pollies came around behind her and sniffed at him again.

"Could we go into the next field?" he asked. "I'm a bit nervous of those lads. I always was uncomfortable around cattle. Even as a boy."

They climbed a wall and into a field where the ewes and their lambs were grazing. "You'll feel more at home here," she said, "with the sheep of your flock."

He laughed briefly at that and then put his serious pastoral face back on again. "Surely you, of all people, know it's gravely sinful to have sexual intercourse outside of holy wedlock. And even worse to conceive a child in those circumstances."

"I'm not convinced of that, Father."

"How could you not be convinced?" He raised his hands in supplication to heaven. "Thou shalt not commit adultery! That's the sixth commandment, for God's sake, woman."

"How do you know it was adultery? I'm not married, and if the father wasn't, then it wouldn't . . ."

"Well, if it wasn't adultery it was fornication. And that's still mortal sin. The point, Mary, is—and 'tis well you know it—children should be conceived and born within the bonds of marriage."

"I don't know any such thing, with all due respect to your reverence. I'm of the opinion that a woman has the right to have a child as long as she can properly rear it and take care of it. Whether or not there's a father around to help her."

"Oh, God help us!" Total despair in that supplicating cry. "What's got into you at all, Mary? Where on God's earth did you come up with such an idea? You know the teaching of the church! Marriage is the sacrament for those whose primary purpose on entering it is the procreation of children. We don't beget promiscuously like dogs or cats. Or for breeding purposes like sheep or cattle. We are the children of God, and we procreate our offspring according to the laws of God."

She hesitated for a moment, seeking the right words for a solid rebuttal. But the parish priest smelled victory from her silence. "Now look, Mary." He put his hand on her shoulder. "We can straighten this out easily enough. You just tell me who the father is and I'll have a word with him and we'll have the wedding bells ringing in no time flat. For the second time in as many months in Kildawree parish church." The grin of sacred triumph suffused his cheerful mug.

She let him savor his victory for a moment. Then she asked, "Who says that children must be born within the bonds of marriage?"

"It's the law of God." Spoken with the quiet conviction of unquestioning faith.

"And what about Abraham and Isaac and Jacob, to name but a few? They all begot children out of wedlock, and God blessed them for it."

"Now, now, Mary, that's the Old Testament. They did some things in those days that the Almighty just put up with because of the times. But not anymore. We're in the new covenant now, and that sort of thing can't happen again."

She laughed. "Father, do you want to know what I really think?"

"Tell me, Mary. It's a time for good honest talk between us. And I'll give it to you straight from the shoulder as well."

"Well, to tell you the God's honest truth, I don't believe anymore in the church and all its works and pomps. And as for the Bible, I think it's a fabulous collection of stories and homilies, but it's certainly not the word of God. A God who would be as hard and as cruel as the fellow described in the Old Testament is not a God I'd want to have anything to do with. I believe that if there is a God out there, he doesn't care very much what happens to us. We're on our own in this vale of tears, and all we can do is try to love each other and help each other as best we can and do whatever we think is best for ourselves and everyone else."

Father John Patrick stood facing her. As blasphemy followed blasphemy, the eyes closed, the mouth opened, the forehead wrinkled, the fists clenched, the body became rigid, until at the end he could have been a statue for all the movement that was out of him. He remained that way for so long that she began to think he had gone catatonic. She had read once about someone that happened to after being told some tragic news. "Are you all right, Father?"

"I am not all right," he shot right back, the eyes still shut tight. "And I don't think I'll ever be all right again." He raised his arms towards heaven and threw back his head. "Father, forgive her, for she knows not what she says." And he stayed in that supplicatory position for a full minute or more. Then slowly the arms dropped, the eyes opened, and he looked at her with a face as sad as the crucified Christ in the stations of the cross on the chapel wall. "Tell me, Mary," he said, and there were tears in his eyes, "that I didn't hear what I heard. That it was the blood going to my head from climbing all those walls that made me imagine you said such terrible things."

She almost cried herself then. Not for what she had said but in sympathy with John Patrick's doleful face; for causing this kindly man such terrible pain. "I'm sorry if I upset you," she said. But he mistook the tears in her eyes for remorse.

"Ah, sure, you didn't really mean it at all. I can see that. Sometimes we say things in a fit of pique and just as quickly regret them." The words came rushing out of him, tripping over each other, as if to wash away by their exuberance all trace of the heresies she had mouthed.

She turned away and resumed walking. "I'm afraid I meant it all. Can I make you a cup of tea?"

"But how could you think such things, Mary? After all you've been through in the convent? You've had the advantage of a profound religious training and experience. You've practiced the spiritual life in a way that was designed to bring you as close to God as any human being can be. How can you say you no longer believe?"

"Ah! Belief, Father! That's the crux of the whole matter, isn't it? I thought once that I could never possibly not believe. But that's the very nature of belief, isn't it? When you believe, you can't imagine being in any other state. Then one day I found I no longer believed. I don't know how it came about, any more than I know why I believed in the first place. But there it was: unbelief, loss of faith. And I noticed that I held it with the very same conviction that I possessed the faith."

"'Twill come back again," he jumped in. "It's just a temporary aberration due to the shock of your leaving the convent, you see. Prayer! That's the answer. Ask and you shall receive. Seek and you shall find. Knock and it shall be opened to you. Promise me now that you'll pray. Say the rosary every night. And you do go to mass."

"You can't force belief, Father." They stepped through a gap into the field behind the barn. The ducks and geese were at the pond, some of them swimming, others picking for tasty creatures in the clay. "You'll have a cup of tea now," she said again.

"No, no tea today." And they walked in sober silence back to the yard. Getting into his car, he said, "I'll be back to see you soon again. And don't forget what I said about the prayers."

They finished planting the spuds and the children had a feast of tea and currant cake afterwards. And Wattie stayed to chat for a while after they had straggled across the yard towards home, too tired to run anymore. That night, sitting by the fire trying unsuccessfully to read a novel, it was neither the spuds nor the argument with Father Mulroe that were distracting her. She felt the loneliness close in on her as never before, and her thoughts drifted, without direction, to Kitty. A sharp-tongued, domineering woman she was, yet Mary felt a nature for her that she experienced for no one else. "You're playing with fire," the voice within her said.

Early next day she cycled back to the village. The morning sickness that had nauseated her for weeks was gone. Passing the school, she heard the sounds of children reciting arithmetic tables in unison. Her child would be there one day. Kitty was home. "Come in," she said. "You're an unexpected visitor." But there was welcome in her eyes. From a Kitty she had never seen before, dressed in a faded flowered frock and flat-heeled shoes, without stockings or powder or lipstick, the long blond hair unbrushed. She liked her better this way. "Don't mind me; I'm a mess," Kitty apologized.

"I just dropped in for a chat." It was her first visit to the new home.

"Come into the kitchen and I'll make a cup of tea." Kitty poured water from a large bottle into the kettle, which she placed on the stove. This action too was new. The daughter of Henry Malone would have had the maid perform that service.

"And how is married life agreeing with you?"

Kitty got down the cups and saucers from the dresser. Out to the pantry and in with a jug of milk and a dish of butter. Humming to herself. Back to the pantry and forth with a plate of scones. "They're still warm; I just took them out of the oven a while ago." Over to the dresser for a pot of jam. More humming.

"I'm sorry," Mary said. "I shouldn't have asked a question like that."

"Married life," Kitty said, standing over her, "if you divide it into four parts, is one part fun and three parts a pain in the arse."

"Well, tell me about the part that's fun."

"I haven't found it yet." Kitty's brittle laugh was more like a cry of pain.

"You're not sorry that . . ."

"No! Not at all. It's about what I was afraid it might be but sort of hoped it wouldn't, if you know what I mean."

"I remember Mammy and Daddy," Mary said. "They hardly ever talked to each other—at least not when I was around. But they never seemed to fight either; just ignored each other. Is that the way marriage is supposed to be?"

"I was hoping it might be more like what Nadinha and I had. At least the first four years. That last year, when she was sick, was terribly sad."

145

"Do you think that women get along better with each other than they do with men?"

It happened so suddenly: one second Kitty was standing over her, the next she was slumped in the chair on the other side of the stove with a hand over her eyes, convulsing with sobs. Mary instinctively knelt in front of her and put her arms around her, letting Kitty's head rest on her shoulder, cheek against hers. She rocked her gently back and forth like a mother would a crying baby. It was an extraordinary experience! So distressing, yet so comforting. She wanted Kitty's pain to stop but her dependence to last. She stroked her hair, those long blond tresses she had sometimes envied. Her fingers gently rubbed Kitty's nape. She caressed her cheek with the back of her hand. She kissed her forehead, her tear-dewed eyelids, even the moist tip of her pointed nose. All the while murmuring silly, nonsensical words and phrases: "It's all right, my dear! You're not alone, *a leanbh!* I'm here with you, *a stor.*" Soon *she* was crying too. Though more a sympathetic keen to Kitty's misery than an independently justified bawl of her own.

There was no sudden end to this symphony of weeping. It just sort of faded out. Mary bent her head to see how her friend was doing. And that was when Kitty lifted *her* head, reached out with both hands, held Mary's face, and kissed her lips. Now, except for *him*, Mary had never been kissed by a man, much less a woman. This kiss of Kitty's was so different from *his*. How could her thin lips be so soft and yielding, yet so intense? And how could she herself, who had so recently made love to a man, react with such passion to the touch of a woman?

She had little time to savor it. Kitty shot to her feet in the abrupt way she did so well. "I shouldn't have done that." She grabbed the kettle and pushed it to the side of the stove, then strode to the window and stood staring out.

"Aren't you going to make the tea?" Mary asked.

"If you don't mind," Kitty said, still with her back turned, "I think I need to take a walk across the fields now and do a bit of thinking. I'll come back to see you in a couple of days."

On Friday Mary had another visitor. He came while she was in the middle of dinner. Not much of a dinner indeed: a fried egg, fried pota-

toes, beans, and a glass of milk. "Come in, love," she shouted, thinking
from the timid knock that it was Fidelma. Mick Burke stuck an embarrassed face in the door.

"God bless," he said, removing his cap. "I hope I'm not bothering
you."

She made him tea and they discussed the weather and Kitty's wedding. Eventually he said, "I suppose you're wondering what brings me
here?"

"Musha, you're always welcome, Mick. You know that. With or
without a reason."

"I know that, faith." Though her response seemed to choke him up
for a minute. "But I have a particular reason for coming today." He
stopped again, as if looking for encouragement. She said nothing. "I have
a thousand pounds in the bank."

"Aren't you the rich man," she responded.

"'Tisn't an awful lot, indeed." He spoke softly and leaned across the
table, as if to keep the matter confidential. "But it would buy a power of
cattle and sheep, if you know what I mean?"

"I'm afraid I don't quite follow you."

"I heard them say that you were interested in buying more stock."
He cocked a quizzical eyebrow at her.

"I am, though I don't know where you could have heard it."
Nothing! but nothing! was private in this parish. The minute you even
thought of something, everybody knew about it.

"Well, anyway, I thought a thousand pounds might be some help to
you."

"You'd lend it to me, Mick? Well, on my word, isn't that terribly nice
of—"

"I wasn't exactly thinking of a loan." The sweat glistened on his forehead, though it wasn't a warm day. "It would be yours for the keeping if
we were to get married."

Even though she had a strong sense that this was coming, it still
caught her off guard. "Oh, Mick!" was all she could manage.

"You'll do it!" he misinterpreted. There was fierce excitement in his
voice and he looked ready to leap across the table.

"I can't, Mick." It pained her to have to say it to the creature. He slumped like a sheep with the staggers. "I thought we had been over this before," she added.

He raised his head. "We have," he admitted. "We have indeed. But," and he managed the most woebegone grin a man ever put on, "a fellow can always hope for a change of heart."

She cried a bit, then. And again that night before she went to sleep.

13

The boys and girls of Kildawree National School looked at each other in delighted amazement. Mr. Tarragh had just announced as they lined up after lunch that they could go home today at two o'clock. It was unheard of! Though it *was* the second Thursday in May, the day of the Ballinamore races. But still! Mr. Tarragh had never before bowed to the pressure of this frivolous event. Had the young scholars known the real cause they would have given three cheers for the schoolmaster's new wife. It was she who had coerced him into releasing them at such an early hour. "I'm afraid I couldn't do that, dear," was his first response. They were in the middle of dinner the previous evening.

"Of course you can," was her commonsense reply as she peeled a potato.

"Ah, now, it wouldn't do at all." She winced as he cut into his steak— which he had cooked himself. "Bad example for the children, you see."

"Tom! The meeting starts at three o'clock. Unless you're out of that school by two we won't have time to look at the horses and put our bets on."

"What's your hurry? There'll be five more races. And it takes only fifteen minutes to get there in the car."

"I will never speak to you again, Tom Tarragh, if you don't get me there in time for the first race." So he did. And made a lot of children happy by so doing. And a bookmaker as well, who collected Kitty's losing bet on Hot Potato in the opening event, a two-mile hurdle. Mary McGreevy fared better: she put her money on a little-fancied filly named Cold Feet that cantered to a three-length victory at eleven-to-two. "Aren't you the lucky one," Kitty said enviously.

"Smart, not lucky," Mary corrected cheekily. "I've been following form in the *Irish Independent*."

It was Kitty's idea to invite Mary to go with them. "Do you think that's wise?" Tom had asked.

"Why wouldn't it?" She looked at him askance. "What are you afraid of?"

"Well, now, people might talk."

"Because of her condition?"

"People are funny that way, you know."

"But why should they talk about us? We haven't done anything strange or extraordinary. Or have we?" She was watching him carefully.

"No. Of course not."

Mary herself was delighted. "I haven't been to the races for seventeen years," she said when Kitty came by to invite her. She was kneeling out in the front garden weeding her flowerbeds. "I always loved to go with Daddy. And I knew the form of every horse in the country."

Kitty leaned her bike against the wall and squatted down beside her. "How are you doing at all?"

"Fit as a fiddle, bedad. The stomach was a bit delicate in the mornings for a while, but that's all gone now."

"Who's going to do the work for you?"

"Musha, I'll do it myself for the time being. Later on, Wattie and the lads will do whatever I can't manage."

"Isn't it a bit dangerous for you to be working like this?"

"Divil a bit." Mary got lightly to her feet. "I remember Mammy saying that in her mother's time women would be out working until the day the baby was born. And out again the very next day."

"So, Miss McGreevy, tell me the winner of the second race," Tom said. They were watching the horses parading in the paddock behind the grandstand, Kitty listening for any nuance that might indicate a special relationship between the pair.

"Blue Bird would be my fancy," Mary said. "He came in a good second in Killarney a couple of weeks ago."

"Blue Bird it is, then," said Tom. "How much should I put on, do you think?"

Kitty met her father at the Tote, where she always did her wagering: you got better odds there than from the bookies. Though Mary preferred the latter and had just stopped at Joe Byrne, Turf Accountant, to place bets for herself and Tom. "I've seen bigger crowds," Henry remarked, left hand leaning on his stick, the right behind his back.

"Oh, it's not a bad crowd at all, Daddy. Better than last year, I think."

"'Tis the fine day," Henry said. "They're all in the bog." He himself would never miss a race meeting. "Was that Miss *McGreevy* I saw you with just now?" Emphasizing the last name.

"It was. Doesn't she look great?"

Henry stared into the distance. "My advice to you now is the less you are seen with that woman the better." He tapped his stick on the ground to add weight to his words. "And the same applies to your husband, only more so."

"Oh, Daddy! Don't be so old-fashioned. Mary is—"

"I have no doubt that she has her own reasons for doing what she did. But they're not reasons that most people around here would approve of."

"But it's her own business and no one else's, Daddy. People should—"

"People will decide for themselves one of these days who is responsible. And whoever they decide on, rightly or wrongly, mind you, will have a poor welcome in Kildawree for a long time to come. So you two be careful, now. That's all I have to say. Put a few shillings on Fatal Choice in the fourth race." And off he headed in the direction of the grandstand.

She was too upset to place her bet on Moorish Prince. Which was just as well, since the horse finished last in a field of eleven. They watched the race from the rails in front of the stand. Blue Bird came in third. "I had money on each way." Mary leaned across to tell Tom the good news. "So we'll collect a few bob anyway."

"Aren't you great," said Tom. Kitty had never seen him so animated, and it deepened her depression no end. It was all very well to say

Daddy was old-fashioned and to dismiss what he said. But if any man in the parish knew the pulse of its people, it was Henry Malone. What if the consensus of the gossips was that Tom was the father? *She* knew he wasn't, but they might say he was, and for all practical purposes that would be just as bad. The principal of Kildawree National School! The most respected man in the parish after Father Mulroe himself. It would all be worth nothing if those lying tongues prevailed. Tom and she would have to leave Kildawree. And Mary, stubborn woman, would stay, and then she'd never see her again. Wasn't that strange, now, brooding over the feared loss of the very person who was about to be the cause of her misery in the first place? Look at the two of them! Heads together going through the race card. Laughing and joking and the sky about to fall in on them. But she couldn't be mad at them, now, could she? Weren't they both hers!

"How are you, Tom?" said a voice from behind. Jack Banaghan, the embarrassment red on his face.

"Did you win?" Mary asked him.

"I got a second place on Up the Rebels." A shy grin opening up.

"Tom and I had money on third place." Mary smiling back at him. "We'd better go and collect it."

"I'll come with you," Kitty said quickly. Jack was on her list of suspects.

She was watching Mary waiting for Joe Byrne's attention when Maureen Garvey wandered by. "Well, hello, Kitty. How are you at all? Are you enjoying the races?" Maureen was gushy: Henry Malone was always a good customer of hers, and no doubt she expected Mrs. Tarragh would be too.

"Musha, I'm not winning too much. And yourself?"

"Well, you know, not doing too—" It was then that she spotted Mary McGreevy turning around to them, a pound note in her hand. "If you'll excuse me now," Maureen said hastily. "There's someone waiting for me over at the stand." And off she fled.

"That woman looks as if devils with red-hot pokers were chasing her," Mary said. "And they probably are."

"What do you mean?"

"Can't you see she's just been in close proximity to a scarlet woman, the Lord save us from all harm?" Real malice in Mary's laugh. "But I'm getting used to it."

"Well, if she won't talk to you, then I won't talk to her. And I'll tell her that too."

"Two bob and my money back," Jack Banaghan announced, joining them.

"The girls will all be chasing you for your wealth," Kitty told him.

"I'd like to have a chat with you sometime." Jack looking at Mary, dead serious.

"Of course, Jack! Any old time." Mary's head was in the race card. "I think I like Prince Hal in the next race."

"Daddy gave me a tip for Fatal Choice," Kitty said.

"I'll drop back some evening, then." And Jack Banaghan disappeared into the crowd.

"What's bothering *him*?" Kitty looking into Mary's card even though she had one of her own.

"Is it Jack? He's just terribly shy, the creature. Sometimes I want to take him by the scruff and shake him."

"I'll bet he wants to marry you. He has that sick-calf look about him."

"How much will you bet? Two-to-one, bar one! Even money Jack Banaghan."

Fatal Choice did win the fourth. Tom had followed Mary's advice and backed Prince Hal, which finished out of the money. Kitty left the two of them commiserating and went to collect her winnings. When she returned to the rails Tom was no longer there. Mary was talking to a woman she vaguely recognized. "I don't believe a word of it," the woman was saying. Loudly: she seemed very agitated. "He was seen coming out of your house on more than one occasion, let me tell you. And where there's smoke, they say there's always fire."

"You believe what you want, now, Brideen." Mary was perfectly calm.

"Bad cess to the both of you," the woman yelled. "And to your bloody bastard as well!" She swung around suddenly and walked off, pushing a man out of her way as she went.

Kitty waited a bit before approaching. "Who was that you were talking to?" Not letting on she had heard anything.

"That was the great Brideen Kelly. She owns a draper's shop up on Castle Street." Mary didn't seem in the least put out.

"What's so great about her?"

"Not much indeed. We went to the convent school together. She was Brideen Costello then. Her family had money, and she always let us poor peasants know it."

"And she recognized you after all these years! Well, isn't that flattering?"

"Not really. She didn't know me from Adam the day I walked into her shop. If you must know the whole story, she married the boy I was keen on before I went into the convent."

"Ah! So Mary McGreevy has an old sweetheart!"

"Water under the bridge, Kitty. Long gone out to sea."

"But you have seen him since you came home?"

"Once or twice." Her tone said, I don't want to talk about it. "Let's go look at the horses for the next race."

The following day, while Tom was in school, Kitty went back to see Daddy and Mammy. They had just finished dinner, and Henry was sitting by the fire reading the paper. "The Costellos," he told her, taking off his glasses and resting the paper in his lap, "used to be squireens in the old days. Gentleman farmers. Lads that lived beyond their means. Brideen's father was a friend of mine. Died last year, the Lord have mercy on him. He had to sell his land about twenty years ago—five hundred acres or more down near Claremorris—to pay his debts. Then he bought a shop in Ballinamore for the daughter with what was left. Brideen has a good head on her, mind you. She does a good business. The husband was at your wedding: Kevin Kelly. One of the Ballynew Kellys; his mother was a Corcoran from Castlebar. A bit of a wastrel, the same lad. They tell me he never did a day's work in his life. But a decent poor devil. Though they do say he's a lady's man." He put the glasses back on and picked up the paper.

"So what does he do, if Brideen runs the shop?" She tried to be casual.

"What a lot of town lads do: stand at street corners holding up buildings." He opened the paper wide and folded back the front page.

"Really, Daddy! What else does he do? He must have a job of some sort!"

He looked out at her over his reading glasses. "Divil a job, now, so far as I know. Except help out in the shop, I suppose. And drink Guinness. He's always in Murphy's on Saturday evening when I go in for my pint."

"The pot calling the kettle black," Kitty murmured under her breath. She found Mammy in the front garden pruning the rosebushes.

"I'm worried about himself," Mammy said. "He's off his food."

"Do you know Kevin Kelly?"

"Why wouldn't I? We were at the wedding when Brideen Costello married him."

"What kind of a man is he?"

"A nice lad, mind you. A great talker entirely. He'd charm the birds off a bush, as they say." Mammy's face lit up: she too had apparently been charmed.

"Daddy says he's a bit of a ladies' man!"

"Arrah, that man listens to too much gossip in Murphy's on Saturday evenings." She snipped viciously with her pruning shears. "He'd be better off if he didn't go in there at all."

"Amen to that."

"But he never listens to me. I told him to see Doctor Walsh about not eating, but sure, he won't do it."

"So you don't think Kevin Kelly is a ladies' man?"

"Maureen Garvey told me he was back to see Mary McGreevy several times since she came home. What do you think of that, my dear?" Mammy smiled and raised her eyebrows to indicate wasn't this all very amusing. "They used to be great friends before she went into the convent. So that's it, now."

On Monday Kitty drove around Ballinamore looking for corner boys. She spotted a few near the courthouse, but they were either too young or too old or too disheveled to fit her image of Kevin Kelly, ladies' man. She went into the draper's shop in Castle Street. The woman who had scolded Mary McGreevy at the races was behind the counter. "Good day!" Kitty put on her sweetest, though she really wanted to slap the vixen's puss.

"Good day to you," Brideen answered politely, looking up briefly from the paper she was writing on. "And what can I get you today, ma'am?"

"I need the makings of a frock." She didn't, but maybe she'd make one for Mary.

"To be sure." The woman put the paper and pencil away under the counter. "Did you have any particular color in mind?"

"Well," leaning her elbows confidentially on the counter, "it's not for myself."

"I see." Brideen took a half step back, as if to indicate a lack of interest in any confidences her customer might have to offer. "And do you know what kind of frock this person wants?"

Kitty lowered her voice to a confidential tone. "I might as well tell you the whole story." All that acting in *The Playboy* was coming in handy now. "A friend of mine has this neighbor, you see. A girl who's got herself into trouble, if you know what I mean?"

"I know what you mean," said Brideen with a certain amount of vehemence. "It's happening all too often these days." She retraced the half step back towards the counter.

"Mind you, this is a good girl. Every Sunday at the altar. Confession every month. The nine Fridays. You couldn't ask for more." She was getting to be a terrible liar.

"Faith, 'tis my experience that the holy Marys aren't any better than the rest of us," said Brideen. "Sometimes they're the worst."

"True for you. True for you, indeed. But not this one. The nicest girl you could meet, they say—though I don't know her personally. Well, anyway, she went to the dances here in the Town Hall."

"A bad place," Brideen put in quickly. "The curse of God on it! A den of iniquity if ever there was one. My girls will never be caught going there, I can tell you. And if they do go, they'll get the stick."

"Anyway, this girl met a townie there. Not that I have anything against the lads from the town, of course. Far from it! Some of them are good boys. But . . ."

"I know what you mean," Brideen said fervently.

"They say this blackguard was married! Would you believe it? Leaving a wife and children at home on a Sunday night and going dancing as if he hadn't a care in the world." She was watching Brideen carefully.

"They're the very worst kind." The draper was getting red in the face.

"The poor wife!"

"'Tis the good name you'd be most worried about," Brideen said darkly. "Once you've lost your reputation, you can't get it back again."

"What would a woman do at all with a man like that?"

"Horsewhipped, the like of them should be," said Brideen in great agitation.

"Anyway," Kitty said, "this frock is for the girl so her condition won't show for a bit."

Passing the church a short while later she decided on impulse to talk to the parish priest. She had met him once in Galway when she was with Stephen. Canon Gilroy, his back to her, was pacing briskly around the perimeter of the building, his head in his breviary. She followed him tentatively, high heels clacking on the cement path. The priest stopped, looked back, saw her. "I'll be with you in a few minutes." He resumed his walk. A tall, thin, slightly stooped man. Seventy-five if he was a day, Stephen had said. Steel-rimmed glasses. Gray hair overflowing his biretta. Said to be terribly stern.

It was more like fifteen or twenty minutes. Six times he passed the front of the church where she stood waiting, never once even glancing in her direction. She was sorry she had decided to stop and was beginning to feel real annoyance by the time he finally came around with his breviary closed. "What can I do for you, now?" The brusque tone of a man accustomed to subservience. Well, he'd get none of that from Henry Malone's daughter.

"I'm Kitty Tarragh, Canon, Father Stephen Malone's sister." She proffered her hand. "I met you in the Great Southern in Galway a few months ago, if you remember?"

"Ah, yes!" The hard stare fading into slow recognition. He took her hand, held it limply for a moment. "Yes indeed. Father Malone. I know him well." The voice was deep and nasal. "In South America, isn't it? A missionary? Is he still at home?"

"He went back last month, after the wedding."

"They're great men, these missionaries. Great men altogether. Laboring in the steaming jungles of the Lord. But sure, we have our own missions here at home too."

"I'm friends with one of your parishioners," she said. "Brideen Kelly. I'm sure you know her. She owns the draper's shop in Castle Street."

"Ah, Brideen! Yes, to be sure. A fine woman. She does the flowers for the altar. Good family too. The children, God bless them, are the best."

"And her husband, Kevin, of course."

"So what can I do for you? Miss Malone, is it?"

"Mrs. Tarragh now. I'm married to Tom Tarragh, the principal teacher in Kildawree."

"Yes, yes. I have met Mr. Tarragh. A good man. A good man indeed. He wrote a little history book, if I recall."

"The history of Kildawree parish." She could feel the pride in her voice.

"I'm writing a history of Ballinamore myself," the canon said. "A somewhat more elaborate work than your husband's. But anyway, what is it you wanted to see me about?"

"It's about Kevin Kelly, Canon. Brideen's husband. The woman I was just talking about."

"Indeed! And what is the matter with him?"

Lord God! Did she have the right to say what she was going to say? "I have a friend. A woman. She's got herself into trouble. In a family way, I mean."

"I see." The canon stared into the distance. "Is she a girl or a woman?"

Kitty stared blankly at him. "I don't understand, Canon!"

"Is she very young? Or is she a woman of your own age?" There was a testy quality to the priest's tone.

"Oh! About my own age, Canon, I'd say." A black lie, of course: Mary McGreevy was eight or nine years younger.

"Go on, then."

"Well, Canon, I have reason to believe that Kevin Kelly is the father." Was she really saying this? But she had to be right: her instincts were always good about people.

"Have you, now, indeed?" The priest's stare was uncomfortable. "The woman herself told you, I suppose?"

Oh, Mary! Why couldn't you say who it was and be done with it? "Not really, Canon. She refuses to tell anyone who it is. But Brideen Kelly knows. I overheard her taking this woman to task about it."

The priest turned to face the church. "I see," he said, and then he said no more.

When she could stand the silence no longer, she said, "My question for you, Canon, is what to do about the situation? There's a danger, you see, that innocent people may get the blame and be slandered if this man doesn't own up to his misdeed. Indeed, there are signs that this is happening already. Have you ever come across a case like it before? Sure, you must have, a man with your experience."

The canon turned, and again she felt the discomfort of his stare. "I have, unfortunately, over the years come into contact with all too many cases of this kind. However, since the most of them are related to the seal of confession, I'm not at liberty to say much. But I'll tell you this: it is my practice to instill a holy terror of the Almighty's wrath into blackguards of that sort. I don't mince words with them. They are not usually amenable to coaxing or appeals to their better nature. Hardened sinners like them rarely are. So I tell them in no uncertain terms what awaits them on the other side of the grave if they fail to stand up now and do their duty."

"And 'tis yourself, I bet, can put the fear of God into them!" She felt nauseated at her own sickening sycophancy. "So what would you advise *me* to do, Canon, in this particular case?"

He removed his biretta, looked into it, shook the tassel a bit. "Well, I'll tell you this much: it isn't a job for a woman at all. My advice to you now would be to tell everything to your own parish priest and let him handle that end of it. Women generally do more harm than good by interfering in such delicate matters. I'll personally take care of Mr. Kelly." He put the biretta back on his head again. "Good day to you now, Mrs. Malone. I have matters to attend to." And off he headed towards the priest's house on the far side of the church, leaving her fury to rise unseen.

Well, wasn't he the pompous ass! God forgive her for cursing the clergy. But she'd show him. Just let her get hold of Kevin Kelly herself. Around with her immediately to Murphy's on Cornmarket Street. She'd bring him outside—she couldn't say what she had to say in the cozy atmosphere of a pub. Unfortunately, he wasn't inside to start with.

"I'd say now that at this time of day you'd find him down at the railway station, ma'am." This from the solitary customer, an old man with a mustache sitting on a high stool looking into the remains of a pint.

"He's more likely out fishing in the lake," the publican behind the bar cleaning glasses offered.

"Arrah, 'tis not a good day for the fish to be biting," the customer growled. A bit belligerently, as in the opening salvo of an argument. "I'd try the station first if I were you."

She parked by the high cut-stone wall near the station entrance. The place looked deserted. The Dublin train wasn't due until later in the evening. She walked down to the ticket office anyway. On the far side, two men were sitting on the platform, feet dangling over the edge, cigarettes in the corners of their mouths, their heads turned to watch her approaching. Really, it was embarrassing the way they were staring at her, the eyes moving up and down on her as if she were a prize cow.

"I was looking for Kevin Kelly." Though she recognized him immediately from the wedding. He had been dancing with Mary McGreevy.

"I'm him." He got to his feet, a big middle-aged man in a tweed jacket and no tie. "Can I help you, ma'am?" A wide, friendly smile on him. Not bad-looking, though a bit too heavy about the middle for her taste. Then recognition lighted his face. "Aren't you Kitty Malone that married Tom Tarragh? Arrah, wasn't I at the wedding? Well, bad cess to me, I didn't know you for a minute."

"I'd like to speak to you, if you have the time." Though now that she was in the presence of the blackguard she didn't know how she was ever going to lambaste him face to face the way she had been doing it in her head.

"Plenty of time, ma'am; around here we have nothing but time on our hands." She said nothing. The silence was awkward. Finally he said, "What did you want to see me about?"

"Could we talk in private?" Glancing at his companion, a younger fellow in a raincoat and felt hat, still sitting on the platform watching her.

"To be sure." He pointed along the platform. "We can take a walk to the other end." He winked at the felt hat. "I'll be back in a bit, Matty. Don't go away."

"Don't do anything I wouldn't do," Matty shouted after them.

"Well, now, isn't that a coincidence meeting you here?" He was effusive. "It was a lovely wedding. Of course, 'twas Brideen that was invited. Your father and she are great friends. I was only let go because she didn't trust me to mind the shop for the day."

"I'm a good friend of Mary McGreevy." She adopted a cool tone that would permit harsh words to be soon said.

"Well, is that a fact?" He beamed. "Ah, sure, Mary and I are friends for the longest time. A grand girl entirely." The smile changed suddenly to anxiety. "Is she all right? There's nothing . . ."

"She could be better," she said severely.

"Oh, Christ!" It was a cry of anguish. "Is she sick? Or did she hurt herself? Or—"

"I think you know perfectly well, Mr. Kelly, what's the matter with her." She was not going to beat about the bush with the lout. Surprise was the best tactic. It might elicit a confession before he had time to think of lies.

"What in God's name are you talking about? I haven't set eyes on Mary since the wedding. She was in great form that day. I had a couple of dances with her. I was even going to give her a lift home, only your father was taking her. Will you tell me what's wrong?"

"When was the last time you were out to see her?" Good on Mammy, anyway, for producing that bit of information.

"Must be a couple of months." He stopped suddenly. She stopped too. There was a sort of wild look in his eye. "How did you know I was there? Did she tell you?" Accusingly, as if his visit were a secret Kitty ought not to know.

That was as good as an admission of guilt! She faced him. Stared him down till he looked away. "And what was the purpose of all those visits to Mary McGreevy?"

She could see him getting back control of himself. The shoulders straightening. The arms dropping to the sides. The wrinkles going from the forehead. "Well, now, I'd say," he said coolly, "that would be a private matter between herself and myself. Especially since—"

"I don't think it's a terribly private matter anymore in the light of what's happened to Mary."

"For God's sake, will you tell me what's wrong with her!" Arms akimbo, the mild face suddenly belligerent.

"Mr. Kelly! There's no need anymore to play the innocent. I'm sure you know perfectly well what has taken place as a consequence of your visits to Kilduff."

"Jesus Christ, woman! Will you say it!" He was shouting at her. Was it possible he didn't know? Maybe Mary hadn't told him. And since he lived in Ballinamore he mightn't have heard the gossip.

"Mary is in the family way." She watched him as she said it and would ever after remember his reaction. Comical, if it weren't for the tragedy of the situation—the slow metamorphoses from shock to disbelief to anger to horror to fear to tears. The latter were the real thing, suddenly welling up in the light-blue eyes and dribbling down the ruddy, unshaven face on either side of his nose.

"Oh, God! No!" A dramatic whisper.

"Yes, indeed!" She could feel no pity for the wretch.

There he went again, that quick pulling himself together. He removed the tears with flicks of his index fingers, took a handkerchief from his pocket and blew his nose, then stared red-eyed at her till she had to look away. "Well, I know damn well now what you're thinking, Mrs. Tarragh. And I can't say I blame you for it. But you're dead wrong. Honest to the good God, you're wrong. I have fathered six children of my own with Brideen. But I have never done anything with Mary McGreevy, and I don't believe I ever will. To be honest with you, it wasn't for want of trying. But it didn't happen, so it didn't. Whoever did it, I can tell you it wasn't Kevin Kelly. And God is my witness to that."

There was a terrible sincerity to his denial that shook her certainty to the core. She wasn't convinced of his innocence, but she could no longer be sure of his guilt. So she left him at the end of the platform with neither reiteration of the charge nor apology for her accusation. Or admission, either, that she had accused him of the crime to his own parish priest. God alone knew what would happen when the canon confronted him.

On the way home she examined the alternatives one more time. Father Stephen she dismissed out of hand. Tom Tarragh she would not consider again. The Banaghan lad was an obvious suspect, but her instincts told her it could not be the repressed and bashful Jack. She lay beside her husband that night, wondering if she should discuss the matter tomorrow with Father Mulroe. But then her last dozing thought was whether even John Patrick himself could be safely ruled out.

14

Father Mulroe was a busy man. With the parish mission scheduled to begin in two weeks, there was much to attend to. A pair of Redemptorist fathers all the way from Dublin would be guests in his house during the first three weeks of June. Bridie May was scouring the place from top to bottom, front to back. Floors polished and buffed. Walls and ceilings painted. Furniture dusted and waxed. The good china taken down and washed. Linen scrubbed, hung out to dry, and ironed. The poor priest was lucky to get his meals with all the activity. And the worry of ensuring the mission's success rested ultimately on his shoulders. He fretted that those most in need might not come. So he mentally reviewed every family in the parish and visited those whose practice of the faith was least consistent.

Mary McGreevy was one of those. "Fine day, thank God," he greeted her. She was down the yard feeding the chickens.

"Not bad, now." Barefoot in the muck, and the hem of her skirt tucked into her belt so that she displayed leg halfway up to her thighs. Father Mulroe had trouble maintaining custody of his eyes. She scattered fistfuls of oats from a basin and the hens crowded around, squawking and picking. "I didn't see you at the races last week."

"His Grace does not permit his clergy to do such frivolous things." A touch of sarcasm. The races were a sore point with Father Mulroe: he loved the horses.

"Arrah, sorra bit of harm it would do you." She emptied the basin with a wild swing. The hens clucked and flapped their wings madly. "Except for all the money you'd lose. Would you like a cup of tea?"

"Ah, no, thanks. No tea now. Maybe we could take a walk back the fields. There's a few things I'd like to say."

"Out this gate, then, Father. That way we won't go near the cattle. They were asking for you," she added mischievously.

He had to smile at that, his eyes straying of their own accord to her bare legs. She spotted the glance.

"I'd better let my frock down and not be leading you into temptation."

John Patrick felt the flush in his cheeks. "Sorry. Very sorry. We're all human, I suppose." It was going to be a difficult conversation.

And it was. After their last talk in these same fields a few weeks ago he had gone home feeling quite disheartened. Her faith and morals were so bollixed up it was hard to know where to start. He had put in hours thinking and praying and reading and trying to find ways of dealing with her apostasy. Because that's what it was, for sure. This fine-looking woman walking across the fields with him in her bare feet, with her lovely green eyes and her gorgeous red hair and her impish laugh that would put knots in a celibate's stomach, was a runaway from the faith of her fathers. In the early church she would have been excommunicated. And in the time of the Inquisition she'd have been burned at the stake. But sure, God didn't desire the death of the sinner, only her repentance. So it was the duty of the priest to try to bring her back to the fold.

But how? She had an answer to his every argument, a riposte to his every probe. And a humorous turn of phrase that suggested she was laughing at his efforts. Mind you, she was polite on the surface: no disrespect at all. It was yes, Father this and no, Father that. But at the same time you couldn't help wondering if she were just playing with your words instead of paying attention to them.

A thought that had entered his mind a couple of times over the past week, only to be rejected out of hand, returned now as they climbed a stile into a field of rocks and boulders and sparse tufts of grass where not even sheep were grazing. The power of the devil! The influence of Satan on fallen man, and woman. Wasn't it a dogma of faith that the evil spirits sought to do us moral injury through temptation to sin? The adversary going about as a roaring lion seeking whom he might devour! Was this charming girl at his side, recently a bride of Christ Himself, now a victim of Satan's wiles? No, not a victim, because she had the free will and the grace of God to resist. A willing accomplice, then? It wasn't possible, was it? Yet, to what else could you attribute her sudden fall from grace?

"Do you believe in the devil?" he asked suddenly.

Again the musical, girlish laugh that stirred senses a priest must forever leave dormant. Was that from the devil too? Using her charms to trap even the minister of God? "Arrah, indeed I don't, Father. The devil is a great notion for frightening children and simpletons into behaving themselves. But I think the rest of us have to take responsibility for what we do, the bad as well as the good, and not be blaming our sins on an invisible creature with horns and a tail."

There, you see! One of the cleverest tricks of the devil was to convince the sinner that he, Satan, didn't exist. "So you don't believe in either God or the devil?"

"Not correct, Father." She frowned at him. "I don't believe in the devil. But I don't know whether God exists or not. I have an open mind on that subject."

"How can you not believe in God, Mary? Apart altogether from the faith, there are sound philosophical proofs of His existence. Even the so-called pagan, Aristotle, established that fact. Have you read his five arguments from reason, elaborated and improved on by Saint Thomas himself?" That should hold her for a while.

She plucked a couple of cowslips and sniffed them. "Those are arguments as to why you might reasonably believe there is a God. But they can't convince you of God's existence. Any more than Sartre's arguments could persuade you He doesn't exist. For belief you need what Kierkegaard called an existential leap. And I seem to have made that leap backward. Smell these. Aren't they wonderful?"

Christ Almighty! How could a mere nun know such things? Could it really be that the devil *was* in her? For the past week he had been denying the possibility. But he wasn't so sure anymore. "Where did you learn all that stuff?" Maybe he could trap her into some admission of diabolical influence. Or was Satan able to know what he, Father John Patrick Mulroe, was thinking and so stymie him there too?

"Musha, here and there, Father. I was always a bit of a reader. And I've had a special interest for the past few years in the existence of God." She stopped and faced him, hands on hips. "You know, I didn't lightly let go of my faith. It was slipping away for a long time, and I kept trying to hold on to it with my reading and meditating. But it went anyway. And do you know something? I'm not a bit sorry it's gone. I can be who I am now instead of always debasing myself before an almighty figment of my imagination."

There was a brightness in her eyes as she talked that frightened Father Mulroe. Surely he was in the presence of the Angel of Light, the Prince of Darkness! How else could a simple nun speak so persuasively against the very foundation of her faith? And tempt even the priest of God with her brazen display of naked legs. For the rest of the week he spent more time worrying about what to do with Mary McGreevy than he did about the success of the parish mission. Of one thing he was becoming firmly convinced: she was diabolically possessed. She had to be.

Jack Banaghan was a bank clerk from Monday to Friday. Saturdays he helped his brother Packy on the farm after attending Father Mulroe's nine o'clock mass. He'd go to mass every day of the week, only he'd be late for work. Mass and communion were the great comforts of his soul, and God knew he needed comforting.

On this particular Saturday morning he came home from church as usual and had his breakfast. But then he headed out the door again without so much as changing his clothes.

"Where are you off to?" Carmel asked.

"A bit of business," he said vaguely and escaped before she could question him further. It was a gray dismal day with a hint of a mist. He spotted Mary McGreevy in a field near the boreen, on hands and knees between rows of drills. "God bless the work," he shouted, stepping gingerly over the soft ground, trying vainly not to get his Sunday shoes dirty.

"Jack! What are you doing here?" Kneeling upright and pushing the hair back from her face.

"I came over to give you a hand, of course."

"If you did, faith, you didn't dress too well for the job." Her knees on a dirty sack, clay on her face, and mud on her hands: he thought she looked ravishing.

"The turnips are good; they're getting plenty of rain anyway."

"I'm behind with the thinning," she said. "These should have been finished a week ago. 'Tis hard to keep up." She got to her feet. "God! I hate this job. Do you know, I like everything about farm work except thinning turnips. It's so slow and you break your back and it always seems to be raining when you're doing it."

"If you'll marry me you'll never have to do it again." He couldn't believe he said that. It came out of his mouth so easily. It fit into the conversation so naturally, he supposed. And a good thing too. If it hadn't happened this way it could have taken him hours to get around to it. And even then he might not have had the courage.

"Jack! This is so sudden!" She was smiling. As at a joke. She thought he was fooling. Bad cess to her, anyway!

"I mean it," he said. Very quietly: people took you more seriously when you spoke softly.

"Oh, God!" That wiped the smile off her face for a minute. Then it came back again. "You're such a joker, Jack Banaghan. No wonder the girls are all mad about you." She dropped to her knees on the sack and ripped out a few more budding turnips.

"I'm not joking this time." The same quiet, sober tone.

She sat back on her haunches then and stared up at him for so long that he had time to put his hands in his pockets, take them out again, and run his fingers through his hair. She was like a woman peering into the infinite void, never blinking an eye or changing her expression. Eventually, she said, "Musha, I believe you *are* serious."

"Why wouldn't I be serious? I've been wanting to ask you this for the past six months." He could feel the trembling inside him, as if he were cold.

But it wasn't cold he was. His whole life depended on what this woman was going to say next, and his natural pessimism told him it would be negative.

"I don't know what to tell you," she said. "I'm sure that you—"

"You don't have to give me an answer straightaway," he put in hurriedly, afraid she was going to reject him there and then. "Take your time and think about it." He gave her that sad-cow look of his that his sister-in-law had once told him would melt a stone.

"I don't . . ." she began, and stopped. "All right. I'll think about it. But don't get your hopes up too much."

"I'm going home now to change," he said. "And then I'll be back to help you thin those turnips."

"This mission," Father John Patrick bellowed from the pulpit, "will add fervor to your faith, grace to your soul, and peace to your heart. Let not a man, woman, or child among you miss a single minute of it."

Afterwards in the sacristy as he pulled the chasuble over his head the memory of those stirring phrases generated warm satisfaction in his innards. What sinner, be he ever so hardened, could resist such a powerful appeal to reform? That sermon was as good, he'd bet, as anything those Dublin Redemptorists were likely to preach. Indeed, he could have been a missioner himself if he had been so minded.

He was still kneeling at his prie-dieu in the sanctuary saying his thanksgiving when the visitors arrived. Out of the corner of his eye he spotted the black forms at the back of the church and swept down the nave, soutane swishing, to give them a warm welcome.

"Father Aloysius Heron, C.Ss.R.," the older of the two whispered in measured tones. A gaunt man with a shiny pate and sad eyes whose hand responded like a dead fish to Father Mulroe's hearty squeeze.

"Jack Kilbride," the younger fellow said with no attempt at all to lower his voice in the house of God. He was ruddy, chubby, red-haired, and grinning, more like a fellow you'd play cards with than a Redemptorist missioner.

"You must be starved," the parish priest said, being famished himself after fasting since midnight.

"Ah, not at all," Father Aloysius whispered. "We had breakfast before we set out."

"I wouldn't say no to a cup of tea myself," said Jack Kilbride.

"If you'll come down to the house now, you can freshen up and I'll see if Bridie May has the dinner ready."

Bridie May did not have the dinner ready. "You said to have it at one o'clock, Father, and 'tis only twenty past twelve yet."

So Father Mulroe entertained his guests in the parlor while they waited. "Maybe a little brandy for the stomach," Father Aloysius allowed. "It's quite delicate, you know. I've had several operations."

"I'll take a glass of wine, if you have it," said Father Jack.

The parish priest, himself a lifelong member of the Pioneer Total Abstinence Association, had bought a bottle of brandy for the occasion and even borrowed a half bottle of Jameson from Tom Tarragh—"For God's sake, don't let on to Kitty that I had this in the house," a nervous Tom had warned him—but he had not anticipated a request for wine. "I have some altar wine, if that will do?"

"It'll be grand," said Jack Kilbride.

"Tell me, Father, what are the principal vices that you observe in your parish?" Father Heron crossed his legs and sniffed his brandy and eyed the parish priest with the air of a man looking forward to a good juicy story.

"Well, now!" Father Mulroe sipped his mineral in agitation: Why in God's name hadn't he anticipated that question? "'Tis hard to say, mind you. There don't seem to be any what you might call serious vices. At least—"

"I'm thinking," said the Redemptorist, "of the predominant sins that you hear in the confessional. In a place like Dublin, for example, it's mostly impurity and dishonesty."

"Fornication and theft," Father Jack agreed with a grin.

"Ah, well, you won't get a lot of that kind of thing here," Father Mulroe defended his parishioners. "Though you'll get some, mind you." He wasn't going to tell them about Mary McGreevy, of course: he reserved that particular sinner to himself. "A certain amount of sheep-stealing goes on; even an occasional bullock. And sometimes turf gets taken from the wrong stack in the bog. Shopkeepers, too, have their own problems with weights and measures. And farmers' wives have been known to sell rotten eggs."

"Impurity," said Father Heron, "is the principal vice of the human race. Surely the parish of Kildawree is not immune to it?"

"No. No. Of course not. We have our share. But I wouldn't say it's a terrible vice in this parish. In fact, the opposite seems to be the problem at times. We've had only one wedding in the fifteen months that I've been parish priest here."

"Ah!" The older Redemptorist's sad eyes looked almost animated. "It is my experience from very many missions in rural parishes throughout this island of saints and scholars that the placid surface of bachelors and spinsters hides a seething dunghill of onanism, sodomy, and bestiality. The rampant impurity and promiscuity country people observe in the behavior of animals desensitizes them and leads them to commit the most heinous and unnatural acts themselves. Acts whose wickedness and depravity they are often unaware of until we preach about them in our missions. Isn't that so, Father Kilbride?"

"Ah, yes, to be sure." Father Jack drained the generous glass of altar wine the parish priest had poured for him.

"Well, now," said Father John Patrick as he refilled the glass for his guest, "I wouldn't expect to find too much of that kind of thing in Kildawree. We're dealing here with simple farming people who do their work and say their prayers and go to mass on Sundays and do their duty when they're told to. You won't hear much in the confession box about the sixth or ninth commandments other than the usual bad thoughts and looks and touches. I sometimes think that the whole of the west of Ireland is one big monastery or convent in that respect."

Father Aloysius shook his head vigorously. "I guarantee you, Father, that we will make your parishioners aware of sins they have committed that they never knew about before. Isn't that right, Father Kilbride?"

"We'll make them blush all the way down to their toes," said Father Jack. "Which raises the following question." He put down his wine glass and folded his arms. "Since ignorance of the wickedness inherent in the act precludes subjective guilt for it, ought we, as priests, to enlighten people's minds and thereby plunge them into sins they would otherwise be innocent of? Or should we leave them in their oblivious state with their souls pure in the sight of God, despite their objective guilt? Do you understand what I'm driving at?"

"Nonsense!" Father Heron took a sip of his brandy. "We have a mandate from Christ Himself to preach the gospel: the truth, the whole truth, and nothing but the truth. We must not leave people in ignorance of their faith."

"That's a very interesting point you raise," said Father Mulroe. "I myself—"

"What if," the younger Redemptorist interrupted, "the only effect of our preaching was to make people aware that their acts were sinful? Suppose it wouldn't stop them from committing them anyway? We are then taking them out of the state of grace and into the state of mortal sin with consequent danger to their eternal salvation."

"Our mission," said Father Aloysius sternly, "is to preach the gospel in all—"

"Dinner is ready," said Bridie May from the doorway. The priests rose in unison. A golden-skinned roast chicken occupied pride of place on the dining table, flanked by dishes of mashed potatoes and carrots, whole onions, and a jug of steaming gravy. All atop Father Mulroe's best linen tablecloth and surrounded by the china and Waterford crystal his home parish had given him as a present for his ordination twenty-two years ago. Bridie May had spared no effort in the preparation of this feast, and she stood now at the dining room door like a mother goose watching her offsprings' first sally into the water. The parish priest motioned Father Heron to sit at the head of the table.

"Nevertheless," said Father Jack, resuming the debate as he took his seat, "I think—"

"My compliments to the cook," said Father Heron graciously, first eyeing the table and then nodding with what could almost be construed as a smile in the direction of Father Mulroe's housekeeper.

"Have you been preaching missions for long?" Father Mulroe quickly asked the younger man so as to head off further theological discussion.

"This will be my third." Father Jack looked embarrassed. "I was ordained only last year."

"Father Kilbride will be preaching to the women next week," his companion said. "They tell me he has a great way with the ladies." Not even a hint of humor in Father Heron's sad eyes. "I myself will preach to the men and the children."

"Faith, it's Father Kilbride has the hearty appetite," Bridie May commented on Monday morning to Noreen Macken. There was nobody else in the post office. "But poor Father Heron hardly ate a thing. He has a weak stomach, the creature."

"And how is himself doing?" A sly look on Noreen's face.

"Musha, fine, thank God. He's staying with Mr. Tarragh while the mission is on. Father Heron has his bedroom, you see."

"Bridie May," said Noreen, "you know I'm not the one to gossip. I mind my own business and keep what I see and hear to myself."

"Sure, I know that," said Bridie May. God forgive the liar, she prayed silently.

"But there are times," Noreen continued, "when a person has a duty to speak up. It was Father Mulroe himself I remember said that in a sermon."

"You have something to tell me," said Bridie May.

"It's very hard to say it, mind you, and I know it's not true. But other people are saying it, and I think you ought to know about it, seeing that it's your job to look after himself."

"Tell me it," said Bridie May brusquely.

"They're saying," said Noreen, "that the parish priest is spending too much time visiting a certain person over in Kilduff who is in the family way. You know who I'm talking about, I'm sure."

"Are they, now?" Bridie May's scowl would frighten off a bull. "Well, there are people in this parish who spend far too much time talking about other people's business instead of minding their own." And she swept out of the post office without another word. But she brooded all day on what Noreen Macken had said and hardly slept a wink that night thinking about it. Of Father Mulroe's unblemished character she had no doubts whatsoever; what worried her was the terrible potential for harm to the good man's name from mindless gossip. Of course Noreen might be exaggerating—it wouldn't be the first time. Bridie May decided to keep her ear to the ground for the present but say nothing. No use disturbing himself unless it was absolutely necessary.

She might, however, have decided that it *was* necessary had she known what took place up the street the very next afternoon. In Father Mulroe's morning post came the rescript from Rome that granted a dispensation from her perpetual vows to Sister Mary Thomas, who was thereby reduced to the lay state, stripped of her name in religion, and henceforth to be known as Mary Margaret McGreevy. He must inform her immediately, of course. And continue his investigation of possible diabolical possession.

So at two o'clock, while Father Heron was preparing his evening sermon and Father Kilbride was reciting his breviary, Father Mulroe set off in his Baby Ford to deliver the message from Rome. He didn't have far to go. Halfway up the village he spotted her coming towards him on her bicycle. He stopped the motorcar and waved to her.

"Musha, good afternoon to your reverence," she said cheerfully. As if she didn't have a care in the world. Sitting on the bike in the middle of the road with one foot on the ground, and showing quite a bit of well-shaped leg in the process.

"I was just on my way back to see you," he told her.

"Well, is that a fact? Sorry, Father, but there'll be no tea this afternoon. I'm on my way into town to do a bit of shopping."

"That's too bad, now." He smiled at her.

"You like the cup of tea, don't you, Father?"

"It's the currant cake more than the tea. Even Bridie May doesn't make one as good as yours."

"Well, that's high praise indeed." Mary McGreevy chortled, her laughter reverberating through the quiet street. Which caused a couple of lace curtains on nearby windows to be peeked through in disapproving curiosity. "One of these days I'll make one especially for you and bring it back. Do you think Bridie May would mind?"

"You'll have to sneak it in unbeknownst to her. Which won't be easy, I can tell you." And it was Father Mulroe's turn to laugh.

"I'll leave it at the church door and you can say you found it." Mary McGreevy thought this idea hysterically funny.

"A foundling cake," said the parish priest, and they both howled with merriment. "I have something for *you*," he added when he recovered his composure.

"I didn't know you were a baker too, Father." And Mary McGreevy laughed again.

"This is something the Vatican cooked up," the priest said. "Or should I say baked?" He chuckled, marveling how she was able to bring out the irreverent even in him. Could this possibly be the devil at work? "It's your rescript," he announced seriously.

"My what?"

"Your dispensation. They call it a rescript. God knows why."

"You mean to tell me they finally came through with it?" He handed her the document. She glanced briefly at it and then gave him a look that was suddenly almost hostile. "To tell you the God's honest truth, Father, I don't give a tinker's curse anymore. When it mattered to me, they wouldn't send it. So they can keep it now for all I care."

"We must try not to let annoyance with God's servants come between us and God Himself." Father Mulroe picked his words carefully.

"Oh, I have nothing whatever against yourself!" Her face was all contrition. "You're the nicest man I know."

"Ah, I wasn't thinking of me at all, Mary. But there's a danger that you might let your anger with the institutional church interfere with your duty to the real church, the Body of Christ. That's what concerns me." He had put that rather well, if he said so himself.

"Well, I must be going, Father." She was staring straight ahead. "I have a lot to do before the day is out." Her foot came off the ground. She began to move away.

"You'll come to the mission, won't you?" Shouting after her. "Next week is for the women."

She turned the bike around and cycled back to him. "I don't think I will. It wouldn't do me any good." She looked straight at him, and he leaning out the car window.

"Why wouldn't it? You know yourself as well as I do that many a person has found God waiting for them again at a mission or retreat."

"He's not waiting for me anymore. That stage is gone."

"Well, as a special favor to me, then, maybe you'd come at least the first couple of nights? I'd be most obliged." He was embarrassed at the plaintiveness of his plea.

She gave him the impish grin that had turned the heart crossways on him the first time he went to see her. "To oblige you, Father, I'd stand on my head here in the middle of the road."

All afternoon he was acutely aware of the residual effects of her smile. Several times he halfheartedly tried to get rid of them. But he was not, he was also aware, sufficiently perturbed at his failure to do so. Not even when he considered the possibility that both the smile and his reaction might indeed be the work of the devil.

The last thing Kitty Tarragh expected was to find herself in the church that Sunday evening at the women's mission. An even greater wonder was having Mary McGreevy kneeling next to her. A week ago she would have laughed at the notion. But that was before Tom started coming home every night from the men's sessions saying what a wonderful experience it was and what a pity she wasn't going to go herself. Which unsubtle pressure would scarcely have stirred her had not Father Mulroe himself inveigled her with a virtuoso exhibition of *plamas*. He was sleeping in their spare room for the duration and on Sunday morning had asked her if she was going. When she said forthrightly that she wasn't he didn't seem in the least surprised. "I know you're a bit of a skeptic," he acknowledged with that half grin of his. But then he went on, "However, skeptics aren't afraid to hear what the other side has to say. Are they, now? And Father Kilbride is a very intelligent young man. Besides, you can argue with him afterwards if you don't like what he says: he's very easy to talk to." So here she was, instead of being at home by the fire reading her book, immersed in the sound waves of two hundred women responding to the rosary, smelling sweet incense from the benediction thurible, and watching a young man with chubby cheeks and thinning red hair mount the small pulpit and clear his throat. She had no interest in what he was about to say. She was here to please John Pat, as she called the parish priest in her own mind, though never to anyone else except Mary McGreevy.

But she listened to the preacher anyway because there was nothing else to do. His theme tonight, he said, would be *the end for which we were created*. And despite her avowed lack of interest she got caught up in his words. About God, who doesn't need us, making us anyway, just to show us his goodness. And *our* only purpose in life being to acknowledge that goodness with our continual worship. It was teaching she had heard so many times in her youth, but never before expressed with such fierce intensity or conviction. Father Kilbride burned with a fervor that set fire to the congregation in front of him, and his message exploded in her mind like headlines announcing the end of the world. How could she not have been aware of it before? What blindness had kept this soul-awakening news from her? Why had she wasted her life thus far? "Thou hast made us for Thyself alone, O Lord, said Saint Augustine," cried Father Kilbride. "And our hearts are restless till they rest in Thee." She was ready to weep. What had gotten into her? A mere half hour ago she would have scoffed at all this as pious gibberish; now it was sweet food to her ravenous soul, strong drink to her parched emotions.

"Give thanks to God for having created you for so noble an end," the preacher roared.

"Thank God," she cried in an audible whisper that startled her agnostic friend. Mary McGreevy's quizzical sideways glance restored temporary sanity to her mind. "Sorry," she whispered out of the corner of her mouth. "I must have been dreaming."

But she was carried off again by the sweetest fervor when the preacher wailed, "When, O Lord, will I rejoice eternally in the immensity of Thy glory?" There was a new love suddenly inside her that was ravishing her inmost being, its searing flames melting the ice from her hard, cold heart. When the missioner turned and pointed dramatically at the crucifix above the altar and said in a thunderous whisper, "There! There is the purpose of your life. There is the reason for your creation, Jesus Christ crucified," she was suffused with the warmth of a raging fever. Rays of light, like fiery harpoons, were shooting from the tabernacle and piercing her very soul. And all she could feel was immense delight and a powerful impulse to get up and sing and dance in the aisle for sheer exuberant joy.

Father Kilbride preached for a full hour that night. He dared not speak for less with Father Heron sitting in the sacristy, stopwatch in hand. To Mary McGreevy that time was an eternity of boredom; to Rita Feerick on her right it was an hour of peace from crying children; to Kitty Tarragh on her left it was but a few brief moments of ecstasy. Kitty walked from the church blissfully fuddled, waved a vague good-night to her friends, and floated into her house on heavenly air. So bright were her eyes and so silly her smile that her husband, had he not known her better, would have said she was drunk. Which indeed she was—as Father Kilbride might have said, she was drunk in the Lord.

And, like all inebriates, she suffered the aftermath of her euphoric state. She woke in the middle of the night in a sweat of fear. *Our purpose in life is the glory of God.* But she had spent *her* life laughing at God. Despising Him, ignoring Him, mocking His laws. And for that she was going to be damned. If she died this minute she would go straight to hell. The fear welled up inside her, for the hell she had scoffed at ever since her school days was very real at this moment. How stupid of her to laugh! To think that by jeering at God she could make Him go away. "Save me, Lord; I perish!" She had to get out of bed this minute or she would go mad from the pressure inside her skull. Quietly, without disturbing Tom, though she wanted to shake him and ask him for comfort. She must not! Maybe wake Father Mulroe in the spare bedroom down the hall. He would understand better than Tom. Her skin felt bloated, as if about to burst. Her hand raised to knock at the priest's door. No! He would think her cracked in the head! And they'd take her away and lock her up in the lunatic asylum in Castlebar. She held tightly to the banister, wanting fiercely to race down the stairs just to release some of that awful energy of fear. What now? She desperately needed to scream. Damned! She was damned! There was no hope. Any second now she would explode and die and go straight to hell. God's punishment for her wickedness was to let her see her sins when it was too late to repent. "Save me, Lord; I perish!" She crumpled on the kitchen floor, hands wrapped around her head, and slipped into life-saving unconsciousness.

When she opened her eyes again Father Mulroe was staring down at her. She screamed then, for her mind, confused, concluded that she was on her deathbed receiving the last rites—a fear that was confirmed when she tried to move and her body refused to budge. She screamed again. In a moment Tom was looking down at her as well. "What in God's name are you doing there, Kitty?" he asked.

"You should know," she shouted. "You sent for the priest."

"I got up early to say a private mass before the missioners." Father Mulroe spoke very quietly to Tom. "And I found her like this on the floor." Then for the longest time both men gazed down at her, helplessness etched deep into their sympathetic faces.

There was feeling and movement in her legs again. Maybe she could get up. Mustn't let them think she had gone mad. "Sorry," she murmured. "I think I had a nightmare." The panic seemed to be gone. In silence the men helped her up. Tom held her arm as she climbed the stairs to their room.

"You must have walked in your sleep," was all he said.

"I don't remember a thing," she lied.

Father Mulroe was standing at the church door Monday night when the women were coming out from the mission. He liked to mingle with his flock on these occasions. Standing at the bottom of the steps saying good-night and exchanging pleasantries, he refused to acknowledge that his principal concern was to see if Mary McGreevy had attended. He soon spotted her coming out the door, flanked by Rita Feerick and Kitty Tarragh. They all said, "good-night, Father," but made no effort to stop and talk. "I'd like a word with you, Mary." Though he had no idea what to say to her. He wanted to observe her actions and reactions: you had to do a lot of that, he had read, in order to determine if the devil was indeed in control of the person.

"Of course, Father." Her companions kept going. She looked pale and tired and stared at him with what seemed apprehension.

"How do you like Father Kilbride?"

"He gave the fire-and-brimstone sermon tonight. Boring as hell, Father, if you'll excuse the language. I suppose I've heard it too many times."

"Do you realize, Mary McGreevy, that you are a heretic? That's what you are, now." It could be the devil all right.

"*Damnant quod non intelligunt!* Did you know it was the pagan Cicero said that?" Anger in the green eyes. "'They condemn the things they don't understand.' Well, if it was true in Roman times, it's still true today. You have only to step the slightest bit out of the orthodox line and they send you straight to hell. But that's what hell is for, I suppose."

Surely it must be the case! Nuns didn't memorize Cicero in Latin like that. The use of unknown tongues! One of the three signs of demonic possession, according to the *Roman Ritual*. And using arguments away beyond anything he had ever heard of before from a sister! Didn't she quote Sartre and Kierkegaard back in the field the other day! Making known hidden things! The second sign. He was on to something, for sure. There remained only the third: exhibiting a strength out of all proportion with one's age and circumstance! Had he ever witnessed the like in her? Those giant pig pots? Of course! He had always marveled that she was able to carry them the way she did. "Will you let me pray over you?" he asked. He'd have to go to the archbishop for permission to perform a formal exorcism, of course, but he could do a private one on his own.

"What did you have in mind, Father?" A touch of the sardonic in the McGreevy voice and eye.

"I'll be over one of these days and we'll talk about it then."

"I suppose you want to drive the devil out of me? Is that it?"

She was laughing at him! Or was it Satan that was laughing inside her? Anyway, she had him confused. He didn't know what to say. "Right!" Taking his cue from her tone. "We'll send old Nick packing. Drive him into the pigs."

"Oh, no!" Holding up a protective hand. "Not the pigs. They're worth too much. You can have a couple of the old hens if you need them." But he could swear there was a note of anxiety in her banter.

The confessional in Kildawree church was on the left side, halfway between the back wall and the altar rails. By convention the penitent box nearest the rails was for men and boys, the one nearest the back for women and girls. On Saturday evening, the last day of the women's mission, Kitty Tarragh waited her turn. Only six women and two men ahead of her now, and then she'd unload a lifetime of sin into the waiting ear of Father Kilbride. Though terrified that she might die any minute and be hurled forever into the pit of hell, she had, nevertheless, taken all week to examine her conscience. She was determined to confess all, repent of all, and be forgiven for all. She went over her sins again for the umpteenth time. It was a long list. She had transgressed every single commandment that God gave to Moses, as well as the six imposed by the church, not to mention the seven deadly sins. And she had made a bad confession before the wedding.

The queue was moving slowly—five women and one man before her turn would come. She must be patient: the lack of it was one of the many faults on her list. A whole seat of women behind her too, including Maureen Garvey. She'd have to speak softly into Father Kilbride's ear so as not to be heard by that one. They said she could hear people talking in their own houses and she passing by on the road.

Only four women now and no men. The women would be able to use both boxes. She'd soon be in. There was sweat on her upper lip. God forgive her the sins she had committed in all those years. So quiet. Only a dim murmur from within the confessional box. And the rattle of occasional rosary beads. Thank God you couldn't hear what was going on inside. Some priests were known to shout their displeasure, but obviously not Father Kilbride.

Two women ahead of her still. And two men slipped in just now, one of them Mick Burke. She'd like to hear what Maureen Garvey had to tell. God forgive her, it was none of her business. Would she confess to all the gossip she spread? Or to snubbing Mary McGreevy? Stop it—uncharitable thoughts; no more of these. This new life she was starting was going to be hard for a while. None of the liberties she used to allow herself—mostly thoughts and words; she didn't *do* much harm to anyone. Except the sex, of course. Poor Nadinha! Was she in hell? How could she be, who never harmed anyone in her entire life? Yet sex sins were always mortal. All very mysterious really. But she was taking no more chances. Straight and narrow from here on.

Mick Burke had stepped in on the men's side. She was next on the women's. Well, here goes. Dark inside the box. Cushioned kneeler: that was nice. "Want to get married, Father." Oh, God! She could hear Mick. Try not to listen. Deliberate eavesdropping would be sinful. "A nun, Father. I mean, she was a nun." Stop! Cover your ears. That was better. But she'd have to watch for the grill opening on her side. Was she going to remember everything? Please, God, yes!

Father Kilbride was so nice. He listened without saying a thing, then just murmured a few words of encouragement when she was done. And only a single rosary for her penance. She choked when she heard him say, *"Ego te absolvo . . ."* She was clean again, her soul pure in the sight of God. Maybe some purgatory, but she'd work that off with indulgences. She knelt at the back of the church, thanking her Savior for his mercy. And she recalled Mick Burke and what she had heard him say. He wanted to get married. Past time for him indeed. He had said something else too, though she had been trying not to listen. Nun! Used to be! He wanted to marry Mary McGreevy, of course! Well, fat chance with Mary. He wasn't in her class at all. Funny! You never knew what was going on in people's heads.

Then it struck her. Oh, Christ! How could she have missed it? That was why he wanted to marry her! Dear kind Lord, was it possible? Mick Burke the father of Mary McGreevy's baby? But why else would he be talking in confession about marrying her? You didn't have to tell the priest you'd like to get married. Unless there was a major sin attached. Like fornication and getting a woman pregnant. She went home elated— she had saved her soul and resolved her mystery.

After brooding about it all during the mission, the priest's housekeeper decided that her silence not only was the result of cowardice on her part but was probably sinful as well. A hard woman on herself, the same Bridie May. "Can I speak to you, Father?" she said Sunday afternoon when she brought him his dinner. The mission was over and his guests had left after breakfast.

"Of course, Bridie May. And thanks very much again for all you did for the missioners. You'd like the rest of the day off, I suppose. Certainly! You have—"

"It's not that at all, Father." Bridie May turned away and looked out the window. "I'm not good at this kind of thing," she said, and then she had to stop to clear her throat. "But I believe it's my duty to tell you what people are saying about you behind your back."

"Of course, Bridie May, of course. I value your honesty. Go ahead and tell me. I won't be offended."

"They're saying, Father, that you're spending too much time visiting Mary McGreevy." And the housekeeper turned and ran to the kitchen. Father Mulroe, following her a minute later, found her sitting by the fire, her face in her hands and her body shaking with sobs.

"It's all right," he said. "It's all right. People gossip too much at times. Even about their priest. Huh! Especially about their priest. Don't let it bother you."

"I know it's not true, Father," Bridie May managed between sniffles. "But it could destroy your good name. That's what worries me."

Father John Patrick consoled her as best he could and then went back to his dinner. It was well on the way to being cold, but he didn't have the heart to tell her.

15

Reading was one habit of Kitty's that Tom Tarragh favored. Being a bit of a scholar himself, he admired those who took an interest in the intellectual life. And she didn't waste her time with silly romantic novels, either. Serious stuff—history and biography and the great works of fiction, all from the county library in Castlebar. He grew accustomed to her sitting by the fire at night with her head in a book. And he'd smile with amused tolerance when she was so immersed as not to hear him ask a question. He was very pleased altogether when after the parish mission she took to borrowing books on spirituality from Father Mulroe's small library. A religious dilettante himself until after the death of his first wife, he had in recent years begun to take his faith seriously and was now a regular member of the men's sodality. Anyway, piety was becoming in a woman, and he had been a bit disturbed at Kitty's disdain for the rules and practices of holy mother church. He had been particularly upset over the measures she had been taking to ensure that procreation did not occur from their connubial mingling. Measures that included a device she had obtained from a physician in London at the start of their honeymoon. Since that device was strictly prohibited by the laws of the church he expected that its use would now cease. And with the help of God a baby might be on the way in the very near future. "The mission did her a world of good," he told the parish priest on a late August evening. They were sitting in Father John Patrick's parlor discussing material for the latest chapter of Tom's *History of South Mayo*.

Father Mulroe looked pleased. "I've been noticing her at weekday mass lately, all right. And she has been in here browsing through my books several times."

"She's been reading them too. One of these days she'll be coming in teaching yourself theology." They both had a good laugh over that. But the laughter stopped when she began to apply her learning. Not long after, Tom turned to his wife in bed one night and sought the rendering of what theologians called the nuptial debt.

"I can't tonight," she said and turned her back on him. He assumed it was that time of the month for her, so he didn't press the issue. But when refusals continued for the next four weeks he asked for the reason.

"Artificial contraception is forbidden by the laws of the church," she told him, her head on the pillow and she staring at the ceiling. "And I don't want to get pregnant." And she wouldn't discuss the matter further.

After another month of abstinence, Tom went to see Father Mulroe. "She's theologically correct," the priest informed him. "But it would not be reasonable for her to expect you to abstain indefinitely. There is the rhythm method, of course. The church approves its use when there is good and lawful cause."

"I'm aware of that, Father. But I want children. That's the main reason I married her."

"Just so," said the priest. "Just so indeed. Would you like me to talk to her?"

"Would you ever mind doing that, please, Father?"

The opportunity presented itself a week later when Kitty walked in on him halfway through his dinner. "Sorry for disturbing you, Father," she said. "I'll come back another time."

"Not at all, Kitty! If you'll sit here at the table now for a few minutes, Bridie May will be bringing in the tea." Father Mulroe stuck a large piece of potato in his gob.

"I've been reading some of your spiritual books," Kitty began. "Most interesting stuff, I must say. I wish I had read them a long time ago."

"Well, I'm glad you like them." This was the kind of thing that made a priest feel good about his life's work.

"Tanquerey says mortification of the senses is necessary for perfection."

"Oh, it is indeed. Certainly." Father Mulroe cut a slice off his mutton chop and covered it with mint jelly.

"He says," said Kitty, "that our spiritual growth depends on the measure of violence we do to ourselves."

"That's true," the priest said between chews.

"Well, I have decided," said Kitty, "to mortify *my* senses."

"Good!" He balanced some fresh peas on the back of his fork and transferred them carefully to his mouth.

"I'm going to give up what I'm most attached to." She looked straight at him. "The pleasures of the flesh."

"Yes. To be sure." But he'd prefer to postpone this conversation till he had finished his meal.

"You agree, don't you, Father, that it's a good and meritorious thing to do?" Her left eyebrow defied him to contradict.

The parish priest pushed away the remainder of his dinner. "Well!" He wiped his mouth, rolled the napkin carefully, and shoved it into its ring. "We must, as the theologians say, distinguish. It is indeed a good and efficacious act in itself to mortify the senses."

"There, now," said Kitty.

"However, we must take into account the situation in which it is done. For instance, if by our action we were to injure another party, especially one towards whom we had obligations, then the deed would no longer be good because of the circumstances. Do you see what I mean?"

"I do, Father. And of course I wouldn't dream of doing anybody any harm."

"But don't you think now that . . ." Here Father Mulroe paused to clear his throat. "Wouldn't it be injurious to your husband if you were to deprive him of the pleasures of the marital bed?"

Kitty dropped her gaze demurely to the table. "I've thought about that, Father. And to tell you the truth—and just between ourselves, mind you—

I don't think he has ever got much pleasure out of the marriage bed with me. Anyway," she cocked a sudden eye back up at him, "he wouldn't be any worse off than he was before we got married, would he?"

"Well, now, all the same!" Father Mulroe joined his hands, leaned back in his chair, and stared at the ceiling. "If I may speak frankly and without putting a tooth in it, your husband acquired the right to carnal intercourse with you by virtue of the sacrament of marriage. So it would be unlawful for you to deny him that right for any prolonged period of time without his consent. Even if the reason was a virtuous one." He glanced at Kitty. "Do you understand my point?"

She was staring at him but not seeing him. Her eyes seemed focused on an object infinitely distant. And she was silent for a long time. Then she said, "I think I'd like you to hear my confession now." She knelt on the dining room floor, her elbows on the table. "Bless me, Father, for I have sinned. It's—"

"I'm very sorry," the priest interrupted. "But we're not allowed to hear women's confessions anywhere except in the confession box in the church. If—"

Bridie May opened the door and walked in. She looked suspiciously at Kitty, still on her knees. "Sorry, Father! I didn't know that . . ." She sniffed audibly. "I'll come back later."

Kitty resumed her seat and glared at the housekeeper's departing back. Father Mulroe stood. "We're going over to the church for a few minutes," he shouted after Bridie May. "Maybe you can bring the tea when we get back."

"Why can't you hear my confession here?" Kitty demanded.

"It's a law of the church. To preserve the virtue of priest and penitent." They walked in silence across the narrow path. Their footsteps rang loud and hollow inside the empty church. "Are you ready?" the priest asked.

She stepped into the men's box. "Bless me, Father, for I have sinned. I made a good general confession at the mission in June and have been making good confessions every week since."

"Yes," said the priest encouragingly.

"However, I discovered in my reading that to contract a valid marriage in the eyes of the church a person must have the intention of having children. Isn't that true, Father?"

"One must at least not have a positive intention of not having children," Father Mulroe finely distinguished.

"Well, I did have a positive intention."

"Not to have children?"

"Yes."

"Oh, good God!"

"So that means we're not married in the eyes of the church? Doesn't it?"

Deep silence from the priest.

"So we can't lawfully have marital relations, then? Amn't I right?"

More silence, even deeper, from the other side of the grill.

"You understand my position, Father?"

"We'll have to validate the marriage," the priest said eventually. "You're willing to have children now, I take it?"

"Oh, no, Father. Not at all. I could never have children." Nadinha had convinced her of that. "That would be impossible for me."

Another protracted pause from the priest. "But you understand, you *must* be willing to have children in order to validate the marriage."

"But surely there's no law, Father, that says a woman must have children? Provided she's not married, of course. And I'm not married now, am I?"

A long, deep sigh from the priest's side of the grill. "But you do want to be married to Tom, don't you?"

"Well, now that you ask me, Father, I don't."

This time the confessor's breathing was akin to a release of steam from the Dublin train. "You went through a marriage ceremony, anyway. So you'd have to ask for an annulment. From the pope himself in Rome. That would cause a lot of scandal, I can tell you."

"I've been reading about that kind of situation in your theology books, Father. Couldn't we go on living together as brother and sister, so no one need know we're not married?"

After another lengthy pause the priest said, "You could, I suppose. As long as Tom agrees to it."

"Oh, I wouldn't want to tell Tom at all. It would only upset him, you see. And it might disturb his conscience too. Better to say nothing there, Father."

Much more deep breathing ensued before Father Mulroe said reluctantly, "That could be the case indeed."

"This way, nobody knows about it except you and me. Even you don't know anything, Father, since it's under the seal of confession."

"Mention some sin from your past life," said the confessor wearily, "so I can give you absolution."

There was a cattle fair in Ballinamore the first Friday in October. Wattie Feerick, though he had no animals to sell, cycled in about ten o'-clock to see what calves were fetching. And to have a chat or a pint with any acquaintance he might come across up Main Street. A most garrulous man, the same Wattie. He was on his way home about two in the afternoon when he decided to pay a visit to Henry Malone. The spuds were almost ready for digging, and maybe he could borrow Henry's horse-drawn digger, the only one of its kind this side of the parish. Henry was down the yard with one of the workmen examining a horse's hoof when Wattie rode up. "That'll need the services of Mr. Graney," Henry said, letting go of a fetlock and straightening his back.

"How are you, Henry?" Wattie said cheerfully. He was feeling good himself, with a couple of Guinnesses inside him. But Henry just stared as if not recognizing him and then suddenly collapsed in a heap on the ground. "Cripes!" Wattie and the workman dropped to their knees beside the prone farmer. "Are you all right, Henry?"

Not a stir out of the man, or a sign of life. "Jaypers!" said the workman. "Is he alive at all?"

Wattie put his finger to the old man's throat. "I think we'd better take him up to the house." The workman got a cart crib and some sacks and they lifted Henry onto the makeshift pallet. "Easy does it, now," said

Wattie as they carried their burden up the path. The maid screamed when she opened the door and saw them. Missus came running. No hysterics with her. "Put him on the sofa in the kitchen," she said hurriedly but calmly. She felt for his pulse, put her ear to his mouth, her hand over his heart. "Would you mind going for the priest?" she said quietly to Wattie.

"I will, to be sure, ma'am. And I'll ring for the doctor too." He didn't want Henry to die, was going through his mind as he pedaled furiously back to the village. He'd miss him something fierce. Everybody would. Father Mulroe was walking up and down in front of his house saying his breviary. But by the time Wattie got to the post office he was already heading up the road in the Baby Ford.

Noreen Macken rang for Doctor Palmer, the new man who had just taken over old Doctor Walsh's practice in Ballinamore. "He'll be out in no time at all," she said when she got off the telephone.

"I think it'll be a wasted journey," Wattie said.

"I'd better run over and tell Kitty." Noreen was already on her way out the door.

Wattie cycled home slowly, getting his wind back and meditating on what had just happened to poor Henry Malone. To be carted off to eternity just like that, without a minute's notice. But maybe it was better that way. He was in heaven now, for sure. Providing, of course, he was ready. Wattie himself wasn't ready to go this minute if he was called, and that was a frightening thought. There were times when he doubted the very existence of heaven, but at this moment he believed in it very firmly.

Henry Malone's sudden death was the talk of the parish. A terrible sad thing entirely for Missus and Kitty, everyone agreed. As for poor Father Stephen, it would take a whole week to even get the news to him out in Brazil. Missus was restrained in her grief, it was noted at the wake. "She's taking it well, the creature," Rita Feerick remarked to several women neighbors sitting around the table in the Malone kitchen sipping tea. A sentiment that was repeated by many in the course of the evening.

But if Missus mourned quietly, Kitty did not. She sobbed openly every time someone condoled with her. And she never once wiped the tear streaks from her face during the entire night. She sat next to her mother near the bed that had been moved into the dining room and stared and stared at Henry's dead face and pulled the beads of her rosary without ceasing through her fingers. Tom Tarragh would come in now and again to see her and put his arm around her shoulder, but she would ignore him and he would soon return to the parlor and his glass of whiskey and the company of the men of the parish who had come to say good-bye to Henry Malone.

Only twice during the night did Kitty rise from her chair and engage in conversation. The first time was early in the evening when Mick Burke, after kneeling by the bedside of the deceased to pray, got up and told her he was sorry for her troubles and then left. She followed him into the hall. "Mick," she called out, "can I have a word with you?"

"We're all going to miss him," said Mick. Which commiseration brought on a fresh burst of sobbing from Kitty.

"We are," she managed eventually. "Can we take a walk outside? It's a bit crowded in here."

"'Tis cold out there," he warned. "You'd need a coat, I'd say."

"This won't take very long." Kitty pulled her cardigan tight and folded her arms and stepped outside. "I hear you want to marry Mary McGreevy," she said softly after pulling the front door shut.

Mick's reaction in the dim porchlight was instant and comical. Eyes widened, mouth opened, and nostrils flared. "Christ Almighty! Where did you hear that?"

"Never mind where I heard it. What I wanted to say—"

"She told you herself? Fook it! She said she wouldn't say a word to a soul." He turned his back on her and headed rapidly down towards the yard.

"Mick!" She raced after him. "Mick! She didn't tell me a thing. On my word of honor!"

That stopped him. He turned and faced her. "Then who in God's name told you?" There was seething anger in his voice.

"Listen now, Mick. Don't be mad at me, because it wasn't my fault. At the time of the mission I was in the confession box waiting and I heard you telling the priest."

"Cripes Almighty!" A wail of purest anguish. "The whole fooking parish knows about it, then."

"You don't have to worry," she soothed. "Nobody else heard. You weren't talking that loud. And I didn't tell anyone."

Mick stood there staring at her. But the anger and the anguish were slowly fading. Until suddenly his expression switched back to doubt and suspicion. "Why are you telling me, then?" he demanded.

"Will she have you?" Kitty countered.

"Indeed she won't. She says she's not going to marry anyone. But the way of it is she thinks she's too good for me. And bejasus, I don't doubt that it's true for her. What would she want with the like of me anyway?"

"It's a shame," said Kitty mercilessly, "that you didn't think of that before you got her into trouble."

She was getting used to his expression of comical agitation. "You're daft," he said, and then he cackled loudly. "Do you think that I . . ." And he looked up at the sky and cackled some more. "To tell you the truth, I wish it was. Honest to the good God, I do!"

"If it wasn't you, then why do you want to marry her? I mean, if she's carrying someone else's baby."

"Ah, that's a long story, Kitty." He turned his back on her and put his hands in his pockets. "Would you believe I wanted to marry yourself first, only you were taken?"

"Did you, now? Well, I'm flattered."

"Anyway, it's time for me to settle down, and since yourself is gone there isn't a finer unmarried woman in the parish than Mary."

Kitty dropped her voice to a whisper. "You can confess to me, now, Mick. I won't tell a soul. You *are* the father, aren't you?"

"Jesus Christ, Kitty!" Mick swung around. "What do I have to say? I told you she wouldn't have me."

"Well, obviously she's not marrying the father, anyway. So why couldn't it be you?"

He stared up at the sky. "You better go back inside now or you'll catch your death of cold." He turned and grabbed his bike that was leaning against the wall and quickly cycled off.

When Mary McGreevy arrived some time later, Kitty's sobs augmented. "He was very fond of you," she blubbered, ignoring the memory of Henry warning her not to be so much as seen with the ex-nun.

"He was a good man," Mary said. Seven months pregnant, her condition was showing.

Kitty noted disapproving glances aimed at her friend's back. "I still have my own room upstairs," she whispered. "Let's go up there and we can talk for a bit. That's if you can climb the stairs, of course."

"I'm not entirely helpless yet." There was a noticeable diminution in mourner conversation as they passed through the hall and up the stairs. Kitty sat on the bed; Mary eased herself carefully into a straightbacked chair.

"Why did God take Daddy the way He did—suddenly?" Kitty asked and then cried.

"I don't know," Mary said.

"I have been mortifying myself." She saw Mary's puzzled look. "You must have noticed that I've become very pious since the mission?"

"I've noticed that."

"And I've been reading about the need to mortify the senses. But I'm sure you know all there is to know about that sort of thing?"

"Indeed." Was there a trace of a smile on her friend's face?

"What I find hard to understand is that God, instead of accepting the sacrifices that I have been making to him, chose to impose Daddy's death on me instead."

"They say God's ways are inscrutable." Mary's face at that moment was also a bit on the enigmatic side.

"Mary McGreevy, you're no help to me at all." Kitty stretched out on the bed and folded her arms. "You gave up on God yourself, didn't you?"

"I don't want to disturb your faith with my lack of it."

"Oh, you needn't worry about me." Kitty sat up and rested her back against the headboard. "I'm madly in love with Jesus right now. But He's still on probation. Taking Daddy hasn't helped His case at all." She sobbed again. "Do you believe in hell?"

Mary smiled. "Why does everyone want to know if I believe in hell? Father Mulroe keeps asking me the same question."

"Because I'm not sure *I* do. Hell is punishment, right? And punishment is revenge, right? And God tells us that revenge is sinful. And surely God wouldn't commit sin? So there!"

Mary laughed out loud. "God help poor Father Mulroe if he has to deal with you."

"Oh, he has to. I go see him every day for spiritual advice. Bridie May doesn't like that very much, I think."

"You're a gas woman," Mary said.

Kitty leaped off the bed, knelt by Mary's chair, and put her head in her friend's lap. "There'd better be a heaven. I want to see Daddy again." Suddenly she raised her head. "Is that the baby moving inside?"

"Yes."

She put her head back on Mary's lap. "I wish *I* was the father. Then I could marry you and come to live with you." At which thought Kitty first giggled and then cried.

Sitting by the fire in the kitchen slurping pints of Guinness, three farmers of the deceased's own vintage reminisced, ignoring entirely the group of women sitting close by around the table. "Sixty years I've been going to wakes and funerals, and I've never known Henry to miss a one," said the bald one sadly, a small man with a long crooked nose and rounded shoulders.

"And divil a fear that he'll miss this one either," said the mustached one next to him, a heavyset man in a brown suit and shiny shoes.

"A great man for the fair day," said the third, a dignified man who kept his black bowler hat on. "You'd always find him up on Market Street in the late morning, whether he had stock to sell or not."

"Here's to him, then," said the mustache, raising his glass in salute. "We'll miss him, by God!" The others lifted their pints and they all drank deep. And even the women's chatter could not drown the silence they observed in honor of their departed friend and neighbor.

The bald one looked behind him at the table, then leaned forward conspiratorially. "Who do you think will get the place?" Just above a whisper.

"The daughter, I suppose," said the bowler. "'Twill hardly be the priest, anyway."

"Faith, if she does get it 'tis Tom Tarragh will have the calluses on his hands." The mustache breathed heavily in imitation of a laugh. "It isn't Kitty that'll be doing the work, I can tell you."

"Maybe she'll have her convent friend over to give her a hand," said baldy. And he sniggered. "They say she's a power of a man on the farm."

"Bull and heifer all in one, I hear," said the mustache. They all smiled at that.

"Easy does it, now," said the bowler, who had his back to the wall. "You won't believe who just walked in." The other two heads swiveled creakingly to look at Mary McGreevy and Kitty Tarragh. The women's conversation lapsed for a moment, then took off once more.

Kitty walked straight to the fireplace. "If you'll excuse me, now," she said without so much as a greeting. And she picked up one of the several teapots sitting on the hearth and walked back out the door, followed by the McGreevy woman.

"Now there's a heifer ready to calve," said the mustache.

"The question is, who was the bull?" The bald one leaned towards the fire and spat into it. "They're saying it was the schoolmaster himself."

"Arrah, not at all, not at all," the bowler contradicted very calmly. "Mr. Thomas Tarragh is much too respectable a man to do such a disreputable thing. And he just after getting married, to boot."

"Well, if it wasn't him, who was it?" The bald one was belligerent. "'Twasn't any scut of a lad got *her* in a hay shed, I can tell you that."

"I'll tell you who it was." The bowler rested his pint on his knee. "Jack Banaghan! A respectable fellow, you see, working in the bank. But hot young blood, all the same. And the expectation of marrying the girl afterwards and acquiring the farm left to her by the father. The Lord have mercy on Michael McGreevy, anyway. He was a fine man, and he deserved better than he's getting from his daughter. I only hope Banaghan will make a respectable woman out of her one of these days."

"I have it on the best of authority myself," the mustache whispered, laying his pint down on the hearth, "that it was none other than the princess's own brother did the deed." He winked solemnly at the bald one.

"Is it Father Malone?" the bowler ejaculated.

"Will you go easy, now?" the mustache whispered fiercely. "This is just between ourselves. It's a scandalous business entirely, so it is. And for sure this is not to be mentioned up at Queally's in any shape or form. Henry, the poor devil, would turn over in his grave if he knew it was even talked about, much less be the truth."

"We didn't put Henry into his grave yet." The bald one snickered.

"I don't believe for a single minute that it was Father Stephen," the bowler affirmed with great dignity. "I've known him since he was a nipper and—"

"Faith, there are them that know, and they have assured me that it was him all right. They tell me he spent a power of time below in her house when he was at home. So what was he doing there? And she a nun at that!" The mustache retrieved his glass and drained it. "Take my word for it, now, the missionary is your man."

"Well, upon my oath, now, my source is very close to the horse's mouth too," the bald one said. "And he says for sure it was the schoolmaster. And he claims, furthermore, that it's not the first one in the oven for Mr. Thomas."

"Damned if I know about that," the bowler said. "But let no one besmirch the name of Henry Malone by casting aspirations on the reputation of his priestly son." And he rose with great dignity and walked out of the kitchen.

It was the biggest funeral in Kildawree for many a year, everyone said. The church was packed for the mass and those at the end of the procession couldn't even get inside the gate to the graveyard. But they could all hear Kitty bawling her head off when the clay began to thump on her father's coffin. Tom Tarragh had to practically carry the poor creature back to their house. And there she stayed, crying and moping and staring into space. All she could hear was the dirt falling on Daddy, and Daddy's voice calling out to her. All she could see was Daddy standing across the kitchen, one hand behind his back, staring at her; Daddy laughing; Daddy giving advice; Daddy sitting by the fire sleeping, the newspaper in his lap. How could she go on living without him? Tom fed her, then left her alone. Mary McGreevy came to see her twice, but she could hardly talk to her pregnant friend. It was a whole week before she felt well enough to step outside her front door again. Then she went back to Curnacarton and found Mammy coping a lot better than herself.

It was Mammy's calm acceptance of Daddy's death that shook Kitty out of her stupor. She went home determined to get her life moving again. And to get rid of that nagging resentment she was nursing against Jesus for taking Daddy from her. God's reasons were not ours, Mammy said. Kitty decided too to stop being unfair to Tom. Jesus surely couldn't object to her not wanting a baby and at the same time wanting to give her husband his due. For he *was* her husband, she now believed, regardless of Father Mulroe or the theology books, with all their talk of intention and validity and liciety and annulment. One other thing—she was going to satisfy herself once and for all that Tom was not the father of Mary's baby. She couldn't stand the thought of that. But it had more to do with her fondness for Mary, she thought, than with jealousy over her husband's possible infidelity.

She went up to Queally's in the middle of the afternoon to find Mick Burke. Dan Queally himself was behind the counter. "Sorry for your trouble, ma'am," said Dan. "We'll all miss him, that's for sure."

"Where's Mick?" she asked.

"Is it Mick?" said Dan. "Sure, he left us. Why do you think I'm here myself in the middle of the day?"

"Where did he go?"

"To England, ma'am. He packed his bags the day after the funeral and took the train to Dublin."

She didn't ask any more questions. So it *was* Mick! Why else would he run away like that? Especially after what she had said to him the night of the wake. Well, good riddance anyway! He'd leave Mary alone now. Oh, Mary! Why Mick Burke, for God's sake? She could have had any man she wanted. Except Tom Tarragh, of course. At which thought something close to a smile crossed her face, and she walking down the village street.

16

On a cold, clear, frosty Saturday morning in late October they were back in the potato field trying to finish harvesting the spuds, Tess and Brian doing the digging, Wat and Fidelma picking, Mary lending moral support, the most she could do these days. All of them periodically blowing on their fingers to thaw them out. Suddenly Jack Banaghan jumped over the wall, dressed in overalls and with a digging fork in his hand. He barely took time to God-bless the work before he was throwing out stalks and spuds at a rate that would do credit to poor Henry's digger. Tess had to drop her spade so she and Fidelma could pick for him. And by the end of the morning the spuds were all in the pit, a job they had expected would take the whole day.

"Ye'll all come back for dinner now," Mary said. "I have a chicken cooking."

"Mammy said we're to come right home for dinner and not be causing you bother," Tess said primly. And off the lot of them galloped without another word.

"I hope nobody told *you* to go home," she said to Jack.

"Divil a one." She could see the satisfaction in his face that he was going to have her all to himself. Back at the house he made her sit down and get out of her Wellingtons while he put the dinner on the table.

"Faith, you're a handy man to have around," she let out incautiously.

"I'll make you a good husband," he retorted.

"You'll make a good husband for someone, that's for sure."

"For you!" He waved the knife he was carving the chicken with. "*He* wants me to marry you."

"He! Who wants you to marry me?"

"Himself! The Man Upstairs."

"Now, how do you know that, Jack Banaghan? Did you have a private audience with Him or something?"

"Never mind how I know, now." Hacking away at the chicken. "It's a fact."

Mary winced with the pain. "I have a cramp in the back of my leg." She was getting a lot of those lately. "So let me see how good a husband you'd make by getting rid of it for me."

He put down the knife. "Where is it?" Standing over her. "We get them sometimes kicking football and—"

"Rub it!" she yelled. "Rub it!" Pulling up her skirt and slapping the back of her right thigh. "Rub it hard! Hurry!" He grabbed her foot with one hand and started to pat her calf gently with the other. "Not there!" she snapped. "Here!" Sliding forward on the chair till her backside was barely supporting her. She pulled the skirt up all the way over her stomach. "Here! Rub it here, for God's sake! Quick!"

He was on his knees in an instant. Strong, nimble fingers kneading, pressing, squeezing, soothing the delicate nerves of her upper leg. "Thanks, Jack. Don't stop! Please don't stop!" Grabbing him by the shoulder to keep him there.

At which point it appeared Jack became aware of his state. Straddling her leg, his groin tight around her knee, his hands wrapping her soft thigh flesh, and his nose just inches from her exposed knickers. He looked up and there was fear in those soft eyes. She refused to release him. The head went back down and he continued to massage. But in a very short time he convulsed, groaning with the weight of unwanted pleasure. Then he dropped his head onto her swollen belly and cried.

She tried to soothe him. Running her hands through his hair. "It's all right, Jack! It's all right, *a stor.*" But he wouldn't be comforted. His head was pushing into her stomach till she felt pain. She tried to lift him, but he wouldn't move. "You're hurting me, Jack," she said eventually, afraid his weight would do something awful to the baby. He slid off and crouched on the floor, face buried in his hands. She struggled to get up and pull down her dress. "Jack!" she called.

He rose slowly, his back to her. "I'd best be going now." Slouching to the door.

"You'll do no such thing, Jack Banaghan," she said firmly, "till you have your dinner."

He turned and stood there, head down, hands in his overall pockets. "I'm terribly ashamed." He looked as if he were going to cry again. "I don't know what to say at all."

"There's nothing to be ashamed of," she said. "I'm flattered you found me so interesting. Sit down and have a bit to eat."

But he wouldn't stay. "There'll be confessions tonight," he muttered, as he headed out the door.

Kitty didn't visit Mary for weeks after Henry died. When she finally came one afternoon in November, Mary was sitting in, or rather hanging out of, a chair by the fire, no longer comfortable in any normal position of repose. "You look tired," Kitty said straightaway. She had a basket in her hand.

"Musha, you could knock me over with a thrawneen this minute. How are you keeping yourself?"

"I'm all . . ." she began, and then the free hand went up to the face and the bawling started. "I miss him," she blubbered. "But I didn't come over to cry." Drying the eyes with a handkerchief. "I baked you a cake." She lifted it out of the basket and unwrapped the cloth around it. "A fruitcake, with almond paste. And it's got your name on it, see!" "To my dearest Mary" was boldly inscribed in red across the decorative white icing.

"It's gorgeous, Kitty!"

Kitty put it on the table and pulled a chair up to the fire. "How is herself?" Pointing at Mary's belly. She had already decided it would be a girl.

"At the rate she's kicking, she'll be the first girl on the Kildawree football team."

"I know who her father is!" Not an ounce of expression in Kitty's voice, and she staring into the fire.

At it again. Every time she came she got in a remark or a question on the subject. Though this was the first time she had actually claimed to know his name. "Do you, now? He told you himself, I suppose?"

"Arrah, he did not. But I know 'tis him anyway. Why else would he run off to England the very next day after I told him I knew?"

"And how is your mother?"

"You're a great one for wriggling out of a corner, Mary McGreevy!" Kitty smiled. "But we'll let you go this time. Ah, sure, Mammy is doing fine, God bless her. Much better than I am, indeed." The tears were there again, but she staved them off with a shake of the head. "Her strength is in her rosary, I'd say. I wish to God I had some of it myself."

"But *you* have a strong faith now, don't you?"

"I don't know if I do or I don't."

"You're fortunate to have Tom," Mary consoled.

"I'm fortunate to have *you*! Honest to God, I don't know what I'd do without you." She slipped off her chair and knelt, her ear pressed up against Mary's belly, listening. "I think of her as *our* baby," she murmured. "Yours and mine."

Mary stroked her hair, took her face in both hands, and looked at her. "I'm lucky to have you too."

Kitty was on her feet in an instant, leaning over. The caress of her lips renewed the jolt Mary had treasured for months. Then, just as suddenly, Kitty pulled back and covered her face with her hands.

"God help me! I don't know whether I'm coming or going!" She stood there, silent, for a minute. "I'm going to clean the house for you now. That's what I came back to do."

Doctor Palmer calculated that Mary McGreevy would be delivered on the eighth of December. Just the day before that date Rita Feerick, in response to a seemingly solicitous inquiry, let the owner of Kildawree's grocery shop know when the babby was due.

"Well, now, isn't that grand entirely," said Mrs. Garvey, scarcely able to maintain her calm. "On the feast of the Immaculate Conception itself? How extraordinary! And how appropriate, without a doubt." The pious malice on the woman's face belatedly alerted Rita that she had said too much.

Which indeed she had. The Garvey woman lost no time at all in advising her customers that the McGreevy child had been virginally conceived like the Holy Infant Himself and would be born on the Blessed Mother's feast day just to prove it.

In midafternoon of the same day Father Mulroe came sweeping back the Kilduff boreen in his Baby Ford like Elijah in his fiery chariot. "You're looking well," he told Mary. And then for more than a few minutes he talked casually, too casually, about this and that and nothing of any consequence.

Eventually she said, "I'll make the tea for you now, Father."

That was when he put his hand in the inside pocket of his jacket and brought out the slim black book. "I thought maybe I'd bless the baby," he said, eyeing her warily. "Did you know there's a prayer in the ritual for the unborn?"

"Well isn't mother church wonderful." She struggled to her feet and waddled to the fireplace. "She thinks of everything."

"She does indeed. Especially mothers and their babies." He pulled a small purple stole from his side pocket and did a one-handed flip to get it around his neck. Then he opened the black book and blessed himself. "*Adjutorium nostrum in nomine Domini,*" he intoned sonorously.

"*Qui fecit coelum et terram,*" she responded promptly, laboriously picking up the kettle. "You see, I haven't forgotten everything yet." She turned and grinned at him before heading slowly for the back door, carrying the kettle.

Father John Patrick looked crestfallen. "Would it be possible . . ." He stopped. "Maybe the tea could wait until after the blessing," he added mildly.

"Of course it can." But she kept going anyway. "I'll just fill the kettle and put it on the fire." She poured water into it from a shiny tin can on the table by the door. "That way it'll be boiled by the time you've sent the devil scurrying."

"There are many great theologians," the priest said solemnly as she returned to the fireplace, "who hold that not only do we each get a guardian angel to take care of us, but that we also get a fallen angel to excite us to evil. So this prayer is protection for the little one."

She hung the kettle on the crane, then lowered herself gently, wearily, back into her chair. "Proceed," she said.

"*Domine, exaudi orationem meam,*" he pleaded.

"*Et clamor meus ad te veniat,*" she retorted.

"*Dominus vobiscum.*"

"*Et cum spiritu tuo.*"

And then he continued on his own, in his best ecclesiastical Latin. She listened, straining to get the gist of what he was saying. Though no expert in the official language of mother church, she did know more than a smattering of it after five years in secondary school and sixteen years of reciting the Little Office and sundry other prayers and psalms and hymns and spiritual canticles. That knowledge permitted her to understand now that these were no innocent pleadings for the welfare of unborn children the parish priest was blithely muttering: they were hard, uncompromising threats to the evil one to get out of this woman's body or it would be the worse for him. However, she was willing to humor her priest. So she sat there quietly and let him invoke the powers of heaven against the wicked spirits of the damned.

Until he pulled the bottle of holy water from the other inside pocket. She didn't know what got into her then; maybe it *was* the devil. Anyway, as soon as Father John Patrick splashed the holy water in her direction she raised her arms and started screeching, "No! No! Not that! Please don't!" And making faces at him that might well imitate the torture of the damned. But the more she protested the more the man sprinkled, all the while continuing to read calmly from his slim black book. And the more he splashed the sillier she felt, till soon she was laughing hysterically. But that didn't last very long, because the laughing brought on cramps in her poor bloated stomach and very soon she was groaning from the pain. Which seemed to excite his reverence even further—perhaps her behavior suggested he was on the brink of success. So he poured the remainder of the bottle over her head. "Stop! Will you stop!" she screamed, flailing her arms in all directions.

This appeared to be the ultimate inspiration for Father John. He grabbed her hands and shook her. "I adjure thee by the living God to depart from this woman," he yelled, eyes bulging, his face just an inch from hers.

"Will you let me go! You're hurting me," she howled.

"I'll hurt you even more if you don't leave this woman in peace," he roared.

He was out of control and she was getting desperate with the pain. It was then that the experience of a thousand generations of tortured women came to her rescue. Humor him, said the voice inside her. Make him feel he has won the battle. She went limp all of a sudden. "Praise be to God," she croaked.

Standing there, arms raised, holy water bottle poised, Father John Patrick beamed. "Hallelujah!" he shouted. *"Deo gratias."*

All of a sudden she felt totally without energy. Escalating cramps in her lower abdomen. Then wetness on her inner thighs. And water flowing down her legs . . .

So Mary McGreevy's baby *was* born on the eighth of December. At exactly twenty-five minutes past eleven in the morning, according to Wattie Feerick, who looked at the clock on the kitchen dresser the second he heard the first squawk out of the newborn. It was a long and difficult labor, and Wattie and Rita, well versed in such events, had spent the entire time at the McGreevy house. At seven the evening before Wattie had gone to fetch Mrs. Dolan, the midwife. After that, as he always did for Rita, he kept the water hot in the kettle, the tea drawing on the hearth, and his bicycle clips on his trouser cuffs in readiness for a quick ride to the doctor in Ballinamore if that was called for. In the meantime he kept to the kitchen. Rita spent most of her time back in the bedroom with the mother-to-be, doing whatever it was that needed to be done on these occasions.

Wattie was dozing by the fire when Mrs. Dolan stuck her head out the bedroom door. "It's time for the doctor," she said. He made it to Ballinamore in just under half an hour and had to rap on the doctor's door knocker six times before a light went on upstairs. Coming home, the battery of his flashlamp failed just outside Kildawree and he made the remainder of the journey in a light drizzle and almost total blackness.

As night passed into bleak morning and Luke and Brian came down to do the milking and left the buckets at the door and fled, Mary McGreevy's moans advanced to sudden shrieks and occasional prolonged screams. Worse than anything he had ever heard from Rita, although his missus had had a couple of bad deliveries. It was strange how women had such a terrible time bringing forth their children when the brute animals of the field could do it without a bother. Punishment for Adam and Eve's sin, he had once heard a missioner say. Maybe so, though he had his doubts about a lot of things missioners said. Before he had time to develop this thought, the front door shot open and in roared Kitty Tarragh.

"Is she all right? Is the baby born? Where is she?" A furious demanding rush that Wattie hadn't begun to cope with before Kitty opened the bedroom door and charged in. Whether her presence had anything to do with it or not Wattie couldn't tell, but within five minutes of Mrs. Tarragh's arrival the infant let out its first squeal. Great was the scurrying then with basins and hot water and towels and emptying the kettle and boiling it again and stoking the fire and talking and laughing and much cooing and isn't she grand the image of her mother without a doubt in the world and a fine healthy baby she is indeed and would you take care of this Wattie and the bloody basinful that Wattie always had to dispose of and could never bear to look at and the doctor driving away in his motorcar and Rita shouting to make more tea and musha *a stor* you must be starved and Mary McGreevy saying only the odd quiet word and Kitty Tarragh laughing as if she had the hysterics.

"I'll be off, then," Wattie said as soon as it was decent to go. "We took care of the milking," he told Mary, and he standing in the bedroom doorway. It was the first time he had gotten any way close to the scene of the day's great event. Mary looking pale and tired, and her red hair all over the pillow and the babby, smothered in white, lying on her chest.

"Faith, there's a young lady here that'll be doing her own bit of milking soon," said Rita. The others laughed. Wattie fled—a man had no business at all to be standing around when a gaggle of women was talking like that.

Five days later Father Mulroe drove back to Kilduff again. Rita Feerick was sweeping the floor and Mary was sitting by the fire, a shawl over her shoulders. "I came back to see herself." He took a chair across from the new mother.

"She's sleeping," Rita said.

"You're well yourself?" he asked Mary.

"She's fit as a fiddle," Rita answered from near the back door.

"An old, broken-down fiddle," Mary grumbled.

"Do you hear her!" Rita scoffed. "It's a hard time I had this morning to keep her from going out milking."

"Ah, sure, there isn't a thing wrong with me." Mary pushed the shawl back off her shoulders and got to her feet. "You'll have the usual, I suppose?"

"Ah, no, now, you just sit there and rest yourself."

"*I'll* make the tea," Rita said firmly. And she did. Then she left them, saying she had a few things to do at home and she'd look in later on.

"Come back and have a peek at her," Mary said. The priest had just drained his second cup.

"She's the image of yourself." Father Mulroe beamed at the little round face in the crib.

"That's what everyone says."

"Maybe a trace of the father?"

Mary closed the door quietly and returned to her place by the fire. "It would have to be a red-haired man with rosy cheeks, now, wouldn't it?"

"Seriously." The priest sat across from her, leaning forward, elbows on knees. "Some people's reputations are in jeopardy, Mary. Maybe it's time now to say who it is."

"And destroy entirely one person's good name! I couldn't do that."

"So there won't be a father's name on the baptismal certificate?"

"The question is, will there be a baptism?" She was looking straight at him, the old defiance still there.

"Ah, now, Mary, we must baptize the little creature. You wouldn't want her winding up in Limbo if, the Lord between us and all harm, anything were to happen to her?"

"Limbo! Another invention of medieval theologians."

"God bless us! Mary McGreevy, what am I going to do with you at all?"

She smiled then. "Musha, I'd do anything to keep you happy, Father. We'll do it as soon as I'm fit to go out."

Father Mulroe sat back and crossed his legs. "As you know, it's not customary for the mother to attend the christening, so we won't need to wait. Just pick out the godparents and we'll do it straightaway."

"*This* mother will attend her daughter's christening, I can tell you." Her smile disappearing like the moon behind a cloud.

"All the same, now, we wouldn't want to delay the sacrament, would we?" He pushed on. "Just in case . . . And then there's the matter of yourself, of course." He folded his arms. "The new mother has to be churched, as you know, before she takes part again in liturgical ceremonies."

Her brow grew dark then as a sky lowering rain. "There will be no churching this woman," said Mary McGreevy.

"Ah, sure, what's the harm in it? It's the custom. People will be expecting it."

"Churching is a ritual of purification. As if the act of giving birth made a woman unclean. Well, I don't feel unclean, and I'm not going to be churched."

It was Father Mulroe's turn to look grim. The mouth clamped shut and the jaw muscles bulged. For a full minute he stared silently into the fire. Then his shoulders relaxed and the arms uncrossed and he smiled tight-lipped at Mary McGreevy. "Right, then," he said mildly. "We'll have the baptism as soon as you're ready."

PART THREE

17

There was much speculation by the gossips of Kildawree about who would be godfather to Mary McGreevy's child. And opinions were divided as to how the choice should be interpreted. One party held that whoever was selected could definitely be eliminated as the culprit—it wouldn't be right for the father to be the godfather as well, now, would it? But another point of view insisted that on the contrary, who was *that wan*—who for God's sake had already thumbed her nose at everything else that was decent and Christian in the parish—more likely to pick as godfather to her little bastard than the very blackguard himself that sired it? It would be her way of acknowledging the hoor without actually naming him. Fierce verbal battles were fought on the subject for several nights at Queally's pub. And on the evening of the baptism, after the Feericks brought the McGreevy one herself—in defiance of all tradition, mind you—and her baby back to the church, and Mrs. Tarragh held the infant during the ceremony, and the mother pronounced that the child was henceforth to be called Bridget Patricia, and Mr. Tarragh stood on the other side of Father Mulroe while he poured the cleansing waters over the young neophyte's head, the debate at Queally's intensified. The result, however, was a standoff, and the following night the subject was dropped entirely in favor of an argument over the composition of the Kildawree team that had won the O'Hara Cup in 1946.

But, given the penchant of Queally's patrons for flogging a dead horse, the subject of the McGreevy child's paternity inevitably had to be resurrected. That it arose sooner rather than later was due to a remarkable story brought in two nights after the christening by Paddy Carney. Paddy, with only a single pint inside him, on his solemn oath declared to those duly assembled and drinking that his own wife had been told the gospel truth on the matter that very day by her neighbor down the boreen, who got it in person from the midwife who attended the birth. And what was this gospel truth? ten pairs of eyes asked Paddy Carney, though not a man present so much as opened his gob. It was that Mr. Thomas Tarragh himself, said Paddy after taking a long, deep slug on his second pint, was the father of Mary McGreevy's child.

That revelation brought on a general thirst that had Dan Queally and his new curate pulling pints for the next ten minutes. *Well, doesn't that beat the band, now. Mind you, I always suspected as much myself. They say it wouldn't be the first time for our Tom either.* The comments flowed as fast as the Guinness. Adverse judgments were not pronounced, however—Mr. Tarragh was not only respected as principal teacher of Kildawree National School, he was also liked by the men of Queally's for his common touch. Before his unfortunate second marriage, wasn't he almost one of themselves? A man who could raise an elbow to beat the best. Not that they condoned what was done, mind you. Not at all! Not at all! But sure, it was only a private sin. Nobody got hurt. And Tom was a decent sort, the poor devil, regardless of present temporary disgrace.

Unfortunately, his wife, Kitty, did not receive the news with the same equanimity. It was days after Paddy Carney's announcement before she heard a thing, for who in their right mind would risk the venom of that spitfire by telling her? In the end it was Bridie May who passed along the information. Kitty, increasingly annoyed with God over the loss of her father, stopped in to the priest's house on the afternoon of the Sunday before Christmas to give His representative a piece of her mind.

"He's saying his breviary." Bridie May answered the door. "Is it something urgent?"

"No, no indeed. I'll come back again. I wanted to tell him off about something he said in his sermon this morning." Kitty managed a smile for the priest's housekeeper.

"Is that all that's on *your* mind?"

"Well, I think it's quite important to let Father Mulroe know that—"

"Has anyone let *you* know what they're saying about your husband?" Bridie May herself had a terribly sharp tongue at times.

"I'm tired of . . ." But there was a look in Bridie May's eye that stopped Kitty. "What are they saying now? If it's more of the same I don't want to hear it."

"They're saying this," said Bridie May. And she stepped out the door and pulled it closed after her and folded her arms and looked Kitty squarely in the face and told her the version she herself had heard of what Paddy Carney had told the patrons of Queally's earlier in the week.

"I don't believe it," Kitty whispered. But she did. And she turned and walked back to her house without another word. Tom was gone to Ballinamore to visit Canon Gilroy—they had become friends over their mutual interest in local history. She sat in the parlor and stared into the fire. Feeling perfectly calm. And completely numb. Like a general after a lost battle, was the thought that came into her mind. She had done her best—attacked and routed the possibility head on, outflanked the rumors, found a plausible alternative. But she had been defeated anyway. The forces of truth and evil had prevailed in the end. So be it. The fire died slowly before her unseeing gaze. Then she slept.

She woke shivering when Tom walked into the room. "It's chilly in here," he said. "You let the fire die out. Come on into the kitchen. I made the tea." She followed him in. Sat in her place at the table. A long sip of scalding tea revived her a bit. She looked across at him. His mouth was smiling, but there was concern in his eyes. "You must have been tired," he said.

She glared back at him. He had visited Mary the evening before the wedding. Could that have been when . . . ? "Have you heard the latest?" As cold as the east wind that was blowing outside.

"The latest what?" He was buttering a piece of bread.

"About yourself being the little bastard's father, that's what!" She fairly spat the words at him.

"You mean our godchild?" He looked up, weary humor in his eyes, biting into his bread. "I'm flattered, of course. Unfortunately, it's not true."

"It is so true!" She was yelling now. "And what's more, the whole parish knows it's true."

He closed his eyes as if in prayer, chewing slowly. "And how did you all reach this wonderful conclusion?"

She clutched the table with both hands to keep from leaping across and hitting him. How dared he be so calm! "Because Mary herself told Mrs. Dolan, the midwife. That's how! So what do you have to say for yourself now? Huh! Huh!" The top of her head was about to come right off.

"I say it's not true." He finished chewing, took a long, slow sip of tea, put down the cup, and leaned forward. "Listen, Kitty," he said gently, patiently, "whatever you heard is nothing but a malicious joke. Someone trying to get a rise out of you. Or me. It's typical of what these people think is funny. Don't pay any attention to them."

"It's no joke," she screamed. "You went to see her the night before we got married!"

He stopped dead in the middle of cutting a piece of bread. "This has gone far enough." The beginnings of anger in his tone.

Well! She'd show him what anger could be. "I know exactly what you're up to."

"Then for God's sake, tell me. Because I certainly don't know what you're talking about." The temper rising in him as if he were all innocence itself.

"It's her you want, isn't it? Her you always wanted, not me!" The tears were close, but she wasn't going to let him see her cry. "Well, you can't have her, do you hear?" Then she ran from the kitchen up the stairs. Threw herself on the bed, hands covering her ears to block out the terrible screaming inside her head.

He was up after her immediately. "We have to talk, Kitty," he said.

214

Calm now, another voice intruded. She could strangle him this minute for what he had done, but she was going to need him. "Go ahead," she said bleakly, without looking at him. "Talk!"

He sat beside her. "I am not the father of Mary McGreevy's baby." In his most formal tone. "But I do want to be the father of yours." He put a hand on her shoulder. "This is fierce important to me, Kitty."

She wanted to get up and run. From that vision of *her*, spread-legged and bloody in the bed of birth. Whatever the chance of her weakening before, after that sight there was none. "I can't," she said. "I just can't." She wanted to scream, No, a million times no, but she spoke quietly, civilly, as if declining an éclair at a posh afternoon tea.

"Please! Just the one. I won't ask for another." As if he were that child himself begging an éclair.

She sat up. "I can't do it, Tom! How many times do I have to say that?"

He said nothing for a bit, but his breathing was deep and audible. "I need a child," he said eventually. She could feel the restraint in him swelling his body.

"Well, I can't do anything about that," she snapped. And then it came out, even though she had promised herself to say no more on the subject. "Anyway, hasn't *she* already given you one?"

He sat there silently till she was ready to scream. Then, when her endurance was exhausted, he stood and looked down at her. "In that case," he said mildly, "I will ask Father Mulroe to start annulment proceedings." And shut the door softly behind him. His footsteps were muffled on the carpeted stairs.

She waited till he closed the parlor door. Softly down the stairs then. Her fur coat hung on the hall stand, the keys on the table next to it. She saw his head by the pulled-back curtain as she rolled the car down the driveway.

Father Mulroe was sitting by the fire reading a novel when the schoolmaster knocked. "Come in, Tom," he said. Bridie May had gone to bed early. He got the whiskey out for Tom and a mineral for himself and they sipped in silence for a while. "Is everything all right?" Tom was looking a bit down in the mouth, staring into the fire.

"Could be better." But he didn't elaborate.

The priest put his glass on the mantelpiece. "I heard today," he said, stirring the fire with the poker, "that the bishops are thinking of coming out strong against the Mother and Child Scheme."

"I want an annulment," Tom said.

Father John Patrick stood the poker against the tiled facing and retrieved his glass. "I was afraid it might come to that."

"Will I be able to get it?" The schoolmaster's head was bent, examining the fire as if it held the secret to his future.

Father Mulroe sipped his lemonade. "It won't be easy, I might as well tell you. The Sacred Congregation would prefer to part with gold bars than with annulment parchments." It would be a lot easier if he himself could divulge what Kitty had told him in confession. But he couldn't do that, of course.

"What do I have to do?" In the dull monotone of a condemned man inquiring about gallows etiquette.

"To be honest, Tom, I'm not quite sure. It's not something a parish priest does very often. But I'll find out, of course. I believe you'll have to write a letter to His Grace, and then he'll send for you and Kitty to appear before a diocesan tribunal, and they'll examine the case, and if they're satisfied they'll send a petition to the Sacred Congregation in Rome. Something of that sort."

"Will it take long?" A trace of desperation in the schoolmaster's voice.

"Very likely a good while. Those lads in Rome are never in a hurry with anything. Except when it comes to condemning something or someone. They're good at that."

"Is there any way to speed it up at all, do you think? A bit of influence in the hierarchy, maybe?" Tom smiled wanly at his glass. "I have a cousin who is married to the nephew of a bishop out in Indochina. I don't suppose that would help?"

"I wouldn't think it would give you much favor with His Grace." Father Mulroe smiled bleakly. "Though it might help a bit in Rome if he knows someone in the right place. But your first step will be to convince the archbishop. He doesn't like annulments or dispensations of any kind, they tell me. So the important thing is that you have a proper case to present to him."

For the first time since he came in, Tom looked the priest in the face. "I'll need your help with that, Father."

"To be sure. To be sure. Whenever you're ready to start, let me know."

"I'd like to start now." He was staring at the fire again. "There's no point in delaying, is there?"

Father Mulroe could feel the butterflies begin to churn his insides. He hated having to deal with His Grace or the diocesan chancery; they made him feel like a first-year seminarian again. "Well, now, you know what an annulment means, I'm sure, and I won't insult you by telling you. But all the same, it would be just as good if we went over the details carefully, since the lads in the diocesan tribunal will give you the works when you appear before them."

For the next two hours or more they discussed and argued and agreed and speculated, and Tom drank more whiskey than he should. In the morning after mass, Father Mulroe decided to visit Kitty. "You won't have a leg to stand on unless she goes along with it," he had told Tom, and they agreed that it would be best if the parish priest were to act as the husband's emissary in this matter.

On the way to Curnacarton he stopped in to see Mary McGreevy. It was a fine, crisp, frosty morning, and she was feeding the chickens in the back yard. "God bless the work," he said.

"You too, Father." She threw a handful of grain at the cackling fowl, then scattered the remainder from her basin with a two-handed swish. "To what do we owe the pleasure so early in the day?"

"Oh, I just dropped in to see how our new Christian is doing."

"Bridget Patricia is doing very well, thank God. If she'd only learn that night is the time for sleep."

"And the mother? She's doing well too?"

"Ah, sure, not a brack on her. At least I'm able to feed the chickens and make the tea. Speaking of which, I suppose you'd like—"

"Ah, no! No, thanks. I was just passing by and thought I'd say hello."

"Well, come in for a minute out of the cold anyway." She led the way into the house and went straight to the cradle by the wall near the fireplace.

"There was one thing I thought I should mention," he said to her back. And he coughed to clear his throat.

She bent over and made a face at the infant. "Are you awake, *a leanbh?* Your parish priest has something to say to you." She turned her head and smiled at Father John Patrick.

"It's a serious matter," he said. "There is a story going around the parish about you telling Mrs. Dolan, the midwife, that Tom Tarragh was the little one's father."

That straightened her up in an instant. "I did no such thing." Incredulity in her face. "I don't believe . . ." Changing to exasperation. "Who could . . . ?" And then the anger rising, reddening the cheeks. "People are such bald-faced liars! I—"

"I take it you didn't say it?"

"I certainly did not!" And he had to believe her. Whatever her faults, a liar the woman was not. Too truthful, maybe, for her own good at times. But not a liar, no.

"I'll be going, then. I'll tell Kitty what you said when I see her." Going out the door, he could not resist saying, "Too bad I can't tell her who the father really is."

But with the mood Kitty was in, it probably wouldn't have helped.

18

Father Mulroe had admonished his parishioners in advance from the pulpit—"Don't put off your Christmas confession till the last minute. For God's sake and for mine, come the Saturday before if you possibly can." But it didn't make a bit of difference. On Christmas Eve when he came into the church at seven o'clock in the evening—an hour earlier than usual—the queue was already four seats deep on the women's side and nearly three on the men's. And these were just the regulars. The stragglers—the hard cases, the fellows who came only twice a year—would be drifting in at nine, pushed out the door at the last minute by the missus and half hoping they'd be too late already.

He arranged the cushion on his seat and closed the door to the box. It was going to be a long night. He slid back the grill on the women's side, bent his head to the opening, and leaned his shoulder against the wall of the box. A woman's voice whispered urgently, "Bless me, Father . . ."

God forgive him, but confession was his least favorite function in the priestly ministry. It was without doubt God's magnanimous sacrament of mercy, the fountain of reconciliation between man and his Creator, the stream of divine grace to cleanse sinners' souls and heal their bruised spirits; so what service to the Lord or his flock could be more rewarding for a priest? Nevertheless, he, John Patrick Mulroe, endowed by priestly ordination with this supernatural power to forgive, found the task endlessly boring. You heard over and over again the same banal tales of wrongdoing. And trivial wrongdoing at that, for the most part—lies, petty dishonesty, weakness of the flesh, gossip, abuse of others. Sometimes he almost wished for a horror story of magnificent evil. Or at least some complex circumvention of divine or ecclesiastical law that would challenge his theological and canonical learning.

"I had bad thoughts three times," a woman was whispering. "And I told a lie once to my husband."

"For your penance, say three Our Fathers and three Hail Marys. A good Act of Contrition. *Dominus Noster Jesus Christus te absolvat . . .*" He closed the grill and glanced at his watch in the thin sliver of light that slipped in between curtain and box. Twenty minutes to nine and the queue out there still as long as when he started. He switched to the men's side and waited, stifling a yawn.

"Bless me, Father . . ." Not a familiar whisper, this one. Must be one of those twice-a-year lads. It was worse—"It's a year since my last confession, Father." Keep an ear open, now; there was always the chance of real blackguardism from the fellows who stayed away that long. "Had a drink too many . . . lies . . . indecent talk . . . I committed sin with a girl on three occasions. I didn't do my Easter duty this year." And silence after that.

A little bit of probing was indicated. "Did you engage in carnal intercourse with this person?"

"Yes, Father."

Since the man was a year away from confession, the next question was necessary too. "Were there any consequences to the act?" It was fellows like this that caused young girls to go traipsing off to England to have their illegitimate babies.

"Yes, Father." The whisper was strained and tense.

Good God! "There was a baby?"

"Yes, Father."

"And the mother had to go to England, I suppose?" He shouldn't have said that, but it angered his priestly soul that these louts would be taking advantage of foolish girls and ruining their lives.

"No, Father. She stayed at home."

A terrible suspicion formed in Father Mulroe's mind. "Has the baby been baptized?"

"Oh, yes, Father. You christened her yourself."

It was *him!* Without a doubt in the world. "I suppose you're the father of Mary McGreevy's baby?" It slipped out of him, as unstoppable as the west wind, though he ought not to be asking it since it had nothing to do with the man's sins. Or had it, now? Of course it had! Wasn't poor Tom Tarragh looking for an annulment of his marriage this very minute because the lad across the grill hadn't publicly owned up to his sin?

"I am, Father."

Mother of God! What was he to say to the blackguard at all? On the one side, of course, was the seal of confession. But on the other . . . "You'll need to make a public admission of that fact, then."

"Oh, God, no, Father, I couldn't do that." A terrible vehemence in the man's whisper.

"Why not?" Stalling for time till he could determine the correct theological and moral course of action.

"I just couldn't, Father! I couldn't. It would destroy my good name entirely on me."

"You should have thought of that beforehand!" Steady, now. He was letting his bile get the better of him. "Anyway, what about this child? And its mother? Don't you owe it to them to acknowledge you're the father?"

"Ah, no. Sure, the girl herself doesn't want it known, Father."

Without doubt that was true. But he tried another tack anyway. "There's a man's good name being ruined in this parish because people think he's the father. You owe it to that man to tell the truth."

"I'm sorry about him, Father, but sure, there isn't anything I can do about the lies that people go on with."

What more could a priest say? A public confession was not required for the penitent to receive absolution. Father Mulroe settled for a short, fierce admonition that nothing like this was ever to happen again, do you hear? With a rosary every day for a week as his penance. And then absolution for the sin that had caused more gossip in the parish of Kildawree than he had previously heard in his entire twenty-two years as a priest.

He barely restrained himself from peering through the curtain to identify the fellow leaving the box. It was better not to know.

After last mass on Christmas day he raced back to the house and changed out of the soutane into his black suit. He was hurrying out the front door on the way to the car when he spotted Mick Burke walking briskly up the driveway. "Hello, Mick." He waved without breaking his stride. "I didn't know you were home."

"Just back for the Christmas." Mick looked prosperous in a tweed jacket, gray trousers, and a peaked cap. He continued his pace as if racing the priest to the car. "Could I have a word with you, Father?"

"Certainly, Mick. Certainly." The man was blocking the car door on him. "But it's not the best time in the world right now. I'm on my way back to the ma's to carve the goose for her, and I'm already a bit late."

"It won't take a minute, Father," said Mick. With a look on his face that said he'd die on the spot if he couldn't have that minute.

"Could we talk tomorrow?"

"The way it is, Father, I have to leave first thing in the morning."

Cripes! The ma would be in a terrible state waiting for him. Eighty-two last birthday, hardly able to walk from the arthritis, she'd have been sitting by the fire watching the clock on the dresser ever since she hobbled home from first mass. "We'll be expecting you at one o'clock," she had said in her last scrawled letter. It was almost one now, and it would take an hour in the car to get home. But what could he do? "All right," he said. "What is it?"

"It's about Mary McGreevy, Father." Mick took his cap off, tucked it under his arm, and ran his fingers through his hair.

"Indeed," said Father Mulroe.

"I want to marry her." Mick licked his lips and stared at the ground.

Something that had been sputtering in the priest's brain suddenly sparked. This could be the voice he had heard in the confession box. "You do? Well, is that a fact? Well, well! Does Mary herself know about this, or is it a sudden decision on your part?"

"Ah, no, not at all, Father. I've been asking her for the past year. But she won't have me. That's why I went to England."

It *could* be him. "So why are you telling me about it?"

"Well, Father, I was hoping maybe you'd put in a word for me. They say you're good friends with her."

The fellow in the confession box had had that same kind of slightly hoarse voice. "I will indeed, Mick. I can't promise you anything, of course. Women have minds of their own on these things, as I'm sure you know."

"But you'll tell her I'm a man with a good character and that I'd make her a great husband? You'll tell her that, won't you, Father?"

"I will indeed."

"And tell her I'll write to her from England."

"I will, Mick. I must be—"

"And that I'll be back again in a couple of months with a lot of money in my pocket. And then we'll do some serious talking about getting married."

"Right you be, Mick. I have to go now."

On Saint Stephen's Day he drove back to Kilduff in the afternoon. Mary, the baby in her arms and half her left breast exposed, fled to the bedroom without a word the second he put his head in the door. From inside she shouted, "I'll be out in a minute, Father!"

"There's no hurry at all." He settled himself in a chair by the fire, just a little bit flustered by what he had seen.

"Make yourself at home," she shouted a bit later.

"I will." He crossed his legs.

"There's some tea in the pot. Get a cup from the dresser and help yourself."

"Right so." He poured himself a cup. It looked strong. He glanced around, wondering where to get the milk and sugar.

"The sugar is on the top shelf, and if you'll open the door on the bottom you'll find a jug of milk." You'd think she was watching him, although the bedroom door was closed. She came out about ten minutes later, all composed and without the baby. Motherhood was agreeing with her if you could judge by the color in her cheeks and the sparkle in her eyes. "She's sleeping now," she said. "That's all she does, eat and sleep." She went over to the cupboard near the back door and pulled out part of a Christmas cake with white icing and a sprig of holly on the top. "Rita made this for me." She held it up for his inspection. "The children were down this morning and they ate the half of it." She eyed him with that humorous look of hers, as if he were one of the children himself. "I don't suppose you'd like a piece?"

"I wouldn't mind a bit, thank you very much." She took a plate from the dresser, put the cake on the table, and cut him a thick wedge. He tasted it. "I love the almond icing," he said appreciatively. "Did you know Mick Burke was home for the Christmas?"

She flopped into the chair on the other side of the fire. "Was he indeed? And how is poor old Mick doing at all?"

"Not too good, mind you, now. Though he's looking prosperous. He tells me he wants to marry a certain lady, but she won't have him." He broke off another piece of cake and put it into his mouth. Great taste altogether. He should visit the Feericks more often. God forgive him for such a gluttonous thought.

"Poor Mick," said Mary fervently. "I wish he could find himself a suitable girl."

"'Tis you're the suitable girl he's looking for, according to himself."

"So he has told me, more than once."

"He asked me to be sure to tell you he's a man of good character."

"So what would he want with the likes of me, then?" The teasing smile rippled his priestly innards.

"Maybe he just wants to marry the mother of his child?"

Dead silence for a minute after that. Then, "Aren't you the cute one, Father Mulroe?" She was looking into the fire. "You led me right up to that, didn't you?"

"I did," he admitted. "And for a very good reason."

"I thought we had been over all this before, Father."

"Mary! Listen to me." The priest put the plate on his lap, covered his face with his hands, and sat motionless for a while. "I'm going to tell you something in the strictest confidence," he said eventually. "It must never go past your lips."

"I think you know by now, Father, that I'm fairly good at keeping my mouth shut."

"Tom Tarragh is petitioning to have his marriage annulled. It's a long, sad story, but it came about in the end because Kitty believes that Tom is the father of your child."

"After all Kitty told me, I'm not surprised about the annulment."

He remembered what she had said back in the potato field months ago about Kitty having no intention of being a mother. That time he hadn't wanted to hear about it. But he should have listened and talked to Kitty on the spot; it was his priestly duty. He had a bad habit of avoiding the unpleasant. "Maybe it won't happen if you were to tell Kitty that Tom is not the father." This time he was going to face his responsibility.

She poked the fire with the tongs, then grabbed two sods from the hob and threw them on it. Sparks flew up the chimney. White flames licked the new turf. "Father, I have a dilemma here. For myself, I don't care anymore who knows. I honest to God don't. But I made that man a solemn promise that I would never, ever reveal his name to anyone in the entire world. And I have kept that promise. And I must continue to keep it. I have—"

She was interrupted by a very loud knocking on the back door. "Come in," she shouted. The door shot open. In spilled half a dozen short figures who immediately joined hands and started dancing around the floor. Their faces were masked in sacks, with holes cut out for eyes. Ragged clothes and straw bands about their waists gave an appearance of moving scarecrows. The tallest of them squeezed a concertina in and out to the tune of "The Irish Washerwoman" while the rest cavorted wildly, narrowly missing the dresser and falling over each other several times. A lot of giggling came from inside the masks. Eventually they stopped and delivered a decent rendition of "The Croppy Boy," high and low voices blending tunefully. When they finished Mary clapped loudly. "Aren't you all great entirely." She went over to the dresser and took some pennies off a shelf and held them out to the nearest ragamuffin.

"Oh, no, thanks, Aunt Mary," a girlish voice said. "No! Not at all!" And the whole threadbare crew raced out the door as fast as they had come in.

"The Feerick children," Mary explained. "They're the first mummers I've had all day."

"There'll be more," the priest said. "I passed several groups coming over the road. Now, back to what we were saying . . ." But before he could get the conversation cranked up again, another group of mummers arrived. These lads had a melodeon and they danced a four-hand reel as if they had rehearsed it well. One of them, a nipper with a very sweet voice, sang "Who Fears to Speak of Ninety-eight" with great verve. "You're a great singer indeed," the priest told the lad and gave him a tanner for himself in addition to the pennies Mary gave each of them. Which act of generosity elicited no end of giggling as each mummer individually said, "Thank you very much, Miss McGreevy and Father Mulroe."

"Now, what were we talking about?" was all Mary had time to say before there was another knock, this time at the front door. "Come on in," she shouted, and a fellow the parish priest vaguely recognized God-blessed and stepped into the kitchen. Mary was on her feet in an instant. "Kevin Kelly! What are *you* doing here!" And she hurrying across the floor to shake his hand.

"How in the world are you, Mary?" The fellow looked excited too. The priest was wondering where he had seen him before.

"Father, I'd like you to meet an old friend of mine, Kevin Kelly." Mary's face the color of beetroot behind the smile. "Kevin, this is Father Mulroe, my parish priest and the nicest man you could meet anywhere."

"Didn't I meet you before, Father! At a wedding I was at earlier in the year." Kelly's hand was as soft as his own; he wasn't a farmer, anyway.

"The Tarraghs, I suppose?"

"Sure! My missus was great friends with old Henry Malone, the Lord have mercy on him."

"Pull up a chair to the fire, Kevin." Mary still flushed in the cheeks.

226

"You're not from Kildawree?" Father Mulroe thought he knew all his parishioners by now.

"Kevin has a draper's shop in Ballinamore," Mary explained.

Kelly took a chair from the kitchen table and placed it in front of the fire between the two of them. "Mary and myself were going to school in Ballinamore at the same time," he said. "That was how we met."

"He had a terrible crush on me," she said, mischievously, it seemed to the priest. She was watching Kelly, one eyebrow raised and half a smile on her cherry lips. "Only I left him to go into the convent. And then he went and married a draper's shop." She made a face and laughed deliciously, causing the butterflies to flutter again inside Father Mulroe. Kelly laughed too, but there was no joy in it for him, you could see that.

"I went to the Brothers myself," the priest said. "In Westport. A ten-mile ride on the bike each way. We were hardy lads in those days."

"We were indeed," Kelly agreed.

"Well, do you hear him?" Mary guffawed. "How would you know? You were a townie. You only had to walk two streets to school."

"And run like hell—excuse the French, Father—to get around to the convent gates before you got out."

The banter was making the priest feel just a bit uncomfortable; she was making free with this fellow in a way she never did with himself. And God forgive him for it, but he was resenting that. "I suppose it's time for me to be going." He hitched up his trouser legs in anticipation of rising.

"Arrah, not at all! Not at all! Why would you, Father? Sure, what's your hurry? I'm going to make the tea now in a few minutes, and you'll stay for that. Rashers and eggs and black pudding. And there'll be more Christmas cake too." She gave him such a roguish look that what could the poor man do except allow that he would stay? The baby cried just then, and she jumped up, raced across the floor, and vanished into the bedroom.

"I came out to see the babby," Kelly, standing, shouted in at her.

"And I thought you came to see me," she yelled back over the wailing of the child.

"Ah, sure, it's tired of looking at you I am." Such repartee seemed to the priest a bit unseemly for a married man.

"Well, you'll have to wait now till her ladyship is fed before you can see her." Suddenly the crying ceased and Father Mulroe had to make a terrible effort not to imagine white breasts being exposed to the suckling infant.

"She's a grand girl." Kelly lowered his voice, speaking into the fire.

"She is indeed." Could this possibly be the voice he had heard in the confessional on Christmas Eve?

"I love babbies, Father. That's a fact. Some of the lads tell me they can't stand the crying and them waking you up in the middle of the night, but it never bothered me a bit."

"So you have children yourself?" He had been so flustered in the confessional he had forgotten to ask the fellow if it was adultery or fornication he had committed.

"Six of them, Father. I'd have more, but herself says that's enough."

There was silence in the kitchen for a bit. And no sound at all from the bedroom. "I suppose you come out to see her often," the priest murmured. As if talking to himself.

"Ah, now and again. For old time's sake, you know."

The conversation lapsed once more. It might indeed be him. And then again, it mightn't. It was hard to compare a remembered whisper from the confession box with the present voice of a man speaking out loud. Anyway, what good would it do to know?

"Would you like me to put the kettle on?" Kelly shouted at the bedroom door.

"Do that, please, Kevin. Good lad, yourself." The fellow took the kettle off the hob, filled it from a bucket just inside the back door, and hung it from the crane over the fire.

"She needs a range," he said to Father Mulroe, rubbing soot from the kettle off his hands.

"Sorra range indeed, Kevin," came immediately from the bedroom. "I prefer the open fire."

"Isn't she one of a kind?" Kelly whispered, the admiration glowing in his face. Then his expression changed suddenly and he eyed the bedroom door through what looked awfully like tears. "Sorry, Father, and God forgive me for it, but I wish she never went into the convent in the first place. I'd have been a happier man today, so I would."

"What's done is done," the priest said gruffly. He could never stand people whingeing about the past. You took whatever it was God sent you and you made the best of it, and that was that. But before he had time to say more on the subject the bedroom door opened and Mary came out carrying the baby.

"Well, isn't she a grand little girl!" Kelly was on his feet, his head almost touching the mother's bosom and his nose barely an inch from the baby's turned-up button; it was a wonder the tiny creature didn't burst out crying.

"You can mind her now while I'm getting the tea." Mary handed him her precious bundle. "And you can ga-ga away at her to your heart's content." She winked at the priest.

Kelly retreated to his chair by the fire and stared and grinned and made faces at the baby. A bit later when she got restless he waltzed around the kitchen with her, crooning softly a lovely lullaby, *"Caislean Drum an Oir."* He even insisted on holding her during the tea, managing to eat quite well himself with just the one free hand. He was still making ridiculous clucking noises at her an hour later when Father Mulroe said good-bye and went home.

19

The mummer with the sweet voice did more than sing patriotic songs on Saint Stephen's Day. He went home that night, his pockets jingling with pennies and Father Mulroe's tanner, and told his mother about finding the parish priest visiting with *that one*. It was the clinching proof as far as Maureen Garvey was concerned. She had spent months speculating and theorizing and gathering information. Her suspicions as to who the father of the McGreevy bastard might be had rested on no less than seven men at one time or another. However, by degrees she had eliminated all but one of them for good and sufficient reasons. And for some time now the parish priest had been her only suspect. So her son's report that night merely confirmed her own intuitive certainty.

She wasn't alone in pointing the guilty finger at Father Mulroe. No fewer than three of her cronies from different corners of the parish had come to the same conclusion. Independently of one another, they maintained, although the length, intensity, and frequency of their discussions together on the subject might have led an impartial observer to entertain at least the possibility of a degree of mutual influence. Be that as it may, a few days after Saint Stephen's, when the four women met again in the Garvey kitchen, all that remained to be discussed was the proper course of action to be taken now that certainty had been attained.

"It's a terrible disgrace to the parish," said Crony One. Well advanced in years, the same woman, and her wrinkled face pinched with the cold. She kept on her black coat and black hat.

"But 'tis mostly the McGreevy one's fault, if you ask me," Crony Two observed. "A holy man the like of Father Mulroe wouldn't do that kind of thing without a lot of provocation, I'd say." She was known to be a very pious woman herself.

"Hmph!" Maureen Garvey snorted. "You haven't been watching this priest the way I have for the past two years." She stood and wiped her hands on her apron before going over to the fireplace to get the teapot. "That man has a wicked eye for the ladies, let me tell you. I've seen him looking at ankles on more than one occasion. And he always stares you right in the eye. Sure, old Father Moran, the Lord have mercy on him, would never so much as glance at a woman's face. Priests are not supposed to, you know! I was told that once by a missioner."

"Well, is that a fact, now?" Crony Three was a pleasingly plump woman of middle years with rosy cheeks and long black hair tied up in a bun. In her younger days many's the lad in Kildawree had panted after her before she married the biggest *amadhan* this side of Castlebar. "He certainly looks at *me* every time I meet him. Although, mind you, the ankles are not what they used to be, I'm afraid." She laughed and stretched out a chubby leg to prove her point.

"His Grace will have to be informed, then," Maureen pronounced in the middle of filling Crony Two's teacup.

"Faith, that's for sure," Crony One agreed instantly.

"Saint Joseph protect us!" ejaculated Crony Two. "But can we be absolutely sure he is the one? It would be a terrible thing to accuse a person falsely, you know." She sipped her tea in great agitation.

"Oh, bad cess to you, Breeda," scorned Crony One. "You're always afraid of your shadow, you are. To be sure we're sure. Why wouldn't we be sure? Isn't there a babby to prove it?"

"And how is His Grace going to find out?" Crony Three asked.

Maureen Garvey replaced the teapot on the stove. She wiped her hands again on her apron. "I've given some thought to that, ladies. This is what we'll do, now. . . ."

His Grace the Most Reverend Dr. Joseph Quinlan, D.D., archbishop of Tulach, looked every inch the prelate that he was. When he'd come to Kildawree, which he did every three years for the confirmation, and walk up the aisle wearing his ecclesiastical robes and the mitre on his head, and he swinging his wicked-looking crozier, you might be inclined to think it was God the Father Himself who had appeared in the parish church. Or at the very least Saint Patrick. "He has a dignity that makes you proud to be one of his flock," a sanctimonious old cod said above in Queally's after the archbishop's last pastoral visit three years ago. A sentiment that nonetheless brought a blasphemous retort from a fellow drinker who had been privy to another side of His Grace's character. This latter patron had had the naivety to confess a certain matter to Father Moran one Christmas. "You did what?" the old priest shouted in a voice the entire queue of waiting sinners could and did hear. He himself was quite deaf.

"Poteen, Father," the lad whispered again. "I made a drop of poteen. They tell me it's a sin, Father?"

"Sin!" Father Moran shouted. "It's not just a sin, my boy. It's a re-served sin! You'll have to go to the archbishop himself to get absolution from that." And over to Tulach the poor man had to go. Two hours on the bicycle. And knock on the archbishop's door. And wait in the cathedral for another four hours till the great man appeared and took his place in the archiepiscopal confession box. And get a fierce lecture on the evils of drink from His Grace. And wind up with the stations of the cross every night for a week as his penance.

If the lads from Queally's had been able to look into the archbishop's study late on a Monday morning in the middle of January 1952, they would have been privy to yet a third side of His Grace's character. He had just been reading the day's mail, brought to him on a tray a little while ago by his housekeeper. There was a letter from his sister asking him to come down to Limerick and bless his niece's new house. And a tardy

Christmas card from an old Maynooth classmate who was now a monsignor in Mobile, Alabama, U.S.A. But it was the four letters from the parish of Kildawree that inspired the thunderous frown on his episcopal visage. He sat there for a long time, clutching them fiercely in his right hand and staring across his shiny mahogany desk into the licking flames of the turf fire. Eventually he shook himself like a stallion after rolling in the summer grass and went to the door of his study. "Mrs. O'Connor!" he bellowed.

The housekeeper came running down the hall. "Yes, Your Grace!"

"Find Father Tuohy and tell him I want to see him at once."

"Yes, Your Grace." A minute later Father Tuohy arrived, out of breath and patting down his soutane to make sure everything was in place.

"I want to see Father Mulroe from Kildawree parish, and I want to see him today."

"Yes, Your Grace." Within another minute Father Tuohy was on the telephone trying to get a connection to Kildawree. But it was early afternoon before the Tulach operator rang him back and said, "I have Kildawree on the line now, Father." The postmistress in Kildawree said, "Certainly, Father, I'll run over and get Father Mulroe for you." But eons later when she returned it was to say that unfortunately Father Mulroe was out and wouldn't be back until later in the afternoon. Father Tuohy was in the process of instructing her to have Father Mulroe telephone the archbishop's palace the minute he returned when he was interrupted by His Grace himself passing by in the hallway.

"Did you contact Father Mulroe?" The lowering archiepiscopal brow was terrifying to Father Tuohy, a young man only a couple of years out of the seminary.

"They said he's out for the afternoon, Your Grace."

"I want to know where he is. And I want to know who he's with." And His Grace moved regally on.

"Can you find out where he went?" Father Tuohy plaintively asked the postmistress. Half an eon later the good woman returned to say that Father Mulroe was paying a pastoral visit to one of his parishioners. Father Tuohy was about to hang up when he remembered the second half of His Grace's command. "Hello, hello," he shouted in panic into the phone. But the postmistress had already taken her leave. It took another half hour to get reconnected. And more waiting time while Miss Macken went across the road again to the parish priest's house. "His housekeeper says he's with a family by name of McGreevy." There was a nuance in the postmistress's delivery of this information that entirely escaped Father Tuohy. But the mere mention of the parishioner's name produced an ominous "Indeed!" from the archbishop.

"Listen to me now, Father Tuohy. I want you to talk to Father Mulroe's housekeeper yourself on the telephone. And I want you to tell her to go to the house where Father Mulroe is at this very minute and to tell him he is to come here immediately." His Grace breathed heavily. "With no ifs, buts, or ands. Do you understand me?"

Father Tuohy followed instructions to the letter. As indeed did Noreen Macken and Bridie May. Father Mulroe too, even though it meant he had to leave the last piece of Mary McGreevy's Christmas cake untouched on his plate.

What in God's name could the archbishop want to see him about so urgently? The parish priest examined his recent conduct as he passed through the village of Castletown. His conscience was clear—at least regarding anything His Grace might be interested in. Maybe he was about to be offered a bigger parish! There were those priestly colleagues of his who had always said he would go places. A canon, certainly; maybe even a monsignor. Not that he himself was the least bit ambitious. And he would be sorry to leave Kildawree so soon, and he just about settled in.

It was going on five o'clock when he reached Tulach. Mrs. O'Connor said, "Come on in, Father; His Grace has been expecting you all afternoon." He entered the sacred portals with a spring in his step, but the minute he spotted the archbishop's face he knew it wasn't a promotion he was here to receive.

"Come into my study, Father." There was a deep melancholy in the man's voice that had the feel of heavy rain in the offing. Father Mulroe sat in front of the great mahogany desk, just as he had almost two years ago when His Grace had informed him he was to become parish priest of

Kildawree. That had been a proud moment for him. "And how is your parish, Father?"

A much more relaxed tone this time. Maybe everything was all right after all. They had always told him in Maynooth that he was a terrible man for worrying needlessly. "'Tis doing fairly well, now, Your Grace. I have no complaints at all. The Christmas dues were down a little bit, but that was due entirely to the weather, I'd say. The spuds didn't—"

"Do you have a woman in the parish by the name of Mary McGreevy?" His Grace's head was leaning to the left, and there was a quality in the episcopal eyes that caused several butterflies to flitter simultaneously just below Father Mulroe's sternum.

"I do."

"Tell me about her." The archbishop settled back into his big leather armchair.

Father Mulroe cleared his throat. "She used to be a nun, but she left the convent a couple of years ago and came back home when her father died. He left her the place, you see."

"And since she was a nun I suppose you would be good friends with her, Father?" Not an iota of an expression on the man's face.

Come into my parlor, said the spider to the fly, went immediately through Father Mulroe's head. The archbishop was known to be a stickler for correctness when it came to relationships between his priests and the opposite sex. "Not at all, Your Grace," he retorted. "I observe the proprieties with her, as I do with all my female parishioners."

"But you do visit her, of course?"

Ah! Somebody had been talking about himself and Mary McGreevy! The back of his neck was feeling hot, although it was a cold day. "In a pastoral way, yes indeed, Your Grace. I visit all my parishioners from time to time in that way. As of course I should. It is my—"

"I understand you were at her house today when I was looking for you?"

That cold stare was beginning to unnerve him. "I was. The woman has serious spiritual problems, you see." Better to justify his position now without waiting to be asked. "She has fallen away from the sacraments, she has doubts about the faith, and she—"

"And she has an illegitimate child, Father! Isn't that so?"

The room was getting fierce warm. He could feel the sweat under his shirt. "She has, God help us. A sad case indeed. So I've been trying to help her return—"

"And who is the father of this child?" The archbishop leaned forward again, elbows resting on his gleaming desk, eyes boring through Father Mulroe's all the way to the back of his skull.

Where in God's name was this conversation leading to at all? He had not been remiss in regard to the seal—not as much as a hint to anyone about what he was told in confession on the subject. And anyway, he still didn't know who the culprit was. "Now, that's a great puzzle to everyone, Your Grace. The mother refuses to divulge his name, and the father himself has not stepped forward to take responsibility. Unfortunately, as a result, there has been much gossip on the subject. One man in particular has—"

"I have received certain information," said His Grace, "that the father of this illegitimate child is none other than yourself." He leaned back in his chair again. "How do you account for that?"

Father Mulroe had the momentary impression of being rushed ashore on the crest of a giant wave heading straight for the cliffs of Moher. He could no more escape from a false accusation of this sort than he could keep from being dashed against those timeless rocks. Once uttered, the suspicion would always remain, no matter what he replied. He wanted to scream, It's a terrible lie! It's totally and absolutely ridiculous! I have always been faithful to my vow! Anyway, the father has admitted his sin to me in confession! But he said none of these things. "I am not the father of that child, Your Grace. Or of any other child, for that matter." Amazed at the quiet dignity with which he managed to articulate his denial. His calm and candid tone certainly ought to satisfy his accuser.

It didn't. "Then why is the entire parish of Kildawree convinced that you are?" The archbishop pounded the desk with the side of his fist, folded his arms tight across his chest, and lowered those threatening brows of his till they half covered his eyes.

"Indeed, it is no such thing, Your Grace!" Such a lie, and whoever the blackguard was that asserted it could not go unchallenged. "As a matter of fact, a lot of people are convinced, entirely without justification, I must say, that the culprit is the principal teacher of Kildawree National School. The poor man is—"

"Father Mulroe, it saddens me to tell you this. I have received letters from several of your parishioners stating categorically that you are the father of this illegitimate child. And furthermore that the whole parish is aware of the fact. The letters state also that you have been a frequent visitor to the house of this unfaithful nun ever since she returned to Kildawree."

Father Mulroe stood. He felt the skin tighten on his face and prickly sensations run down his back. "I assure Your Grace on my solemn word as a parish priest that I am not the father of that child. I'll make my confession to you now if you wish." He pushed back his chair and knelt.

"Get up, Father. I don't want to hear your confession. I want you to tell me the truth of this matter."

"I *have* told you the truth. What is in those letters is a terrible lie, God forgive the people who wrote them."

The archbishop sucked in a long, audible breath. "Then answer me this, Father. Why are you such a frequent visitor to the house of this woman?"

"She has strayed, Your Grace, from her Father's House. And we know that the good shepherd leaves his ninety-nine sheep in the desert and goes searching for the one that is lost."

"But if thy right eye scandalize thee, pluck it out and cast it from thee!" The archbishop stood now, too, and fairly hurled the words at him. "Father Mulroe, you may deny till you are blue in the face that you are the father of that illegitimate child. And in the end it is only Almighty God Who will know the full truth of the matter and judge you for it. What is incontestable here and now is that you have given great scandal to your flock. Your parishioners expect, and they have every right to expect, exemplary conduct at all times from their priest. What you have done at the very least, by leaving yourself open to the suspicion of immoral conduct, is to betray that trust." He seated himself slowly, picked up a fountain pen from the desk, and stared at it. "And it is for that reason, much as I regret having to do it, that I am removing you now from your post as parish priest of Kildawree."

Kitty Tarragh was upstairs getting ready for bed when she heard the knock. Bad cess to whoever was at that door, anyway, and it nine o'clock at night. The maid was gone out for the evening—a dance in Castletown, she said—and Mammy had been asleep for the past two hours. She considered ignoring the knock at first, but then the thought crossed her mind that it might be Tom, perhaps coming to repent his impetuosity in seeking an annulment of their marriage. So down she went, wearing nothing over her silk nightgown.

"I'm terribly sorry to disturb you, Kitty." Father Mulroe had the posture and the speech of a man in a trance. He took not the slightest notice of her dishabille. "Can I come in for a minute?"

She led him into the parlor. He slumped into a chair. "Are you all right, Father?" She had never seen him like this. He was always so cheerful.

"I'm not. No! I'm not all right at all. I just got the sack." In a featureless monotone that was barely audible. His eyes had the fixed stare of a dead herring.

"You what?" Her brain could make no sense out of what he said.

He bent over, chin in hands, elbows on knees. "His Grace of Tulach, my ecclesiastical superior, has just told me that I am no longer the parish priest of Kildawree. I have been drummed out, discharged, given my walking papers, sent as a curate to the other end of the diocese." He looked up briefly at her. "Not even allowed to stay the three weeks till after confirmation day."

"Are you drunk, Father, by any chance?" It was the only thing that might possibly explain this behavior. She had once seen a bottle of whiskey in his dining room and worried for days about it.

He leaned back, resting his head on the top of the chair in a very tired sort of way. "No, Kitty, I'm not drunk. I'm a Pioneer, as you know. I was called over to the archbishop's palace in Tulach this afternoon. And there I was accused by His Grace of being the father of Mary McGreevy's child. And then I was forthwith dismissed from my parish. So you'll excuse me, please, if I'm not too coherent."

His despondency shook her out of her own lethargy. "Oh, shite!" she shouted, heedless of waking Mammy. "Oh, blast it to hell! Oh, fecking damnation! Excuse the language, Father, though I think this catastrophe calls for it." Good God Almighty! Was there no end to the damage this bloody child was causing? "I think I'm going to go out of my unfortunate mind right now, Father. My bleddy head is about to blow apart like a fecking bomb." She pressed both hands down tightly on her skull. Father Mulroe covered his face with *his* hands. They sat that way in silence for a long time.

"He didn't even give me a chance to defend myself," the priest murmured eventually. In that hopeless, helpless tone of a resigned but tortured Christian.

"Well, we're not going to take it lying down!" The old rebellious Kitty suddenly leaped to her feet. "We'll . . ." She stopped, arms raised in declamation. "Who told the bugger that cock-and-bull story in the first place?"

"Some of my parishioners, it seems. God da—! No! I will not condemn them. We'll leave that—"

"Well, if you won't, Father, then I bleddy well will." She marched barefoot to the fireplace, swung around and faced him, then placed an arm on the mantel in a formal pose. "God damn and blast the bloody buggers!" she shouted. "May they never have a day's luck for the rest of their miserable lives. And may they burn in hell after dying a thousand fearsome deaths."

The priest bowed his head. "I suppose we ought to be forgiving." Though he didn't seem at all convinced of this sentiment.

"The hell we ought! And you know something? I think I know who those slimy, crawling creatures are."

"Better we should not know," the priest said mildly.

"You're the only friend I have left, Father," she said. "And now they have destroyed you. Well, as God is my witness I will find them, whoever they are, and I'll show them up for what they are!"

"I'll have to go now." Father Mulroe dragged himself out of the chair.

"Oh, no, Father! It's early yet. Can't you stay a while?" She needed his company now more than she needed sleep.

"I'm not supposed to be here at all. I only got permission to come and pack a suitcase." He was looking down at the floor. "But I had to say good-bye to you. I'll drop in on Mary as well when I'm driving back."

She looked at him defiantly. "I never want to see that one again." But the immediate woebegone expression on his face knocked the fight right out of her. For a moment she thought he was actually going to cry. His chin quivered and he turned his head away from her and stood facing the fireplace, not moving.

"Don't, Kitty! Please! There's been enough harm done." He turned back to her then, a fierce sadness in his eyes. "Mary is your friend. She didn't say to anyone that Tom was the father. I know that for a fact. And if she could have told you more, she'd have told you. So make it up with her, please!"

It was like a dying man's wish. What could she say but that she would? She didn't know if she could, but she said it anyway.

"Why don't you come with me now," he said, "and we'll go to see her together. That way it'll be easier for both of you." But he was pressuring her, and that got her back up, despite all the sympathy she had for him at this moment.

"I can't now," she said. "I'll do it tomorrow."

"I'd be awfully obliged, Kitty, if you'd come with me tonight." He was staring over her shoulder, as if off into outer space. The hands were joined as if in prayer, and there was surely moisture in those soft brown eyes. "I can't go to her house again, you see, unless there's someone with me."

Contrariness and sympathy joined in sudden sharp, brief conflict. Sympathy emerged victorious but bloody. "I'll have to get dressed," she said, half in a huff, and left him standing there.

"Take your time," he shouted after her, and she trudging up the stairs. She did, dawdling over dressing while she hashed and rehashed her grievance against Mary McGreevy. And feeling towards her that special hatred that is reserved for those one loves. Father Mulroe was waiting for her outside, the headlamps of his car aimed at the front door. "If you wouldn't mind driving your own car," he suggested. "I'll be continuing on to Tulach afterward."

The rain started before she could get to the Vauxhall. She followed him at a distance to avoid the mud. A couple of local lads passing on bicycles gaped at them as they were turning onto the road. There would be speculation and gossip in Curnacarton tonight.

In other circumstances Kitty would have laughed at the sight of her friend: the long red hair hanging loose over the shoulders of a white nightshirt, the baby cradled tightly in her arms, the white legs showing from above the knees down to bare feet. And the mouth streaming invective at the slanderers of Father Mulroe. Mary McGreevy's fury at the gossips of Kildawree was equal to Kitty's own. "That bunch of narrow-minded, spiteful, hate-mongering, craw-thumping, lying hoors! The curse of God and all his filthy devils be upon them! May they be lamed and deafened and blinded! May they turn black from an attack of the plague! May they burn in hell for all eternity!" Kitty followed Father Mulroe inside, but she waited near the door, leaning against the wall with her arms folded. The priest stood in the middle of the kitchen floor in hat and coat listening to the diatribe as if it were his due. "Come and sit by the fire now, Father," Mary said in a calm voice when she had finished cursing. It was only then that she noticed Kitty. "Mrs. Tarragh, what in God's name are you doing down there? Will you come up to the fire before you catch your death of cold."

Kitty, determined though she was to remain hostile, could not resist that friendly scold. She came halfway.

"I can't stay," John Patrick said, standing with his back to the blaze. "I just came in to say good-bye." His voice cracked a little on that last word. "But I would like you to do one thing for me before I go." He was looking at Mary, standing beside him, rocking the baby gently in her arms. "Would you tell Kitty now what you and I know to be the truth?"

"Holy God!" Mary turned away and faced the fire. She stood there motionless.

"Please?" the priest said after a while. He put his hand on her shoulder. "For my sake, do it."

Kitty wanted to run. She'd wanted to be told this for so long, but now she couldn't bear to hear it. Mary swung around. "Kitty, as God is my witness, Tom is not her father." She held the baby out at arm's length. "I am so awfully sorry for all that has happened." Then she collapsed into her chair on top of the book she had been reading and sobbed quietly, one hand held over her face.

Kitty felt no pain, just a heavy numbness over all her body. It wasn't him. Then . . . But of course it had to be him. The woman was lying. "I don't believe you," she heard her own voice shouting.

The hand came off the face. Hair and tears and tortured green eyes. "I swear to God, Kitty! He's not. As a matter of fact, I did ask him to because he is the nicest man I know. And I thought somehow his being the father would make you and me better friends. But he refused."

"You're just making it up!"

"I am not!" She wiped her eyes with her sleeve. "He was sitting right there at that table having a cup of tea when I asked him. And he just got up and walked out the door."

"She's telling you the truth," Father Mulroe said. "I know it for a fact."

"Are you telling me then that Mrs. Dolan, your midwife, as honest a woman as you could meet, made up a lie?"

"No. But I think I know what happened." Mary gently rocked the baby, who was beginning to whimper. "I was lying in the bed, admiring my beautiful newborn infant. And I remembered that Tom Tarragh had turned down the chance to be her father. And I said—to myself, mind you, not thinking anyone would hear me—that even the schoolmaster would have been proud to call this baby his own."

A hot wetness, like boiling soup, spilled over Kitty. She couldn't breathe. She couldn't scream. But she could move. She ran for the door and out into the cold, black, wet night.

20

Snow drifted silently to earth throughout the night. Its clear white coat, covering field and house and road, gleamed in the late-dawning day and dazzled the eye in the unexpected midday sun. Rita Feerick trudged through it down the boreen in the afternoon and shook it from her boots before entering Mary McGreevy's kitchen. "I brought you some black pudding." The contents of her plate had the appearance of a coiled black headless snake.

"You're wonderful." Mary was sitting by the fire knitting, a ball of white wool on the floor between her shoes, the baby in the cradle beside her. "I thought I heard the pig squealing the other day. But I was hoping it might have been the archbishop that was in pain." She smiled grimly at her friend.

"Bad cess to him anyway." Rita removed her coat and draped it over a chair. "God forgive me for saying it."

"I hope God won't forgive *him* lightly for what he did." Serious venom in Mary's tone.

"I know I shouldn't ask you." Rita pulled a chair up to the fire and warmed her hands at the flames. "And I'm quite sure it wasn't, of course. But could you tell me anyway that Father Mulroe . . ."

"It was *not* Father Mulroe." The hard rasp of anger softened when Mary added, "Though I wished many a time that it could have been him."

"It was awful wrong to send the poor man away like that."

"Oh, Rita! I feel so terrible about it. It's as if my dearest friend has died. Or been killed, which is worse. I want to cry every time I think of him. And then I want to lash out and hit whoever is the cause of it. Last night I had this fierce urge to go out searching for him and bring him back. I looked out the door before I went to bed and saw the snow coming down and I was terrified that he was out there somewhere, wandering about without a roof over his head or a bit of food to put in his mouth. And I wanted to scream into the darkness 'Come back!'"

"Ah, sure, he'll be all right, the creature," Rita comforted.

"He will not be all right! There's no use saying he'll be all right. His good name is destroyed. And his parish is gone that he was so proud of. The poor man can never raise his head again for the rest of his life without remembering the shame of his departure from Kildawree. Unless someone convinces that bloody fellow over in Tulach that he committed a horrible injustice to the nicest man I have ever known." There were tears in Mary's eyes.

"Would it help if we wrote letters to the archbishop, do you think? Telling him we're sure Father Mulroe is innocent? Wattie and I would be glad to do that. At least I *think* Wattie would; he liked Father Mulroe."

"It'll take more than letters," Mary said. "Archbishops are like angels: they can never change their minds. They're all infallible, you see. What we need is—" She stopped suddenly, listening. The knock at the back door was repeated. "Come in! Come in." Biddy Moran, the Malones' servant girl, stepped in and closed the door quickly. "How are you at all, Biddy? Come up to the fire and warm yourself."

"My boots are all snow, ma'am," Biddy said, staying by the door. A small, neat girl, not more than about sixteen. But a real treasure, according to Mrs. Malone.

"Never mind that," Mary said firmly. "Come on up out of the cold."

Biddy came, timidly but obediently. "Mrs. Tarragh sent me down to give you this." She pulled a light blue envelope out of her pocket.

"She couldn't come herself, I suppose," Mary grumbled. She ripped open the envelope with her finger and pulled out a sheet of paper. After staring at it for a while she stared into the fire for another while. "Tell her I'll be there," she said abruptly.

"Yes, ma'am." And Biddy took off as if a dog were chasing her.

Silence followed her departure. "A nice girl, Biddy," Rita managed eventually.

"Apparently I'm forgiven." Mary renewed her knitting at a furious pace. "That was an invitation to the manor on Sunday evening for tea with their ladyships." She grimaced at Rita. "Maybe you could ask Deirdre if she'd mind her nibs here for me. Mrs. Tarragh takes exception to crying babies."

By Sunday the snow had cleared. Kitty greeted her as if no angry word had ever passed between them. Tea for three in the dining room was served by silent Biddy. A cold plate of chicken and ham and salad, with brown bread and homemade butter. Followed by scones, apple tart, and fruitcake. And constant refilling of teacups. But only the most innocuous conversation, totally bereft of reference to what most preoccupied both Mary and Kitty. When they were done, Kitty said, "Let's sit in the parlor. There's a nice fire going."

"I have some things to take care of," Mrs. Malone said, looking meaningfully at her daughter. "I'll join you in a while."

"Would you like a glass of sherry?" Kitty closed the parlor door behind them.

Mary hesitated. "Maybe I'll try one." It would be her introduction to intoxicants—apart from a stolen sip of Guinness when she was about fifteen. Then, suddenly, she remembered. "I thought you were teetotally against drink?"

"I was. I was indeed." She filled two glasses at the sideboard. "I'm so glad you came." They sat in easy chairs on either side of the fire. "Here's to us." She raised her glass.

"Good on you," Mary sniffed the sherry the way she used to see her father sniff whiskey. It lightly stung her nose. She closed her eyes and sipped. Prickling and burning tongue and palate and throat. And then, marvelously, before she could decide she didn't like it, dripping soothingly down her esophagus like sweet, warm oil. "Not too bad at all," she admitted.

"I'm agreeing to the annulment," Kitty said abruptly, staring into her glass.

"Uh-huh." The safest response she could think of. This was indeed a surprise.

"I now believe you—and Tom. About the baby, I mean."

"Well, I'm glad to hear that anyway." She couldn't help letting a shade of tartness pervade her response.

"I really should have known better than to doubt you, Mary. I'm awfully sorry." Kitty's tone wallowed in remorse.

"We'll say no more about it." Mary took another sip. "I wish we could get Father Mulroe back now."

"Ah! So sad. Such a nice man. I'll miss him." Kitty took a long sip, then leaned forward confidentially. "There's something else I want to talk to you about. So I asked Mammy to leave us alone for a bit. You know, so we can say what's on our minds without having to be polite."

"And since when did anyone ever stop you from saying what was on your mind?" She was a bit annoyed at Kitty's casual dismissal of Father Mulroe.

"You're a great tease, Mary McGreevy." Kitty emitted her brittle laugh of unease. "Anyway, what I wanted to talk about was the future. Mine and yours." She put her head back and finished her drink. "I think I'll have another sherry." She glanced briefly at Mary's almost full glass and headed for the sideboard. "I've been thinking," she said on return, "that here we are, the two of us, two middle-aged women, both of us with farms and neither of us with husbands." She took a quick slug of sherry. "And neither of us *wanting* a husband, for that matter." She paused. "But we both need company."

"We do, I suppose." Mary indulged in another minute sip. "But then, you have your mother to take care of and I have Bridget Patricia to rear."

"I've thought about that," Kitty said quickly. "And it needn't be an obstacle."

"You've obviously been doing a *lot* of thinking lately." Mary decided to be a bit more adventurous with the sherry. "Phooh!" She gasped after swallowing hastily to prevent herself choking. "That's strong stuff."

"What I'm proposing is pretty strong stuff too," Kitty said.

"And what *are* you proposing, Mrs. Tarragh?" The liquor still sting-ing her throat.

"Miss Malone will do from now on, if you please. What I had in mind was that we share a house, you and I."

Mary looked at her. Kitty gazed right back, her eyes soft, pleading and challenging at the same time. "And whose house would we share, if we *were* to share? If I may ask?"

Kitty looked away, into the fire. "Whichever is more suitable, I sup-pose."

"Well, that would make the choice easy, wouldn't it? I mean, who would hesitate between a miserable *bothan* and a palatial mansion? Between a smelly outhouse and a tiled bathroom? Between—"

"Don't, Mary, please! I wasn't trying to make comparisons." There were tears in Kitty's eyes when she looked up. "I want you, and I only want the best for both of us. If it would make you happy I'd be perfectly willing—"

"Oh, Kitty! You would not, and 'tis well you know it. But tell me, wouldn't this be awfully sinful for you? I mean, how would you recon-cile such an unnatural relationship with the sixth commandment?"

"Don't tease me, Mary, please."

"I'm not teasing. The Kitty Tarragh I've known for the past six months has been a woman of serious spirituality, not to mention ferocious scruples. How could you do these things you're talking about without re-jecting your faith?"

"I'll be honest, Mary. I get a lot of twinges still, and some scruples that keep me awake at night. But the truth is, I don't want to be religious anymore. It gets in the way of living, you might say. But you know that already, don't you?"

Mary tried another slug of sherry. "You're a gas woman, Kitty. Worse than myself, I think. But what would your mother think of all this? She's not about to let another woman into her house. Bad enough to have *two* women sharing a kitchen, but to have three!"

"Mammy is tired. She leaves the cooking to Biddy these days. And as for me, I'd just as soon never darken the door of a kitchen. Actually, I've mentioned the possibility of your coming to Mammy. She won't object.

She doesn't care much about anything since Daddy died. Anyway, she doesn't want to lose me again." She finished her sherry. "So, will you think about it?"

Mary looked into the fire for a long time. "I won't," she said eventually. "I will be your friend, if you'll still have me. And I'll always share my currant cake and apple tart with you. But more than that I cannot commit to, at least for now."

Kitty drew in enough air to expostulate. But then her shoulders slumped. "But maybe later, then?" In a tone that for her was timid.

"Who knows what time will bring?" Mary said. They lapsed into silence. But not for long. A discreet knock on the door, and Mrs. Malone stuck her head in. "May I come in?" she asked, as if she were an intruder in her own house.

The sacrament of confirmation was administered in Kildawree on the first Monday in February every third year. The sacred event's infrequency, the fact that it was presided over by the archbishop himself, and the fearsome test in catechism that accompanied it all combined to make the day memorable for the parish. It was particularly noteworthy, thrilling, and agonizing for the boys and girls whose time had arrived to be made strong and perfect Christians. The great day was preceded by months of hard, and often painful, learning by those children. And by rigorous, unrelenting drilling of the Maynooth catechism into their thick skulls by Thomas Aquinas Tarragh, principal teacher, whose onerous duty it was to present properly trained candidates for the sacrament of Christian maturity. His leather strap scalded and numbed the palms of those who failed to memorize such critical information as the seven deadly sins, the Apostles' Creed, or the nature of heavenly bliss. Curiously, some of the candidates were in even greater terror of the archbishop's unknown hand than they were of the schoolmaster's familiar strap. A slap on the cheek was administered by His Grace, Mr. Tarragh taught them, as an integral part of the sacrament's administration. Its purpose, he explained, was to teach them that they must be brave and unflinching Christians in the face of trial and adversity. Or even martyrdom, should that ultimate sacrifice be required of them. But school lore, slyly assisted by former recipients of the sacrament, attested most solemnly and grimly to the utter ferocity of the wallop meted out by the Most Reverend Dr. Quinlan. Raised welts, swollen jaws, even bloodied noses were among the effects to be expected, they were warned.

Two weeks to the day after Father Mulroe had been sent away in disgrace, a thrilled and proud but extremely nervous group of children arrived at the church in the early afternoon. They were dressed in new clothes bought or made especially for the event and were accompanied by parents and sponsors. Since a new parish priest had not yet been appointed, the responsibility for meeting the episcopal party on behalf of Kildawree fell on Mr. Tarragh. Fortunately, the rain held off and he was able to line up the children, boys on the right, girls on the left, as a guard of honor for His Grace and his entourage of two priestly assistants. The day being cold, the archbishop wasted no time on outside ceremony. After a cursory inspection and blessing, he headed for the sacristy. The candidates and congregation just as quickly entered the church, where they knelt or sat in silent expectation. All rose some minutes later when the archbishop, resplendent in glistening white vestments and mitre and carrying the crozier that symbolized his office, processed onto the altar preceded by his assistants and six of Kildawree's most experienced mass-servers.

Mary McGreevy arrived a few minutes late on her bicycle. Deirdre Feerick, who was to mind the baby for her, had been delayed—she had had to watch her younger sister Tess, who was being confirmed, get into the white frock that Deirdre herself had worn three years earlier. So by the time Mary walked into the church, the archbishop, enthroned in an armchair on the top altar step just to the right of the tabernacle, had already begun his sermon.

"It is unfortunate," were the first words she heard, "that your church is for the moment bereft of its head. The greatest loss a parish can suffer is the loss of its priest. For the priest is the leaven in the bread, the shepherd of the flock, the light in the darkness. He is—"

"And why *are* we without our parish priest?" shouted Mary McGreevy from her seat near the back of the church. She heard herself hurl the words and wondered as she did if it were she who was uttering them. Though her purpose in coming was exactly this—to challenge the archbishop's decision—she had had no idea how she was to accomplish that mission until she heard herself speak.

His Grace paused, turned his head ever so slightly, and gazed sternly in the direction of the voice. "He is," he then continued, as if the interruption had not occurred, "a man sent from God—"

"And sent away by you," Mary McGreevy shouted in anger. "We want to know why."

From the front seats, occupied by parents, children, and sponsors, all heads swiveled. From the middle seats, filled by the merely pious, all heads turned. The necks of mass-servers, seated on the altar steps, strained. The episcopal assistants stared. His Grace focused a wicked eye, accompanied by an awful pause, in the direction of this almost blasphemous interruption. But when sufficient silence had elapsed to suggest that further interference was not forthcoming, he resumed. "A man sent from God to bear witness to the—"

"We want Father Mulroe back in this parish," Mary McGreevy shouted.

A crook of the episcopal finger brought an assistant's head low to catch His Grace's whisper. Immediately the assistant descended the altar steps, opened the gate that led from sanctuary to nave, and marched purposefully down the aisle. His eyes swept the women's side as he went. When he approached the rear he stopped, stared, and whispered, "Who shouted?" He was rewarded with blank stares. Across the aisle on the men's side, Mary McGreevy held her breath. The assistant glowered at the women before slowly retracing his steps.

His Grace continued. "The priest bears witness to the gospel of Jesus—"

"Why was Father Mulroe removed?"

This time the archbishop raised himself from his throne, leaned forward on his crozier, and glared grimly toward the back of the church. "Will the wretched person who is interrupting this sacred ceremony please stand." Gone the reasoned tone of the good shepherd; in its place the bellow of a frustrated man.

All heads turned once more. Mary McGreevy stood and shouted back, "Would your Grace please explain to the people of this parish why you removed Father Mulroe from his post?"

His Grace took in air in the manner of a man about to use it in a hurry. But then he relaxed his shoulders and bent his head as if in deep personal prayer. "I would make three points," he said eventually, the calm restored to his voice. "The first is that I, appointed to be shepherd of this archdiocese by Almighty God Himself through the person of His Holiness, Pope Pius the twelfth, do not have to explain to anyone why I removed your parish priest. The second is that it is a disgrace, a terrible disgrace, to this parish that someone—anyone—would dare to interrupt so sacred a moment in the manner that it has been done, with consequent scandal to the children, their parents, and their sponsors. And the third is a reminder to this person—whoever you are—of the words of Saint Paul himself that women should not so much as raise their voices in church."

"My name is Mary McGreevy." Her voice was loud and clear. "It was, I believe, on my account that Father Mulroe was removed. And I would like to explain—"

"You will not explain anything here," the archbishop thundered. "You will not give further scandal to the children who have come today to be confirmed." He treated himself once more to a soothing intake of air. "Although I do not have to give you a reason, nevertheless, I will do so." In the tone now of sweet reason responding to sad derangement. "When the sacrament of confirmation has been conferred and the children have been dismissed, I will explain my action to whomsoever wishes to hear. But until that time I will tolerate no further interruption."

When she sat her body shook as though with fever. And when the ague subsided she lapsed into a semistupor, neither seeing nor hearing what was taking place at the altar. Had she really done what she had done? Or was it her imagination that had run amuck? Had she actually shouted at the archbishop, he who once had been scarcely less than God Himself to her? In front of the entire parish, at that? And at the top of her voice? They could put her away, so they could. People had been sent to the lunatic asylum for less.

The churning of her intestines increased when the sacred rite ended and the archbishop returned to the sacristy. The children left their seats, genuflected, and marched two by two down the aisle. Tess Feerick, last in the line, waved shyly to Mary as she passed. Wattie and Rita, who were following their daughter, stepped quickly into Mary's bench and sat on either side of her. "Well, weren't you great," Rita whispered, briefly squeezing her hand.

The archbishop was back in the sanctuary, attired now in the somber purple of his rank. He genuflected profoundly, knelt briefly on the lower step in the posture of prayer, then climbed to his makeshift throne at the top. He was followed, then flanked, by his priestly assistants. Hands on episcopal knees, His Grace gazed benignly down at his congregation. Most of the adults had remained in their seats to hear the drama out.

"Jesus tells us in the gospel," he said in the mildest of tones, "that whosoever offends one of these little ones who believe in Him, it were better for that person that a millstone be hanged around her neck and that she be drowned in the depths of the sea." He lowered his gaze to his lap, then raised his head with a jerk as if surprised by what he had seen there. "It must needs be that scandal cometh, Jesus said," his tone suddenly stentorian. "But woe to that man, or woman, by whom it comes." His fearsome stare swept the congregation. "Scandal has been given today to the little ones, here in this very church of God. And scandal has been given to all in this parish in recent times. And I say to you, woe to them by whom that scandal came."

The silence was that of imminent, inescapable doom. No foot was shuffled or throat cleared. His Grace continued inexorably. "It came to my notice two weeks ago that a child had been conceived and born out of holy wedlock in this parish. To a woman who had once been the bride of Jesus Christ Himself. A disgrace to the people of God, a scandal to one and all, and the utmost shame to her who was its cause. But the greatest scandal," here the archbishop's tone rose to a crescendo of outrage, "was the fact that your very own parish priest was named father of this child of sin."

She stood. She couldn't help herself. "Father Mulroe was not the father of my child. And furthermore, she is not a child of sin but a child of love." Then she sat abruptly lest her quaking knees should cease to support her.

His Grace maintained silence for a dramatic moment. "Denial will not avail you," he resumed calmly. "I have it on the most unimpeachable authority that your former parish priest—"

"Well, you have it dead wrong, m'lord." Wattie Feerick on his feet beside her, shouting. "And I should know better than anyone, because I'm the father myself."

Kildawree church seemed to gasp. Mary felt like giggling at the notion. But that instant of relieving lunatic levity was abruptly shattered by Rita's anguished cry on her other side: "Oh, God, no!"

"I don't know who *you* are," the archbishop retorted. "And I don't know what your motive is. And I don't wish to know. But I can assure the faithful of this parish, both present and absent, that your unfortunate priest's guilt has been firmly established beyond all reasonable—"

"This man is telling you the truth." She was on her shaking feet, shouting again.

"Oh, God, help me," Rita Feerick sobbed.

"I can only ask you all," His Grace continued, as though she had not spoken, "to protect the innocent from the scandal that has been caused and to pray for the guilty that they may repent of their sins. In the name of the Father and of the Son and of the Holy Ghost. Amen." Then he rose from his throne, descended the altar steps with measured tread, genuflected profoundly to the Blessed Sacrament, and marched regally into the sacristy.

21

The saddest sight Mary McGreevy ever saw was Rita Feerick's exit from the church that afternoon. The second the archbishop left the sanctuary the woman bolted from her seat as if all the devils in hell were chasing her. Mary followed quickly with the intention of apologizing, groveling, begging pardon on her bended knees of this dear good friend she had so terribly, unforgivably wounded. But as she watched Rita's hunched, dejected shamble down the steps and palpably felt the anguish left in her wake, she turned aside and grabbed her bike and cycled furiously home. Repentance and reparation must wait till the first fierce thrust of pain had passed, till Rita had cried her fill and vented alpha wrath on her faithless spouse.

It was prudence, not cowardice, Mary convinced herself, that kept her for more than a day from facing the anger of the friend she had betrayed. But by the evening of the second day she could bear the strain no longer. To add to her misery, Luke, who had been milking her cows and feeding her pigs for the past three months, did not appear all day. She had to tether the cows by the back door and milk them there, listening all the while for Bridget Patricia's cry. And she left the child alone while she raced down the yard to feed the pigs. This could not go on—she would have to find someone else to help if Rita forbade her son to work for her.

So when Kitty arrived for a visit later in the evening, she pressed her into service. "Just for an hour," she pleaded.

"She'll run you through with a pitchfork," Kitty warned. Like most of the parish she had already heard the scandalous news. But Rita's door was bolted shut when Mary tried the handle. And there was no response to her repeated knocks, though there was light in the kitchen window.

Next morning she was milking her second cow in the yard when Wattie appeared from behind the shed. "Don't get up," he whispered when she made to move.

"Oh, Wattie, I'm so sorry. I shouldn't have got you into this." She continued milking.

"Don't be sorry, now. I'm not. She'll come around herself eventually."

"How is she?"

"I don't see much of her. I'm sleeping in the barn myself. Luke brings me a bit to eat, so I'm not starving. I'm awful sorry he can't come down to help, but you know how it is. Are you managing?"

"I'm managing." What else could she say?

"Listen, I'd best go now. I just came down to see how you were. If I'm caught here, 'tis more than my life is worth." And he vanished behind the shed.

That afternoon she walked back to the Feerick house, carrying the baby, both well wrapped against the February chill. She knocked but got no answer. Nor did she expect any. She knelt on the flagstone outside the door and held that position for a solid hour till her back ached and her knees hurt and her face and fingers were numb with the cold. Several times the child cried, but she kept to her post—it was part of Bridget Patricia's payment for being admitted to the world. During all that time she heard nothing and saw no one. Neither child nor parent entered or left this home that was always filled with noisy comings and goings.

Every afternoon for the rest of the week she repeated her vigil, always with the same result. On Sunday it rained, a steady drenching downpour that left her soaked and Bridget Patricia almost suffocated beneath her sheltering oilskin. Mary got to her feet at the end of her hour and was turning to leave when the kitchen door suddenly opened. "Come in," Rita said, and the misery of the world seemed reflected in those two words.

Mary stepped in wordlessly. When she lifted the oilskin the baby cried. "Give her to me," Rita commanded. "And take those wet things off yourself before you catch your death of cold." She brought the baby up to the fire and sat rocking her gently while Mary removed coat and hat. "Hang them on the doornail and come up and dry yourself."

"Thank you," she murmured. The sudden warmth was almost as unbearable as the cold, driving rain.

"Why Wattie?" No emotion in Rita's voice.

"Because he has character. And good blood. And he's kind. And he has enough children of his own not to bother me again."

"And he hasn't?" A sharp edge to the query.

"Honest to God, Rita, no. He just did me a favor. It was all my fault for asking him."

"I went back to the church last night to go to confession," Rita said, the words tumbling out of her now like stones off a wall. "And I couldn't step into the box because I kept thinking, How can you ask God to forgive you if you yourself don't forgive others? So I forgive you, Mary McGreevy. And I forgive himself too." Then she cried, softly at first but progressively louder as the sobs shook her body. The baby joined in, then Mary, till the kitchen reverberated with their sounds, like the wailing of keeners at a wake.

They were still at it when Deirdre opened the hall door and timidly stuck her head in. "Are you all right, Mammy? Fidelma is in a terrible state because you're all crying."

Rita, still holding the baby, wiped her eyes with her sleeve. "Go out to the barn and tell your father to come in," she said.

"I had a letter from Father Mulroe," Tom Tarragh told her. He came back to visit the day before Saint Patrick's Day. Out in the field across the road from the house she was, searching for a decent sprig of shamrock to wear tomorrow, when his Morris Minor chugged down the boreen.

"Musha, did you, now? And how is the poor man at all?" Pretending to be casual as she walked him into the house.

"Not too good. He didn't put it in so many words, but from the tone of the letter I'd say he's more than a bit unhappy." He removed his coat and hung it on the back of the door.

"And why wouldn't he?" She leaned over the cradle and smiled at Bridget Patricia. "And you're the cause of it all, little angel. Yes you are, too."

"You made your say very well on that occasion, Mary. Your courage was much to be admired. And was, by at least some of us."

"But it didn't do a bit of good, did it? You'll have a cup of tea?"

"I will." His easy acquiescence a sure sign that he came for a purpose and intended to stay a while.

She put the kettle on. "And how are you keeping yourself?"

"I don't know if Kitty told you," he said, not looking at her. "She has agreed to the annulment."

"She told me."

"They tell me I'll have it in about a year." This time he looked steadily at her, as if expecting some sort of response.

"I'm sorry things didn't work out for you." She went about setting the table to cover the awkwardness of the conversation.

" 'Twas all for the best. We never should have got married in the first place."

"Tell me more about Father John Patrick. Where is he? What is he doing?"

"He's a curate in Westport. It's like being in jail, he said—he has to report his every movement to the parish priest. An old fossil, he called the canon. I feel sorry for the poor man."

"I want to see him," Mary said. She warmed the teapot with water from the kettle.

Tom laughed, a harsh, brittle guffaw. "I'd say now that if you were seen anywhere near that man, his next parish would be somewhere in the middle of the Atlantic Ocean."

"We don't have to be *seen* together," she retorted. "If it's done right." She put tea in the pot, her back to him.

"It wouldn't be that easy. Westport is a small town."

"But his friend Thomas Aquinas Tarragh, the noted historian, could take him out to Achill some afternoon to see an ancient ruin." She went over and knelt by the cradle. "Wouldn't Achill be a nice place for Mammy to visit?" she cooed to her child. "You'd do that for me, Tom, wouldn't you?" She got up and stood over him.

He was silent for a bit. "I suppose I'll have to." He didn't stay too long after the tea. And he left, she suspected, without broaching the business he had come about.

He came for her on a Wednesday morning two weeks later. She left the baby with the Feericks for the day. Rita, the saint, had put her residual anger firmly away and accepted Bridget Patricia as one of her own. "I wrote to him," Tom said as they drove through Kildawree, "and invited him to come to Achill for the day. He'll be expecting me, he said." Then, after they had passed through Ballinamore and were on the Westport road, he said, out of the blue, "Would you consider marrying me?"

She ought to have known it was coming. Wasn't it the reason he came to see her a couple of weeks ago? So why was she now at a loss for even a single word? It was who he was, of course, that made it difficult. This was no Mick Burke—a simple, good-natured fellow whose proposal should be treated kindly but not taken seriously. He was a strong character, Tom Tarragh. Intelligent and educated. A person of importance in the parish. Well known and highly respected even beyond its borders. A man whose marriage proposal any woman should be honored to receive. "I'm flattered," she finally managed.

"Does that mean yes?" Eyes on the road, hands firmly on the wheel, only the slightest tension in the voice betraying emotion.

"I made a decision a long time ago that I was not going to marry."

"But you have a child now." The tone even, rational, not in the least pleading, as if he were merely pointing out an error in grammar.

"If I had wanted to get married I'd have waited to have my baby."

"Don't you think she needs a father? I'd be a great father to her. *And* to her brothers and sisters."

"I'm sure of that, Tom. And I'd be most grateful if you would be a father to her. Especially now since Wattie's visiting has been curtailed.

Unfortunately, however, I can't marry you. Or anyone else, for that matter."

"Women are God's purgatory for men," he muttered. And he spoke no more till they reached Westport. "If the old canon sees you in the car now, Father Mulroe's goose is properly cooked," he said grumpily as they approached the church and parish house.

"Drop me off out the Newport road a bit first," she said, "and then go back and pick him up." And she had walked almost half a mile before the Morris Minor caught up with her again. Father Mulroe was in the front passenger seat. When he got out to let her in the back there were tears in her eyes. She wanted to embrace him but instead held out her hand. "'Tis great to see you again, Father."

"I didn't expect to see you," he said.

"I was afraid to tell you she was coming," Tom explained.

"Better you didn't," said the priest. "For my conscience's sake anyway." He seemed calm and composed, but during the long, tortuous drive out to Achill, through Newport and Mulrany and across the Curraun peninsula, Mary sensed the churning of all their emotions beneath the surface-bland conversation. Tom, as a native and a historian, was happy to give them detailed history and geography lessons of the island. Father Mulroe was curious and asked a lot of questions. Mary was content to listen in silence.

"I'm starved," Tom said when they reached Keel. "We can get a decent lunch in the hotel if it's open." It was, and they did, and Tom insisted on paying the bill. When they were leaving he said, "There are a couple of people I have to visit here in the village. Maybe you two would like to take a walk on the strand?"

It was a crisp, dry afternoon, with a chilly wind blowing in off the ocean. "Is it too cold for you?" Father John Patrick asked as soon as they set foot on the hard-packed sand.

"I'll be all right. 'Tisn't often I get to see the fierce waves of the Atlantic."

"You made some fierce waves yourself recently, according to the clerical smoke signals." The priest's tone was sardonic.

"So you heard? Bad news travels fast, I suppose."

"It wasn't all bad, the way I heard it. The fellow that passed it on to me thought it was a pity there aren't more women like you around."

"That sounds almost mutinous, Father. Do I detect a certain antipathy towards a certain archbishop?"

His hands behind his back, he looked out to sea. "I understand you turned down a recent proposal of marriage."

"Poor Tom. I didn't want to hurt him, but what could I do?" She waved her arms melodramatically. "My heart is elsewhere."

"Is that a fact? Listen, Mary, you told me more than once that you didn't ever want to get married. Do you think you could tell me why? I mean, it's the normal, natural state to be in."

"Then why aren't you in it, Father John Patrick Mulroe? What a fine, handsome husband you'd make for a woman!" She picked up a pebble in her stride and threw it into the surf.

"I remember you said something about not wanting to exchange one mother superior for another. But I certainly don't believe you'd have that kind of problem with Tom Tarragh."

"When I went into the convent," she said, "I did so for a reason. I had made a promise, and reason said it had to be kept." She bent, scooped up a large shell, and shook the sand from it. "I didn't let my feelings have any say in the matter. They were screaming at the top of their lungs, 'Don't go, you fool.' But I ignored them. And spent sixteen years regretting it. Until I finally listened to them and escaped." She examined the shell, weighed it in her hand, then threw it into the water. "So I'm taking care to listen to my feelings now. They told me as soon as I came out that marriage was too risky. Probably because of the way I saw my parents live. And they've told me not to marry any man I've met so far who would, or could, have me."

He glanced at her, eyes a mixture of longing and despair. "God help me," he said. And looked away again quickly, distractedly jabbing at a pebble with his shoe. Without hesitation she wrapped her arms around him, patted his back, stroked his neck, and ran her fingers through his hair. He let her, neither encouraging nor resisting. Then she took his head in both hands and kissed his lips, tenderly at first, and when eventually he began to respond, urgently, hungrily, desperately. The cold wind whipped across the strand, but she felt nothing, only the dreadful dissonant ecstasy of that moment.

A distant voice broke them apart. A boy's harsh laugh, followed by a shout and another laugh. "I didn't really intend to . . . ," she babbled. "I—"

"It's all right." He groped for her hand. When she gave it to him he said, "I wouldn't trade this moment for the rest of my life."

The two boys running toward them were laughing and shouting and throwing stones in the water. They slowed to a respectful walk when they spotted the priest, went silently past, and then resumed their run.

"We'd better go back," she said. "The cold is getting to me."

GLOSSARY

A ghradh:	my love;
A leanbh:	my child;
A stor:	my dear;
Amadhan:	a fool;
Bosthoon (bastun):	an awkward, tactless fellow;
Bothan:	a small house or hovel;
Caboclo:	Brazilian term for a backwoodsman;
Cailin Aluinn:	a beautiful girl;
Caiscin:	whole-wheat homemade bread;
Caoineadh:	wailing or lament;
Culchie:	derogatory term for a native of County Mayo;
Eejit:	idiot;
Gradh:	affection, love;
Mar dheadh:	as if it were so;
Plamas:	soft talk, diplomacy;
Pooka (puca):	a hobgoblin or ghost;
Reek:	a mountain. Croagh Patrick, Ireland's holy mountain, is known as *the Reek;*
Slainte:	health.